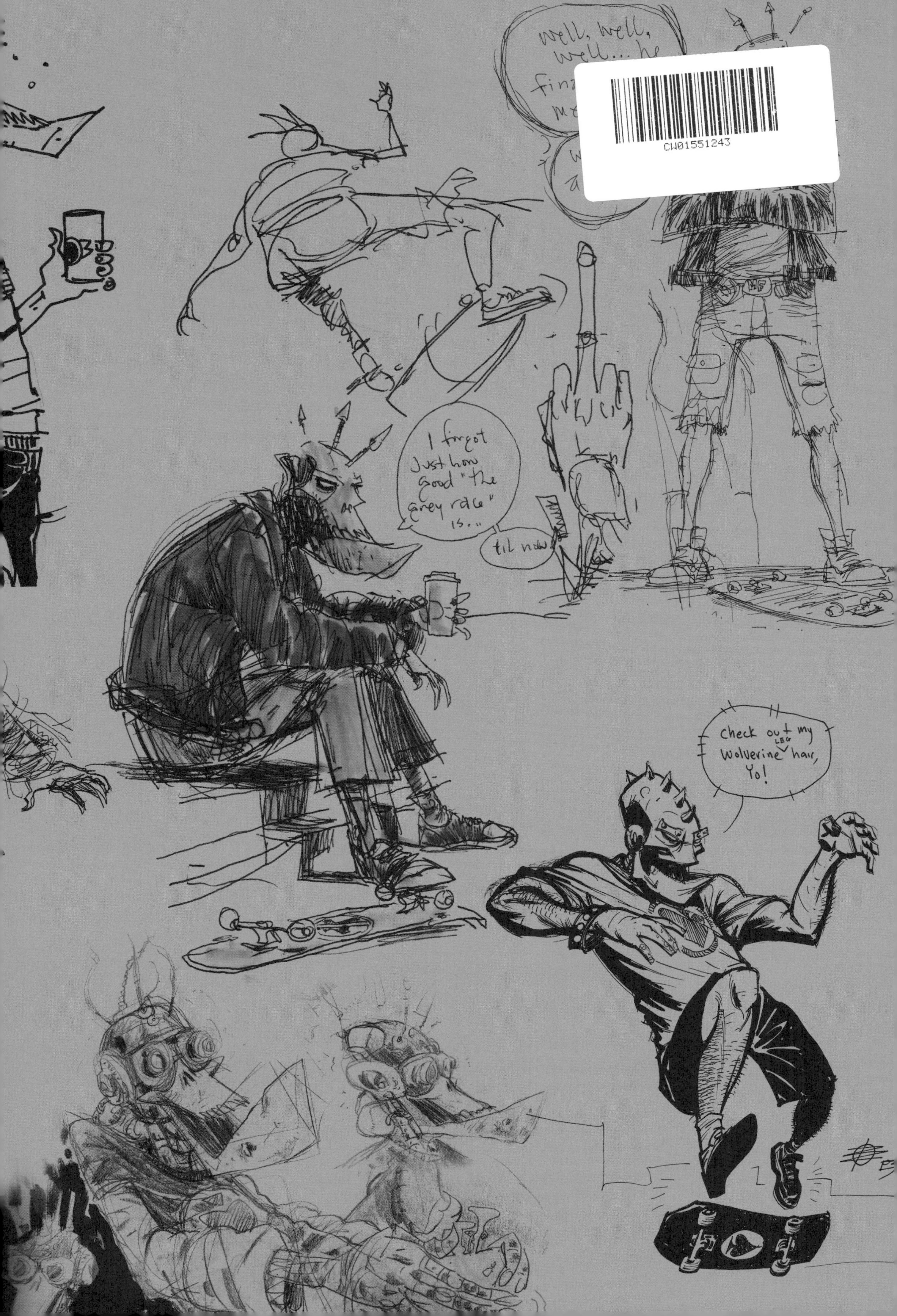

well, well, well... he
I forgot just how good "the grey race" is..
til now
Check out my LEG Wolverine hair, Yo!

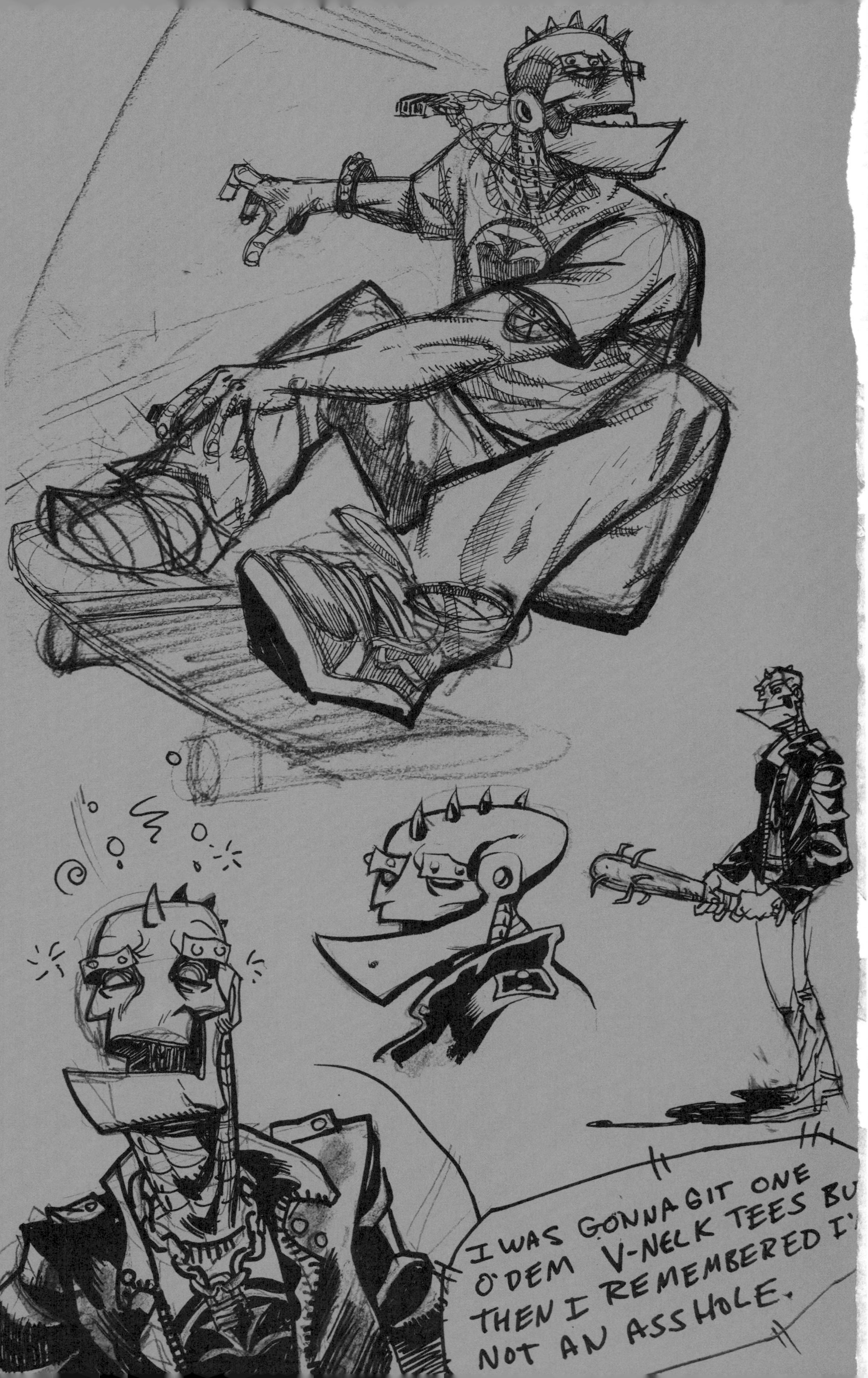
I WAS GONNA GIT ONE O'DEM V-NECK TEES BU THEN I REMEMBERED I' NOT AN ASSHOLE.

BLACK♥HEART BILLY

TWENTY-FIFTH ANNIVERSARY EDITION

Celebrity likenesses appear for satirical purposes; no endorsement is implied.

Brand names and trademarks appear for parody / commentary.

Written by
Rick Remender, Kieron Dwyer & Harper Jaten

Art by
Kieron Dwyer, Harper Jaten, Rick Remender & Paul Azaceta

Cover by
Kieron Dwyer, Rick Remender & Moreno Dinisio

Logo by
Harper Jaten

Edited by
No one (*obviously*)

Layout & production by
Erika Schnatz

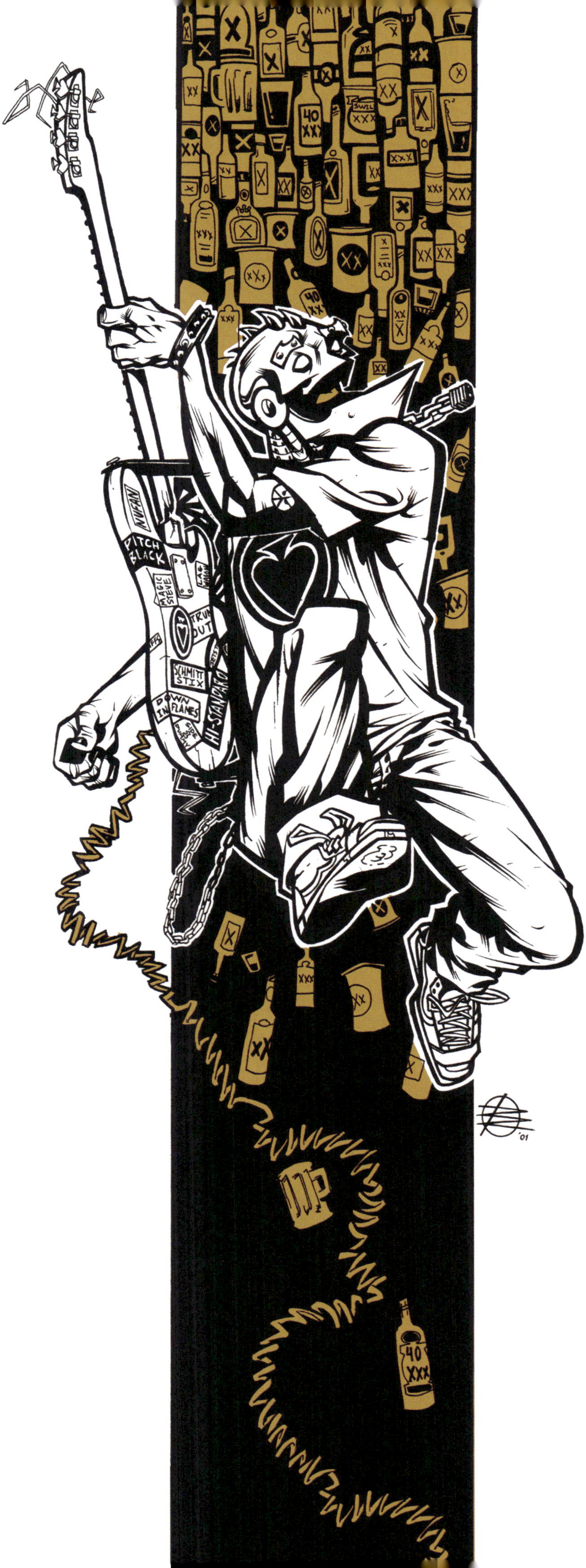
PITCH BLACK
SCHMITT STIX
DOWN IN FLAMES
HI-STANDARD

I never fit anywhere as a kid.

1984 changed that. That was the summer I found skateboarding, punk rock, and comic books. Things that went on to shape my entire life. Scenes built by misfits who didn't fit anywhere else, so they built their own strange new worlds, whole new sports, and songs that said everything I'd kept hidden inside. Thrasher stacked up next to my *X-Men* and *Spider-Man* comics. Powell Peralta and Vision videos replaced MTV. Minor Threat replaced Van Halen in my Walkman. I met other kids who skated and collected comics. We built ramps, skated curbs, and hunted back issues.

From that year on, I spent my time writing, drawing, and reading comics; skateboarding; and voraciously consuming all manner of underground music, and I've spent most of my adulthood frozen in a love of these things. Stunted adolescence and all that.

Fast forward to 1999: I'd dropped out of college, quit a string of jobs, and moved from Phoenix to San Francisco chasing a dream to make personal, absurd, independent comics at any cost.

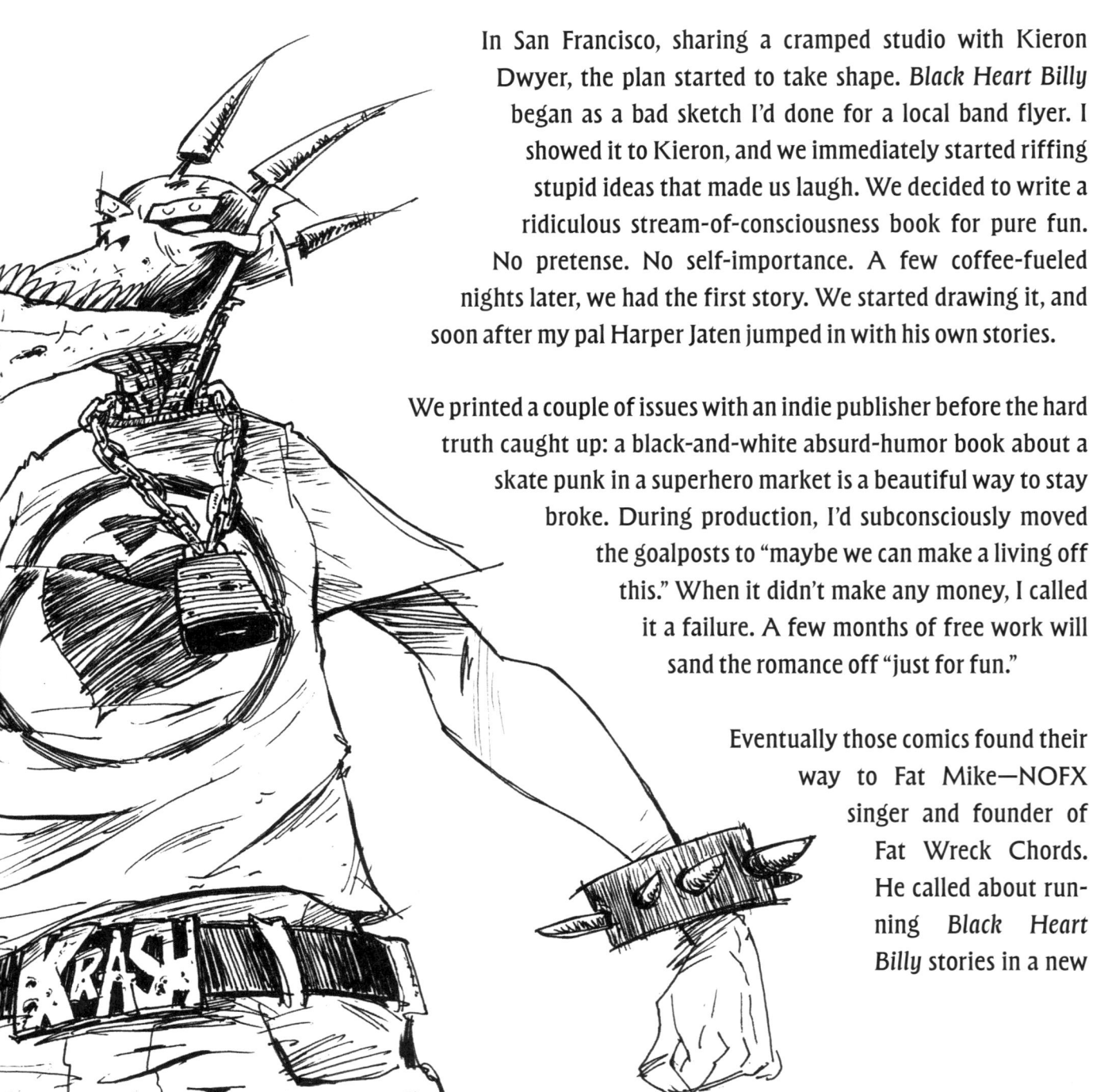

In San Francisco, sharing a cramped studio with Kieron Dwyer, the plan started to take shape. *Black Heart Billy* began as a bad sketch I'd done for a local band flyer. I showed it to Kieron, and we immediately started riffing stupid ideas that made us laugh. We decided to write a ridiculous stream-of-consciousness book for pure fun. No pretense. No self-importance. A few coffee-fueled nights later, we had the first story. We started drawing it, and soon after my pal Harper Jaten jumped in with his own stories.

We printed a couple of issues with an indie publisher before the hard truth caught up: a black-and-white absurd-humor book about a skate punk in a superhero market is a beautiful way to stay broke. During production, I'd subconsciously moved the goalposts to "maybe we can make a living off this." When it didn't make any money, I called it a failure. A few months of free work will sand the romance off "just for fun."

Eventually those comics found their way to Fat Mike—NOFX singer and founder of Fat Wreck Chords. He called about running *Black Heart Billy* stories in a new comic/catalog he was putting together and offered to pay us to bring Billy back and get it in front of punk kids. Under Fat Wreck, we did three new stories co-written with Mike; I also drew a NOFX album cover. Billy got a second chance.

With that financial boost, Kieron and I were able to make some time to finish the story and collect the series through a local hobby press. It didn't sell enough copies to buy groceries. We used the book to pitch an ongoing series across the industry, but no one was interested. So, we set Billy down and moved on. Again. I spent the next seven years working twelve hours a day in extreme poverty, taking any job I could get to fund my refusal to quit comics. My bad wiring called it tenacity. After giving much of my youth to the dream, failure would have proven them right. Every voice that ever said I was wasting my life, not worth a shit, and would never succeed.

Over time, my work found some attention and things got better. The price was heavier than I anticipated, but writing fed my family and kept the original dream alive: to collaborate with people I respect to create whatever inspires us. I don't take that for granted. I honor the cost and still push myself to make new, unique, personal stories—held to a standard no corporate machine can match.

But of all the characters I've created in twenty-seven years of doing this, none carries more weight than Billy. He was born when I was at rock bottom with no reasonable hope of success, and he exists because two friends showed up and did the work with me. Those years spent pushing him on an uninterested world were a metaphor I couldn't see yet.

Billy was me, and I was the thing nobody wanted.

This book was us saying, "fuck you, we're doing it anyway." Pushing forward, white-knuckling through poverty, hopelessness, and rejection.

This deluxe hardcover is for that damaged version of me holding up a burning house, not even sure why he couldn't let it fall. A warm reminder of those late nights with Kieron making pages that made us laugh, and of sketchbook sessions with Harper working up new designs for the editions we swore were coming. No hope, no future, no money. It was pure joy...

The kind you only get when you are trying too hard to make your friends laugh.

—Rick Remender

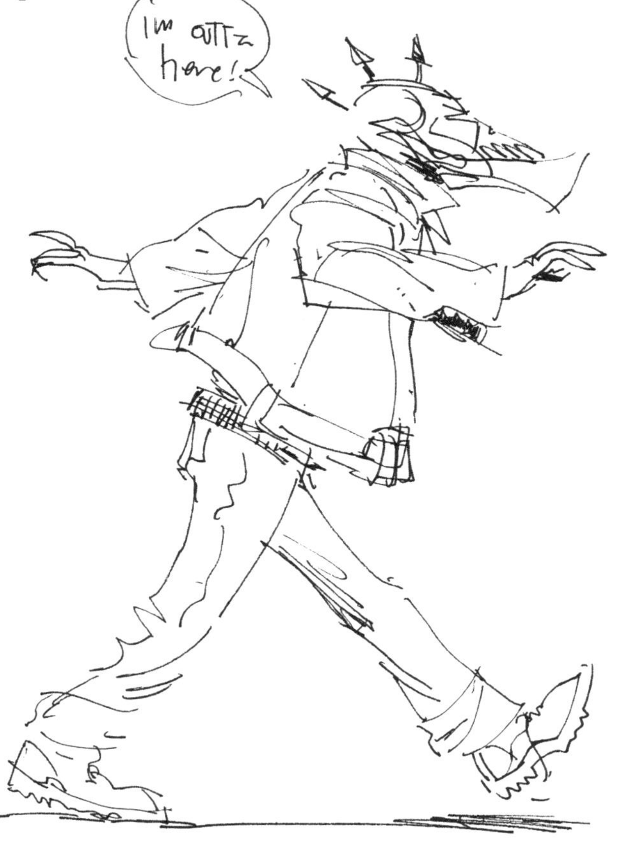
I'm outta here!

CONTENT NOTE

This collection reprints comics made in **1999-2002**. It contains:

- Cartoon violence and reckless stupidity
- Crude language, sexual innuendo, juvenile bathroom humor
- Drug/alcohol use
- Religion-as-foil gags
- Dictator-costume and other era-specific parody
- Musical parody and band send-ups
- Gross ignorance of all varieties
- A wholly irredeemable lead character doing and saying very dumb things
- Degenerate behavior not reminiscent of wholesome corporate superheroes dressed punk
- Period-accurate hippie aesthetics and grooming

The intent then—and now—was **satire**: the punchline lands on Billy (*who is a grotesque idiot*), authoritarianism/Nazis, general hypocrisy, cultural rot, and corporate nonsense, not on real communities. Most jokes will read as dated. We've kept most everything intact to show how the work was built, a quarter century ago, dents and all.

Reader discretion advised

IMAGE COMICS, INC. • **Robert Kirkman:** Chief Operations Officer • **Erik Larsen:** Chief Financial Officer • **Todd McFarlane:** President • **Marc Silvestri:** Chief Executive Officer • **Jim Valentino:** Vice President • **Eric Stephenson:** Publisher & Chief Creative Officer • **IMAGECOMICS.COM**

BLACK HEART BILLY TWENTY-FIFTH ANNIVERSARY EDITION. First printing. December 2025. Published by Image Comics, Inc. Office of publication: PO BOX 14457, Portland, OR 97293. Copyright © 2025 Rick Remender, Kieron Dwyer & Harper Jaten. All rights reserved. "Black Heart Billy," its logos, and the likenesses of all characters herein are trademarks of Rick Remender, Kieron Dwyer & Harper Jaten, unless otherwise noted. Image Comics logo designed by Rob Liefeld. "Image" and the Image Comics logos are registered trademarks of Image Comics, Inc. No part of this publication may be reproduced or transmitted, in any form or by any means (except for short excerpts for journalistic or review purposes), without the express written permission of Rick Remender, Kieron Dwyer & Harper Jaten, or Image Comics, Inc. All names, characters, events, and locales in this publication are entirely fictional. Any resemblance to actual persons (living or dead), events, or places, without satirical intent, is coincidental. Printed in China. For international rights, contact: foreignlicensing@imagecomics.com. ISBN: 978-1-5343-3326-0.

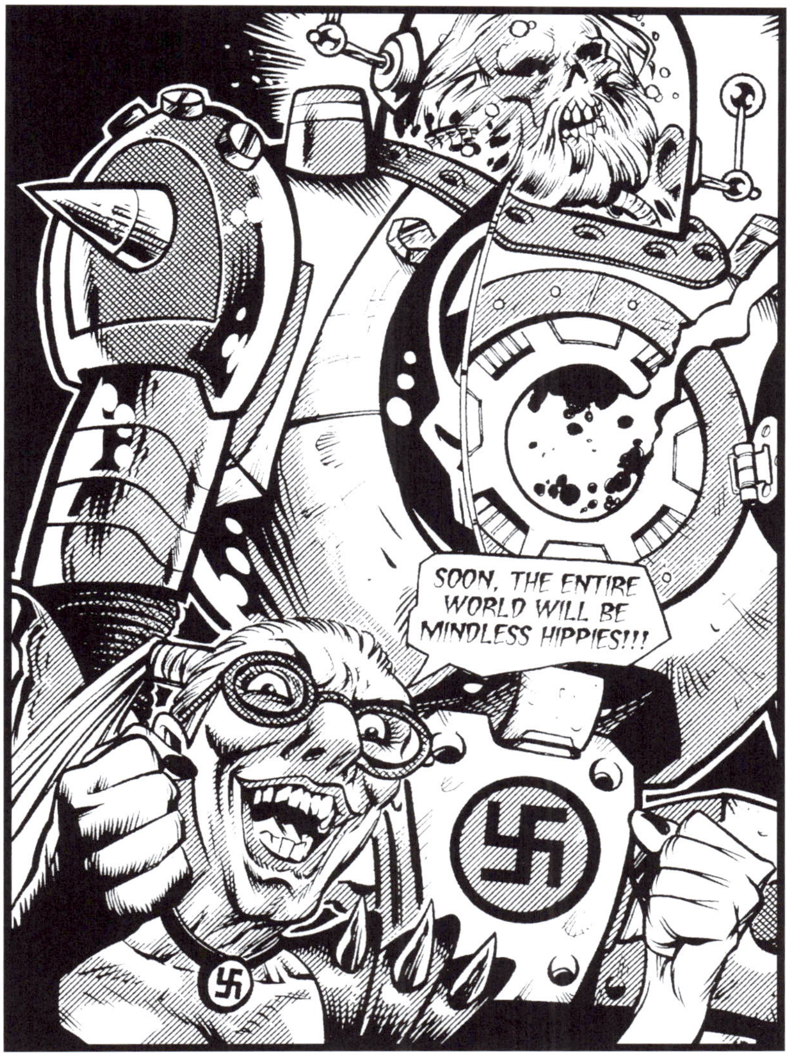
SOON, THE ENTIRE WORLD WILL BE MINDLESS HIPPIES!!!

ONE

THE BALLAD OF BILLY BLACK AND THE GRATEFUL UNDEADHEADS OF THE FOURTH REICH

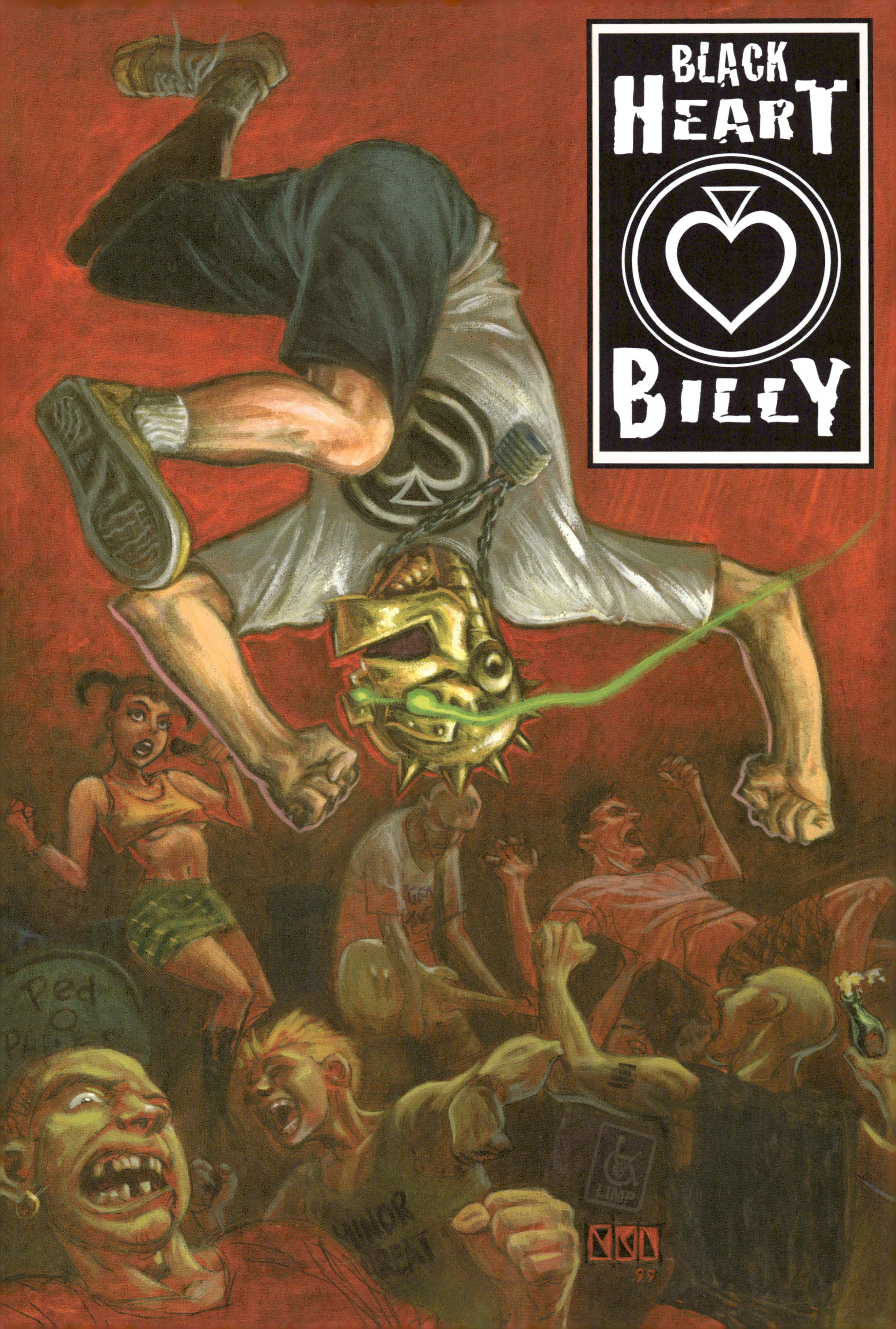
BLACK
HEART
BILLY
LIMP
MINOR

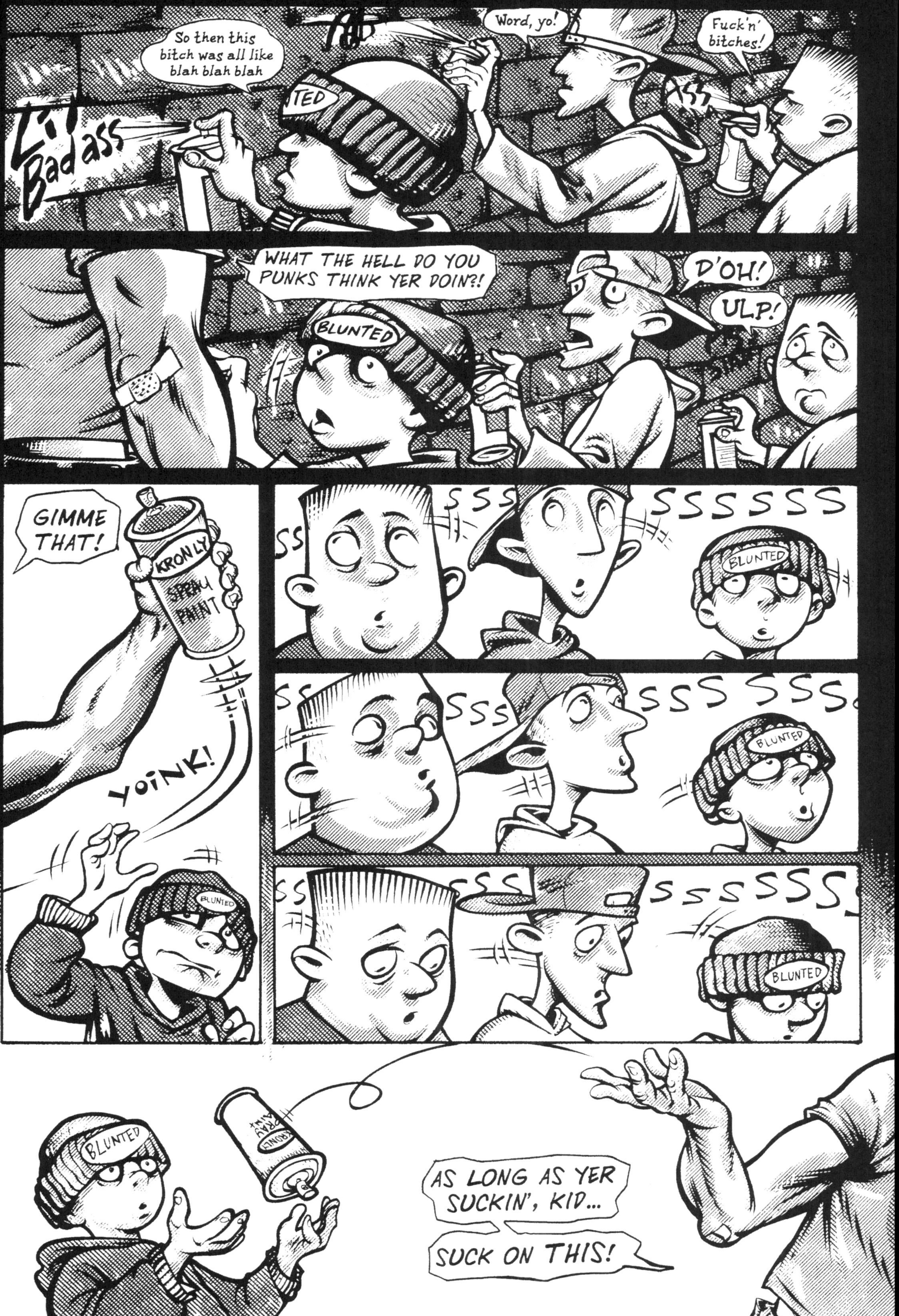

So then this bitch was all like blah blah blah
Word, yo!
Fuck'n' bitches!
Li'l Badass
WHAT THE HELL DO YOU PUNKS THINK YER DOIN?!
D'OH!
ULP!
BLUNTED
GIMME THAT!
KRONLY SPRAY PAINT
YOINK!
SSSSSS
SSSSSSS
SSSSSSS
AS LONG AS YER SUCKIN', KID...
SUCK ON THIS!

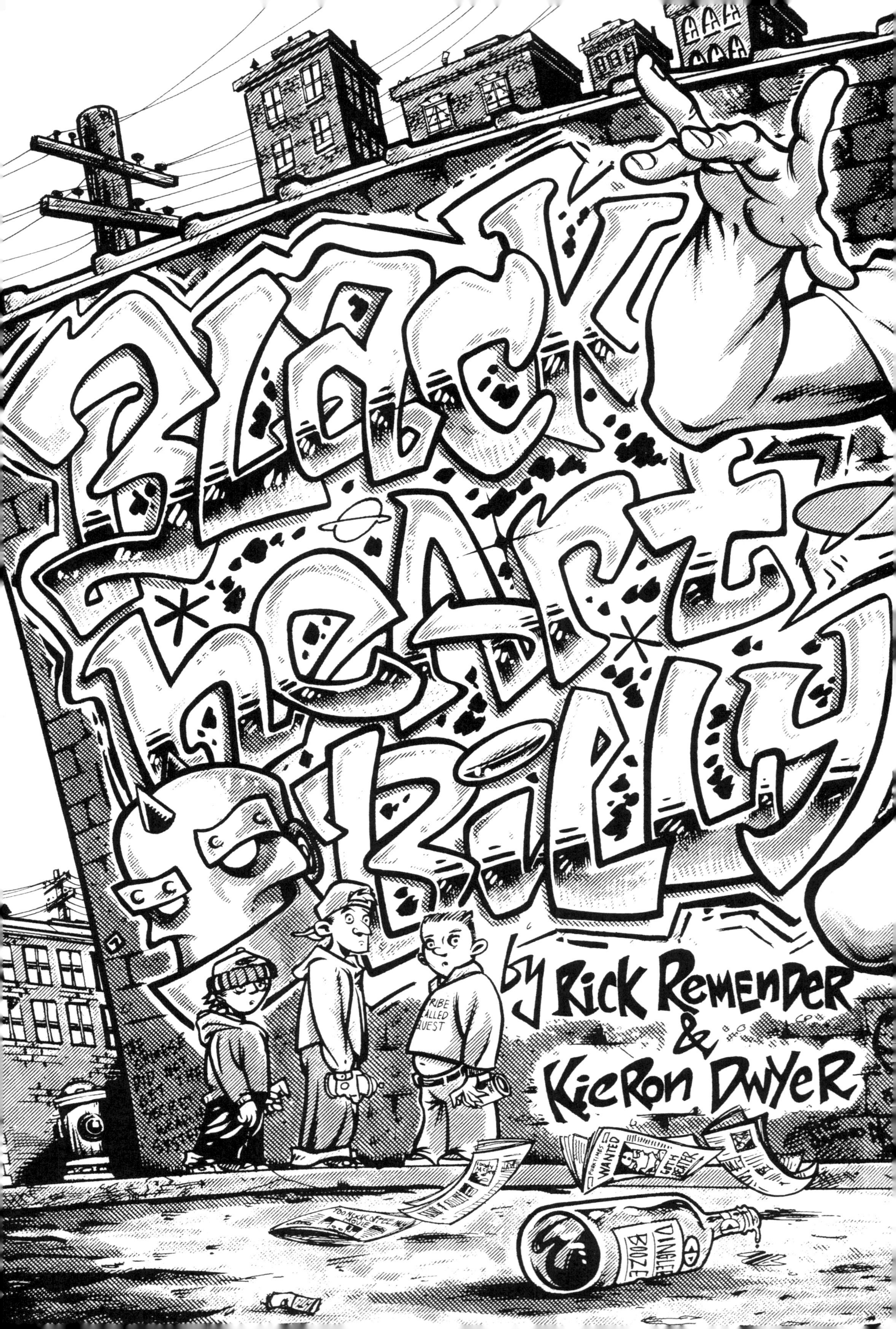

by Rick Remender
&
Kieron Dwyer
TRIBE CALLED QUEST
WANTED
DINGLE BOOZE

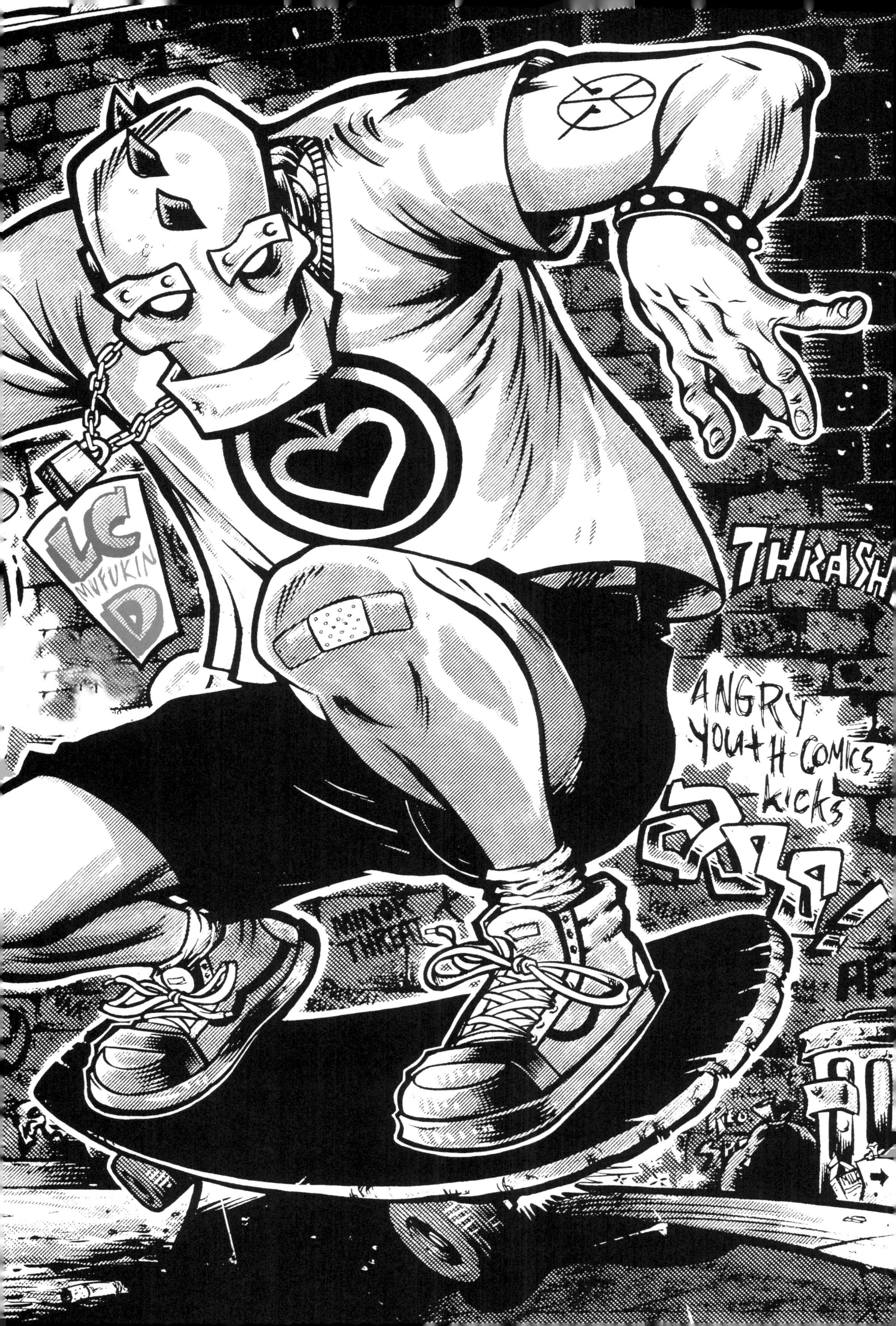

LC
MUFUKIN
D
THRASH
ANGRY
YOUTH COMICS
kicks
MINOR
THREAT

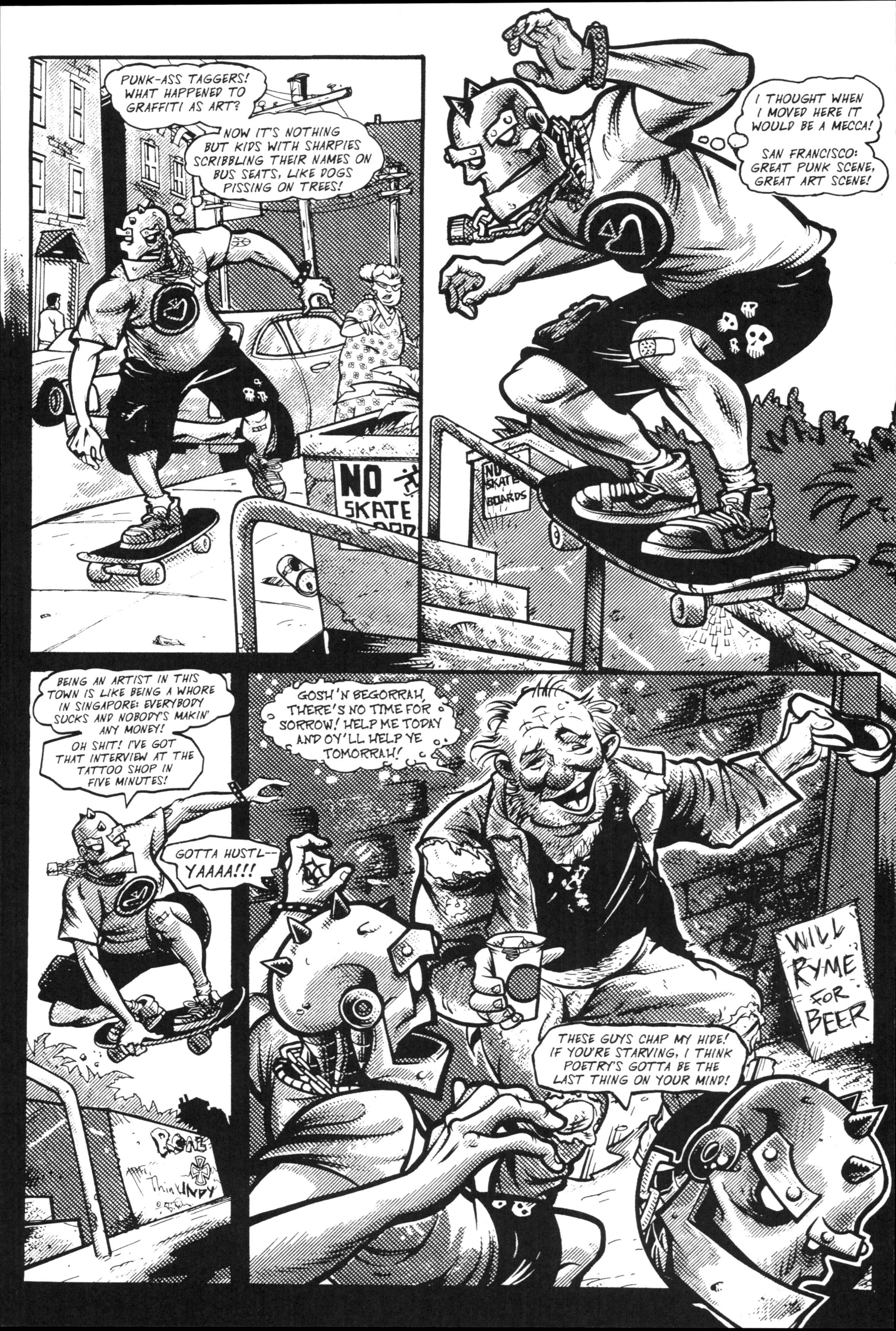
PUNK-ASS TAGGERS! WHAT HAPPENED TO GRAFFITI AS ART?
NOW IT'S NOTHING BUT KIDS WITH SHARPIES SCRIBBLING THEIR NAMES ON BUS SEATS, LIKE DOGS PISSING ON TREES!
NO SKATE
I THOUGHT WHEN I MOVED HERE IT WOULD BE A MECCA!
SAN FRANCISCO: GREAT PUNK SCENE, GREAT ART SCENE!
NO SKATE BOARDS
BEING AN ARTIST IN THIS TOWN IS LIKE BEING A WHORE IN SINGAPORE: EVERYBODY SUCKS AND NOBODY'S MAKIN' ANY MONEY!
OH SHIT! I'VE GOT THAT INTERVIEW AT THE TATTOO SHOP IN FIVE MINUTES!
GOTTA HUSTL--YAAAA!!!
GOSH 'N BEGORRAH, THERE'S NO TIME FOR SORROW! HELP ME TODAY AND OY'LL HELP YE TOMORRAH!
WILL RYME FOR BEER
THESE GUYS CHAP MY HIDE! IF YOU'RE STARVING, I THINK POETRY'S GOTTA BE THE LAST THING ON YOUR MIND!

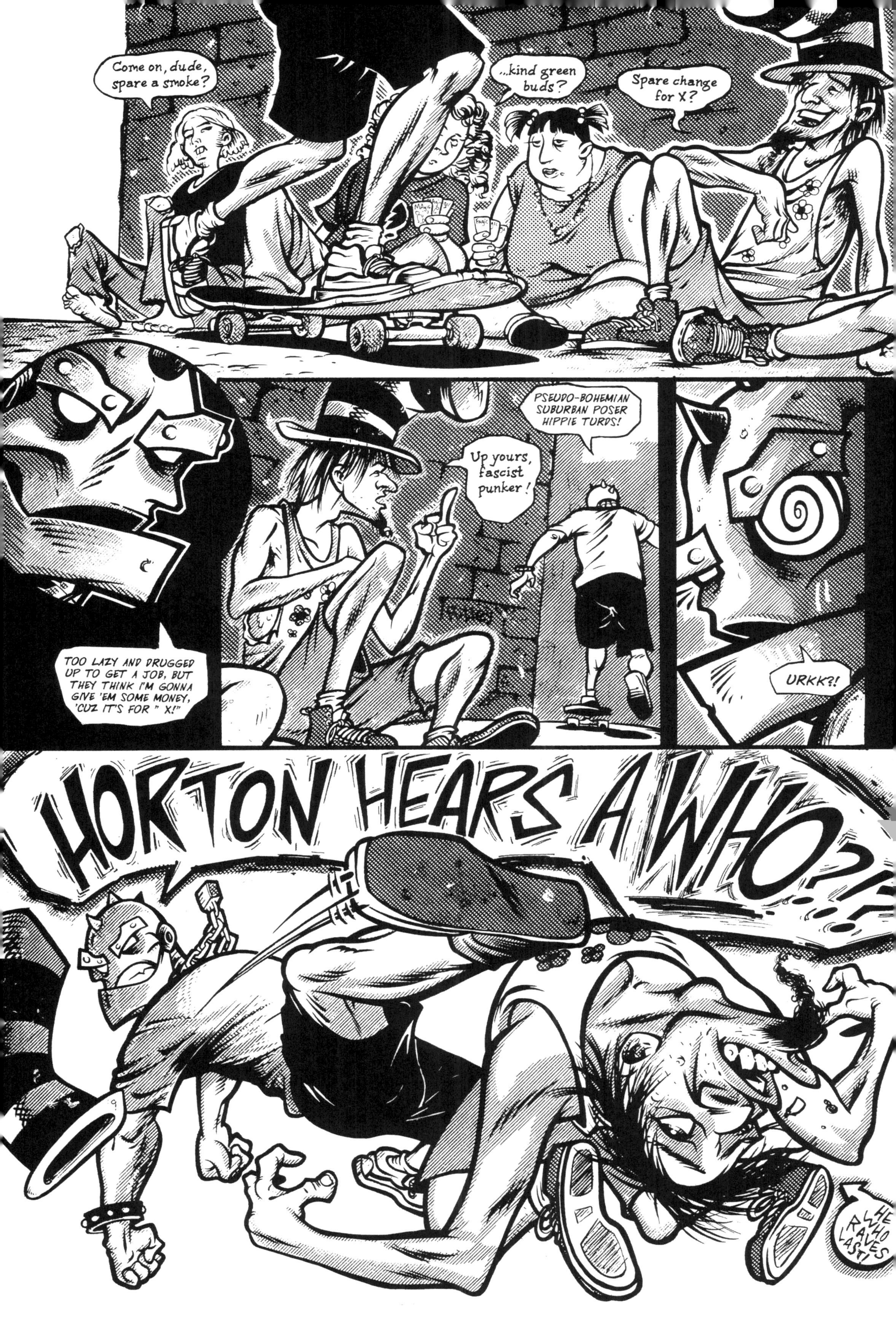

Come on, dude, spare a smoke?
...kind green buds?
Spare change for X?
TOO LAZY AND DRUGGED UP TO GET A JOB, BUT THEY THINK I'M GONNA GIVE 'EM SOME MONEY, 'CUZ IT'S FOR " X!"
PSEUDO-BOHEMIAN SUBURBAN POSER HIPPIE TURDS!
Up yours, fascist punker!
URKK?!
HORTON HEARS A WHO?!!
HE WHO RAVES LAST!

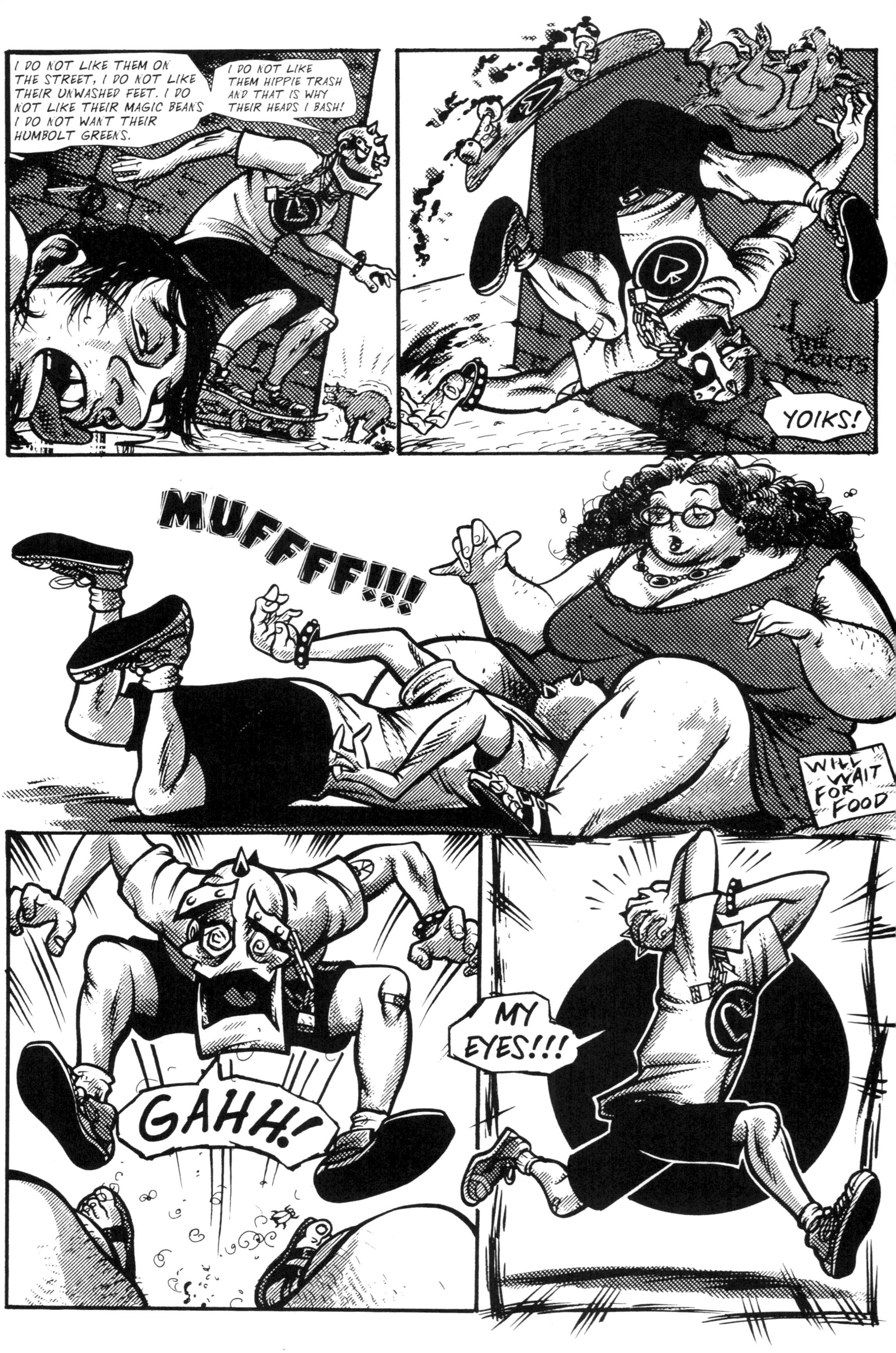

I DO NOT LIKE THEM ON THE STREET, I DO NOT LIKE THEIR UNWASHED FEET. I DO NOT LIKE THEIR MAGIC BEANS I DO NOT WANT THEIR HUMBOLT GREENS.
I DO NOT LIKE THEM HIPPIE TRASH AND THAT IS WHY THEIR HEADS I BASH!
YOIKS!
MUFFFFF!!!
WILL WAIT FOR FOOD
GAHH!
MY EYES!!!

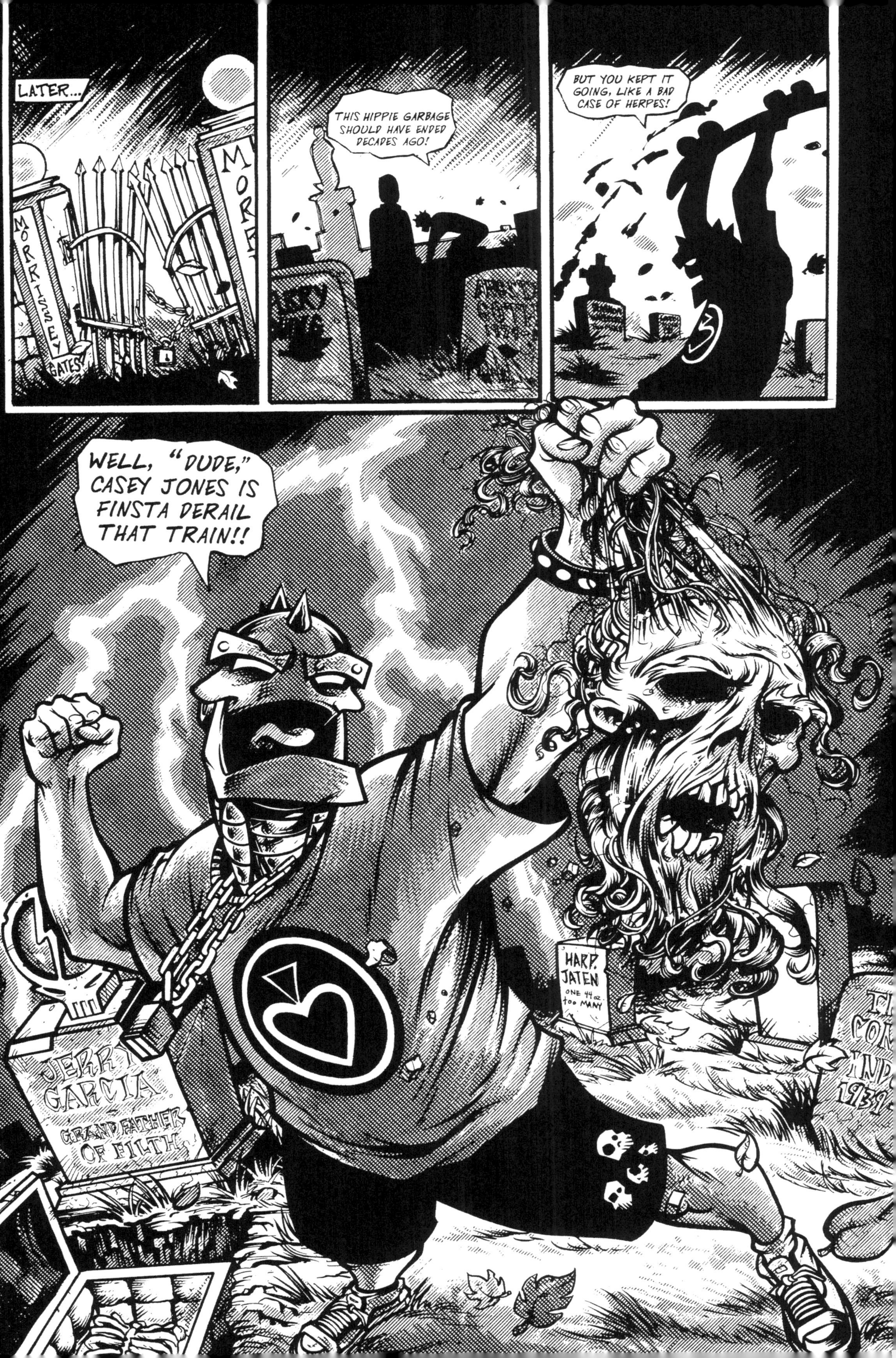
LATER...
MORRISSEY GATES
MORR
THIS HIPPIE GARBAGE SHOULD HAVE ENDED DECADES AGO!
BUT YOU KEPT IT GOING, LIKE A BAD CASE OF HERPES!
WELL, "DUDE," CASEY JONES IS FINSTA DERAIL THAT TRAIN!!
JERRY GARCIA
GRAND FATHER OF FILTH
HARD JATEN
ONE 44 oz too MANY

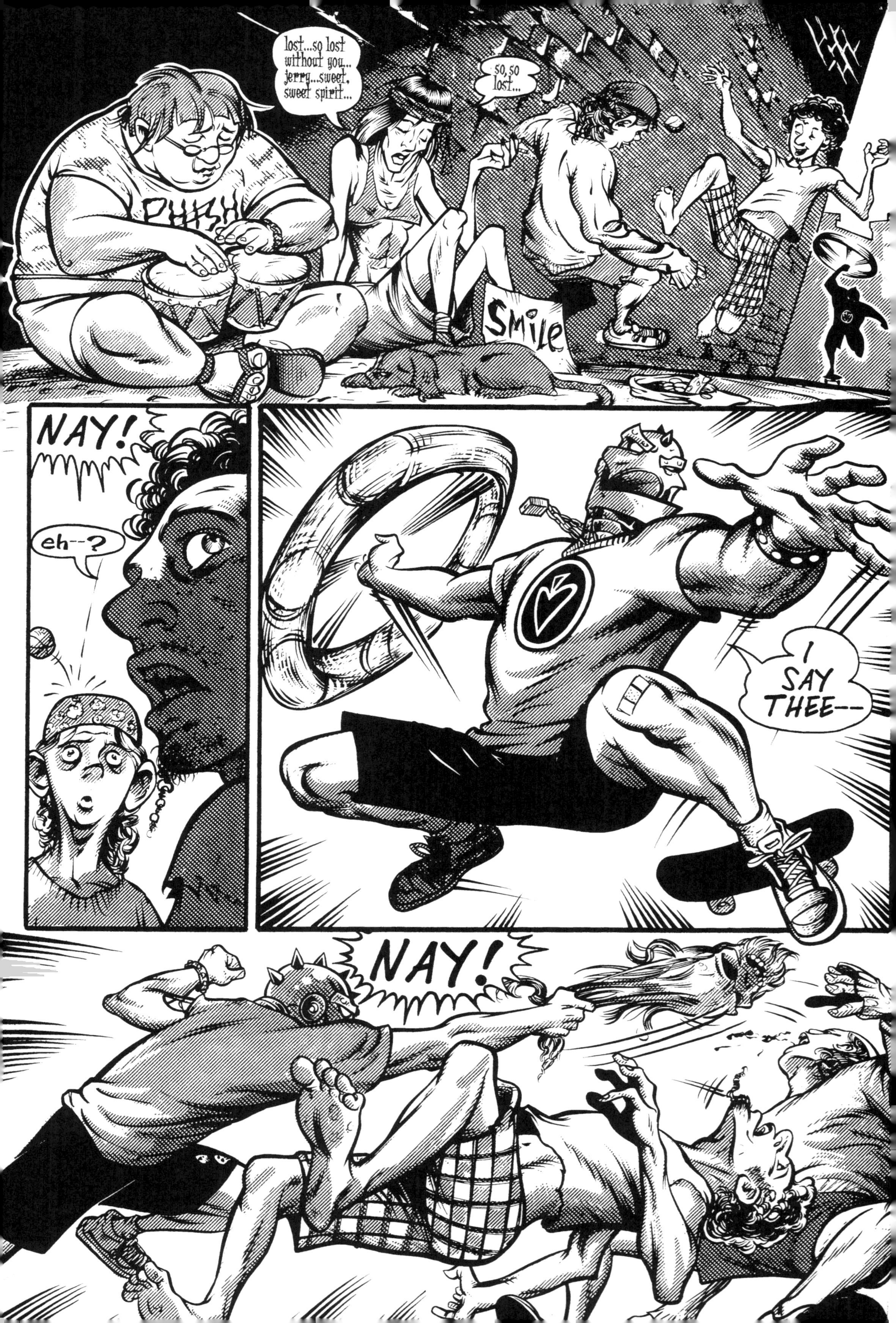
lost...so lost without you... jerry...sweet, sweet spirit...
so, so lost...
PHISH
SMILE
NAY!
eh--?
I SAY THEE--
NAY!

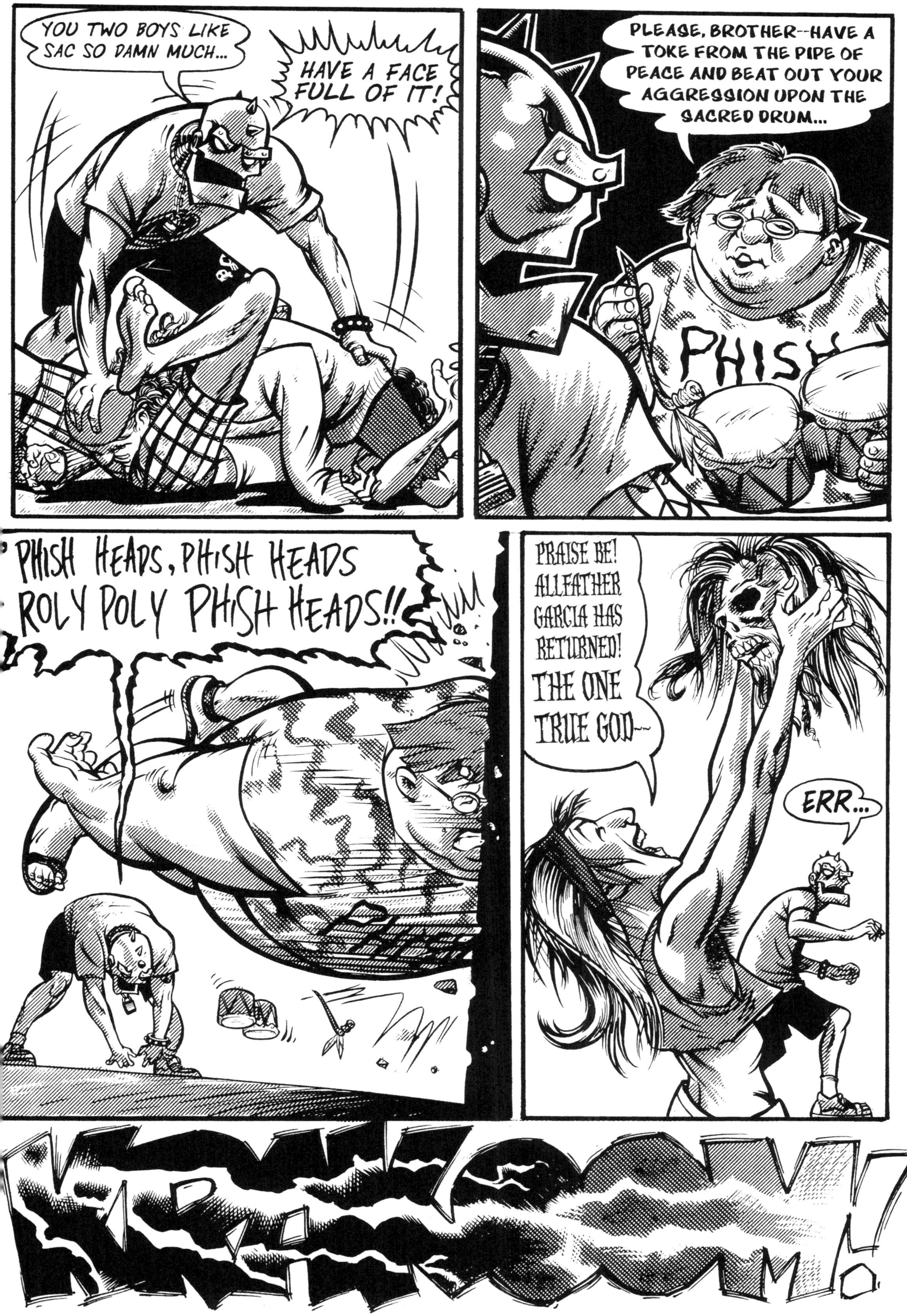
YOU TWO BOYS LIKE SAC SO DAMN MUCH...
HAVE A FACE FULL OF IT!
PLEASE, BROTHER--HAVE A TOKE FROM THE PIPE OF PEACE AND BEAT OUT YOUR AGGRESSION UPON THE SACRED DRUM...
PHISH
PHISH HEADS, PHISH HEADS ROLY POLY PHISH HEADS!!
PRAISE BE! ALLFATHER GARCIA HAS RETURNED! THE ONE TRUE GOD--
ERR...
KRA-KOOM!

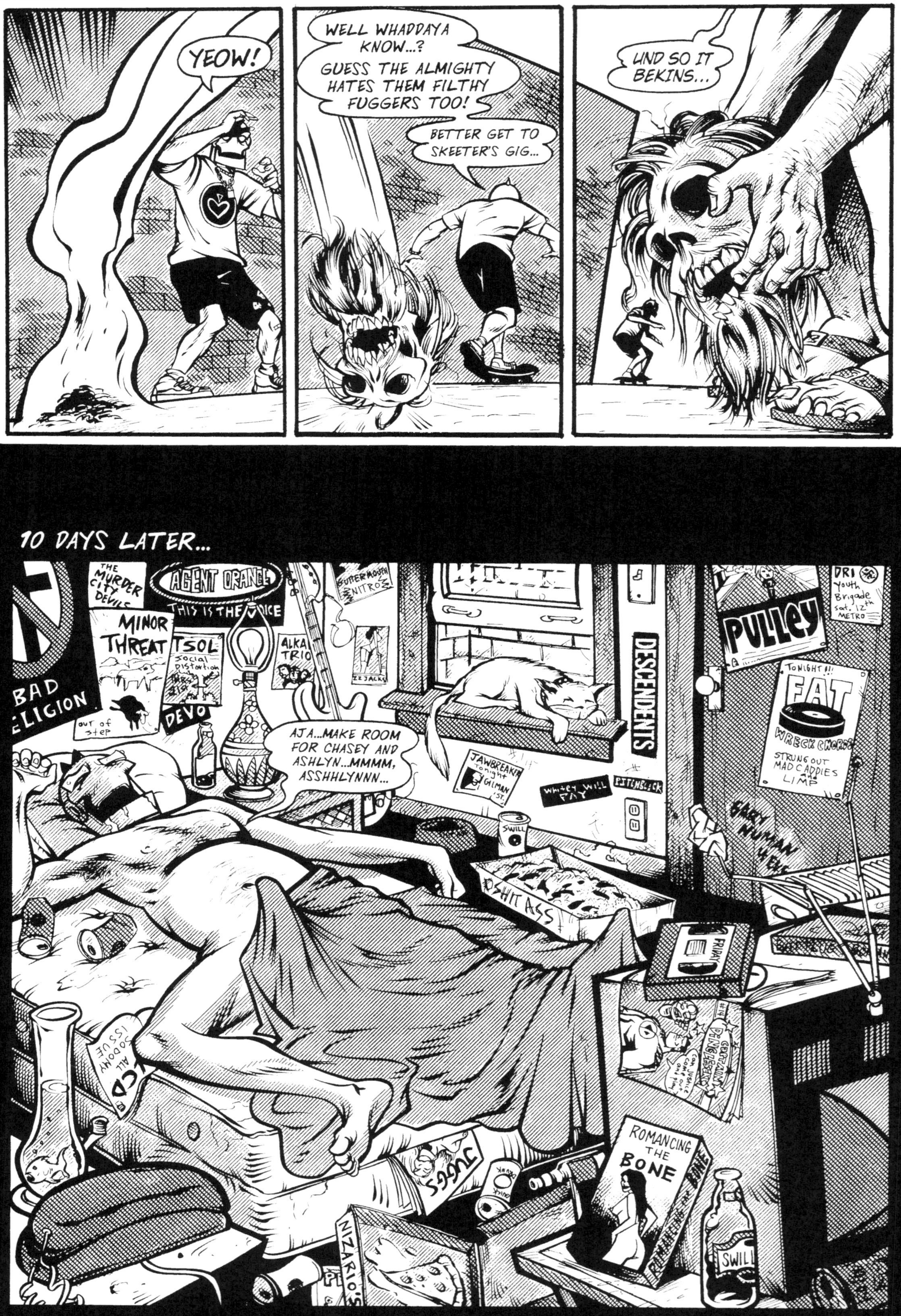
YEOW!
WELL WHADDAYA KNOW...?
GUESS THE ALMIGHTY HATES THEM FILTHY FUGGERS TOO!
BETTER GET TO SKEETER'S GIG...
UND SO IT BEKINS...
10 DAYS LATER...
THE MURDER CITY DEVILS
AGENT ORANGE
THIS IS THE VOICE
MINOR THREAT
TSOL
BAD
DEVO
DESCENDENTS
PULLEY
TONIGHT!!
FAT
WRECK CHORDS
STRUNG OUT
MAD CADDIES
AND
LIMP
AJA...MAKE ROOM FOR CHASEY AND ASHLYN...MMMM, ASSHHLYNNN...
SWILL
ROMANCING THE BONE
JUGGS
NIZARIO'S

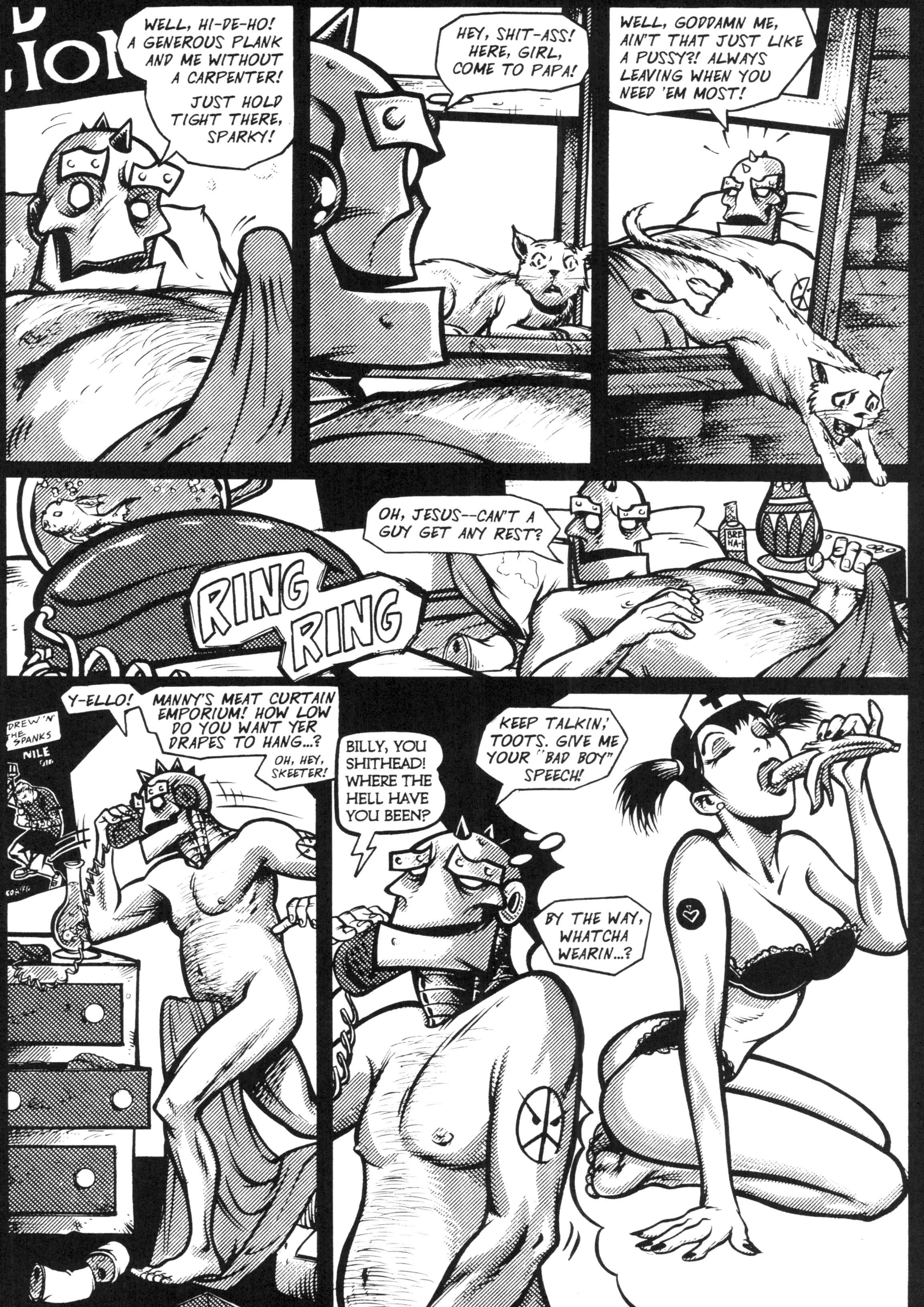
WELL, HI-DE-HO! A GENEROUS PLANK AND ME WITHOUT A CARPENTER!
JUST HOLD TIGHT THERE, SPARKY!
HEY, SHIT-ASS! HERE, GIRL, COME TO PAPA!
WELL, GODDAMN ME, AIN'T THAT JUST LIKE A PUSSY?! ALWAYS LEAVING WHEN YOU NEED 'EM MOST!
OH, JESUS--CAN'T A GUY GET ANY REST?
RING RING
Y-ELLO!
MANNY'S MEAT CURTAIN EMPORIUM! HOW LOW DO YOU WANT YER DRAPES TO HANG...?
OH, HEY, SKEETER!
DREW 'N' THE SPANKS
NILE
BILLY, YOU SHITHEAD! WHERE THE HELL HAVE YOU BEEN?
KEEP TALKIN,' TOOTS. GIVE ME YOUR "BAD BOY" SPEECH!
BY THE WAY, WHATCHA WEARIN...?

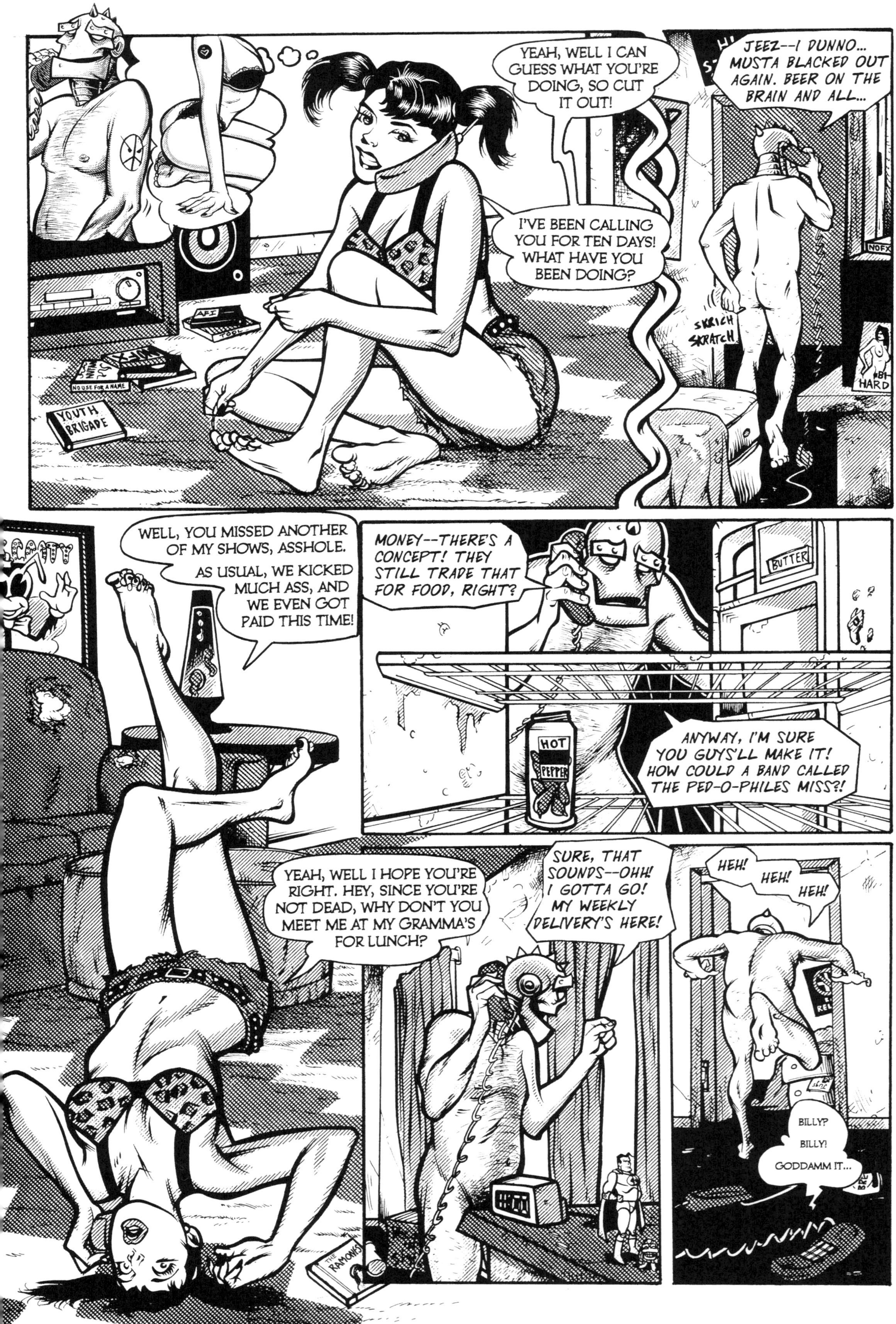
YEAH, WELL I CAN GUESS WHAT YOU'RE DOING, SO CUT IT OUT!
I'VE BEEN CALLING YOU FOR TEN DAYS! WHAT HAVE YOU BEEN DOING?
JEEZ--I DUNNO... MUSTA BLACKED OUT AGAIN. BEER ON THE BRAIN AND ALL...
SKRICH SKRATCH
AFI
TOOL
NOFX
NO USE FOR A NAME
YOUTH BRIGADE
BUTTER
WELL, YOU MISSED ANOTHER OF MY SHOWS, ASSHOLE.
AS USUAL, WE KICKED MUCH ASS, AND WE EVEN GOT PAID THIS TIME!
MONEY--THERE'S A CONCEPT! THEY STILL TRADE THAT FOR FOOD, RIGHT?
HOT PEPPER
ANYWAY, I'M SURE YOU GUYS'LL MAKE IT! HOW COULD A BAND CALLED THE PED-O-PHILES MISS?!
YEAH, WELL I HOPE YOU'RE RIGHT. HEY, SINCE YOU'RE NOT DEAD, WHY DON'T YOU MEET ME AT MY GRAMMA'S FOR LUNCH?
SURE, THAT SOUNDS--OHH! I GOTTA GO! MY WEEKLY DELIVERY'S HERE!
THE RAMONES
HEH!
HEH!
HEH!
BILLY?
BILLY!
GODDAMM IT...

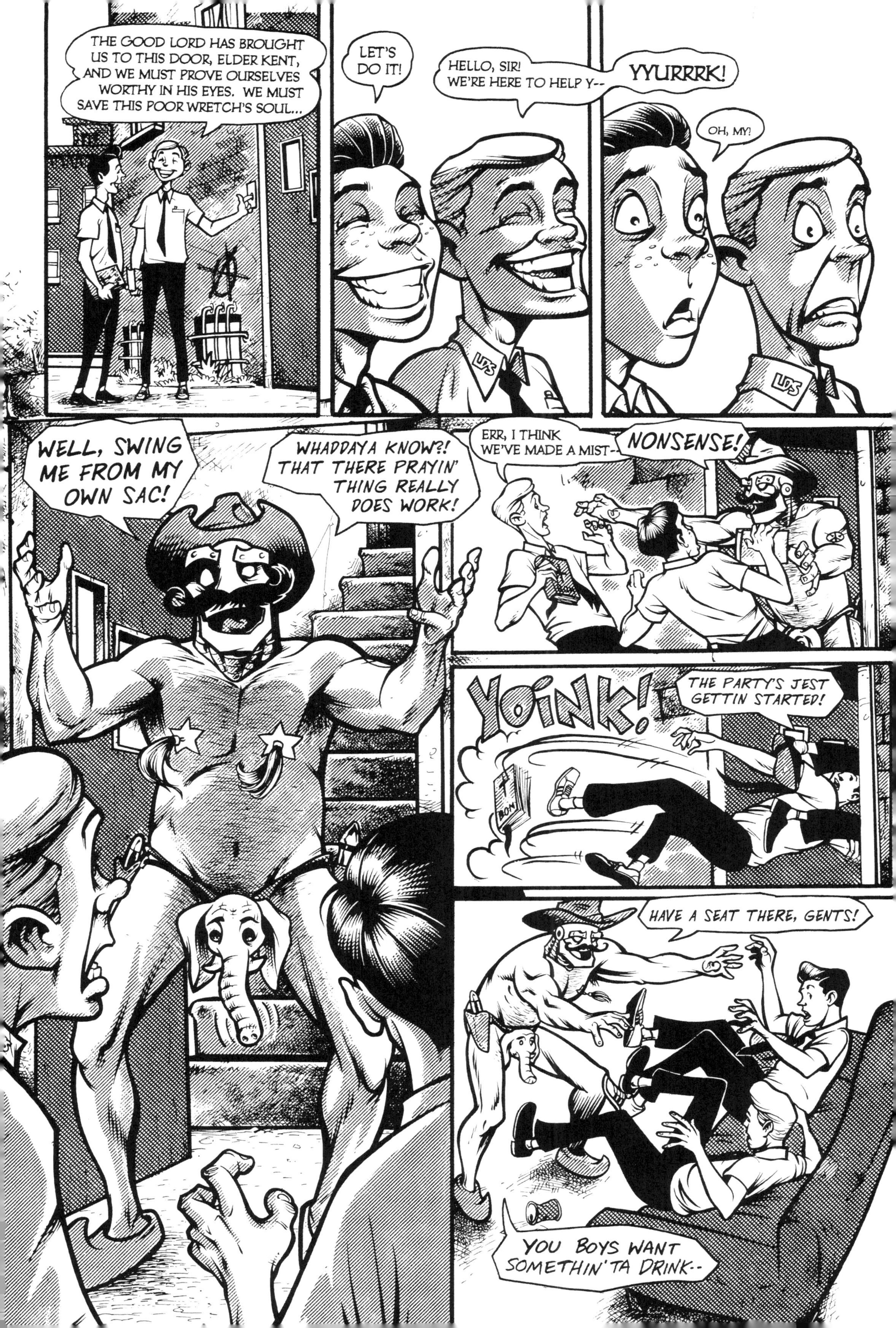
THE GOOD LORD HAS BROUGHT US TO THIS DOOR, ELDER KENT, AND WE MUST PROVE OURSELVES WORTHY IN HIS EYES. WE MUST SAVE THIS POOR WRETCH'S SOUL...
LET'S DO IT!
HELLO, SIR! WE'RE HERE TO HELP Y--
YYURRRK!
OH, MY!
WELL, SWING ME FROM MY OWN SAC!
WHADDAYA KNOW?! THAT THERE PRAYIN' THING REALLY DOES WORK!
ERR, I THINK WE'VE MADE A MIST--
NONSENSE!
YOINK!
THE PARTY'S JEST GETTIN STARTED!
HAVE A SEAT THERE, GENTS!
YOU BOYS WANT SOMETHIN' TA DRINK--

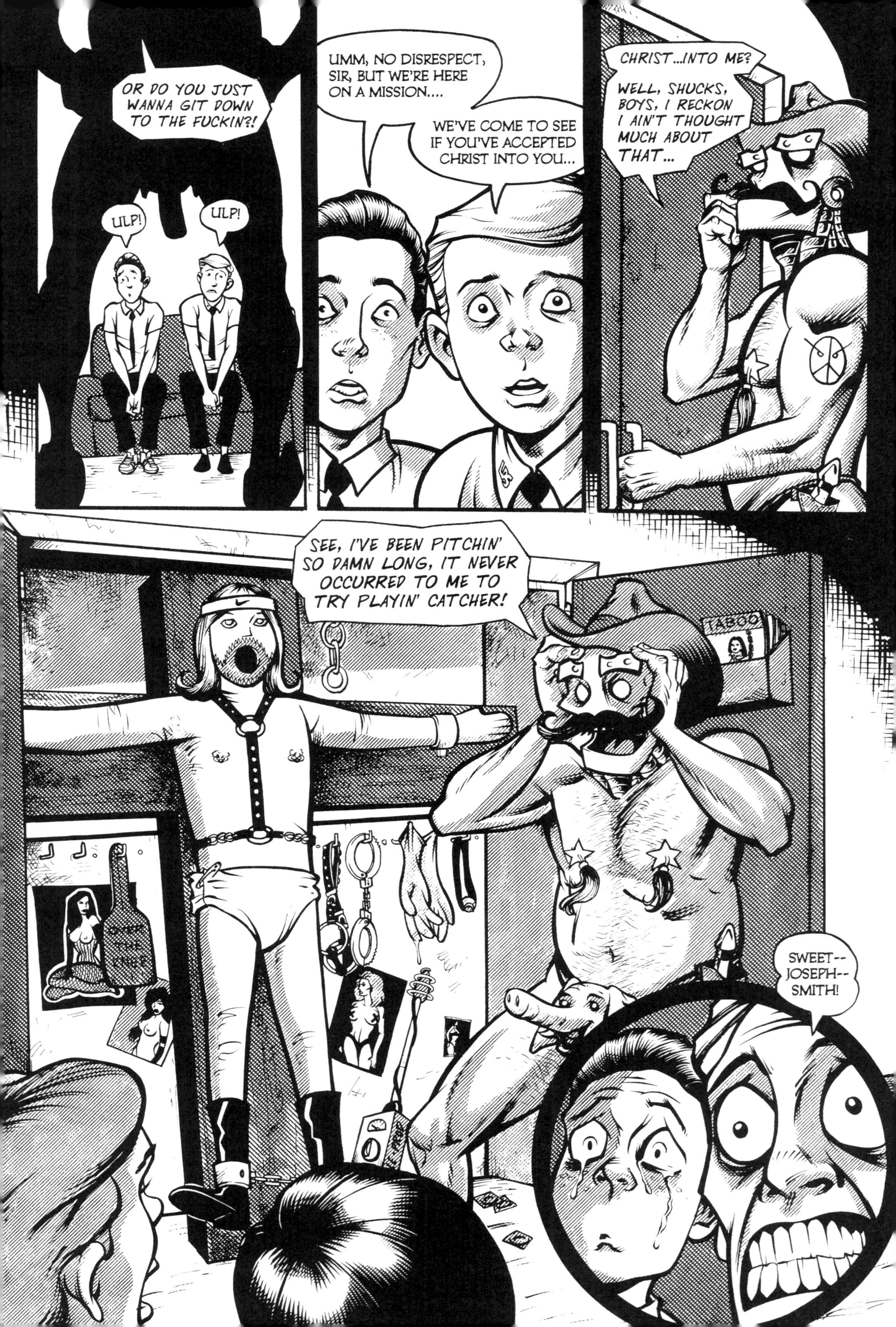
OR DO YOU JUST WANNA GIT DOWN TO THE FUCKIN?!
ULP!
ULP!
UMM, NO DISRESPECT, SIR, BUT WE'RE HERE ON A MISSION....
WE'VE COME TO SEE IF YOU'VE ACCEPTED CHRIST INTO YOU...
CHRIST...INTO ME?
WELL, SHUCKS, BOYS, I RECKON I AIN'T THOUGHT MUCH ABOUT THAT...
SEE, I'VE BEEN PITCHIN' SO DAMN LONG, IT NEVER OCCURRED TO ME TO TRY PLAYIN' CATCHER!
TABOO
SWEET-- JOSEPH-- SMITH!

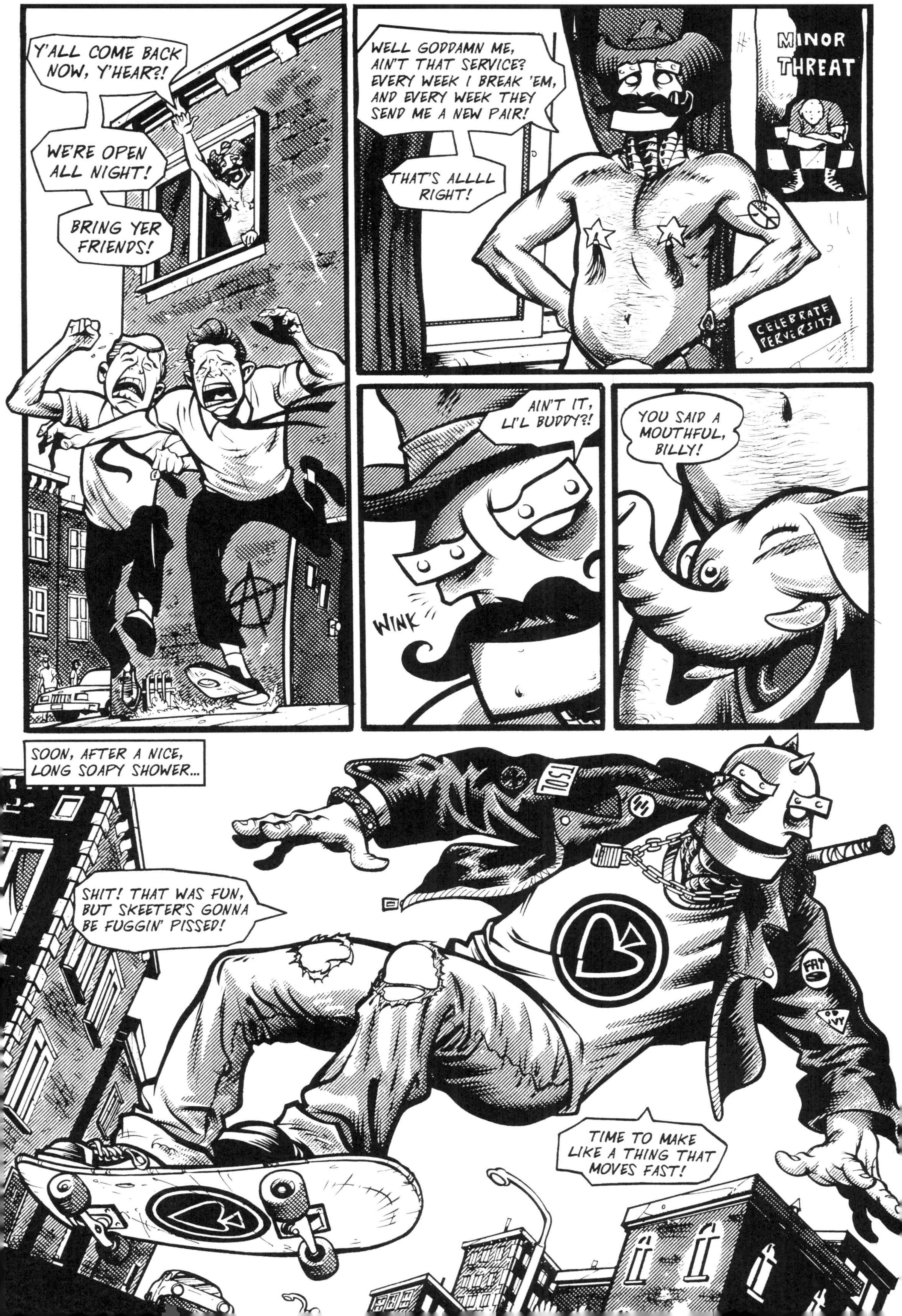
Y'ALL COME BACK NOW, Y'HEAR?!
WE'RE OPEN ALL NIGHT!
BRING YER FRIENDS!
MINOR THREAT
WELL GODDAMN ME, AIN'T THAT SERVICE? EVERY WEEK I BREAK 'EM, AND EVERY WEEK THEY SEND ME A NEW PAIR!
THAT'S ALLLL RIGHT!
CELEBRATE PERVERSITY
AIN'T IT, LI'L BUDDY?!
WINK
YOU SAID A MOUTHFUL, BILLY!
SOON, AFTER A NICE, LONG SOAPY SHOWER...
ISOL
SHIT! THAT WAS FUN, BUT SKEETER'S GONNA BE FUGGIN' PISSED!
FAT
OP IVY
TIME TO MAKE LIKE A THING THAT MOVES FAST!

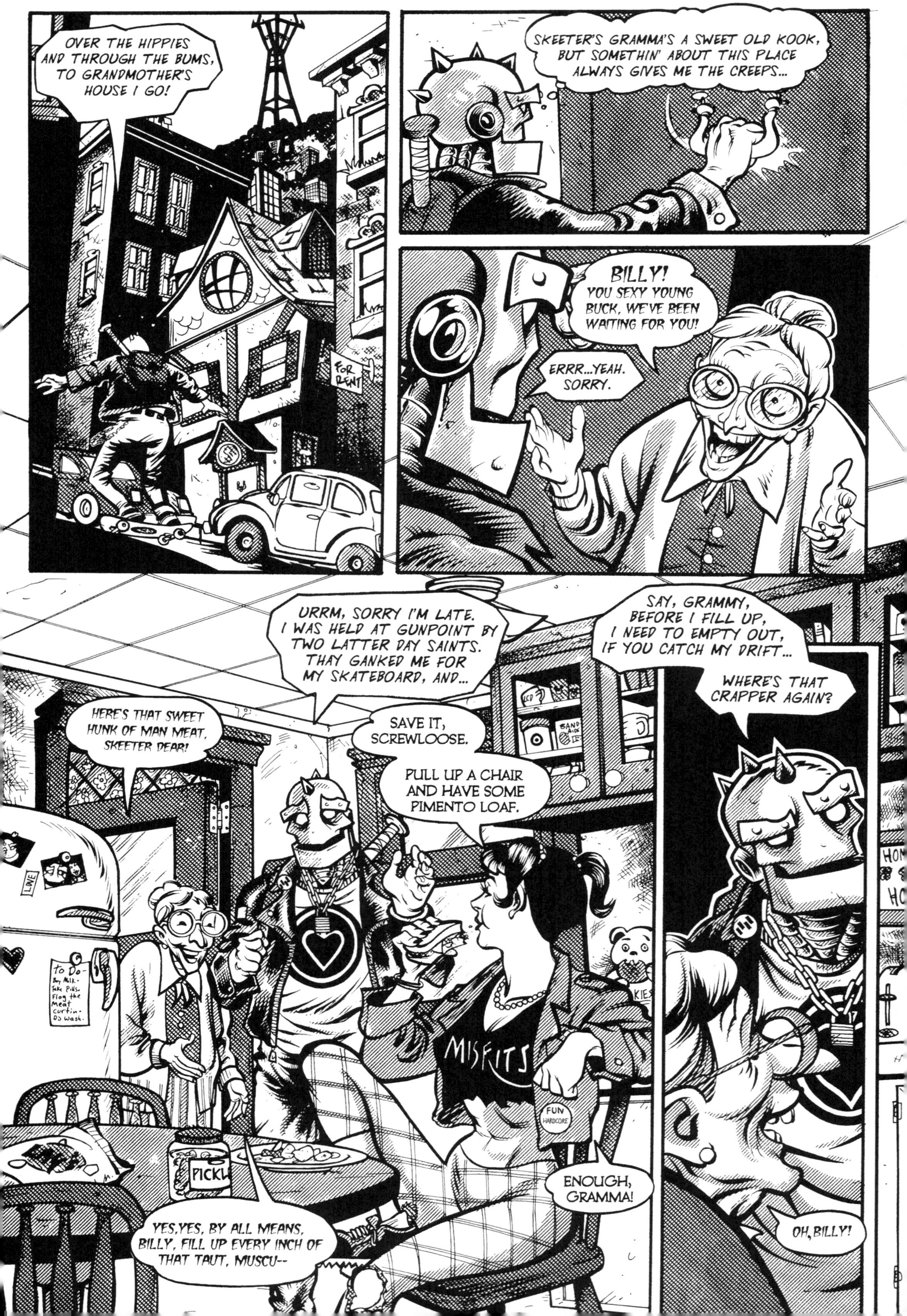
OVER THE HIPPIES AND THROUGH THE BUMS, TO GRANDMOTHER'S HOUSE I GO!
FOR RENT
SKEETER'S GRAMMA'S A SWEET OLD KOOK, BUT SOMETHIN' ABOUT THIS PLACE ALWAYS GIVES ME THE CREEPS...
BILLY! YOU SEXY YOUNG BUCK, WE'VE BEEN WAITING FOR YOU!
ERRR...YEAH. SORRY.
URRM, SORRY I'M LATE. I WAS HELD AT GUNPOINT BY TWO LATTER DAY SAINTS. THAY GANKED ME FOR MY SKATEBOARD, AND...
HERE'S THAT SWEET HUNK OF MAN MEAT, SKEETER DEAR!
SAVE IT, SCREWLOOSE.
PULL UP A CHAIR AND HAVE SOME PIMENTO LOAF.
MISFITS
FUN HARDCORE
YES,YES, BY ALL MEANS, BILLY, FILL UP EVERY INCH OF THAT TAUT, MUSCU--
ENOUGH, GRAMMA!
SAY, GRAMMY, BEFORE I FILL UP, I NEED TO EMPTY OUT, IF YOU CATCH MY DRIFT...
WHERE'S THAT CRAPPER AGAIN?
OH, BILLY!

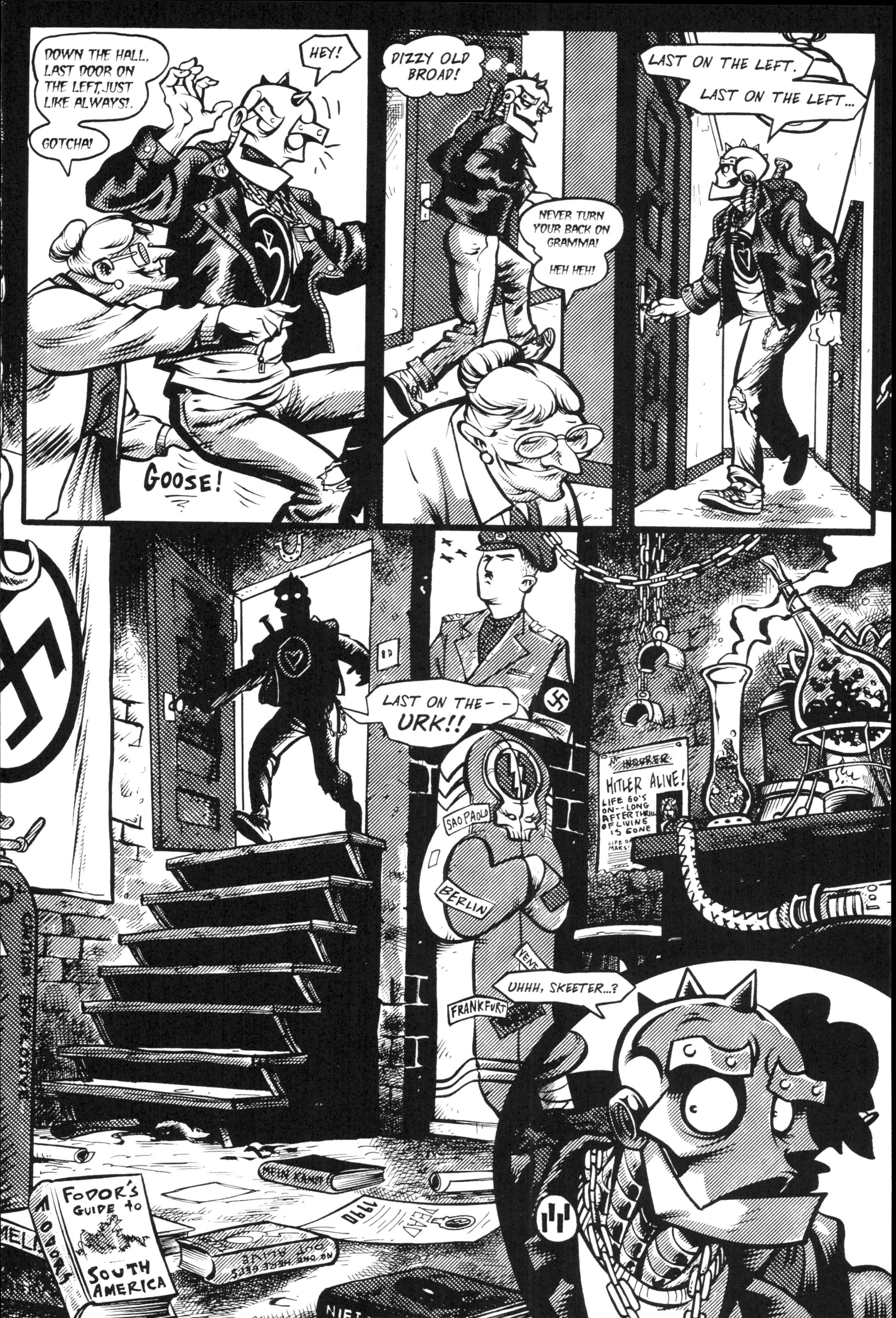
DOWN THE HALL, LAST DOOR ON THE LEFT, JUST LIKE ALWAYS!.
HEY!
GOTCHA!
GOOSE!
DIZZY OLD BROAD!
NEVER TURN YOUR BACK ON GRAMMA!
HEH HEH!
LAST ON THE LEFT.
LAST ON THE LEFT...
LAST ON THE-- URK!!
HITLER ALIVE!
LIFE GO'S ON--LONG AFTER THRILL OF LIVING IS GONE
SAO PAOLO
BERLIN
FRANKFURT
UHHH, SKEETER...?
MEIN KAMPF
FODOR'S GUIDE TO SOUTH AMERICA
NO ONE HERE GETS OUT ALIVE

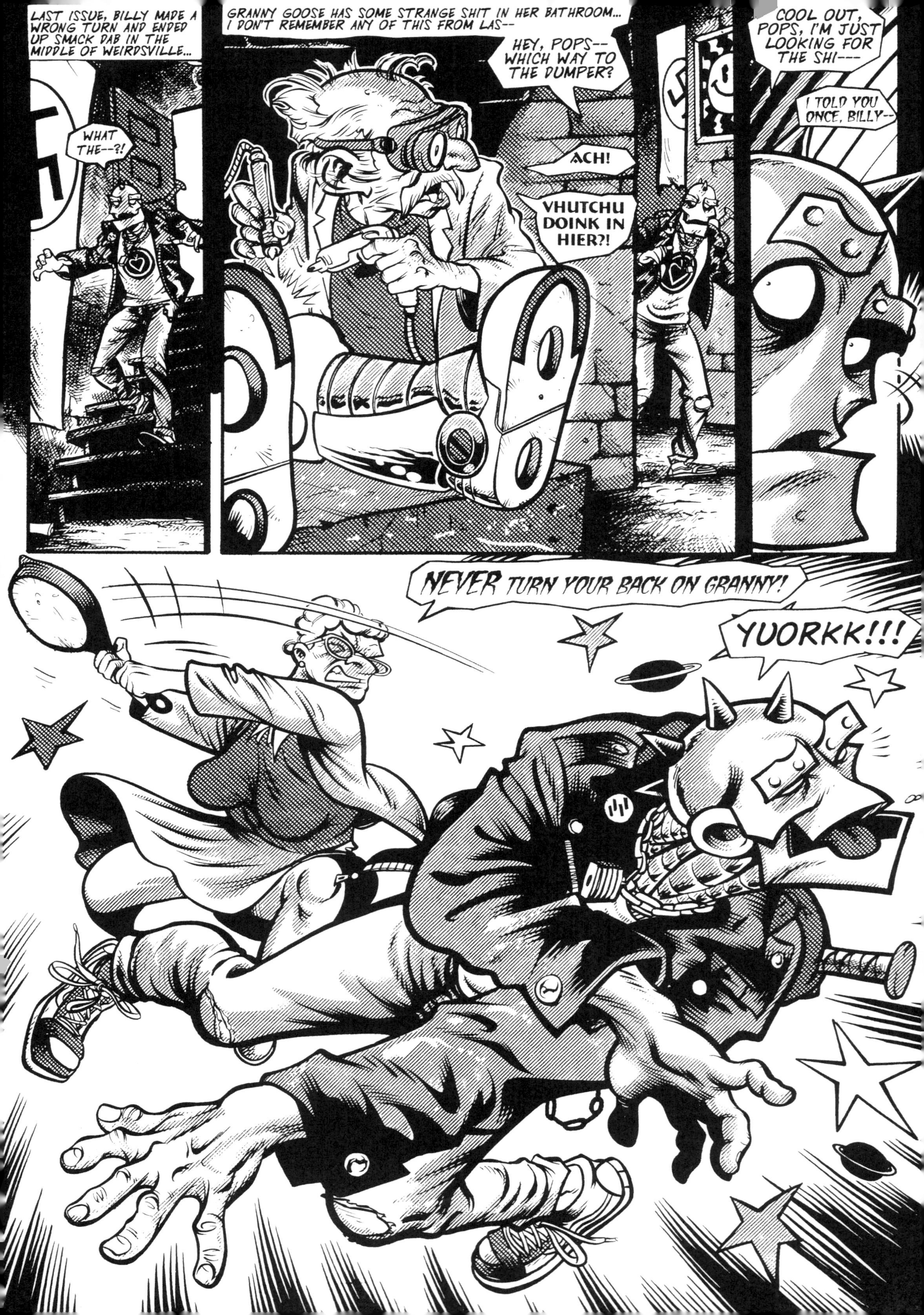
LAST ISSUE, BILLY MADE A WRONG TURN AND ENDED UP SMACK DAB IN THE MIDDLE OF WEIRDSVILLE...
WHAT THE--?!
GRANNY GOOSE HAS SOME STRANGE SHIT IN HER BATHROOM... I DON'T REMEMBER ANY OF THIS FROM LAS--
HEY, POPS-- WHICH WAY TO THE DUMPER?
ACH!
VHUTCHU DOINK IN HIER?!
COOL OUT, POPS, I'M JUST LOOKING FOR THE SHI---
I TOLD YOU ONCE, BILLY--
NEVER TURN YOUR BACK ON GRANNY!
YUORKK!!!

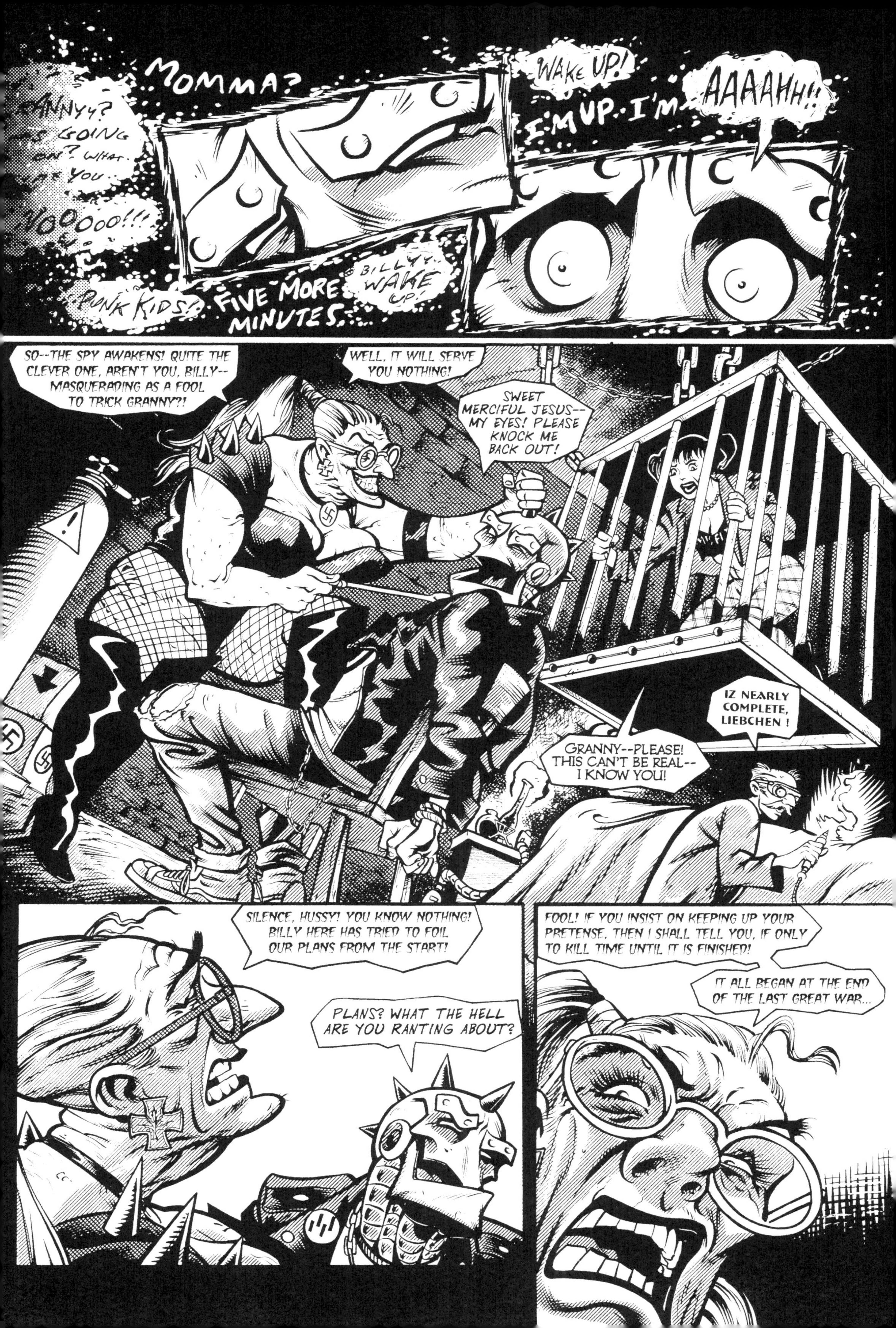

GOING ON? WHAT YOU
NOOOOOO!!!
PUNK KIDS!
MOMMA?
FIVE MORE MINUTES
BILLY... WAKE UP!
WAKE UP!
I'M UP. I'M
AAAAHH!!
SO--THE SPY AWAKENS! QUITE THE CLEVER ONE, AREN'T YOU, BILLY-- MASQUERADING AS A FOOL TO TRICK GRANNY?!
WELL, IT WILL SERVE YOU NOTHING!
SWEET MERCIFUL JESUS-- MY EYES! PLEASE KNOCK ME BACK OUT!
IZ NEARLY COMPLETE, LIEBCHEN !
GRANNY--PLEASE! THIS CAN'T BE REAL-- I KNOW YOU!
SILENCE, HUSSY! YOU KNOW NOTHING! BILLY HERE HAS TRIED TO FOIL OUR PLANS FROM THE START!
PLANS? WHAT THE HELL ARE YOU RANTING ABOUT?
FOOL! IF YOU INSIST ON KEEPING UP YOUR PRETENSE, THEN I SHALL TELL YOU, IF ONLY TO KILL TIME UNTIL IT IS FINISHED!
IT ALL BEGAN AT THE END OF THE LAST GREAT WAR...

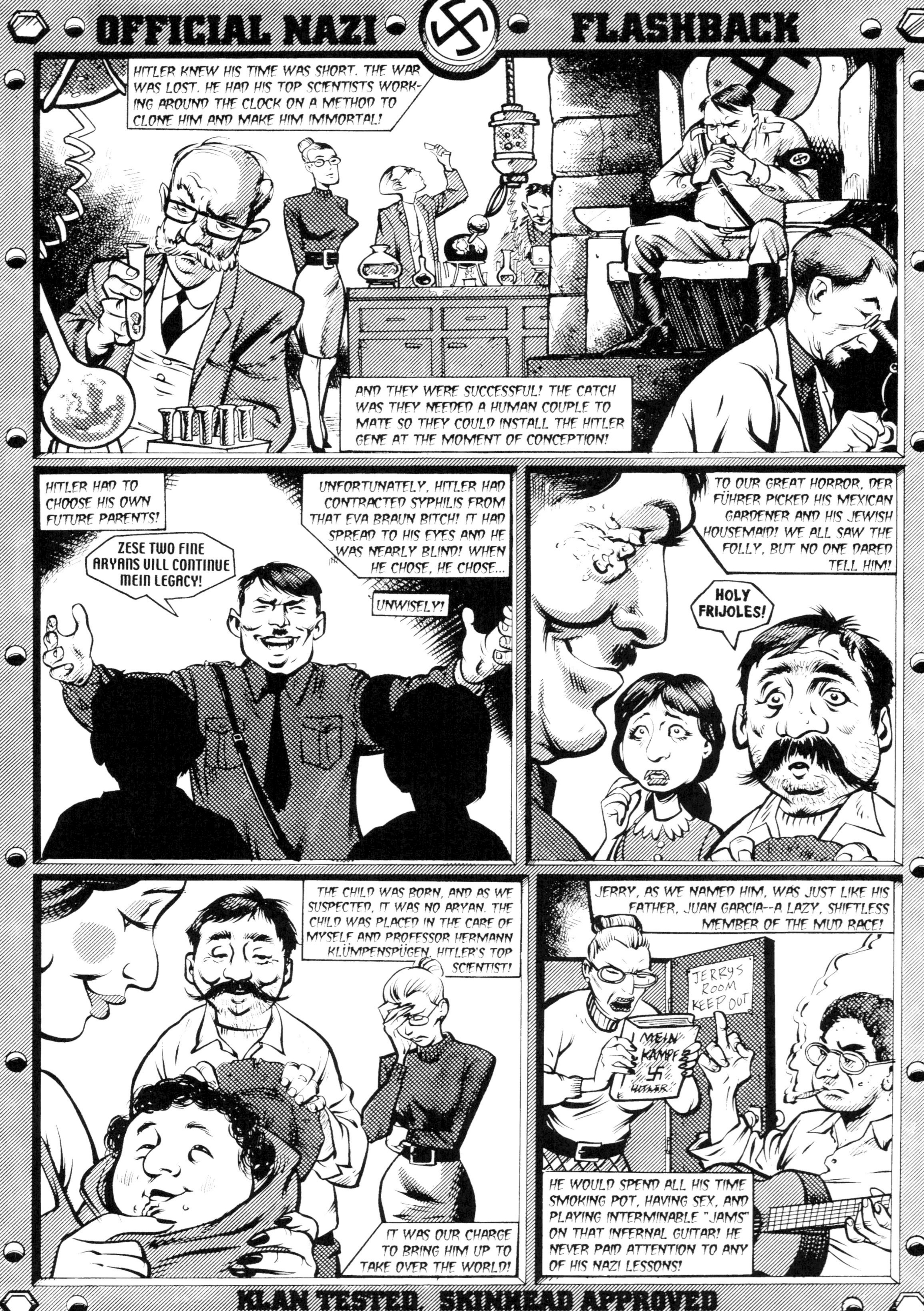
OFFICIAL NAZI FLASHBACK
HITLER KNEW HIS TIME WAS SHORT. THE WAR WAS LOST. HE HAD HIS TOP SCIENTISTS WORKING AROUND THE CLOCK ON A METHOD TO CLONE HIM AND MAKE HIM IMMORTAL!
AND THEY WERE SUCCESSFUL! THE CATCH WAS THEY NEEDED A HUMAN COUPLE TO MATE SO THEY COULD INSTALL THE HITLER GENE AT THE MOMENT OF CONCEPTION!
HITLER HAD TO CHOOSE HIS OWN FUTURE PARENTS!
ZESE TWO FINE ARYANS VILL CONTINUE MEIN LEGACY!
UNFORTUNATELY, HITLER HAD CONTRACTED SYPHILIS FROM THAT EVA BRAUN BITCH! IT HAD SPREAD TO HIS EYES AND HE WAS NEARLY BLIND! WHEN HE CHOSE, HE CHOSE...
UNWISELY!
TO OUR GREAT HORROR, DER FÜHRER PICKED HIS MEXICAN GARDENER AND HIS JEWISH HOUSEMAID! WE ALL SAW THE FOLLY, BUT NO ONE DARED TELL HIM!
HOLY FRIJOLES!
THE CHILD WAS BORN, AND AS WE SUSPECTED, IT WAS NO ARYAN. THE CHILD WAS PLACED IN THE CARE OF MYSELF AND PROFESSOR HERMANN KLÜMPENSPÜGEN, HITLER'S TOP SCIENTIST!
IT WAS OUR CHARGE TO BRING HIM UP TO TAKE OVER THE WORLD!
JERRY, AS WE NAMED HIM, WAS JUST LIKE HIS FATHER, JUAN GARCIA--A LAZY, SHIFTLESS MEMBER OF THE MUD RACE!
JERRYS ROOM KEEP OUT
MEIN KAMPF HITLER
HE WOULD SPEND ALL HIS TIME SMOKING POT, HAVING SEX, AND PLAYING INTERMINABLE "JAMS" ON THAT INFERNAL GUITAR! HE NEVER PAID ATTENTION TO ANY OF HIS NAZI LESSONS!
KLAN TESTED, SKINHEAD APPROVED

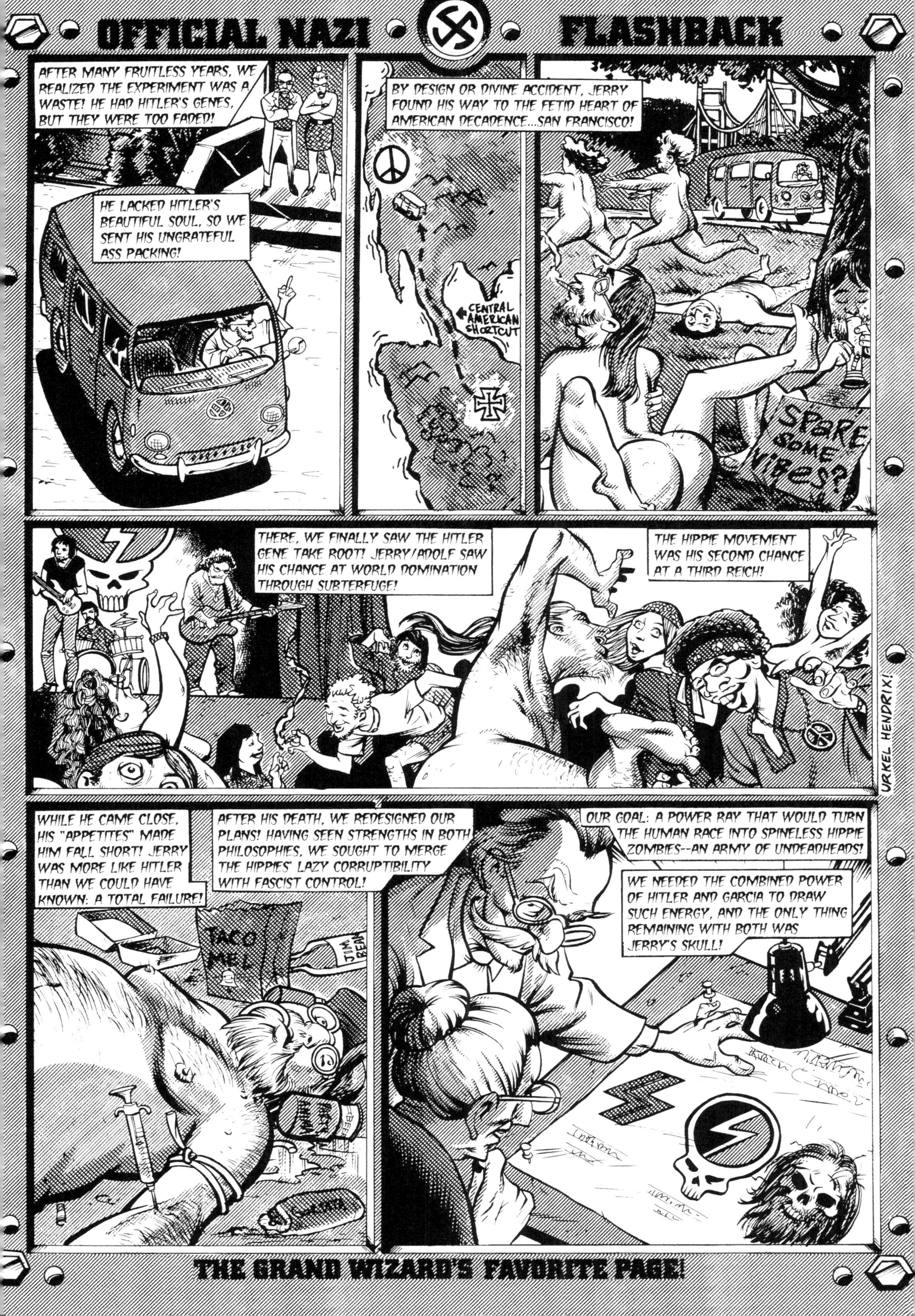
OFFICIAL NAZI FLASHBACK
AFTER MANY FRUITLESS YEARS, WE REALIZED THE EXPERIMENT WAS A WASTE! HE HAD HITLER'S GENES, BUT THEY WERE TOO FADED!
HE LACKED HITLER'S BEAUTIFUL SOUL, SO WE SENT HIS UNGRATEFUL ASS PACKING!
BY DESIGN OR DIVINE ACCIDENT, JERRY FOUND HIS WAY TO THE FETID HEART OF AMERICAN DECADENCE...SAN FRANCISCO!
CENTRAL AMERICAN SHORTCUT
SPARE SOME VIBES?
THERE, WE FINALLY SAW THE HITLER GENE TAKE ROOT! JERRY/ADOLF SAW HIS CHANCE AT WORLD DOMINATION THROUGH SUBTERFUGE!
THE HIPPIE MOVEMENT WAS HIS SECOND CHANCE AT A THIRD REICH!
URKEL HENDRIX!
WHILE HE CAME CLOSE, HIS "APPETITES" MADE HIM FALL SHORT! JERRY WAS MORE LIKE HITLER THAN WE COULD HAVE KNOWN: A TOTAL FAILURE!
AFTER HIS DEATH, WE REDESIGNED OUR PLANS! HAVING SEEN STRENGTHS IN BOTH PHILOSOPHIES, WE SOUGHT TO MERGE THE HIPPIES' LAZY CORRUPTIBILITY WITH FASCIST CONTROL!
TACO MEL
JIM BEAN
OUR GOAL: A POWER RAY THAT WOULD TURN THE HUMAN RACE INTO SPINELESS HIPPIE ZOMBIES--AN ARMY OF UNDEADHEADS!
WE NEEDED THE COMBINED POWER OF HITLER AND GARCIA TO DRAW SUCH ENERGY, AND THE ONLY THING REMAINING WITH BOTH WAS JERRY'S SKULL!
THE GRAND WIZARD'S FAVORITE PAGE!

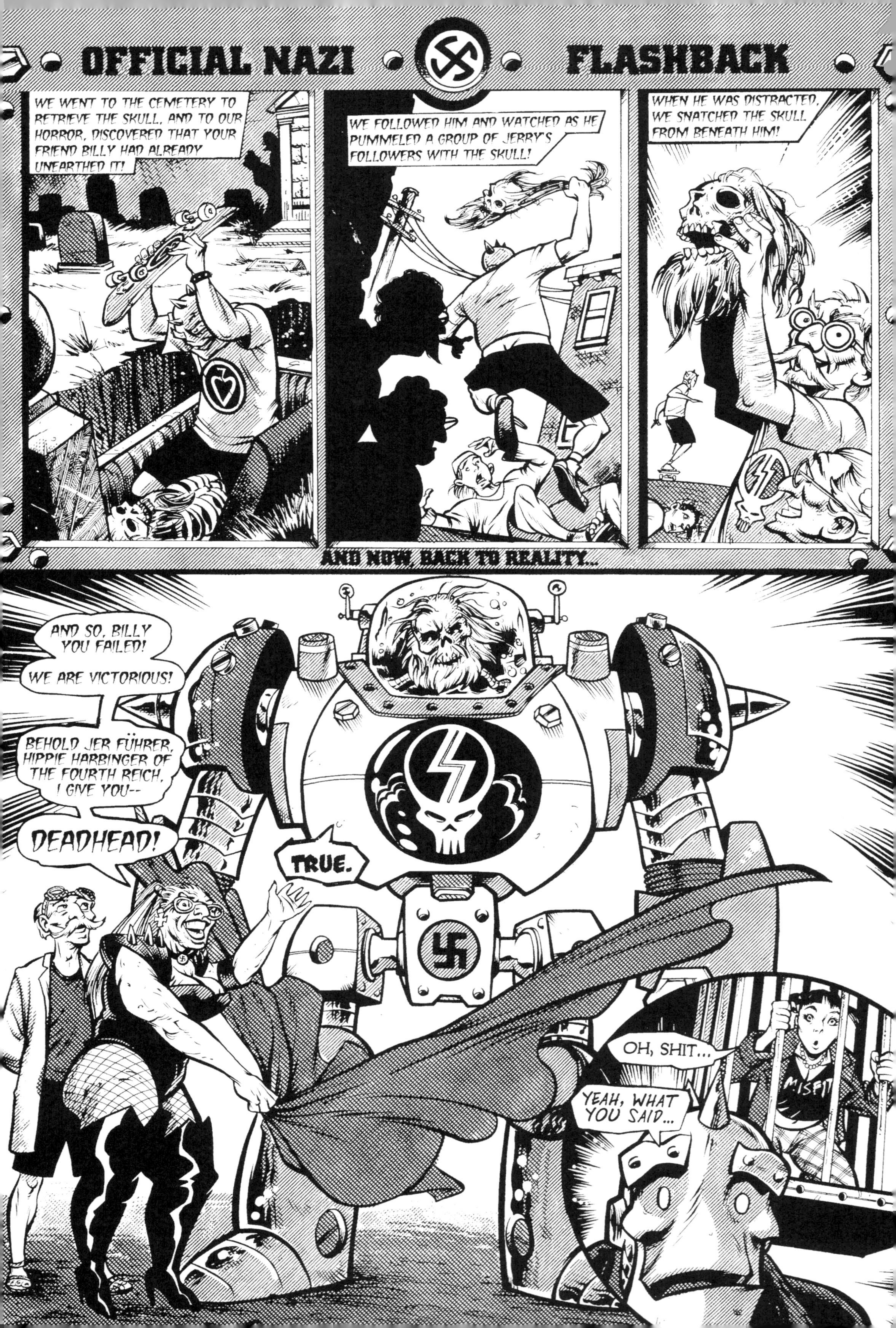
OFFICIAL NAZI FLASHBACK
WE WENT TO THE CEMETERY TO RETRIEVE THE SKULL, AND TO OUR HORROR, DISCOVERED THAT YOUR FRIEND BILLY HAD ALREADY UNEARTHED IT!
WE FOLLOWED HIM AND WATCHED AS HE PUMMELED A GROUP OF JERRY'S FOLLOWERS WITH THE SKULL!
WHEN HE WAS DISTRACTED, WE SNATCHED THE SKULL FROM BENEATH HIM!
AND NOW, BACK TO REALITY...
AND SO, BILLY YOU FAILED!
WE ARE VICTORIOUS!
BEHOLD JER FÜHRER, HIPPIE HARBINGER OF THE FOURTH REICH, I GIVE YOU--
DEADHEAD!
TRUE.
OH, SHIT...
YEAH, WHAT YOU SAID...
MISFIT

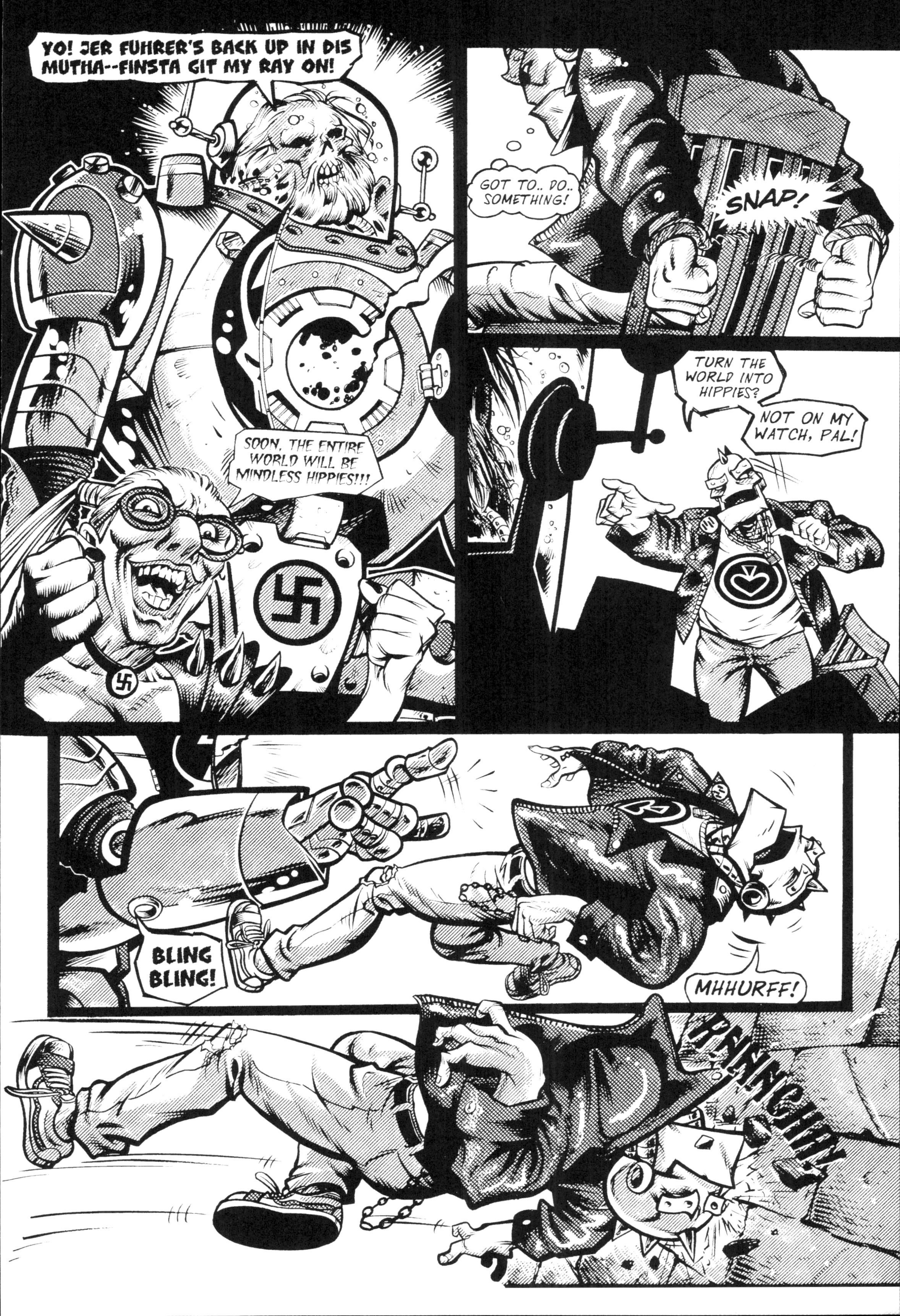
YO! JER FUHRER'S BACK UP IN DIS MUTHA--FINSTA GIT MY RAY ON!
SOON, THE ENTIRE WORLD WILL BE MINDLESS HIPPIES!!!
GOT TO.. DO.. SOMETHING!
SNAP!
TURN THE WORLD INTO HIPPIES?
NOT ON MY WATCH, PAL!
BLING BLING!
MHHURFF!

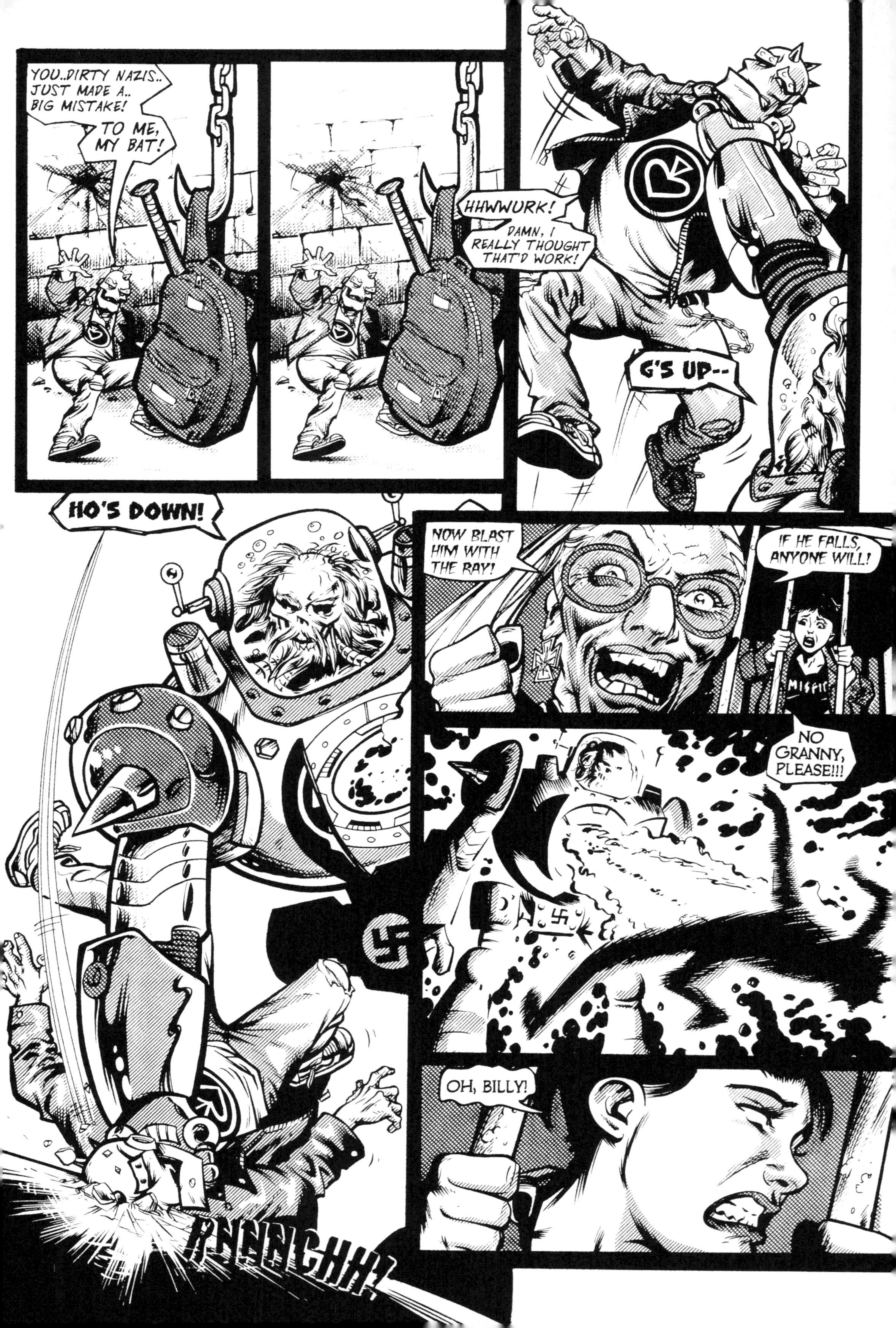
YOU..DIRTY NAZIS.. JUST MADE A.. BIG MISTAKE!
TO ME, MY BAT!
HHWWURK!
DAMN, I REALLY THOUGHT THAT'D WORK!
G'S UP--
HO'S DOWN!
NOW BLAST HIM WITH THE RAY!
IF HE FALLS, ANYONE WILL!
NO GRANNY, PLEASE!!!
OH, BILLY!

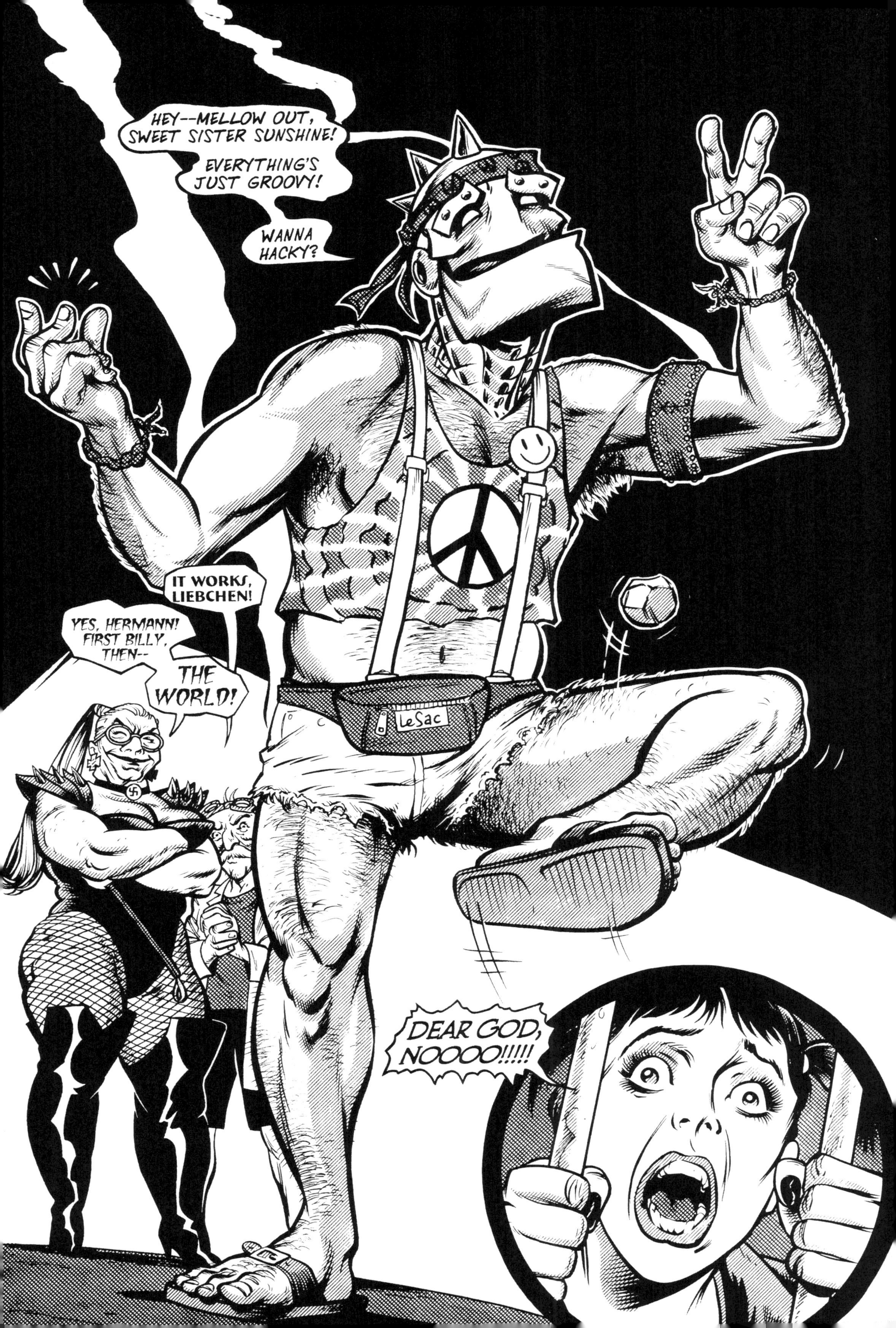
HEY--MELLOW OUT, SWEET SISTER SUNSHINE!
EVERYTHING'S JUST GROOVY!
WANNA HACKY?
LeSac
IT WORKS, LIEBCHEN!
YES, HERMANN! FIRST BILLY, THEN--
THE WORLD!
DEAR GOD, NOOOO!!!!!

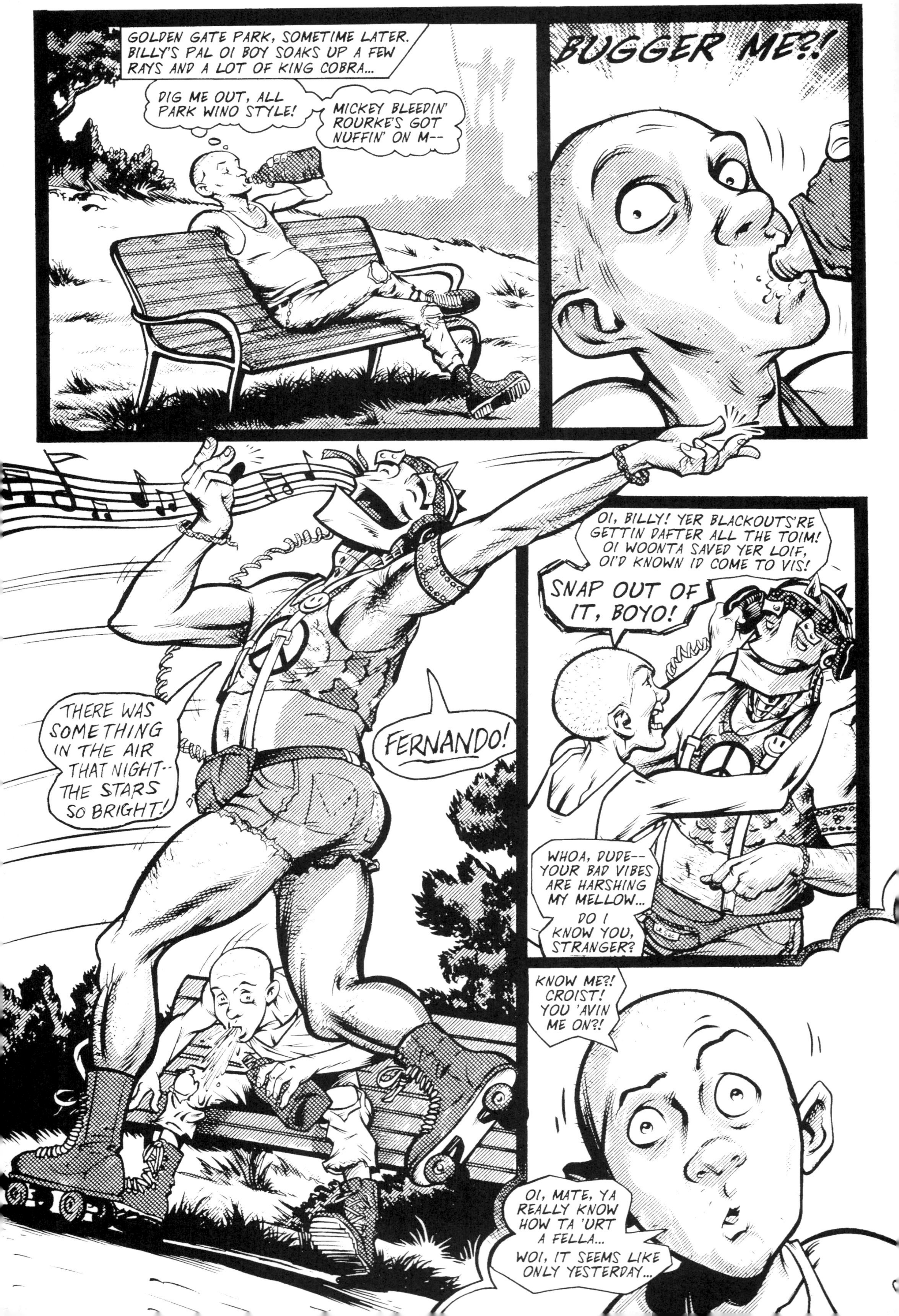
GOLDEN GATE PARK, SOMETIME LATER. BILLY'S PAL OI BOY SOAKS UP A FEW RAYS AND A LOT OF KING COBRA...
DIG ME OUT, ALL PARK WINO STYLE!
MICKEY BLEEDIN' ROURKE'S GOT NUFFIN' ON M--
BUGGER ME?!
THERE WAS SOMETHING IN THE AIR THAT NIGHT-- THE STARS SO BRIGHT!
FERNANDO!
OI, BILLY! YER BLACKOUTS'RE GETTIN DAFTER ALL THE TOIM! OI WOONTA SAVED YER LOIF, OI'D KNOWN ID COME TO VIS!
SNAP OUT OF IT, BOYO!
WHOA, DUDE-- YOUR BAD VIBES ARE HARSHING MY MELLOW... DO I KNOW YOU, STRANGER?
KNOW ME?! CROIST! YOU 'AVIN ME ON?!
OI, MATE, YA REALLY KNOW HOW TA 'URT A FELLA... WOI, IT SEEMS LIKE ONLY YESTERDAY...

OFFICIAL BHB ORIGIN CAM

PHOENIX, AZ--THE METRO CLUB, MINOR THREAT'S LAST TOUR...

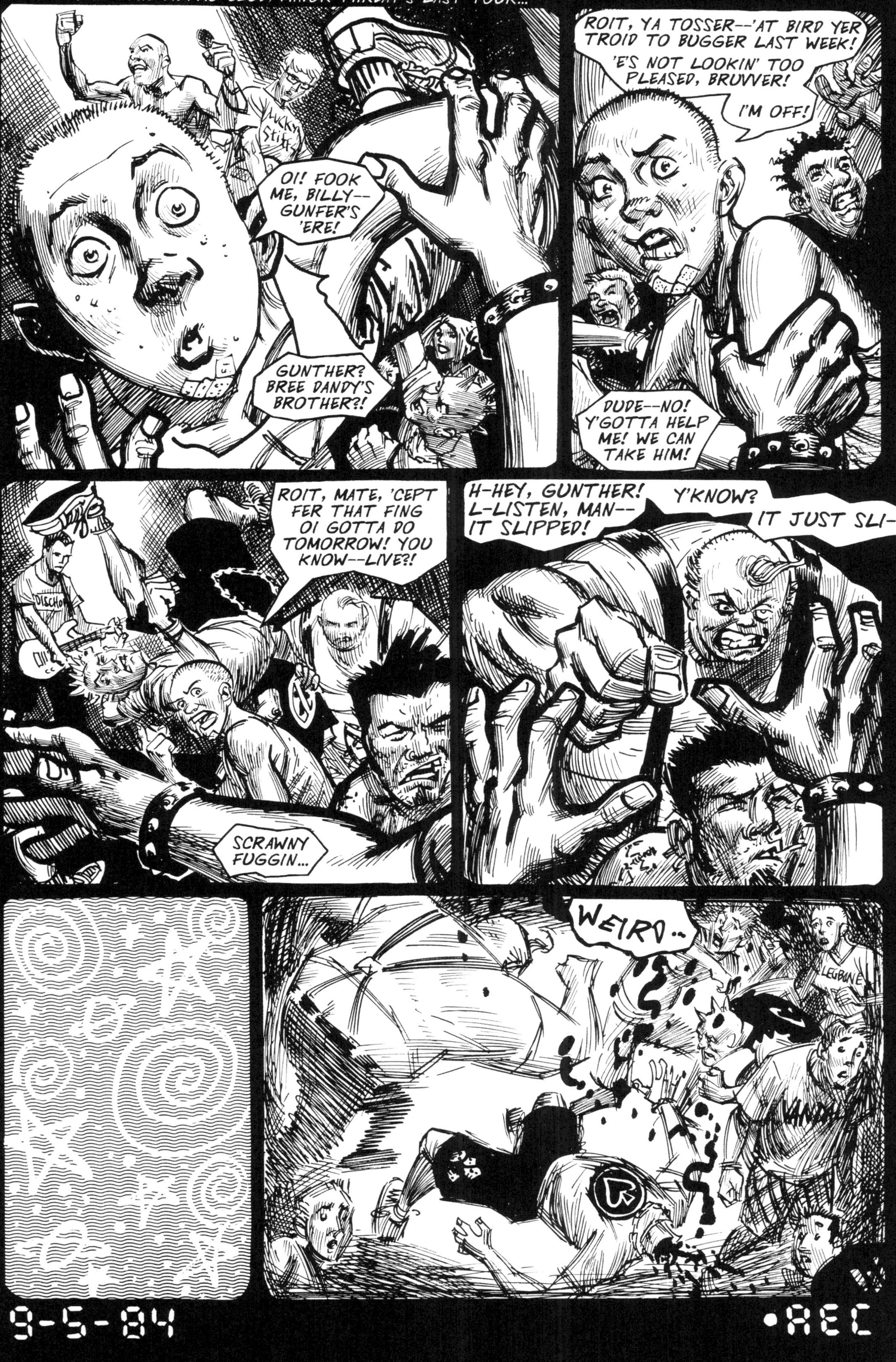
OI! FOOK ME, BILLY--GUNFER'S 'ERE!
GUNTHER? BREE DANDY'S BROTHER?!
ROIT, YA TOSSER--'AT BIRD YER TROID TO BUGGER LAST WEEK!
'E'S NOT LOOKIN' TOO PLEASED, BRUVVER!
I'M OFF!
DUDE--NO! Y'GOTTA HELP ME! WE CAN TAKE HIM!
ROIT, MATE, 'CEPT FER THAT FING OI GOTTA DO TOMORROW! YOU KNOW--LIVE?!
SCRAWNY FUGGIN...
H-HEY, GUNTHER! L-LISTEN, MAN--IT SLIPPED!
Y'KNOW?
IT JUST SLI--
WEIRD..
9-5-84
•REC

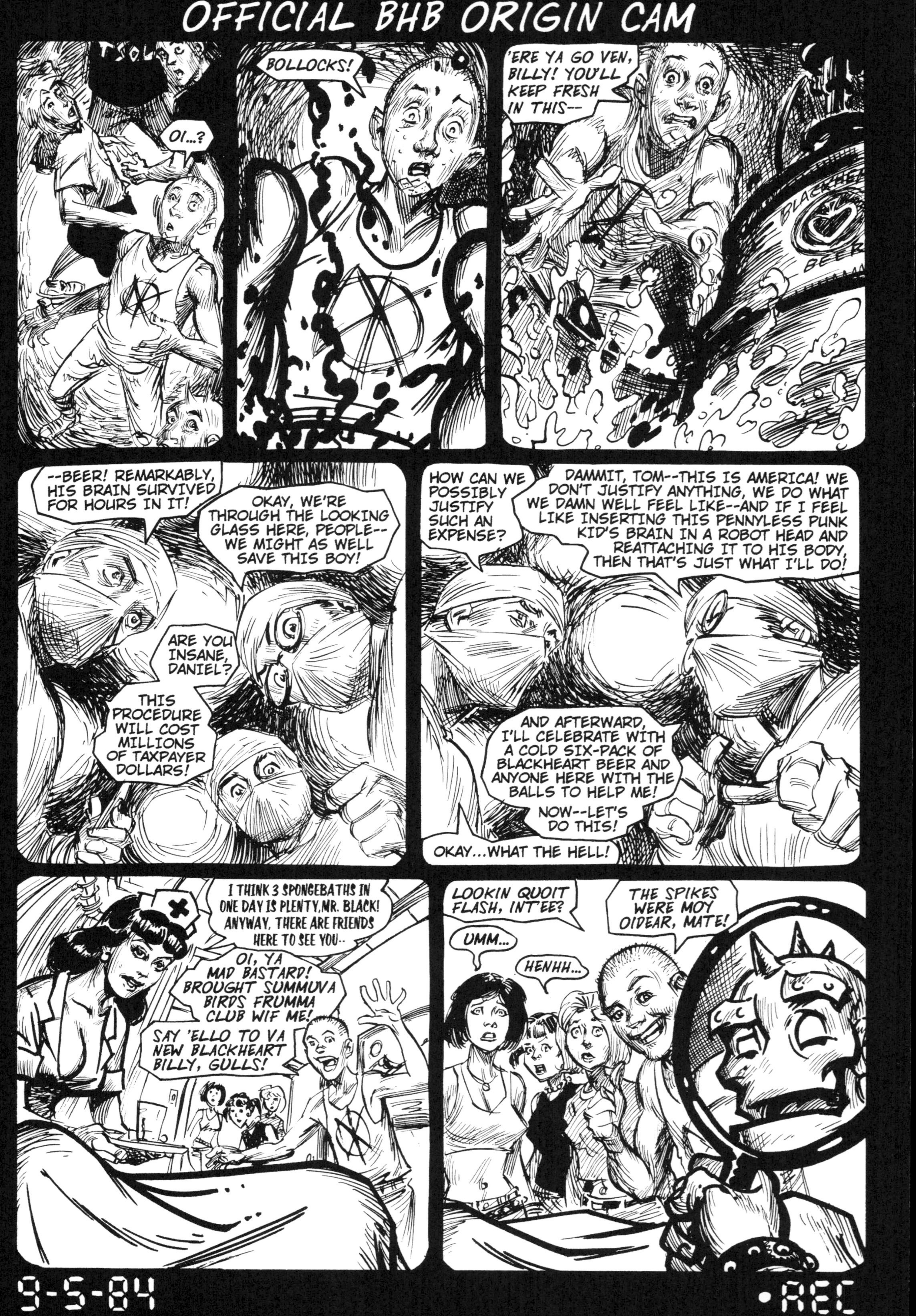
OFFICIAL BHB ORIGIN CAM
OI...?
BOLLOCKS!
'ERE YA GO VEN, BILLY! YOU'LL KEEP FRESH IN THIS--
--BEER! REMARKABLY, HIS BRAIN SURVIVED FOR HOURS IN IT!
OKAY, WE'RE THROUGH THE LOOKING GLASS HERE, PEOPLE-- WE MIGHT AS WELL SAVE THIS BOY!
ARE YOU INSANE, DANIEL?
THIS PROCEDURE WILL COST MILLIONS OF TAXPAYER DOLLARS!
HOW CAN WE POSSIBLY JUSTIFY SUCH AN EXPENSE?
DAMMIT, TOM--THIS IS AMERICA! WE DON'T JUSTIFY ANYTHING, WE DO WHAT WE DAMN WELL FEEL LIKE--AND IF I FEEL LIKE INSERTING THIS PENNYLESS PUNK KID'S BRAIN IN A ROBOT HEAD AND REATTACHING IT TO HIS BODY, THEN THAT'S JUST WHAT I'LL DO!
AND AFTERWARD, I'LL CELEBRATE WITH A COLD SIX-PACK OF BLACKHEART BEER AND ANYONE HERE WITH THE BALLS TO HELP ME!
NOW--LET'S DO THIS!
OKAY...WHAT THE HELL!
I THINK 3 SPONGEBATHS IN ONE DAY IS PLENTY, MR. BLACK! ANYWAY, THERE ARE FRIENDS HERE TO SEE YOU--
OI, YA MAD BASTARD! BROUGHT SUMMUVA BIRDS FRUMMA CLUB WIF ME!
SAY 'ELLO TO VA NEW BLACKHEART BILLY, GULLS!
LOOKIN QUOIT FLASH, INT'EE?
UMM...
HENHH...
THE SPIKES WERE MOY OIDEAR, MATE!
9-5-84
•REC

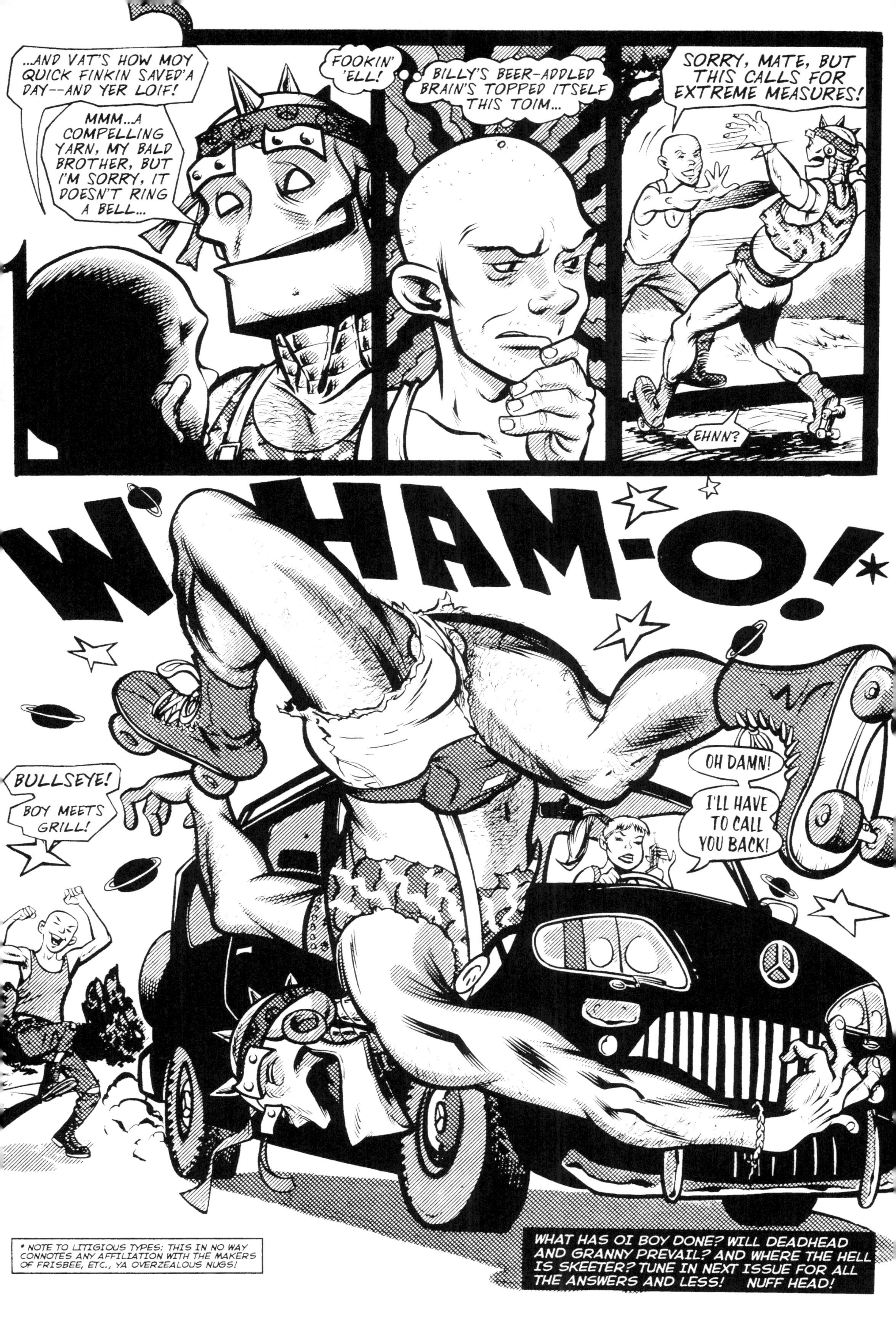
...AND VAT'S HOW MOY QUICK FINKIN SAVED'A DAY--AND YER LOIF!
MMM...A COMPELLING YARN, MY BALD BROTHER, BUT I'M SORRY, IT DOESN'T RING A BELL...
FOOKIN' 'ELL!
BILLY'S BEER-ADDLED BRAIN'S TOPPED ITSELF THIS TOIM...
SORRY, MATE, BUT THIS CALLS FOR EXTREME MEASURES!
EHNN?
WHAM-O!*
BULLSEYE!
BOY MEETS GRILL!
OH DAMN!
I'LL HAVE TO CALL YOU BACK!
* NOTE TO LITIGIOUS TYPES: THIS IN NO WAY CONNOTES ANY AFFILIATION WITH THE MAKERS OF FRISBEE, ETC., YA OVERZEALOUS NUGS!
WHAT HAS OI BOY DONE? WILL DEADHEAD AND GRANNY PREVAIL? AND WHERE THE HELL IS SKEETER? TUNE IN NEXT ISSUE FOR ALL THE ANSWERS AND LESS! NUFF HEAD!

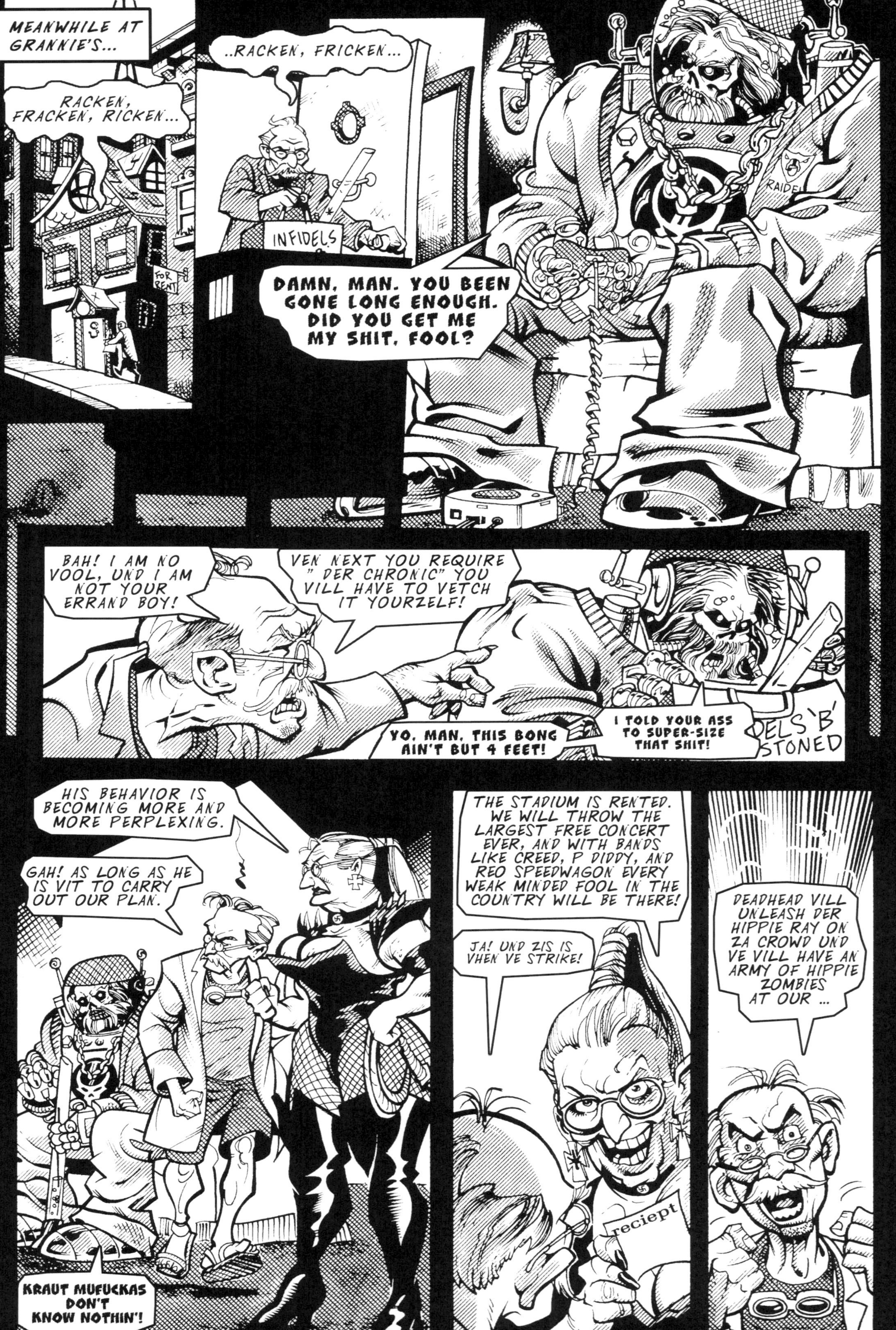

MEANWHILE AT GRANNIE'S...
RACKEN, FRACKEN, RICKEN...
FOR RENT
..RACKEN, FRICKEN...
INFIDELS
DAMN, MAN. YOU BEEN GONE LONG ENOUGH. DID YOU GET ME MY SHIT, FOOL?
RAIDE
BAH! I AM NO VOOL, UND I AM NOT YOUR ERRAND BOY!
VEN NEXT YOU REQUIRE " DER CHRONIC" YOU VILL HAVE TO VETCH IT YOURZELF!
YO, MAN. THIS BONG AIN'T BUT 4 FEET!
I TOLD YOUR ASS TO SUPER-SIZE THAT SHIT!
DELS 'B' STONED
HIS BEHAVIOR IS BECOMING MORE AND MORE PERPLEXING.
GAH! AS LONG AS HE IS VIT TO CARRY OUT OUR PLAN.
KRAUT MUFUCKAS DON'T KNOW NOTHIN'!
THE STADIUM IS RENTED. WE WILL THROW THE LARGEST FREE CONCERT EVER, AND WITH BANDS LIKE CREED, P DIDDY, AND REO SPEEDWAGON EVERY WEAK MINDED FOOL IN THE COUNTRY WILL BE THERE!
JA! UND ZIS IS VHEN VE STRIKE!
reciept
DEADHEAD VILL UNLEASH DER HIPPIE RAY ON ZA CROWD UND VE VILL HAVE AN ARMY OF HIPPIE ZOMBIES AT OUR ...

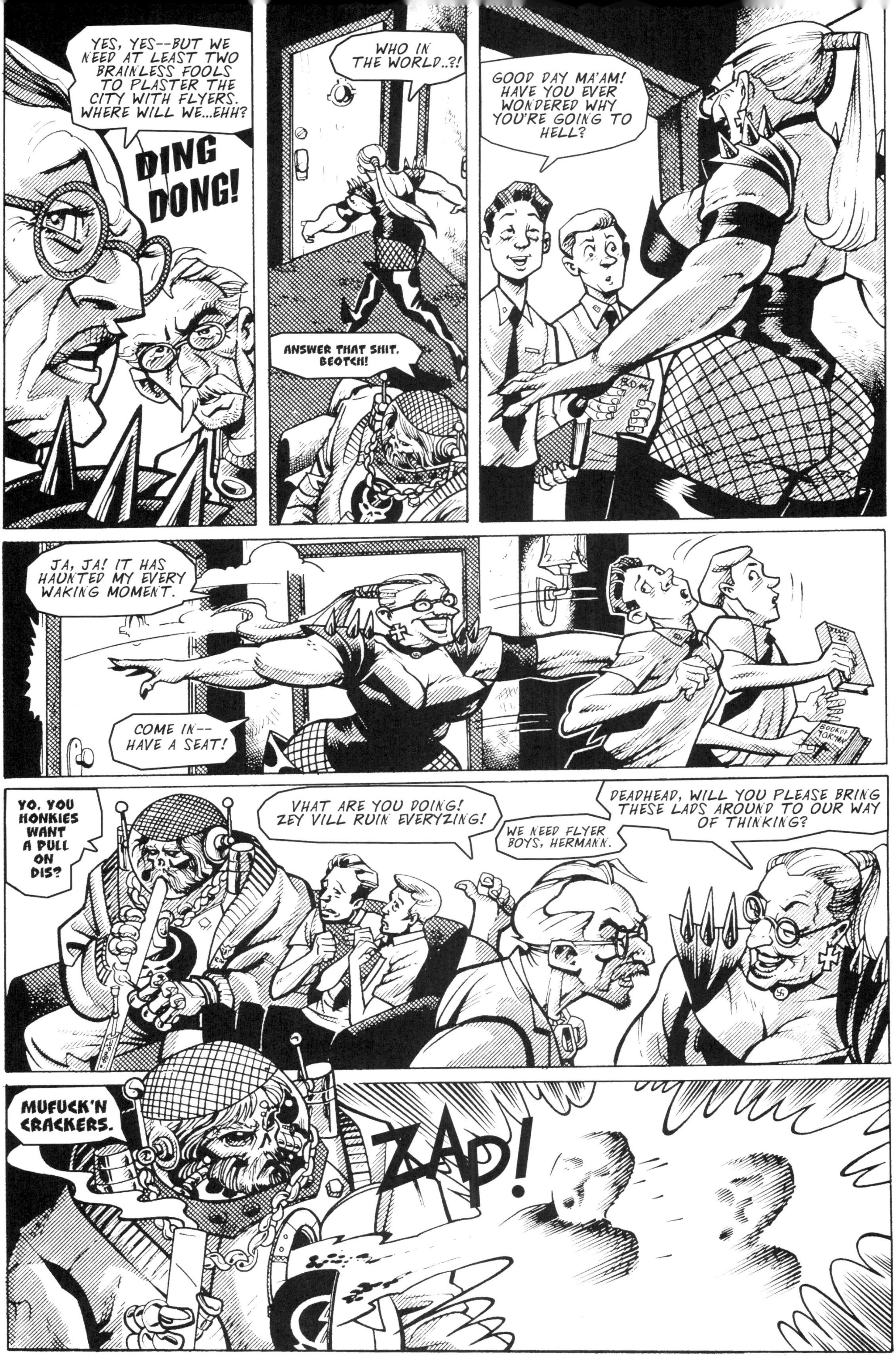

YES, YES--BUT WE NEED AT LEAST TWO BRAINLESS FOOLS TO PLASTER THE CITY WITH FLYERS. WHERE WILL WE...EHH?
DING DONG!
WHO IN THE WORLD..?!
ANSWER THAT SHIT, BEOTCH!
GOOD DAY MA'AM! HAVE YOU EVER WONDERED WHY YOU'RE GOING TO HELL?
JA, JA! IT HAS HAUNTED MY EVERY WAKING MOMENT.
COME IN-- HAVE A SEAT!
YO, YOU HONKIES WANT A PULL ON DIS?
VHAT ARE YOU DOING! ZEY VILL RUIN EVERYZING!
WE NEED FLYER BOYS, HERMANN.
DEADHEAD, WILL YOU PLEASE BRING THESE LADS AROUND TO OUR WAY OF THINKING?
MUFUCK'N CRACKERS.
ZAP!

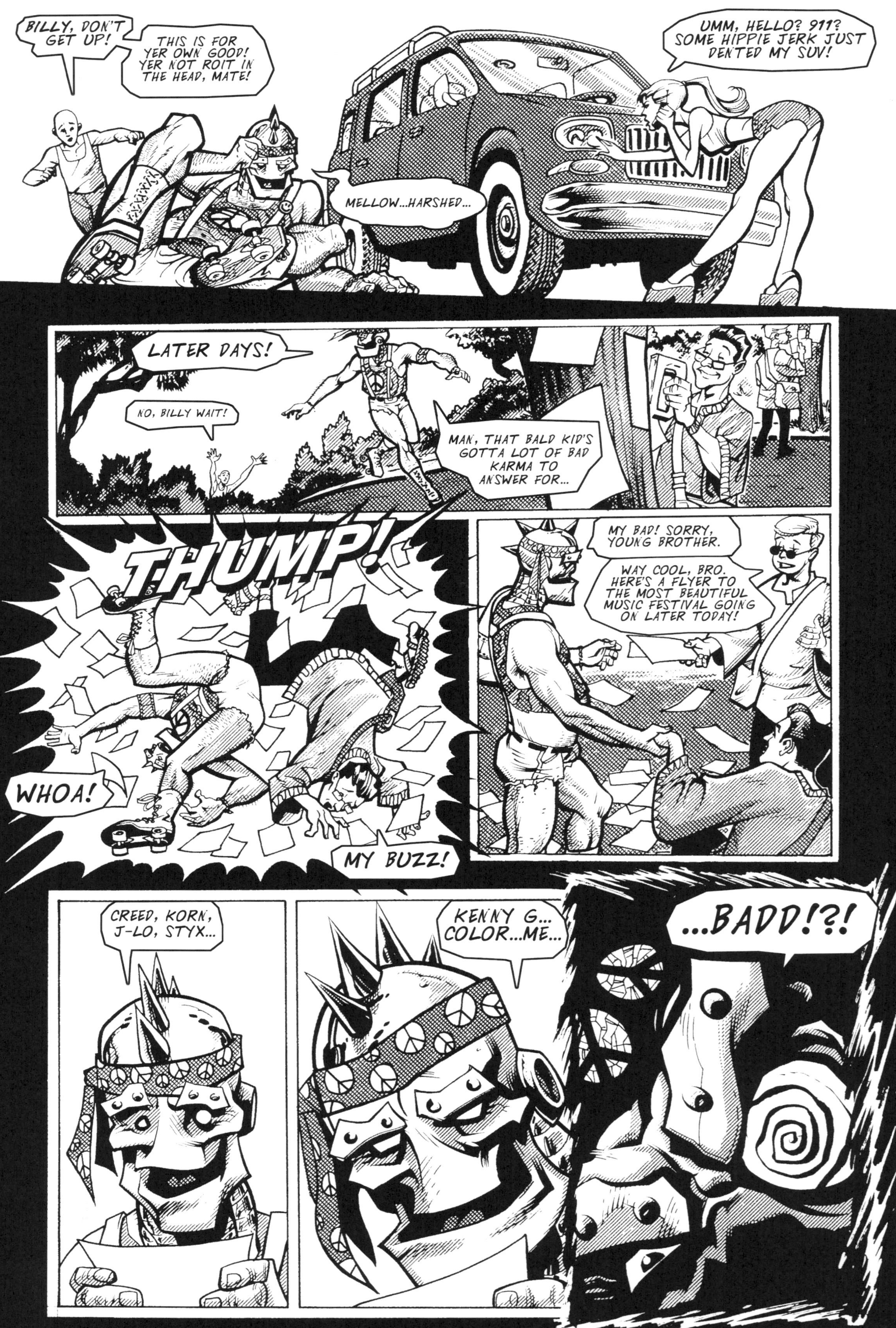
BILLY, DON'T GET UP!
THIS IS FOR YER OWN GOOD! YER NOT ROIT IN THE HEAD, MATE!
UMM, HELLO? 911? SOME HIPPIE JERK JUST DENTED MY SUV!
MELLOW...HARSHED...
LATER DAYS!
NO, BILLY WAIT!
MAN, THAT BALD KID'S GOTTA LOT OF BAD KARMA TO ANSWER FOR...
THUMP!
WHOA!
MY BUZZ!
MY BAD! SORRY, YOUNG BROTHER.
WAY COOL, BRO. HERE'S A FLYER TO THE MOST BEAUTIFUL MUSIC FESTIVAL GOING ON LATER TODAY!
CREED, KORN, J-LO, STYX...
KENNY G... COLOR...ME...
...BADD!?!

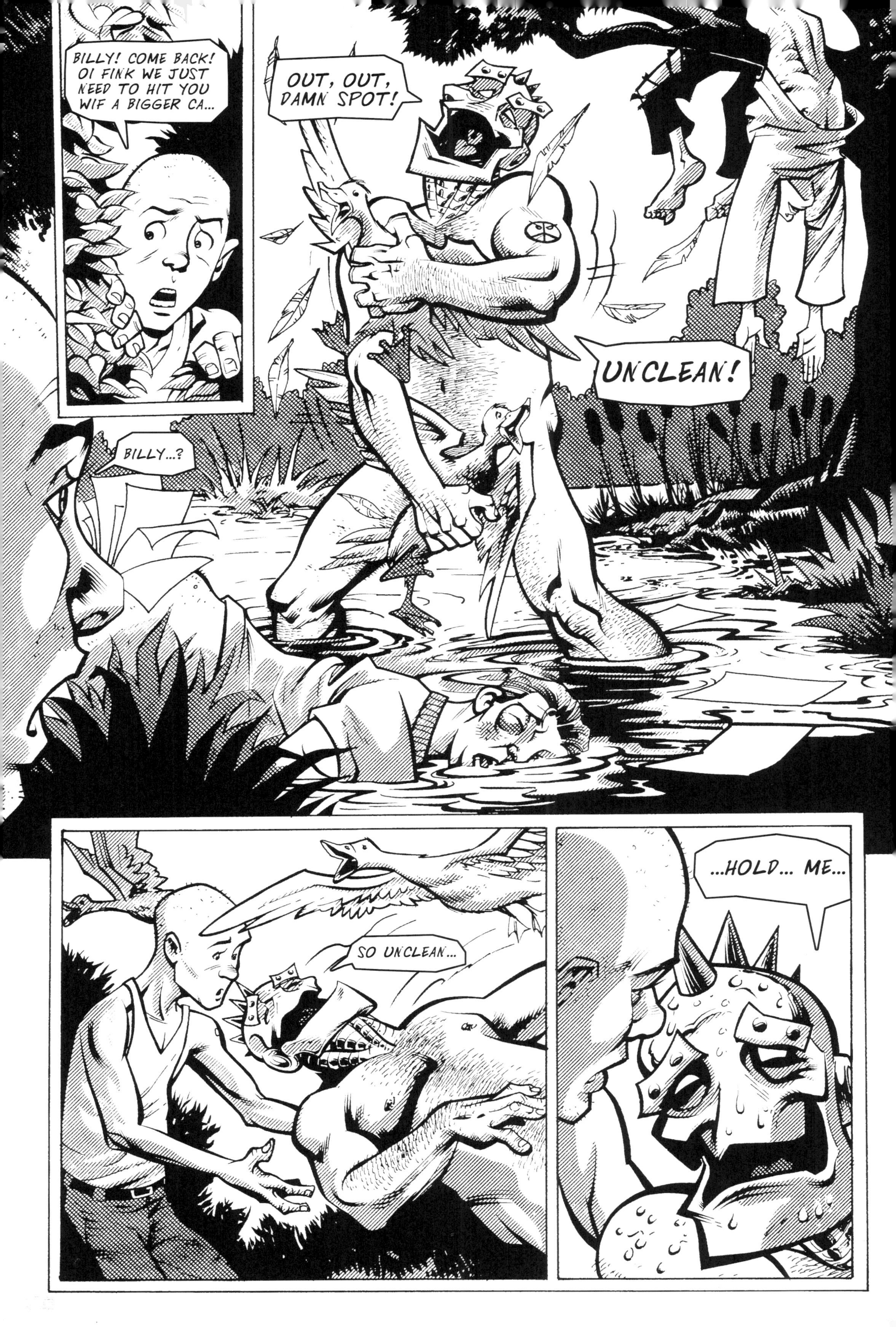

BILLY! COME BACK! OI FINK WE JUST NEED TO HIT YOU WIF A BIGGER CA...
OUT, OUT, DAMN SPOT!
UNCLEAN!
BILLY...?
SO UNCLEAN...
...HOLD... ME...

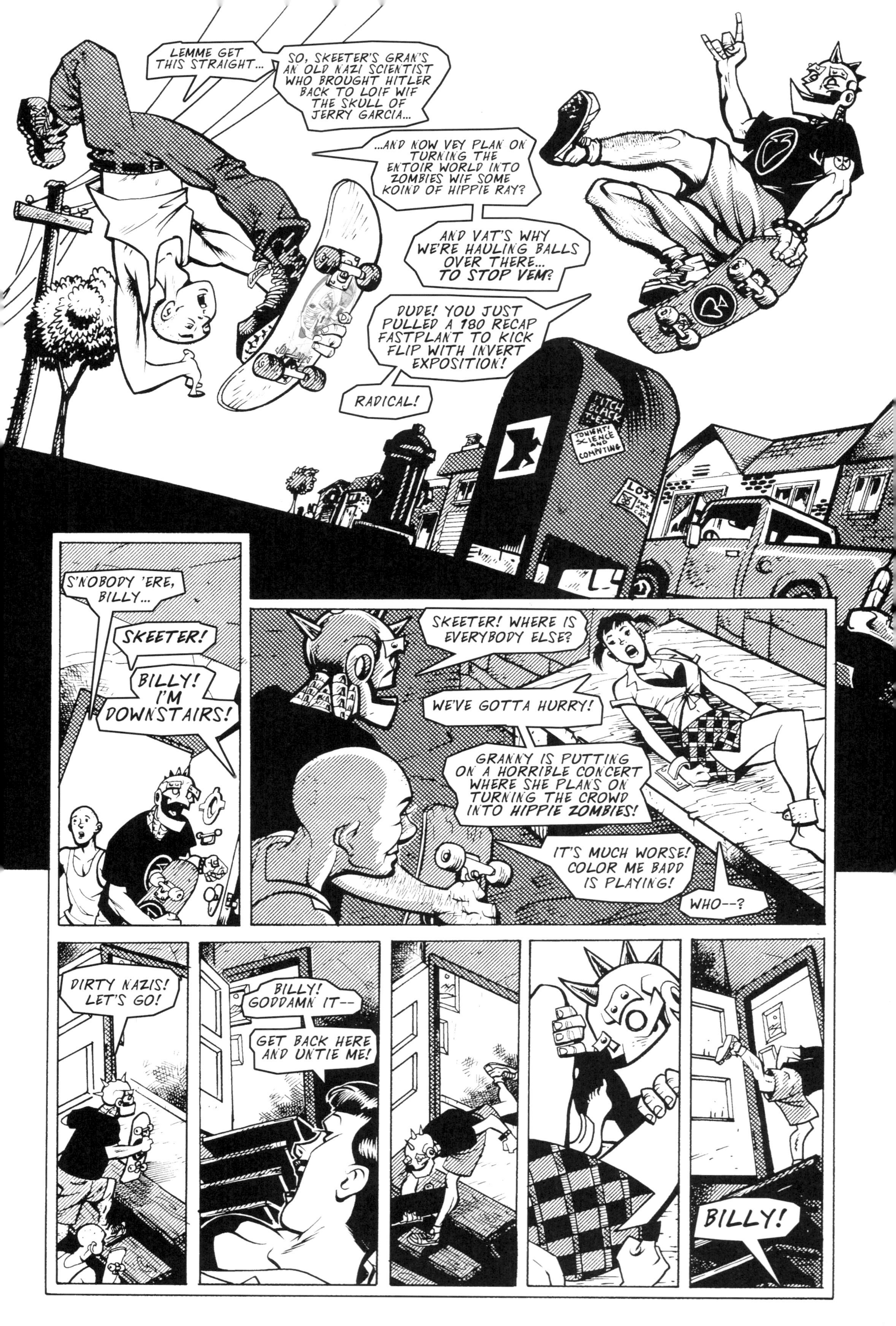
LEMME GET THIS STRAIGHT...
SO, SKEETER'S GRAN'S AN OLD NAZI SCIENTIST WHO BROUGHT HITLER BACK TO LOIF WIF THE SKULL OF JERRY GARCIA...
...AND NOW VEY PLAN ON TURNING THE ENTOIR WORLD INTO ZOMBIES WIF SOME KOIND OF HIPPIE RAY?
AND VAT'S WHY WE'RE HAULING BALLS OVER THERE... TO STOP VEM?
DUDE! YOU JUST PULLED A 180 RECAP FASTPLANT TO KICK FLIP WITH INVERT EXPOSITION!
RADICAL!
PITCH BLACK
TONIGHT! SCIENCE AND COMPUTING
LOST
S'NOBODY 'ERE, BILLY...
SKEETER!
BILLY! I'M DOWNSTAIRS!
SKEETER! WHERE IS EVERYBODY ELSE?
WE'VE GOTTA HURRY!
GRANNY IS PUTTING ON A HORRIBLE CONCERT WHERE SHE PLANS ON TURNING THE CROWD INTO HIPPIE ZOMBIES!
IT'S MUCH WORSE! COLOR ME BADD IS PLAYING!
WHO--?
DIRTY NAZIS! LET'S GO!
BILLY! GODDAMN IT--
GET BACK HERE AND UNTIE ME!
BILLY!

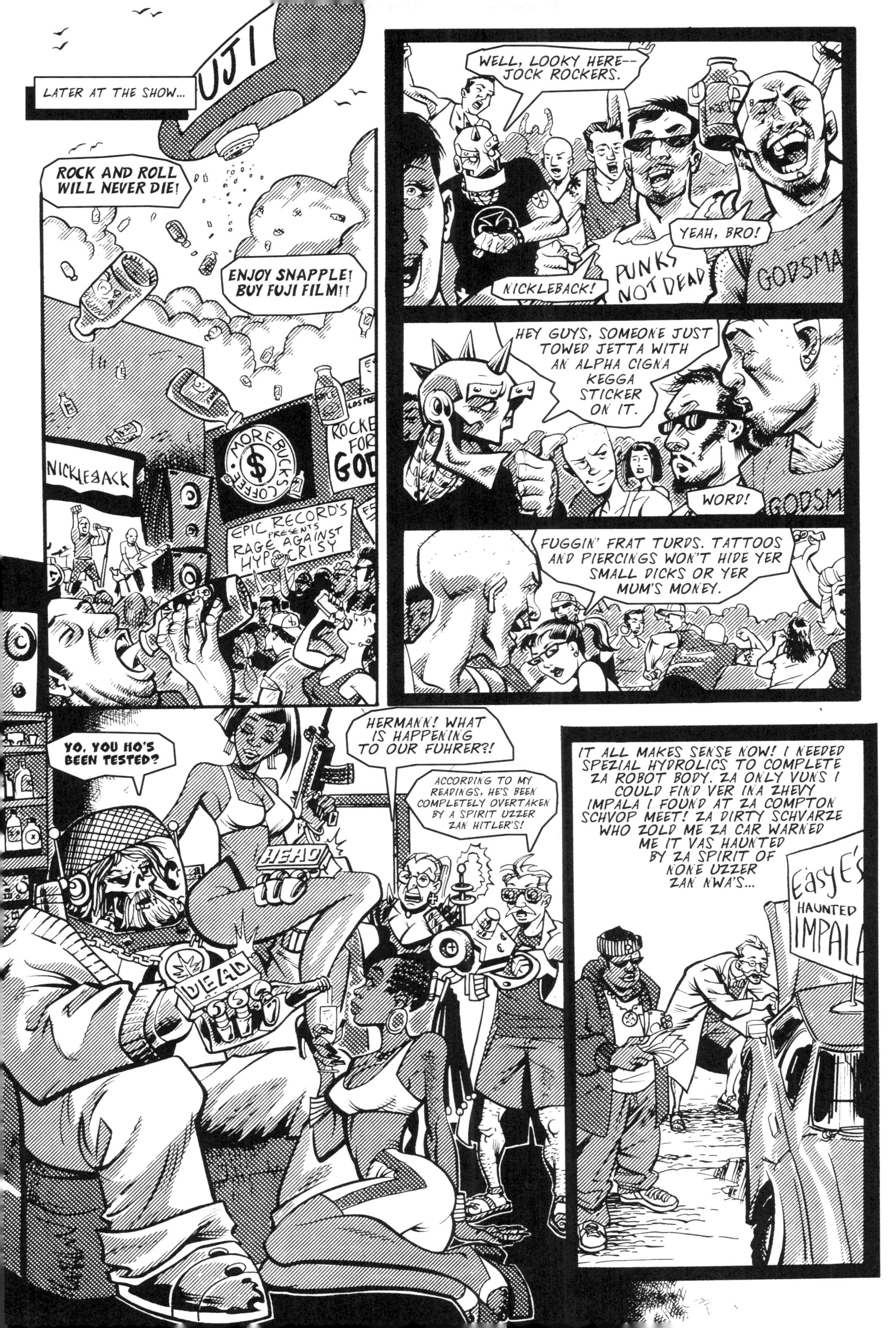

LATER AT THE SHOW...
UJI
ROCK AND ROLL WILL NEVER DIE!
ENJOY SNAPPLE! BUY FUJI FILM!!
NICKLEBACK
MOREBUCKS $ COFFEE
ROCKE FOR GOD
EPIC RECORD'S PRESENTS RAGE AGAINST HYPOCRISY
WELL, LOOKY HERE-- JOCK ROCKERS.
YEAH, BRO!
NICKLEBACK!
PUNKS NOT DEAD
GODSMA
HEY GUYS, SOMEONE JUST TOWED JETTA WITH AN ALPHA CIGNA KEGGA STICKER ON IT.
WORD!
GODSMA
FUGGIN' FRAT TURDS. TATTOOS AND PIERCINGS WON'T HIDE YER SMALL DICKS OR YER MUM'S MONEY.
YO, YOU HO'S BEEN TESTED?
HERMANN! WHAT IS HAPPENING TO OUR FUHRER?!
ACCORDING TO MY READINGS, HE'S BEEN COMPLETELY OVERTAKEN BY A SPIRIT UZZER ZAN HITLER'S!
HEAD
DEAD
IT ALL MAKES SENSE NOW! I NEEDED SPEZIAL HYDROLICS TO COMPLETE ZA ROBOT BODY. ZA ONLY VUNS I COULD FIND VER INA ZHEVY IMPALA I FOUND AT ZA COMPTON SCHVOP MEET! ZA DIRTY SCHVARZE WHO ZOLD ME ZA CAR WARNED ME IT VAS HAUNTED BY ZA SPIRIT OF NONE UZZER ZAN NWA'S...
Easy E's HAUNTED IMPALA

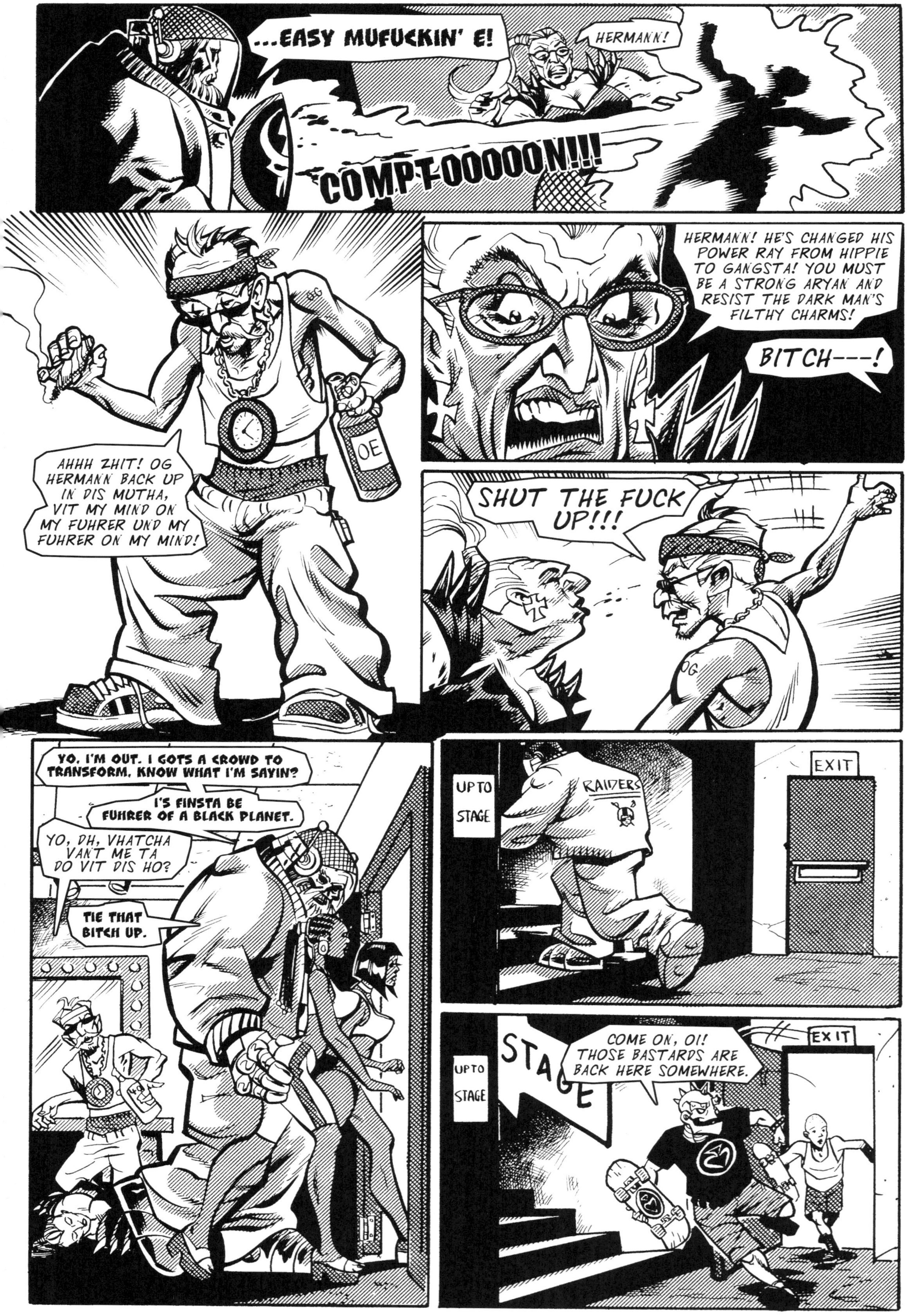
...EASY MUFUCKIN' E!
HERMANN!
COMPT-OOOOON!!!
AHHH ZHIT! OG HERMANN BACK UP IN DIS MUTHA, VIT MY MIND ON MY FUHRER UND MY FUHRER ON MY MIND!
OE
OG
HERMANN! HE'S CHANGED HIS POWER RAY FROM HIPPIE TO GANGSTA! YOU MUST BE A STRONG ARYAN AND RESIST THE DARK MAN'S FILTHY CHARMS!
BITCH---!
SHUT THE FUCK UP!!!
OG
YO, I'M OUT. I GOTS A CROWD TO TRANSFORM, KNOW WHAT I'M SAYIN?
I'S FINSTA BE FUHRER OF A BLACK PLANET.
YO, DH, VHATCHA VANT ME TA DO VIT DIS HO?
TIE THAT BITCH UP.
UP TO STAGE
RAIDERS
EXIT
UP TO STAGE
STAGE
EXIT
COME ON, OI! THOSE BASTARDS ARE BACK HERE SOMEWHERE.

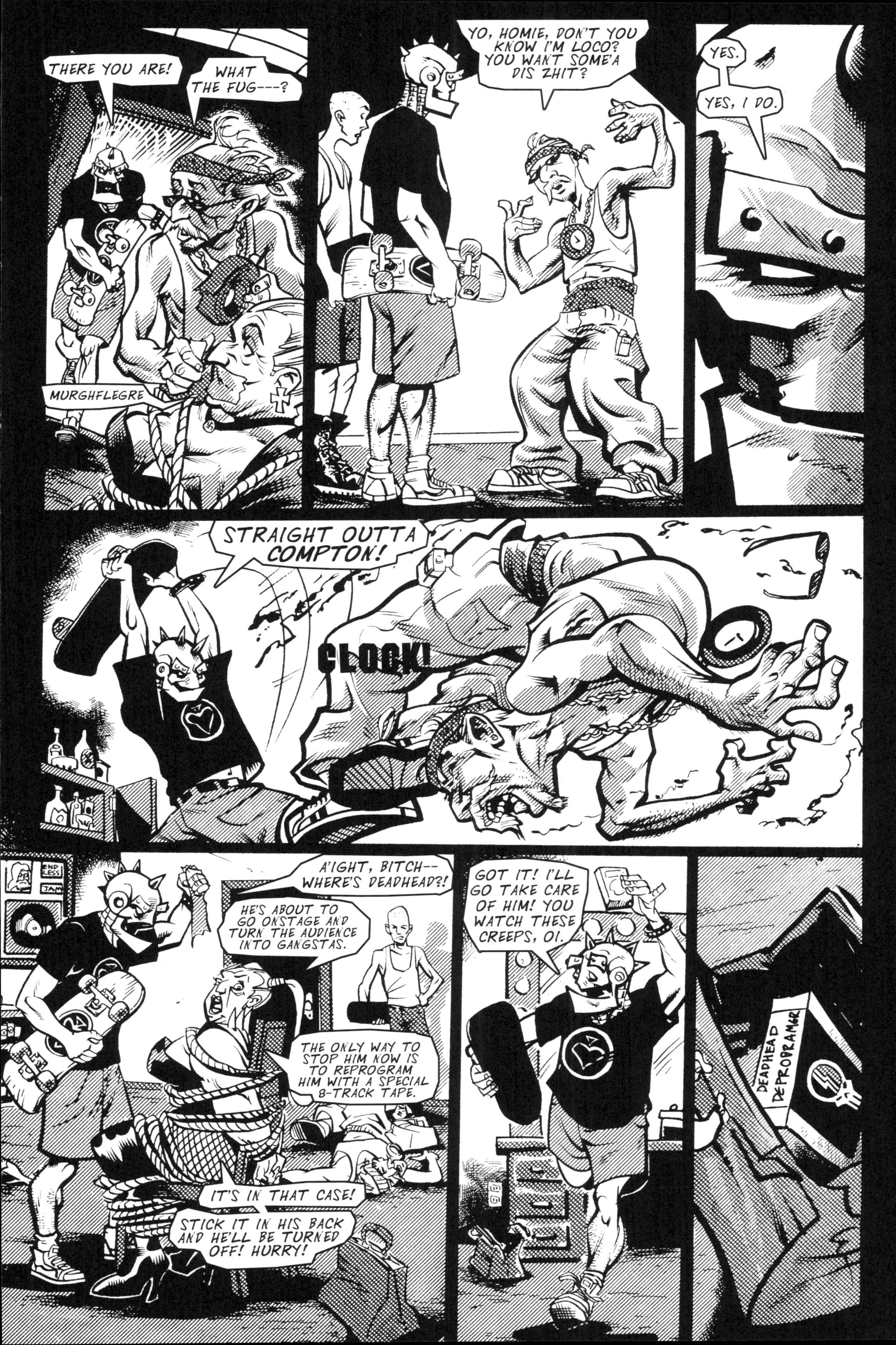
THERE YOU ARE!
WHAT THE FUG---?
MURGHFLEGRE
YO, HOMIE, DON'T YOU KNOW I'M LOCO? YOU WANT SOME'A DIS ZHIT?
YES.
YES, I DO.
STRAIGHT OUTTA COMPTON!
CLOCK!
A'IGHT, BITCH-- WHERE'S DEADHEAD?!
HE'S ABOUT TO GO ONSTAGE AND TURN THE AUDIENCE INTO GANGSTAS.
THE ONLY WAY TO STOP HIM NOW IS TO REPROGRAM HIM WITH A SPECIAL 8-TRACK TAPE.
IT'S IN THAT CASE!
STICK IT IN HIS BACK AND HE'LL BE TURNED OFF! HURRY!
GOT IT! I'LL GO TAKE CARE OF HIM! YOU WATCH THESE CREEPS, OI.
DEADHEAD DEPROGRAMMER

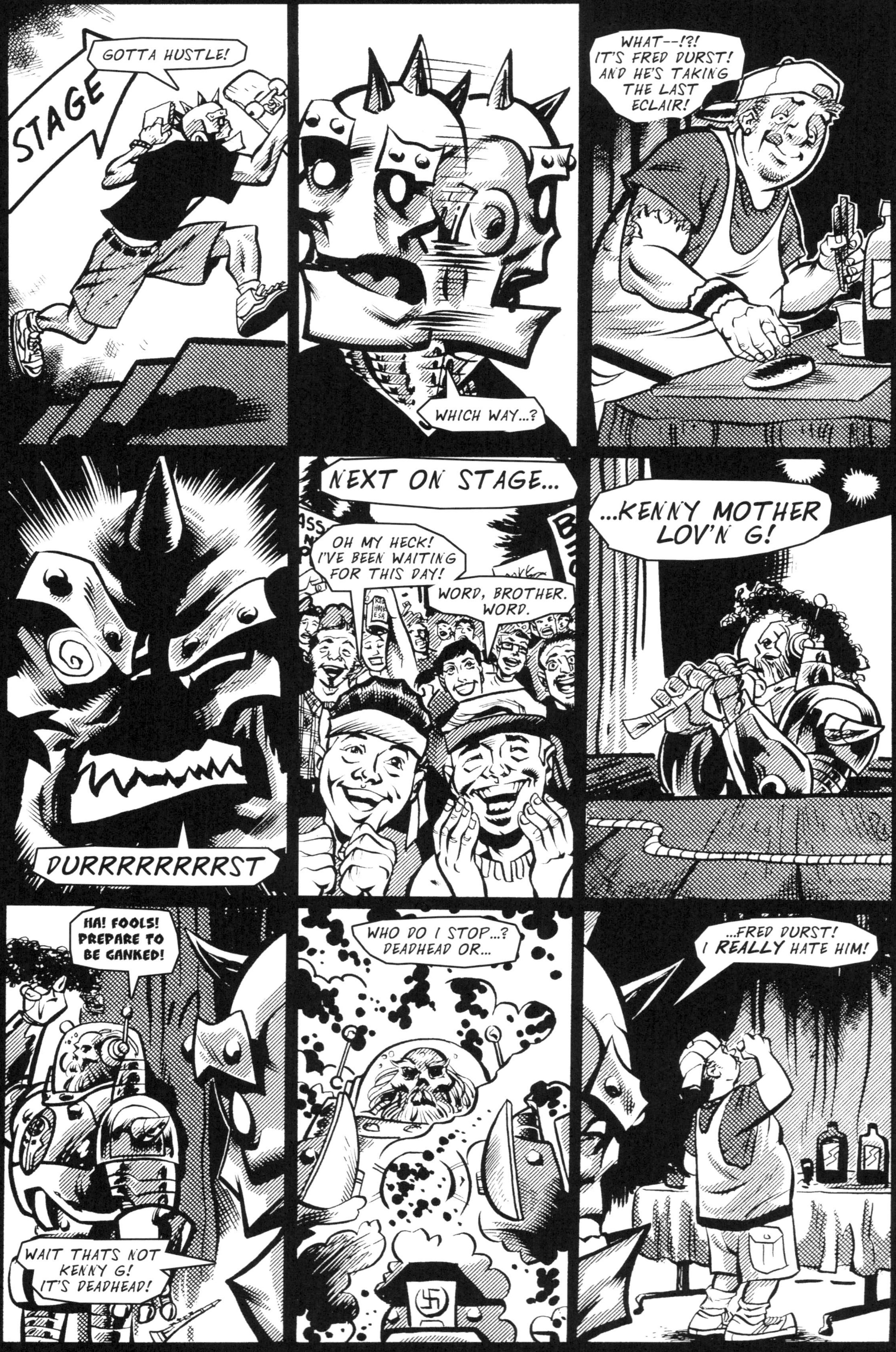
GOTTA HUSTLE!
STAGE
WHICH WAY...?
WHAT--!?! IT'S FRED DURST! AND HE'S TAKING THE LAST ECLAIR!
DURRRRRRRRST
NEXT ON STAGE...
OH MY HECK! I'VE BEEN WAITING FOR THIS DAY!
WORD, BROTHER. WORD.
...KENNY MOTHER LOV'N G!
HA! FOOLS! PREPARE TO BE GANKED!
WAIT THATS NOT KENNY G! IT'S DEADHEAD!
WHO DO I STOP...? DEADHEAD OR...
...FRED DURST! I REALLY HATE HIM!

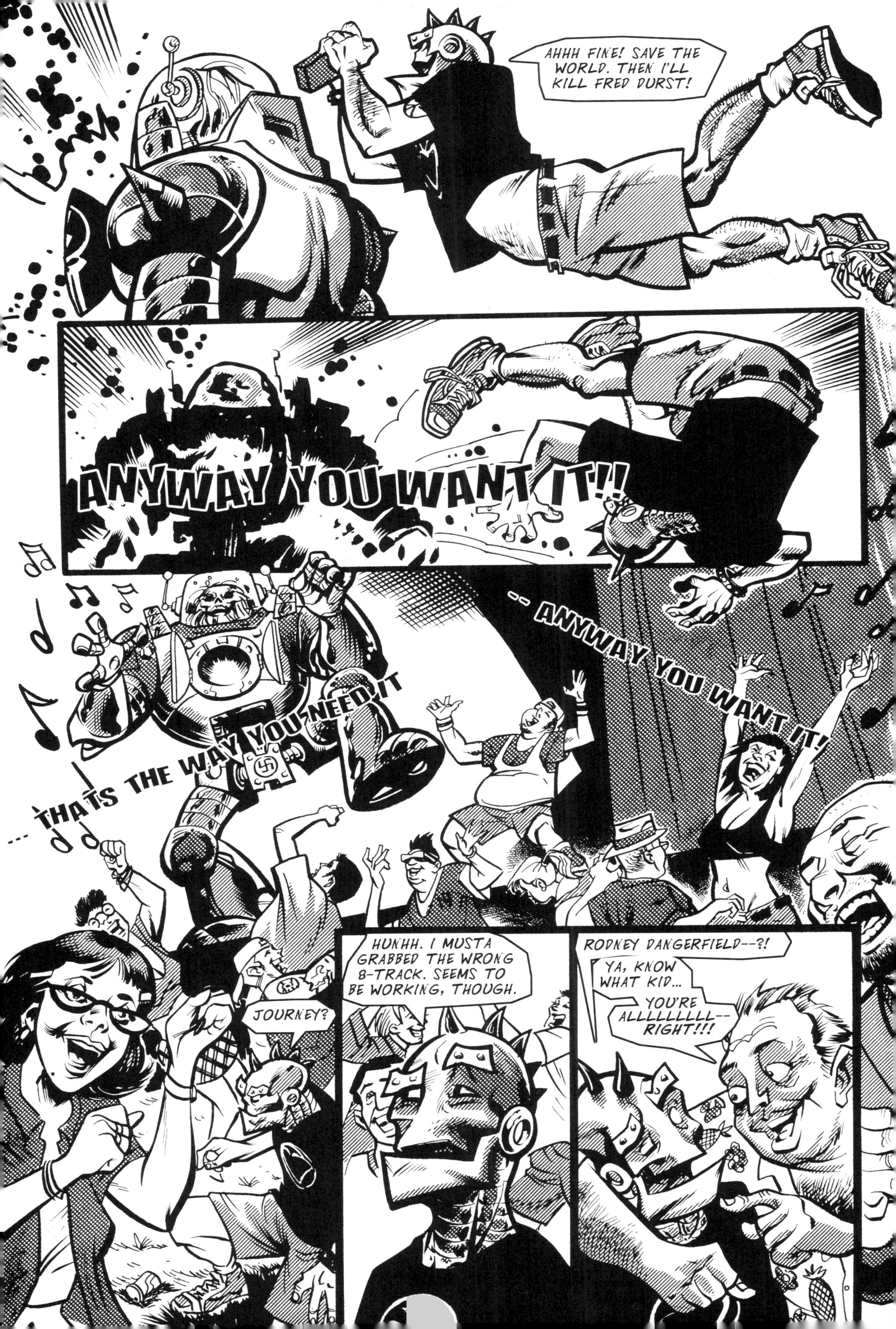
AHHH FINE! SAVE THE WORLD. THEN I'LL KILL FRED DURST!
ANYWAY YOU WANT IT!!
-- ANYWAY YOU WANT IT!
... THAT'S THE WAY YOU NEED IT
JOURNEY?
HUNHH. I MUSTA GRABBED THE WRONG 8-TRACK. SEEMS TO BE WORKING, THOUGH.
RODNEY DANGERFIELD--?!
YA, KNOW WHAT KID...
YOU'RE ALLLLLLLLL-- RIGHT!!!

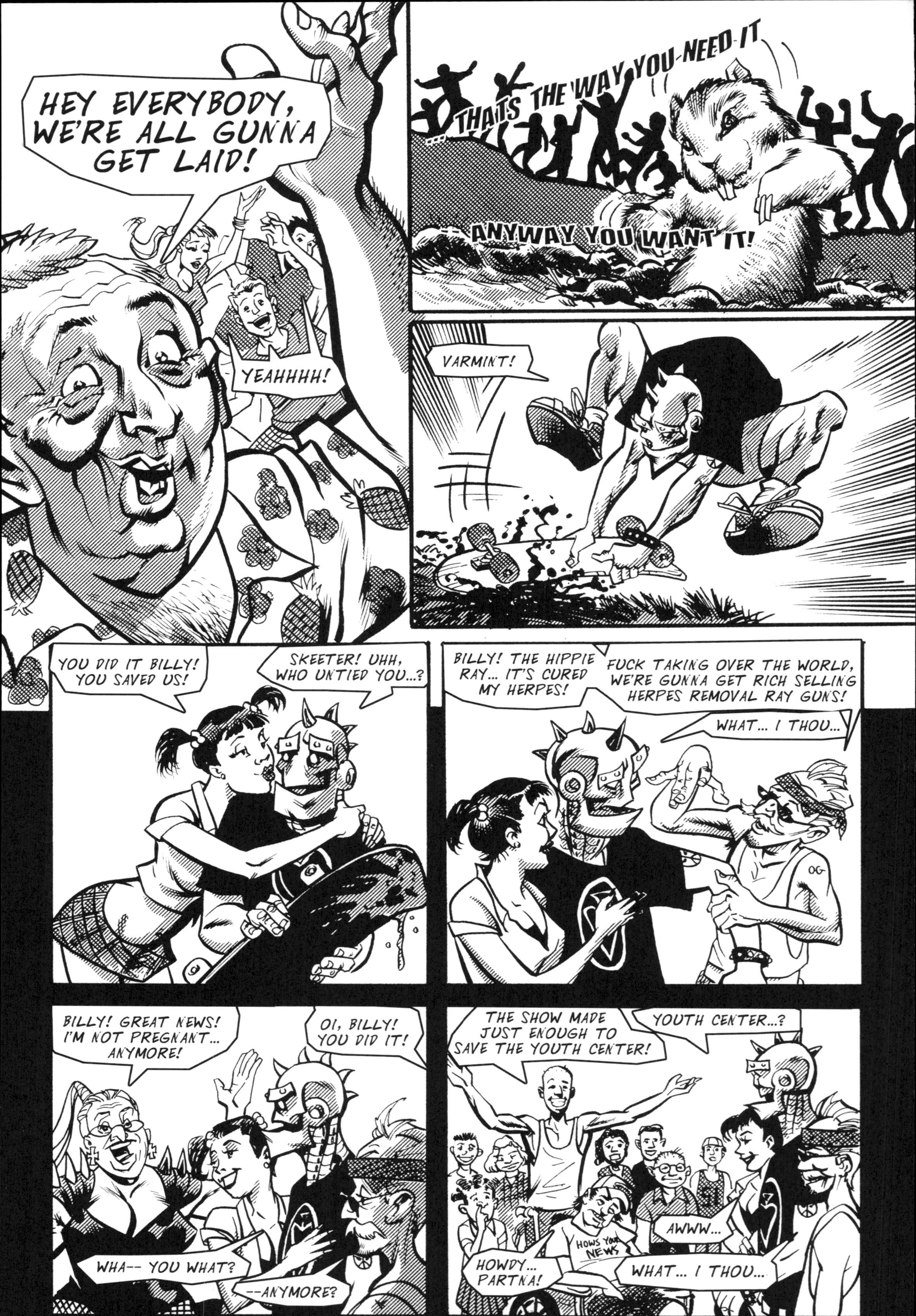
HEY EVERYBODY, WE'RE ALL GUNNA GET LAID!
YEAHHHH!
...THAT'S THE WAY YOU NEED IT
...ANYWAY YOU WANT IT!
VARMINT!
YOU DID IT BILLY! YOU SAVED US!
SKEETER! UHH, WHO UNTIED YOU...?
BILLY! THE HIPPIE RAY... IT'S CURED MY HERPES!
FUCK TAKING OVER THE WORLD, WE'RE GUNNA GET RICH SELLING HERPES REMOVAL RAY GUNS!
WHAT... I THOU...
BILLY! GREAT NEWS! I'M NOT PREGNANT... ANYMORE!
OI, BILLY! YOU DID IT!
WHA-- YOU WHAT?
--ANYMORE?
THE SHOW MADE JUST ENOUGH TO SAVE THE YOUTH CENTER!
YOUTH CENTER...?
AWWW...
HOWS YOUR NEWS
HOWDY... PARTNA!
WHAT... I THOU...

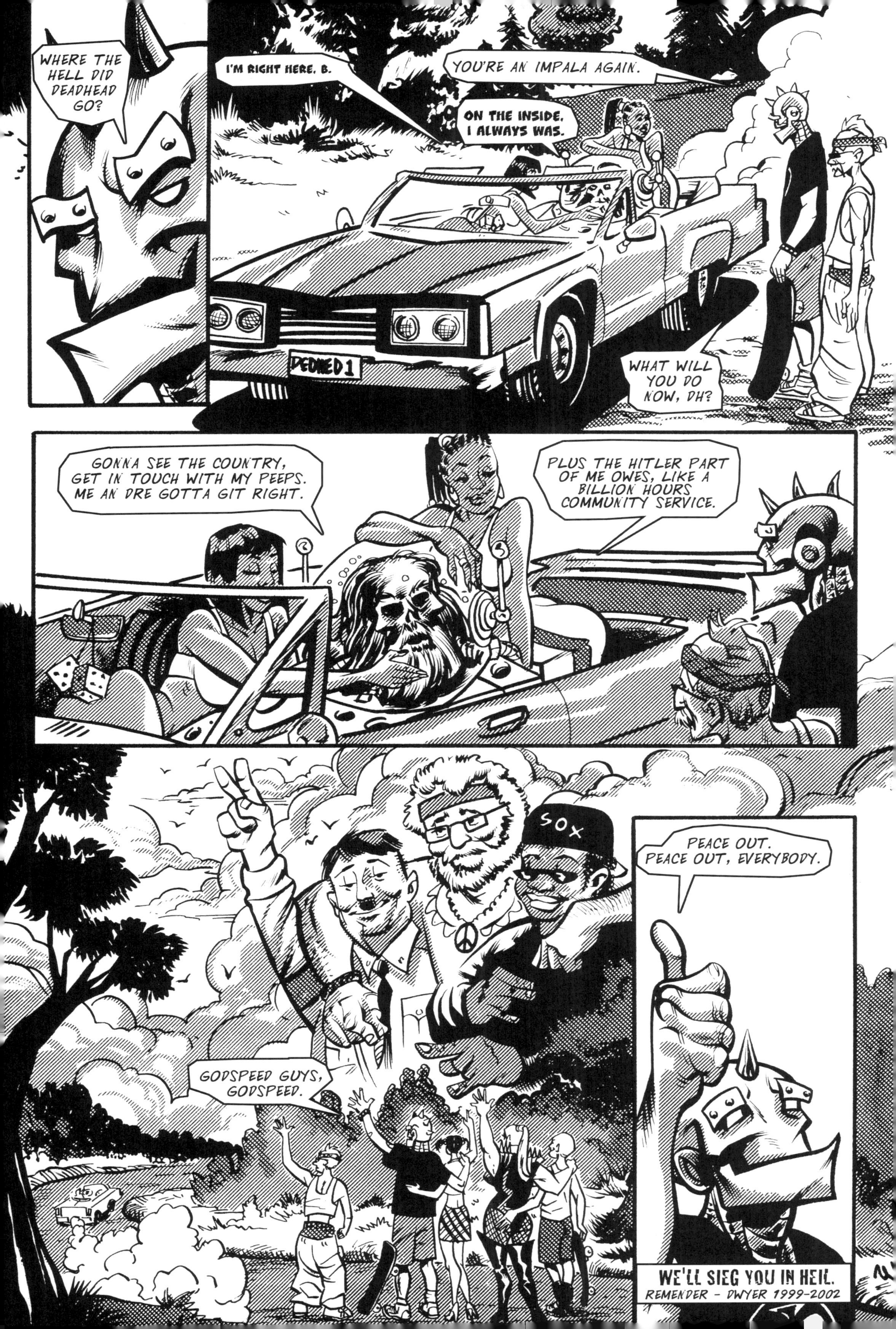
WHERE THE HELL DID DEADHEAD GO?
I'M RIGHT HERE, B.
YOU'RE AN IMPALA AGAIN.
ON THE INSIDE, I ALWAYS WAS.
DEDHED 1
WHAT WILL YOU DO NOW, DH?
GONNA SEE THE COUNTRY, GET IN TOUCH WITH MY PEEPS. ME AN' DRE GOTTA GIT RIGHT.
PLUS THE HITLER PART OF ME OWES, LIKE A BILLION HOURS COMMUNITY SERVICE.
SOX
PEACE OUT. PEACE OUT, EVERYBODY.
GODSPEED GUYS, GODSPEED.
WE'LL SIEG YOU IN HEIL.
REMENDER - DWYER 1999-2002

TWO
BETTER OFF DEAD

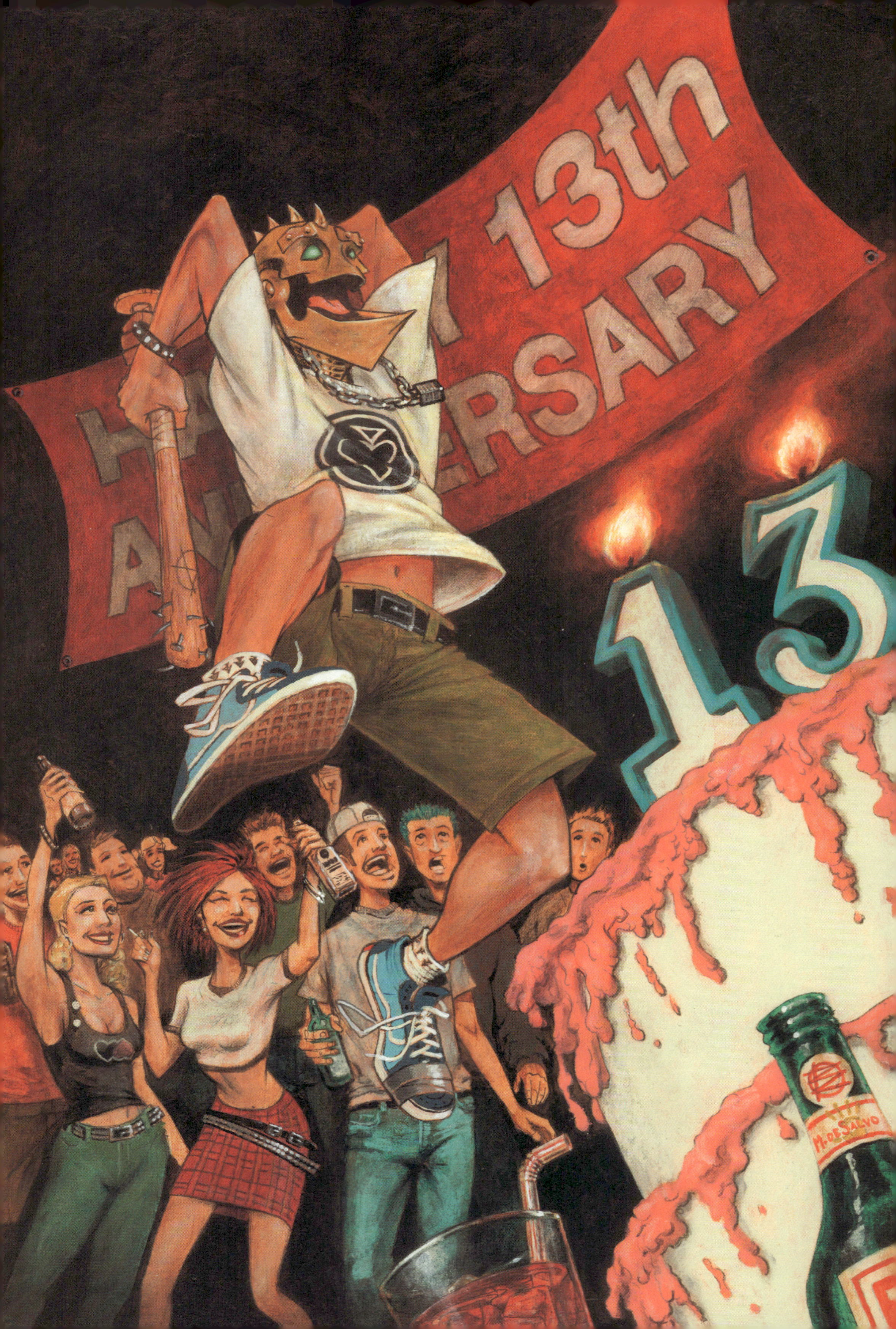

13th
13

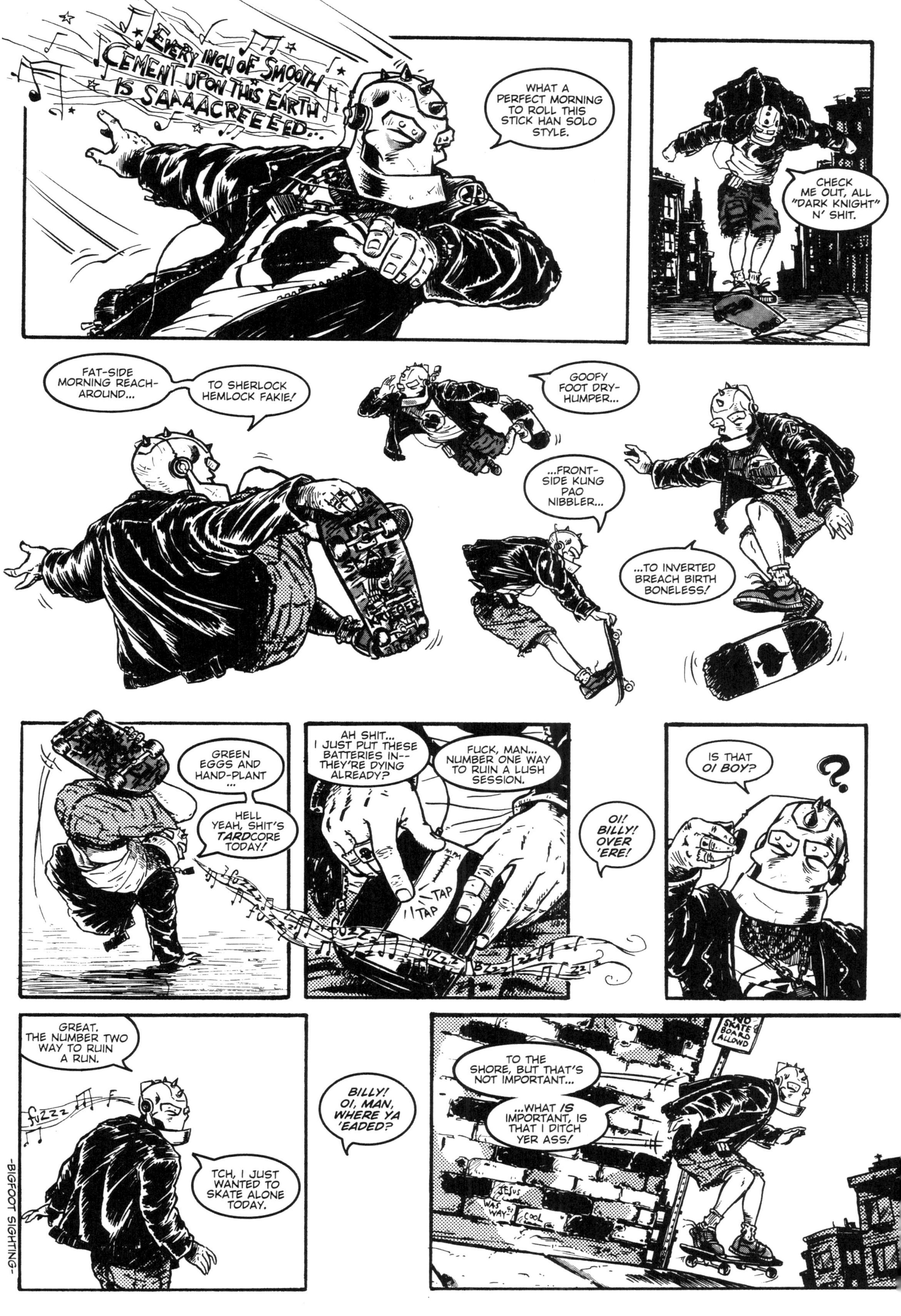
EVERY INCH OF SMOOTH CEMENT UPON THIS EARTH IS SAAAACREEEEED...
WHAT A PERFECT MORNING TO ROLL THIS STICK HAN SOLO STYLE.
CHECK ME OUT, ALL "DARK KNIGHT" N' SHIT.
FAT-SIDE MORNING REACH-AROUND...
TO SHERLOCK HEMLOCK FAKIE!
GOOFY FOOT DRY-HUMPER...
...FRONT-SIDE KUNG PAO NIBBLER...
...TO INVERTED BREACH BIRTH BONELESS!
GREEN EGGS AND HAND-PLANT ...
HELL YEAH, SHIT'S TARDCORE TODAY!
AH SHIT... I JUST PUT THESE BATTERIES IN-- THEY'RE DYING ALREADY?
FUCK, MAN... NUMBER ONE WAY TO RUIN A LUSH SESSION.
TAP
TAP
OI! BILLY! OVER 'ERE!
IS THAT OI BOY?
GREAT. THE NUMBER TWO WAY TO RUIN A RUN.
TCH, I JUST WANTED TO SKATE ALONE TODAY.
BILLY! OI, MAN, WHERE YA 'EADED?
TO THE SHORE, BUT THAT'S NOT IMPORTANT...
...WHAT IS IMPORTANT, IS THAT I DITCH YER ASS!
NO SKATE BOARD ALLOWD
JESUS WAS WAY COOL
-BIGFOOT SIGHTING-

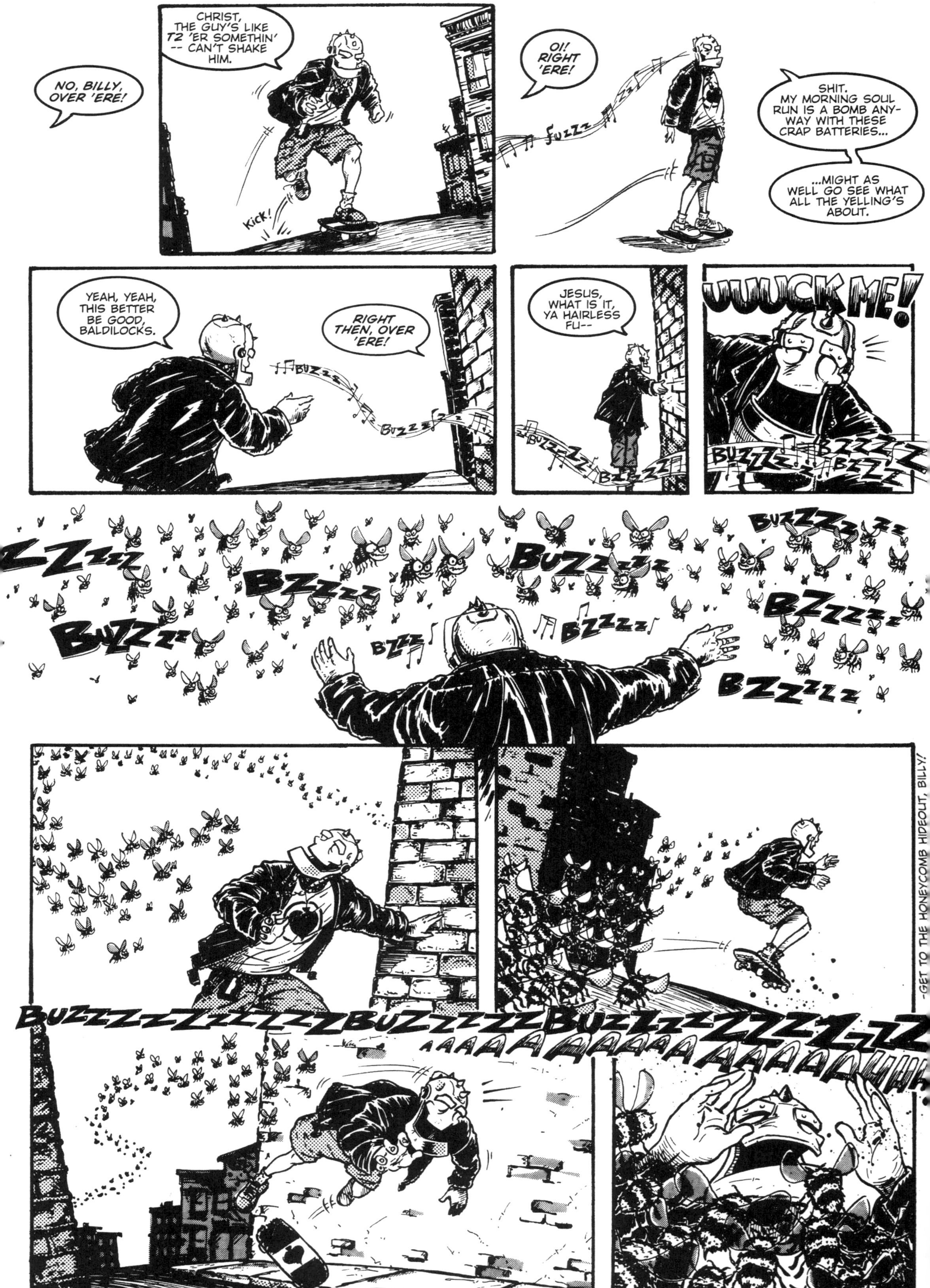
NO, BILLY, OVER 'ERE!
CHRIST, THE GUY'S LIKE T2 'ER SOMETHIN' -- CAN'T SHAKE HIM.
KICK!
OI! RIGHT 'ERE!
FUZZZ
SHIT. MY MORNING SOUL RUN IS A BOMB ANYWAY WITH THESE CRAP BATTERIES...
...MIGHT AS WELL GO SEE WHAT ALL THE YELLING'S ABOUT.
YEAH, YEAH, THIS BETTER BE GOOD, BALDILOCKS.
RIGHT THEN, OVER 'ERE!
BUZZZ
JESUS, WHAT IS IT, YA HAIRLESS FU--
UUUUCK ME!
BUZZZZ
BZZZZZ
BUZZZZZ
BZZZZZ
-GET TO THE HONEYCOMB HIDEOUT, BILLY!
BUZZZZZZZZZZZBUZZZZZZZBUZZZZZZZZZZZ
AAAAAAAAAAAAAAAAAAAHHH

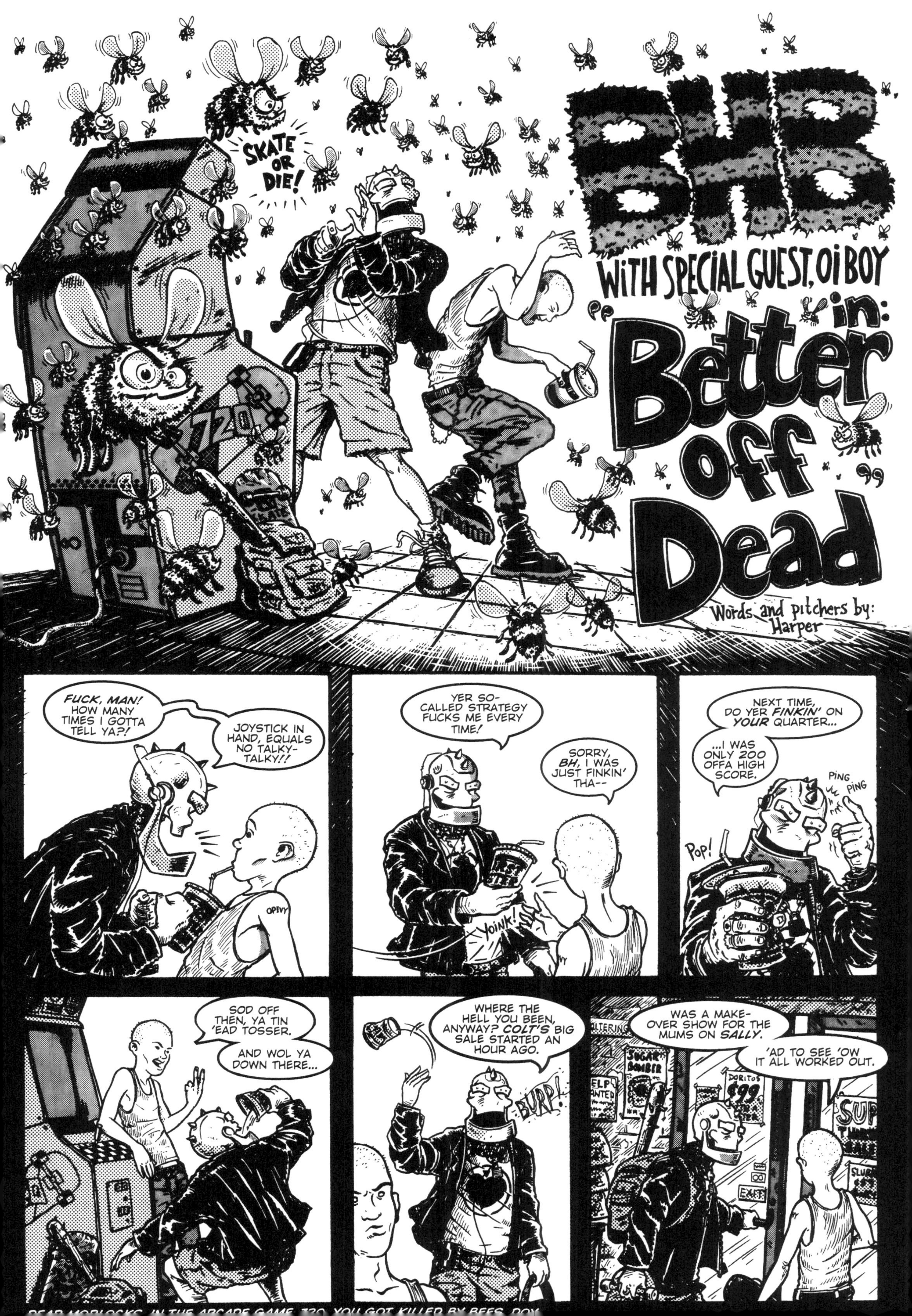
SKATE OR DIE!
BHB
WITH SPECIAL GUEST, OI BOY
in:
"Better off Dead"
Words and pitchers by: Harper
720
FUCK, MAN! HOW MANY TIMES I GOTTA TELL YA?!
JOYSTICK IN HAND, EQUALS NO TALKY-TALKY!!
OPIVY
YER SO-CALLED STRATEGY FUCKS ME EVERY TIME!
SORRY, BH, I WAS JUST FINKIN' THA--
YOINK!
NEXT TIME, DO YER FINKIN' ON YOUR QUARTER...
...I WAS ONLY 200 OFFA HIGH SCORE.
PING PING
POP!
SOD OFF THEN, YA TIN 'EAD TOSSER.
AND WOL YA DOWN THERE...
WHERE THE HELL YOU BEEN, ANYWAY? COLT'S BIG SALE STARTED AN HOUR AGO.
BURP!
WAS A MAKE-OVER SHOW FOR THE MUMS ON SALLY.
'AD TO SEE 'OW IT ALL WORKED OUT.
SUGAR BOMBER
DORITOS $.99
EXIT

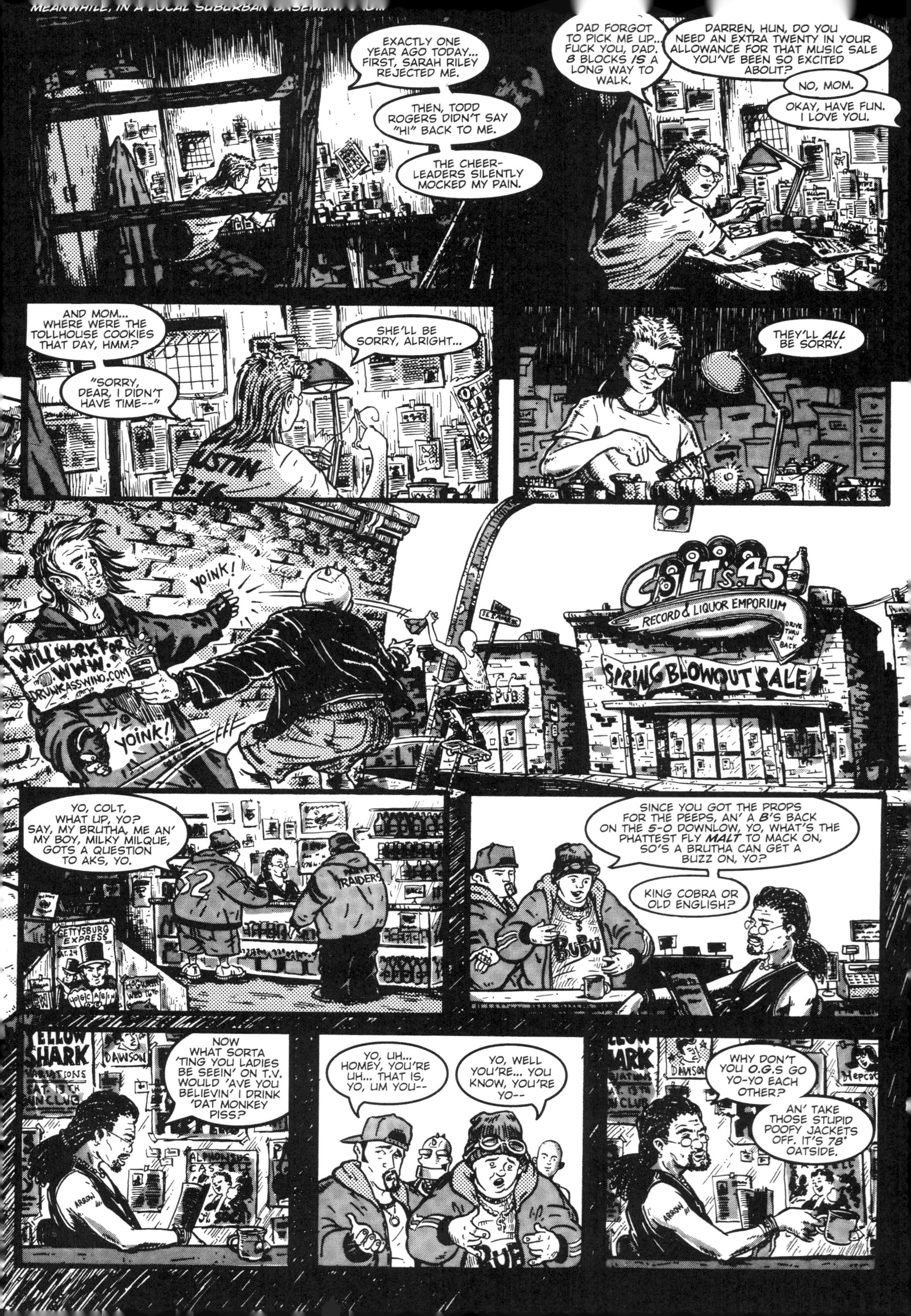
MEANWHILE, IN A LOCAL SUBURBAN
EXACTLY ONE YEAR AGO TODAY... FIRST, SARAH RILEY REJECTED ME.
THEN, TODD ROGERS DIDN'T SAY "HI" BACK TO ME.
THE CHEER-LEADERS SILENTLY MOCKED MY PAIN.
DAD FORGOT TO PICK ME UP... FUCK YOU, DAD. 8 BLOCKS IS A LONG WAY TO WALK.
DARREN, HUN, DO YOU NEED AN EXTRA TWENTY IN YOUR ALLOWANCE FOR THAT MUSIC SALE YOU'VE BEEN SO EXCITED ABOUT?
NO, MOM.
OKAY, HAVE FUN. I LOVE YOU.
AND MOM... WHERE WERE THE TOLLHOUSE COOKIES THAT DAY, HMM?
"SORRY, DEAR, I DIDN'T HAVE TIME--"
SHE'LL BE SORRY, ALRIGHT...
THEY'LL ALL BE SORRY.
WILL WORK FOR WWW. DRUNKASSWINO.COM
YOINK!
YOINK!
COLT'S 45
RECORD & LIQUOR EMPORIUM
DRIVE THRU IN BACK
SPRING BLOWOUT SALE
YO, COLT, WHAT UP, YO? SAY, MY BRUTHA, ME AN' MY BOY, MILKY MILQUE, GOTS A QUESTION TO AKS, YO.
32
RAIDERS
GETTYSBURG EXPRESS
SINCE YOU GOT THE PROPS FOR THE PEEPS, AN' A B'S BACK ON THE 5-O DOWNLOW, YO, WHAT'S THE PHATTEST FLY MALT TO MACK ON, SO'S A BRUTHA CAN GET A BUZZ ON, YO?
KING COBRA OR OLD ENGLISH?
BUBU
YELLOW SHARK
DAWSON
NOW WHAT SORTA 'TING YOU LADIES BE SEEIN' ON T.V. WOULD 'AVE YOU BELIEVIN' I DRINK 'DAT MONKEY PISS?
ARROW
YO, UH... HOMEY, YOU'RE UH... THAT IS, YO, UM YOU--
YO, WELL YOU'RE... YOU KNOW, YOU'RE YO--
WHY DON'T YOU O.G.S GO YO-YO EACH OTHER?
AN' TAKE THOSE STUPID POOFY JACKETS OFF. IT'S 78° OATSIDE.

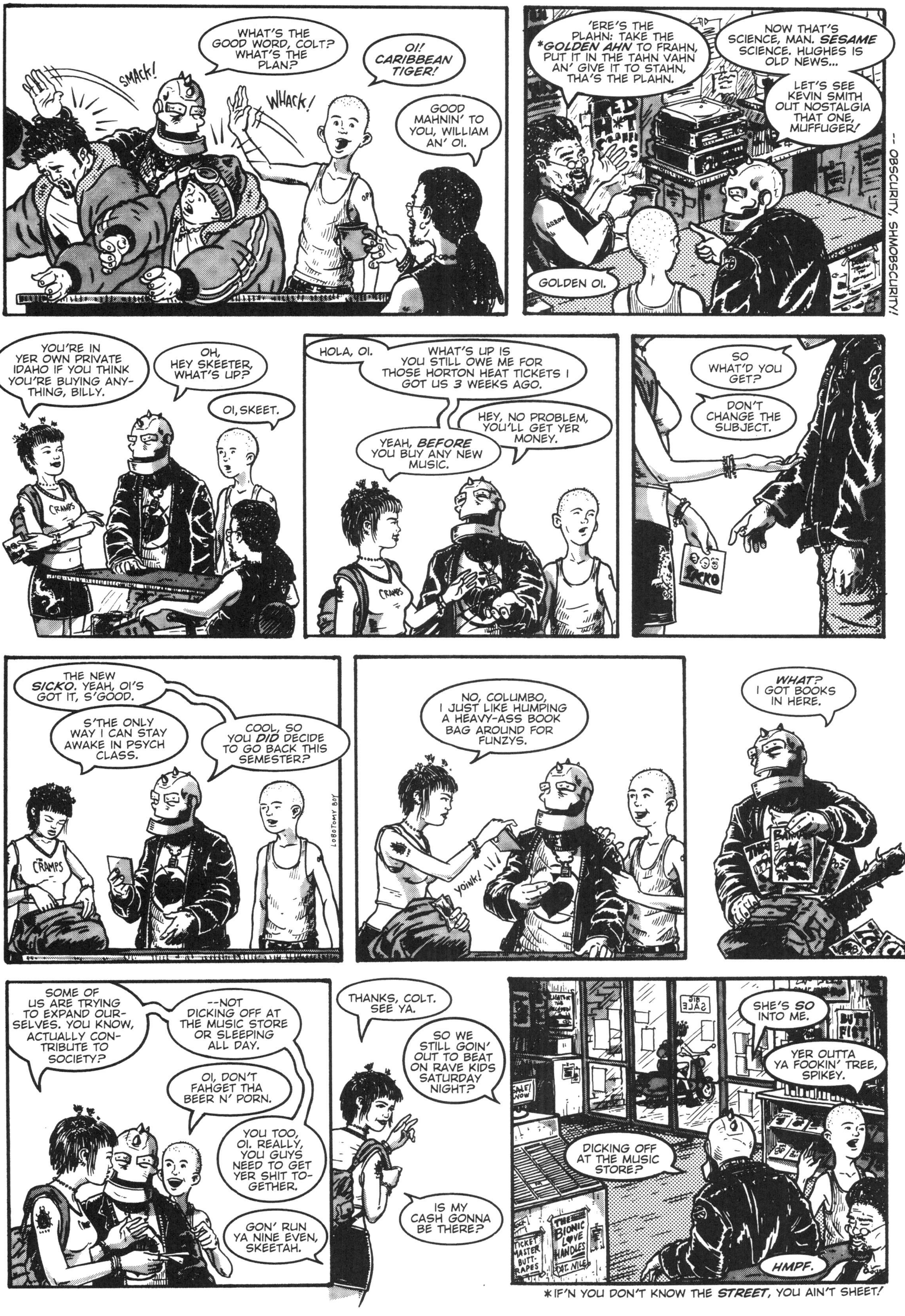

SMACK!
WHAT'S THE GOOD WORD, COLT? WHAT'S THE PLAN?
WHACK!
OI! CARIBBEAN TIGER!
GOOD MAHNIN' TO YOU, WILLIAM AN' OI.
'ERE'S THE PLAHN: TAKE THE *GOLDEN AHN TO FRAHN, PUT IT IN THE TAHN VAHN AN' GIVE IT TO STAHN, THA'S THE PLAHN.
NOW THAT'S SCIENCE, MAN. SESAME SCIENCE. HUGHES IS OLD NEWS...
LET'S SEE KEVIN SMITH OUT NOSTALGIA THAT ONE, MUFFUGER!
GOLDEN OI.
-- OBSCURITY, SHMOBSCURITY!
YOU'RE IN YER OWN PRIVATE IDAHO IF YOU THINK YOU'RE BUYING ANYTHING, BILLY.
OH, HEY SKEETER, WHAT'S UP?
OI, SKEET.
HOLA, OI.
WHAT'S UP IS YOU STILL OWE ME FOR THOSE HORTON HEAT TICKETS I GOT US 3 WEEKS AGO.
HEY, NO PROBLEM, YOU'LL GET YER MONEY.
YEAH, BEFORE YOU BUY ANY NEW MUSIC.
SO WHAT'D YOU GET?
DON'T CHANGE THE SUBJECT.
SICKO
THE NEW SICKO. YEAH, OI'S GOT IT, S'GOOD.
S'THE ONLY WAY I CAN STAY AWAKE IN PSYCH CLASS.
COOL, SO YOU DID DECIDE TO GO BACK THIS SEMESTER?
NO, COLUMBO, I JUST LIKE HUMPING A HEAVY-ASS BOOK BAG AROUND FOR FUNZYS.
YOINK!
WHAT? I GOT BOOKS IN HERE.
SOME OF US ARE TRYING TO EXPAND OURSELVES. YOU KNOW, ACTUALLY CONTRIBUTE TO SOCIETY?
--NOT DICKING OFF AT THE MUSIC STORE OR SLEEPING ALL DAY.
OI, DON'T FAHGET THA BEER N' PORN.
YOU TOO, OI. REALLY, YOU GUYS NEED TO GET YER SHIT TOGETHER.
GON' RUN YA NINE EVEN, SKEETAH.
THANKS, COLT. SEE YA.
SO WE STILL GOIN' OUT TO BEAT ON RAVE KIDS SATURDAY NIGHT?
IS MY CASH GONNA BE THERE?
SHE'S SO INTO ME.
YER OUTTA YA FOOKIN' TREE, SPIKEY.
DICKING OFF AT THE MUSIC STORE?
THE BIONIC LOVE HANDLES
TICKET MASTER BUTT-RAPES
HMPF.
*IF'N YOU DON'T KNOW THE STREET, YOU AIN'T SHEET!

SIX HOURS LATER...

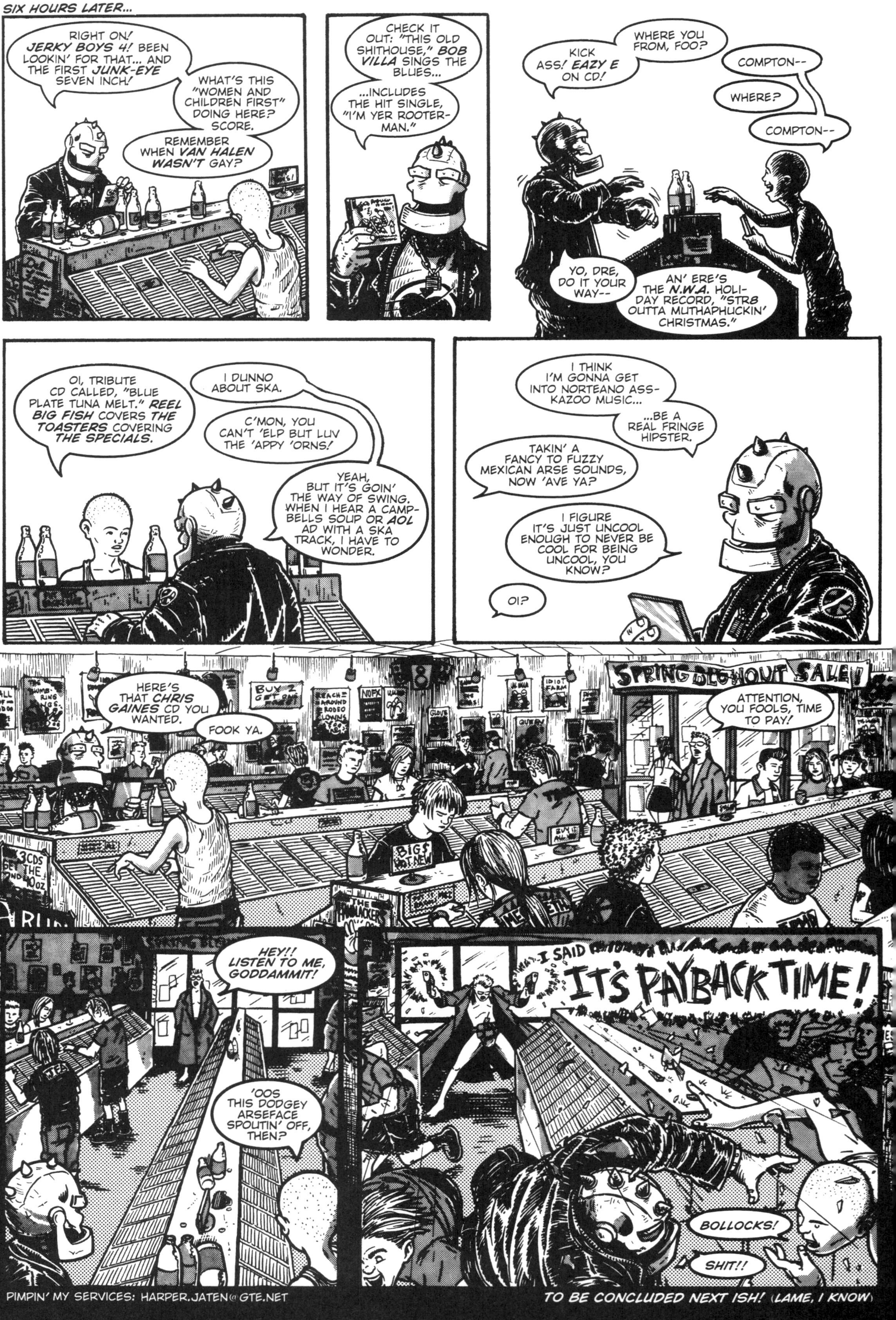
RIGHT ON! JERKY BOYS 4! BEEN LOOKIN' FOR THAT... AND THE FIRST JUNK-EYE SEVEN INCH!
WHAT'S THIS "WOMEN AND CHILDREN FIRST" DOING HERE? SCORE.
REMEMBER WHEN VAN HALEN WASN'T GAY?
CHECK IT OUT: "THIS OLD SHITHOUSE," BOB VILLA SINGS THE BLUES...
...INCLUDES THE HIT SINGLE, "I'M YER ROOTER-MAN."
KICK ASS! EAZY E ON CD!
WHERE YOU FROM, FOO?
COMPTON--
WHERE?
COMPTON--
YO, DRE, DO IT YOUR WAY--
AN' ERE'S THE N.W.A. HOLIDAY RECORD, "STR8 OUTTA MUTHAPHUCKIN' CHRISTMAS."
OI, TRIBUTE CD CALLED, "BLUE PLATE TUNA MELT." REEL BIG FISH COVERS THE TOASTERS COVERING THE SPECIALS.
I DUNNO ABOUT SKA.
C'MON, YOU CAN'T 'ELP BUT LUV THE 'APPY 'ORNS!
YEAH, BUT IT'S GOIN' THE WAY OF SWING. WHEN I HEAR A CAMPBELLS SOUP OR AOL AD WITH A SKA TRACK, I HAVE TO WONDER.
I THINK I'M GONNA GET INTO NORTEANO ASS-KAZOO MUSIC...
...BE A REAL FRINGE HIPSTER.
TAKIN' A FANCY TO FUZZY MEXICAN ARSE SOUNDS, NOW 'AVE YA?
I FIGURE IT'S JUST UNCOOL ENOUGH TO NEVER BE COOL FOR BEING UNCOOL, YOU KNOW?
OI?
SPRING BLOWOUT SALE!
HERE'S THAT CHRIS GAINES CD YOU WANTED.
FOOK YA.
ATTENTION, YOU FOOLS, TIME TO PAY!
NOFX
IDIOT FARM
BUY 2
HEY!! LISTEN TO ME, GODDAMMIT!
'OOS THIS DODGEY ARSEFACE SPOUTIN' OFF, THEN?
I SAID
IT'S PAYBACK TIME!
BOLLOCKS!
SHIT!!

PIMPIN' MY SERVICES: HARPER.JATEN@GTE.NET

TO BE CONCLUDED NEXT ISH! (LAME, I KNOW)

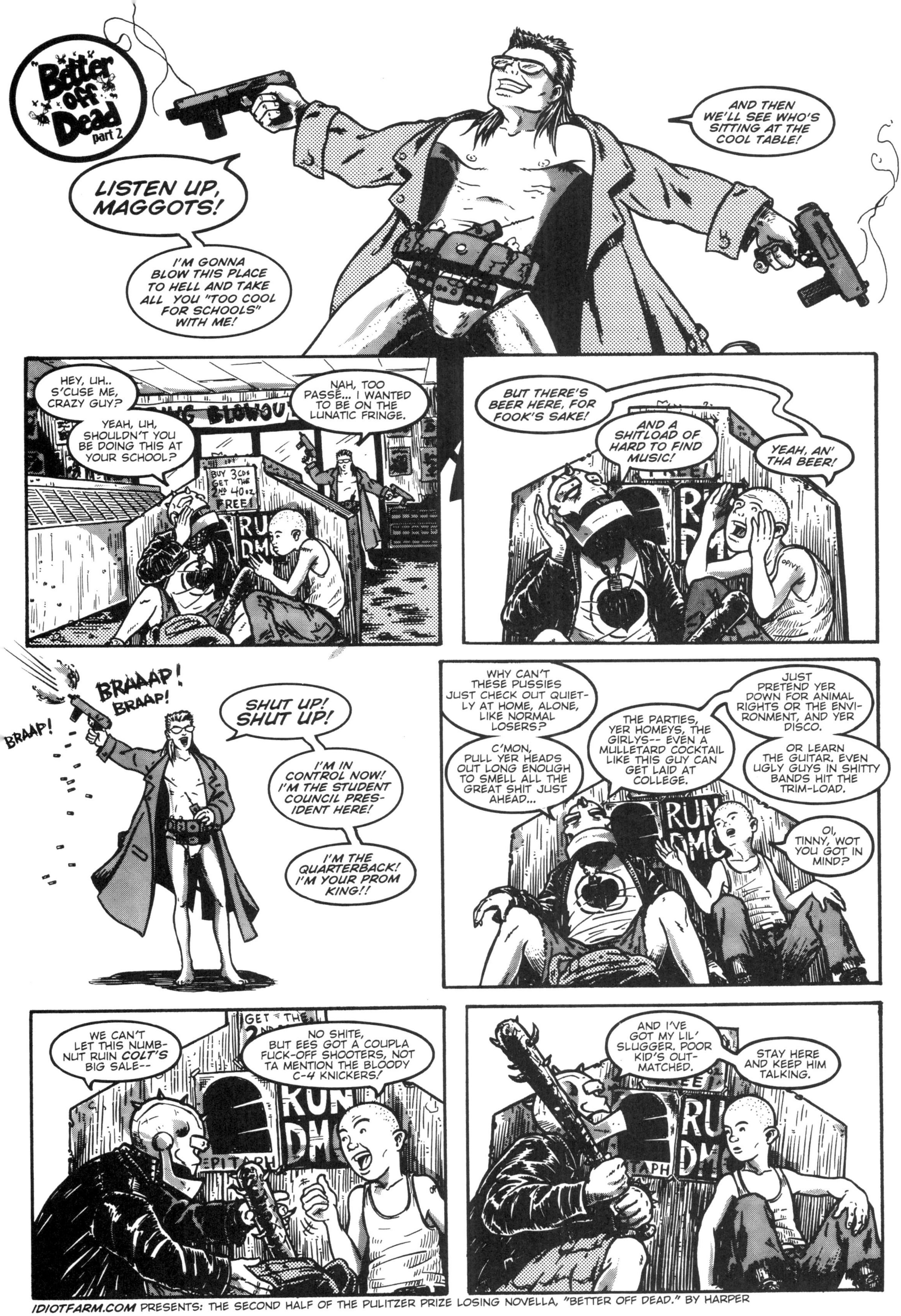
Better off Dead part 2
LISTEN UP, MAGGOTS!
I'M GONNA BLOW THIS PLACE TO HELL AND TAKE ALL YOU "TOO COOL FOR SCHOOLS" WITH ME!
AND THEN WE'LL SEE WHO'S SITTING AT THE COOL TABLE!
HEY, UH.. S'CUSE ME, CRAZY GUY?
YEAH, UH, SHOULDN'T YOU BE DOING THIS AT YOUR SCHOOL?
NAH, TOO PASSÉ... I WANTED TO BE ON THE LUNATIC FRINGE.
BUY 3 CDS GET THE 2ND 40 OZ FREE!
RUN DMC
BUT THERE'S BEER HERE, FOR FOOK'S SAKE!
AND A SHITLOAD OF HARD TO FIND MUSIC!
YEAH, AN' THA BEER!
BRAAAP! BRAAP!
BRAAP!
SHUT UP! SHUT UP!
I'M IN CONTROL NOW! I'M THE STUDENT COUNCIL PRESIDENT HERE!
I'M THE QUARTERBACK! I'M YOUR PROM KING!!
WHY CAN'T THESE PUSSIES JUST CHECK OUT QUIETLY AT HOME, ALONE, LIKE NORMAL LOSERS?
C'MON, PULL YER HEADS OUT LONG ENOUGH TO SMELL ALL THE GREAT SHIT JUST AHEAD...
THE PARTIES, YER HOMEYS, THE GIRLYS-- EVEN A MULLETARD COCKTAIL LIKE THIS GUY CAN GET LAID AT COLLEGE.
JUST PRETEND YER DOWN FOR ANIMAL RIGHTS OR THE ENVIRONMENT, AND YER DISCO.
OR LEARN THE GUITAR. EVEN UGLY GUYS IN SHITTY BANDS HIT THE TRIM-LOAD.
OI, TINNY, WOT YOU GOT IN MIND?
WE CAN'T LET THIS NUMBNUT RUIN COLT'S BIG SALE--
NO SHITE, BUT EES GOT A COUPLA FUCK-OFF SHOOTERS, NOT TA MENTION THE BLOODY C-4 KNICKERS!
AND I'VE GOT MY LIL' SLUGGER. POOR KID'S OUTMATCHED.
STAY HERE AND KEEP HIM TALKING.

IDIOTFARM.COM PRESENTS: THE SECOND HALF OF THE PULITZER PRIZE LOSING NOVELLA, "BETTER OFF DEAD." BY HARPER

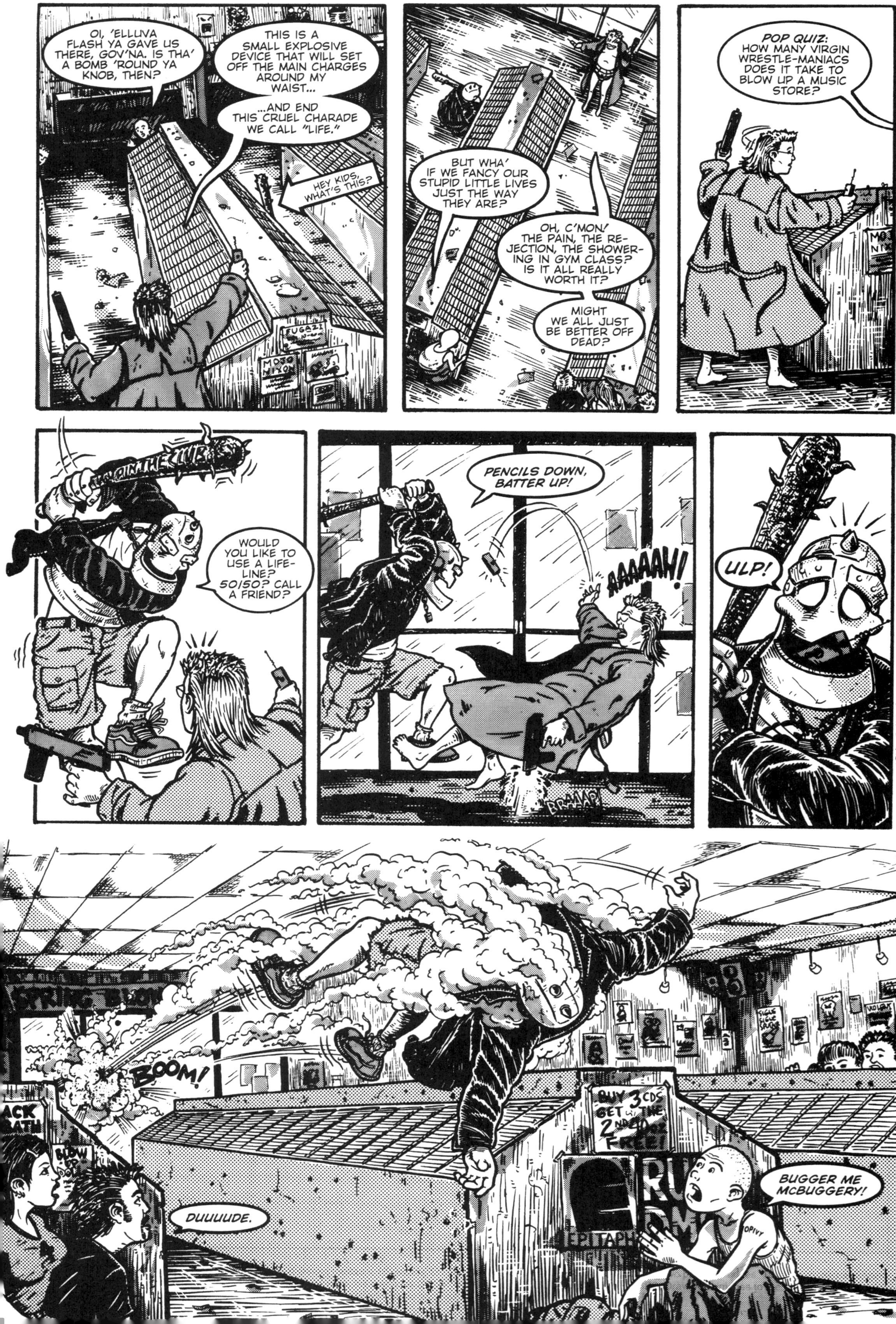
OI, 'ELLUVA FLASH YA GAVE US THERE, GOV'NA. IS THA' A BOMB 'ROUND YA KNOB, THEN?
THIS IS A SMALL EXPLOSIVE DEVICE THAT WILL SET OFF THE MAIN CHARGES AROUND MY WAIST...
...AND END THIS CRUEL CHARADE WE CALL "LIFE."
HEY KIDS, WHAT'S THIS?
FUGAZI
MOJO NIXON
BUT WHA' IF WE FANCY OUR STUPID LITTLE LIVES JUST THE WAY THEY ARE?
OH, C'MON! THE PAIN, THE RE-JECTION, THE SHOWER-ING IN GYM CLASS? IS IT ALL REALLY WORTH IT?
MIGHT WE ALL JUST BE BETTER OFF DEAD?
POP QUIZ: HOW MANY VIRGIN WRESTLE-MANIACS DOES IT TAKE TO BLOW UP A MUSIC STORE?
WOULD YOU LIKE TO USE A LIFE-LINE? 50/50? CALL A FRIEND?
PENCILS DOWN, BATTER UP!
AAAAAH!
BRAAAP!
ULP!
BOOM!
DUUUUDE.
BUGGER ME MCBUGGERY!
EPITAPH
OPIVY

(OH) SHIT-FACED

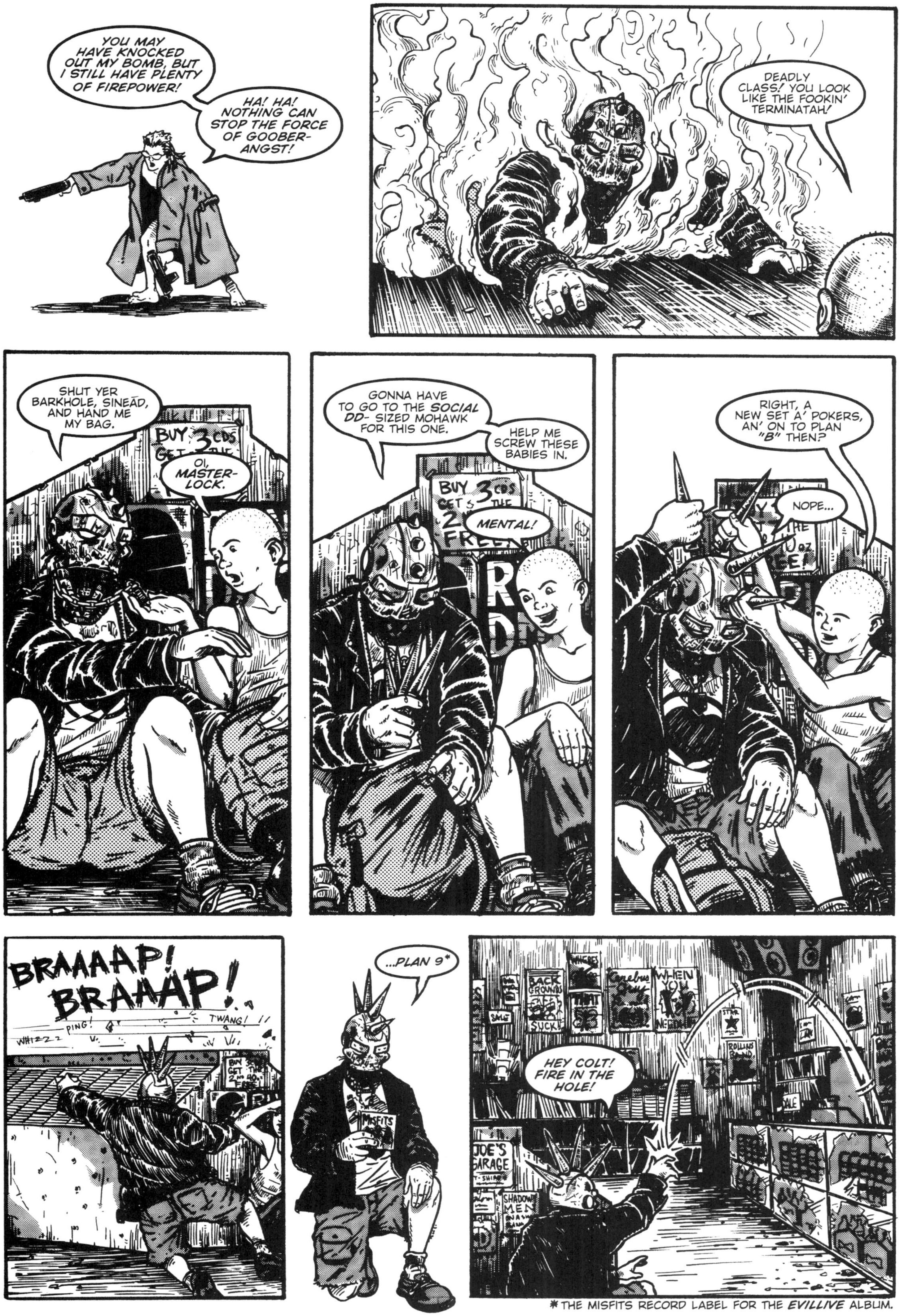
YOU MAY HAVE KNOCKED OUT MY BOMB, BUT I STILL HAVE PLENTY OF FIREPOWER!
HA! HA! NOTHING CAN STOP THE FORCE OF GOOBER-ANGST!
DEADLY CLASS! YOU LOOK LIKE THE FOOKIN' TERMINATAH!
SHUT YER BARKHOLE, SINEAD, AND HAND ME MY BAG.
OI, MASTER-LOCK.
GONNA HAVE TO GO TO THE SOCIAL DD- SIZED MOHAWK FOR THIS ONE.
HELP ME SCREW THESE BABIES IN.
MENTAL!
RIGHT, A NEW SET A' POKERS, AN' ON TO PLAN "B" THEN?
NOPE...
BRAAAAP! BRAAAP!
PING!
TWANG!
...PLAN 9*
MISFITS
HEY COLT! FIRE IN THE HOLE!
JOE'S GARAGE

*THE MISFITS RECORD LABEL FOR THE *EVILLIVE* ALBUM.

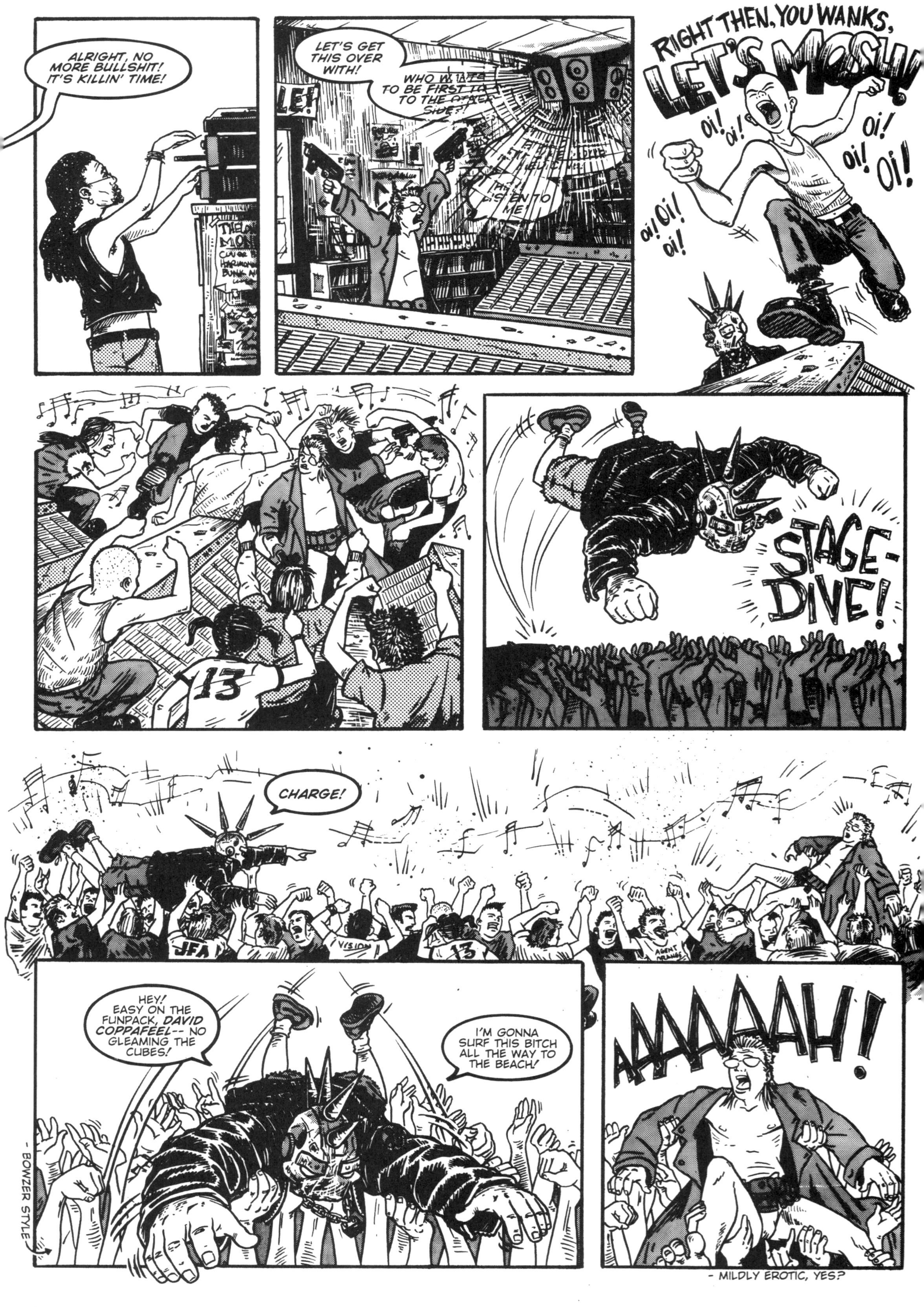
ALRIGHT, NO MORE BULLSHIT! IT'S KILLIN' TIME!
LET'S GET THIS OVER WITH!
RIGHT THEN, YOU WANKS, LET'S MOSH!
OI! OI! OI! OI! OI! OI! OI! OI!
STAGE-DIVE!
CHARGE!
HEY! EASY ON THE FUNPACK, DAVID COPPAFEEL-- NO GLEAMING THE CUBES!
I'M GONNA SURF THIS BITCH ALL THE WAY TO THE BEACH!
AAAAAAH!
- BOWZER STYLE
- MILDLY EROTIC, YES?

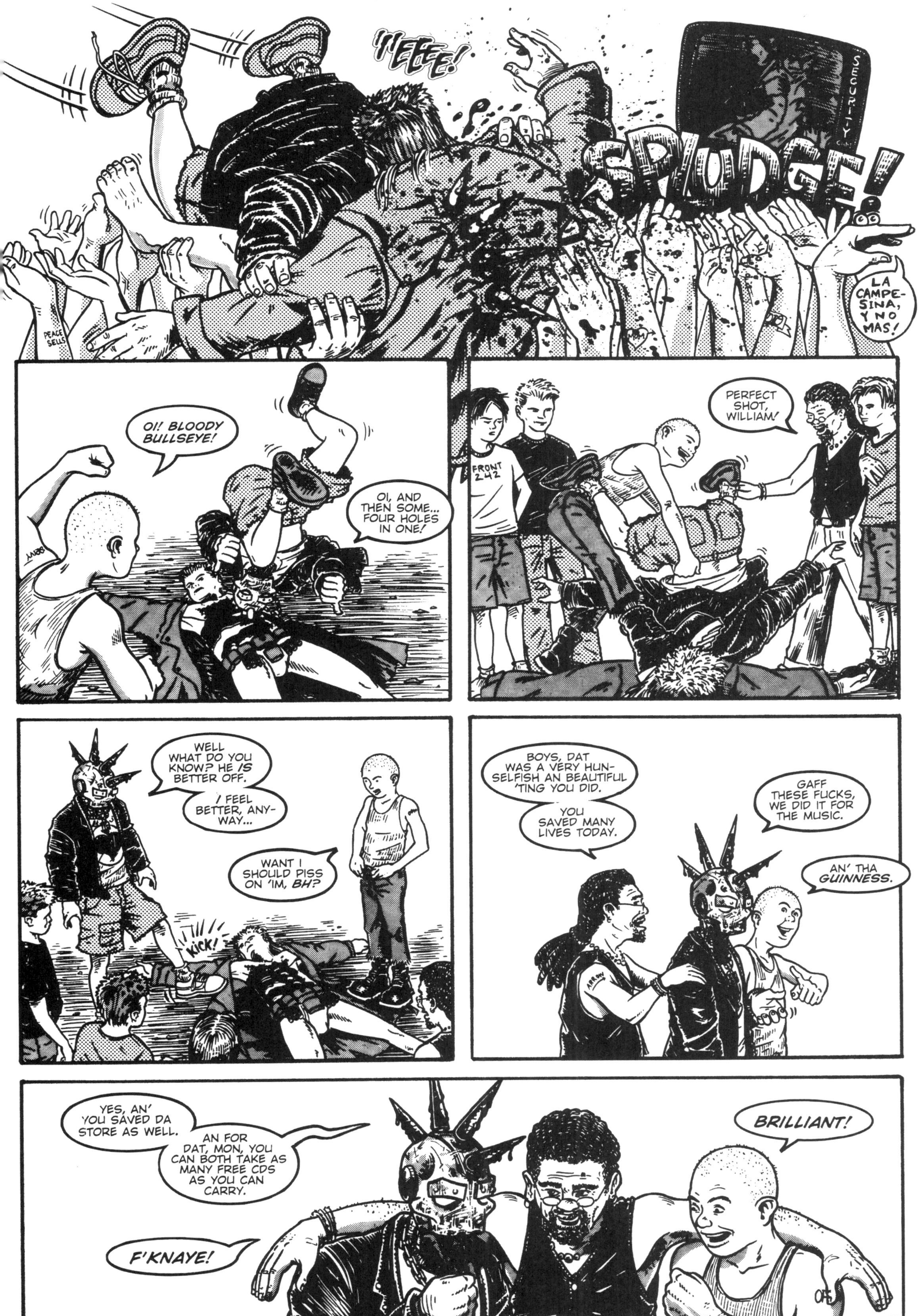

'EEEE!
SECURITY
SPLUDGE!
PEACE SELLS
LA CAMPESINA, Y NO MAS!
OI! BLOODY BULLSEYE!
OI, AND THEN SOME... FOUR HOLES IN ONE!
FRONT 242
PERFECT SHOT, WILLIAM!
WELL WHAT DO YOU KNOW? HE IS BETTER OFF.
I FEEL BETTER, ANYWAY...
WANT I SHOULD PISS ON 'IM, BH?
KICK!
BOYS, DAT WAS A VERY HUN-SELFISH AN BEAUTIFUL 'TING YOU DID.
YOU SAVED MANY LIVES TODAY.
GAFF THESE FUCKS, WE DID IT FOR THE MUSIC.
AN' THA GUINNESS.
YES, AN' YOU SAVED DA STORE AS WELL.
AN FOR DAT, MON, YOU CAN BOTH TAKE AS MANY FREE CDS AS YOU CAN CARRY.
BRILLIANT!
F'KNAYE!

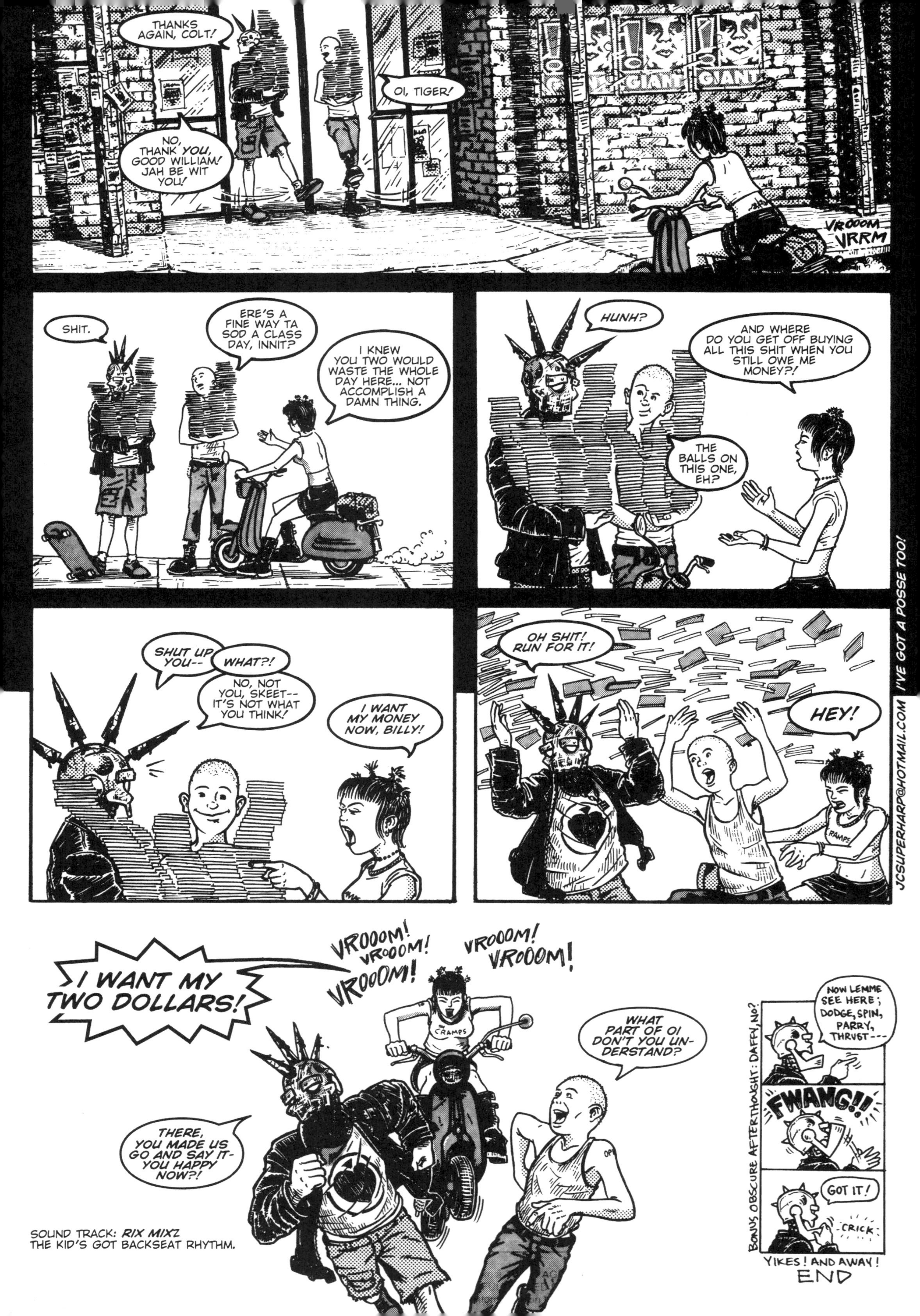
THANKS AGAIN, COLT!
NO, THANK YOU, GOOD WILLIAM! JAH BE WIT YOU!
OI, TIGER!
GIANT GIANT
VROOOM VRRM
SHIT.
ERE'S A FINE WAY TA SOD A CLASS DAY, INNIT?
I KNEW YOU TWO WOULD WASTE THE WHOLE DAY HERE... NOT ACCOMPLISH A DAMN THING.
HUNH?
AND WHERE DO YOU GET OFF BUYING ALL THIS SHIT WHEN YOU STILL OWE ME MONEY?!
THE BALLS ON THIS ONE, EH?
SHUT UP YOU--
WHAT?!
NO, NOT YOU, SKEET-- IT'S NOT WHAT YOU THINK!
I WANT MY MONEY NOW, BILLY!
OH SHIT! RUN FOR IT!
HEY!
CRAMPS
I'VE GOT A POSSE TOO!
JCSUPERHARP@HOTMAIL.COM
I WANT MY TWO DOLLARS!
VROOOM! VROOOM! VROOOM!
VROOOM! VROOOM!
CRAMPS
WHAT PART OF OI DON'T YOU UNDERSTAND?
THERE, YOU MADE US GO AND SAY IT- YOU HAPPY NOW?!
SOUND TRACK: RIX MIXZ
THE KID'S GOT BACKSEAT RHYTHM.
BONUS OBSCURE AFTERTHOUGHT: DAFFY, NO?
NOW LEMME SEE HERE; DODGE, SPIN, PARRY, THRUST---
FWANG!!
GOT IT!
CRICK
YIKES! AND AWAY!
END

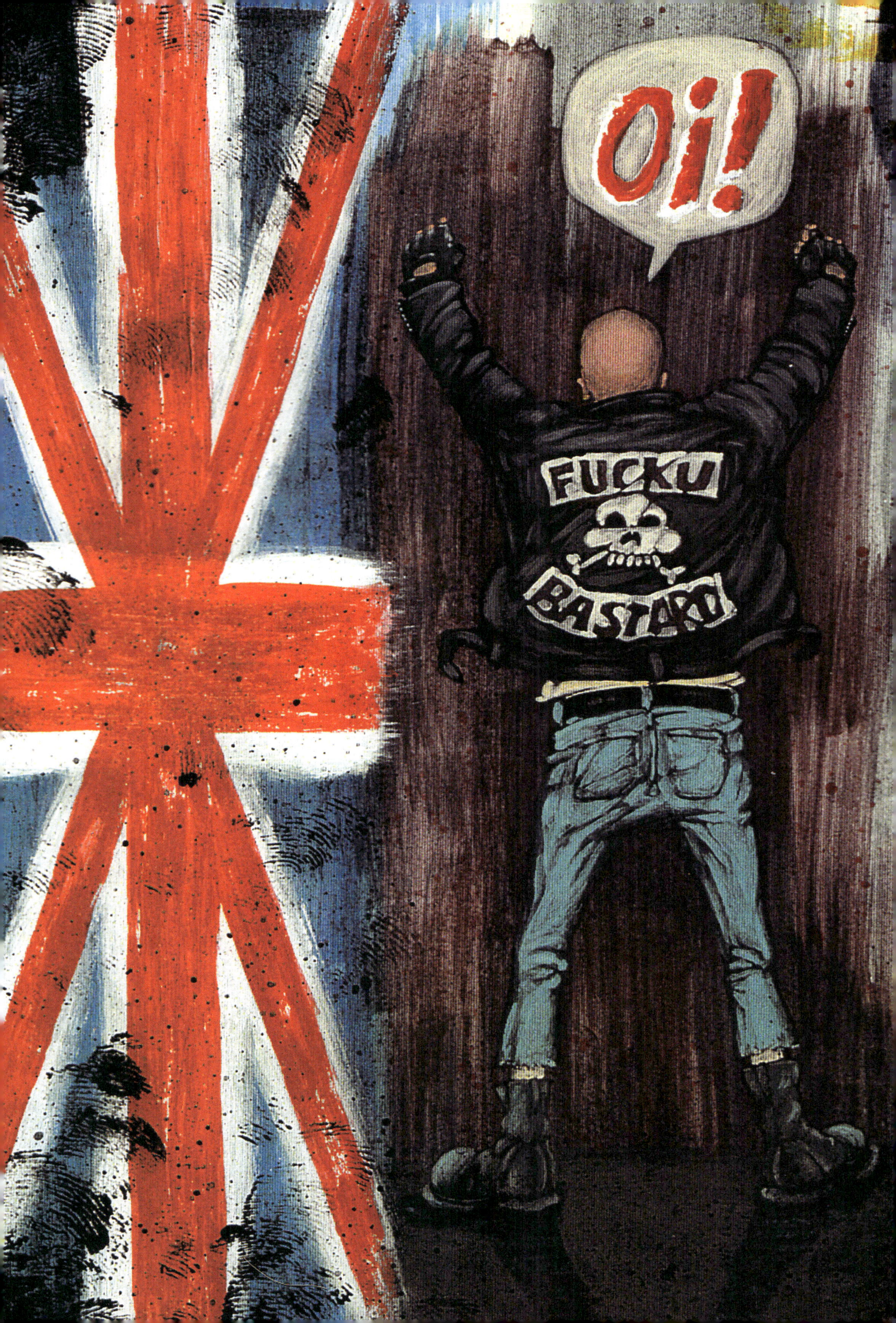
Oi!
FUCKU
BASTARD

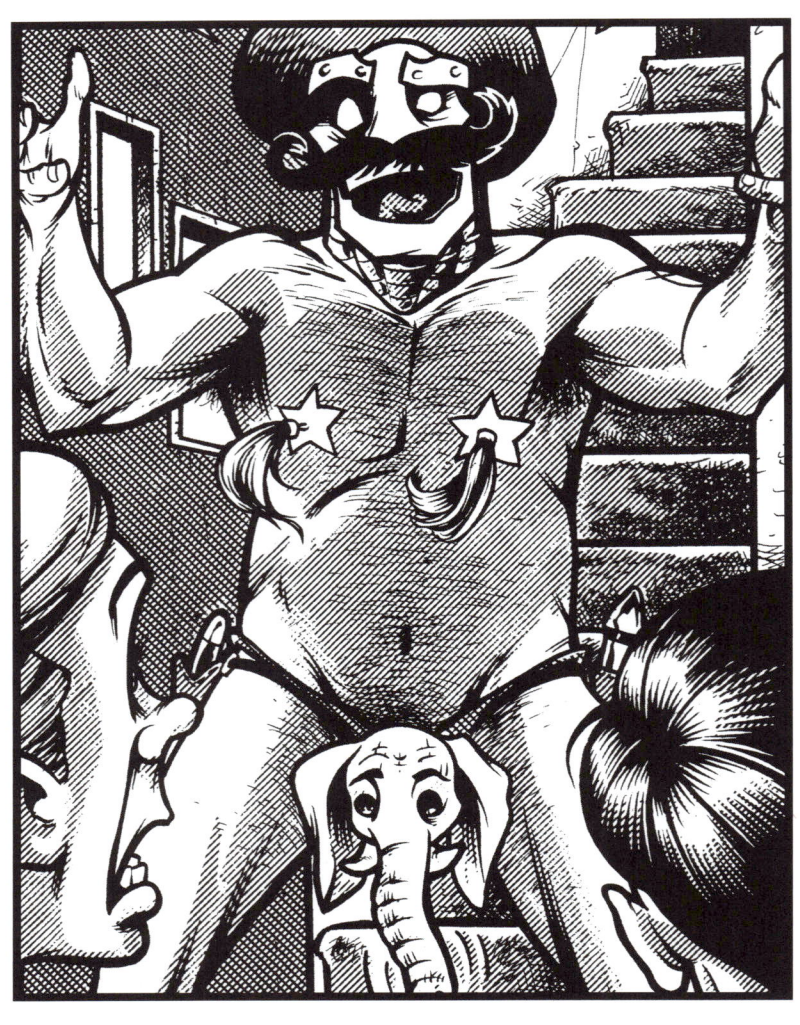

THREE
CAPTAIN DINGLEBERRY SELLOUT CROSSOVER

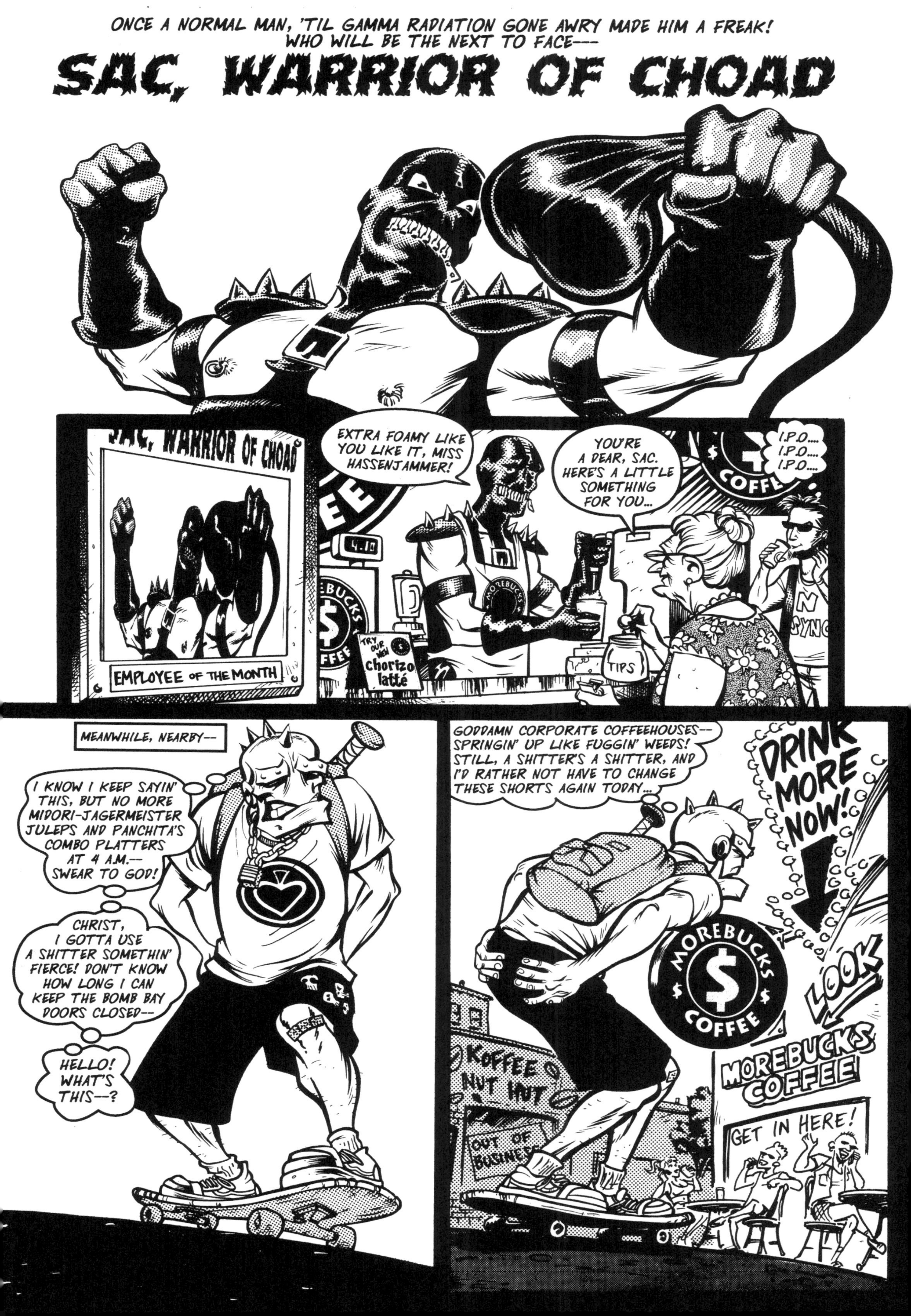
ONCE A NORMAL MAN, 'TIL GAMMA RADIATION GONE AWRY MADE HIM A FREAK!
WHO WILL BE THE NEXT TO FACE---
SAC, WARRIOR OF CHOAD
SAC, WARRIOR OF CHOAD
EMPLOYEE OF THE MONTH
EXTRA FOAMY LIKE YOU LIKE IT, MISS HASSENJAMMER!
YOU'RE A DEAR, SAC. HERE'S A LITTLE SOMETHING FOR YOU...
I.P.O.... I.P.O.... I.P.O....
4.10
TRY OUR NEW chorizo latté
TIPS
COFFEE
MEANWHILE, NEARBY--
I KNOW I KEEP SAYIN' THIS, BUT NO MORE MIDORI-JAGERMEISTER JULEPS AND PANCHITA'S COMBO PLATTERS AT 4 A.M.-- SWEAR TO GOD!
CHRIST, I GOTTA USE A SHITTER SOMETHIN' FIERCE! DON'T KNOW HOW LONG I CAN KEEP THE BOMB BAY DOORS CLOSED--
HELLO! WHAT'S THIS--?
GODDAMN CORPORATE COFFEEHOUSES-- SPRINGIN' UP LIKE FUGGIN' WEEDS! STILL, A SHITTER'S A SHITTER, AND I'D RATHER NOT HAVE TO CHANGE THESE SHORTS AGAIN TODAY...
DRINK MORE NOW!
MOREBUCKS $ COFFEE
LOOK
MOREBUCKS COFFEE
KOFFEE NUT HUT
GET IN HERE!

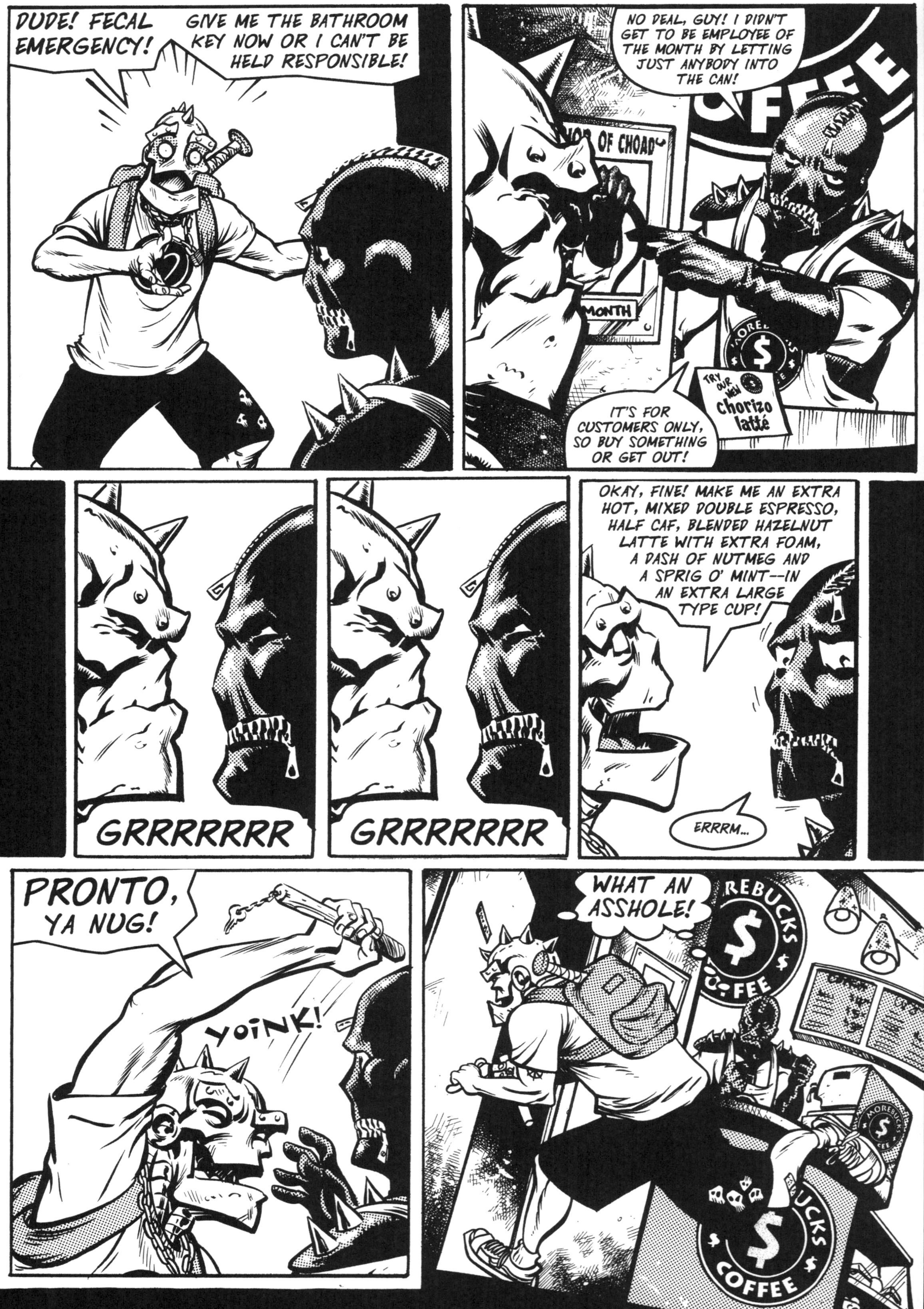
DUDE! FECAL EMERGENCY!
GIVE ME THE BATHROOM KEY NOW OR I CAN'T BE HELD RESPONSIBLE!
NO DEAL, GUY! I DIDN'T GET TO BE EMPLOYEE OF THE MONTH BY LETTING JUST ANYBODY INTO THE CAN!
OF CHOAD
MONTH
COFFEE
TRY OUR NEW Chorizo latté
IT'S FOR CUSTOMERS ONLY, SO BUY SOMETHING OR GET OUT!
GRRRRRRR
GRRRRRRR
OKAY, FINE! MAKE ME AN EXTRA HOT, MIXED DOUBLE ESPRESSO, HALF CAF, BLENDED HAZELNUT LATTE WITH EXTRA FOAM, A DASH OF NUTMEG AND A SPRIG O' MINT--IN AN EXTRA LARGE TYPE CUP!
ERRRM...
PRONTO, YA NUG!
YOINK!
WHAT AN ASSHOLE!
REBUCKS $ COFFEE
BUCKS $ COFFEE

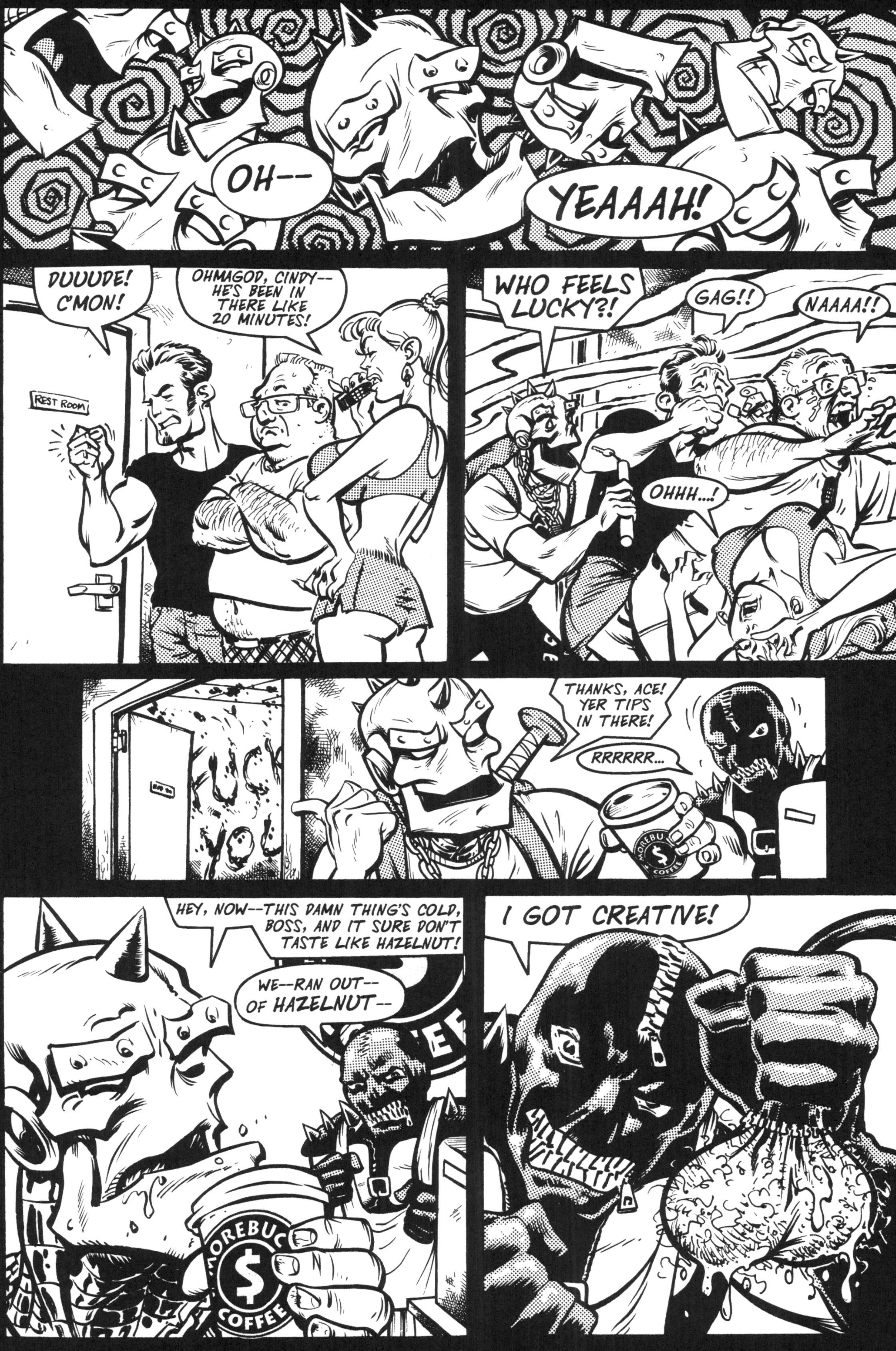
OH--
YEAAAH!
DUUUDE! C'MON!
OHMAGOD, CINDY-- HE'S BEEN IN THERE LIKE 20 MINUTES!
REST ROOM
WHO FEELS LUCKY?!
GAG!!
NAAAA!!
OHHH...!
THANKS, ACE! YER TIPS IN THERE!
RRRRRR...
MOREBUC$ COFFEE
HEY, NOW--THIS DAMN THING'S COLD, BOSS, AND IT SURE DON'T TASTE LIKE HAZELNUT!
WE--RAN OUT-- OF HAZELNUT--
MOREBUC$ COFFEE
I GOT CREATIVE!

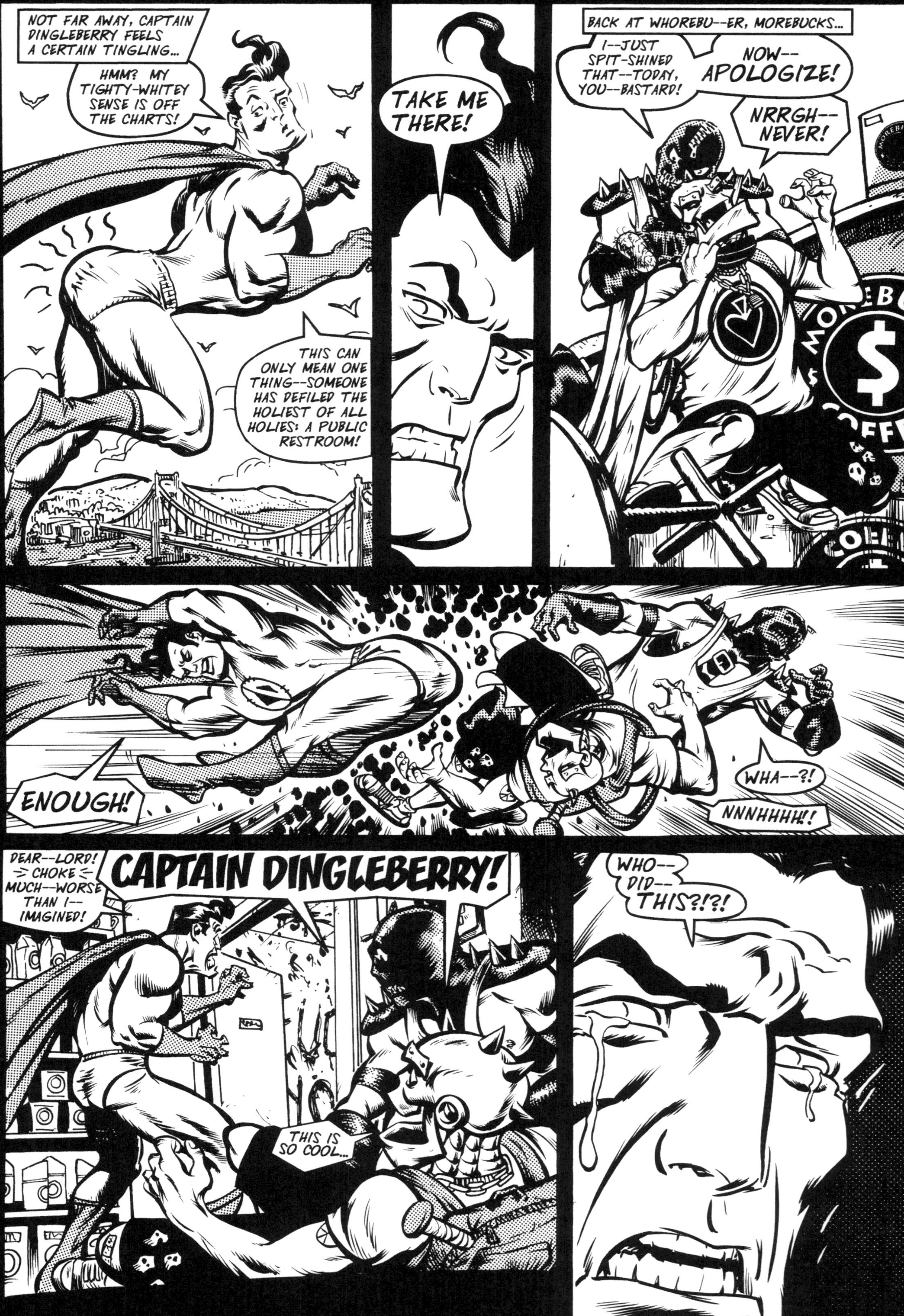
NOT FAR AWAY, CAPTAIN DINGLEBERRY FEELS A CERTAIN TINGLING...
HMM? MY TIGHTY-WHITEY SENSE IS OFF THE CHARTS!
THIS CAN ONLY MEAN ONE THING--SOMEONE HAS DEFILED THE HOLIEST OF ALL HOLIES: A PUBLIC RESTROOM!
TAKE ME THERE!
BACK AT WHOREBU--ER, MOREBUCKS...
I--JUST SPIT-SHINED THAT--TODAY, YOU--BASTARD!
NOW--APOLOGIZE!
NRRGH--NEVER!
ENOUGH!
WHA--?!
NNNHHHH!!
DEAR--LORD! ≥CHOKE≤ MUCH--WORSE THAN I--IMAGINED!
CAPTAIN DINGLEBERRY!
THIS IS SO COOL...
WHO--DID--THIS?!?!

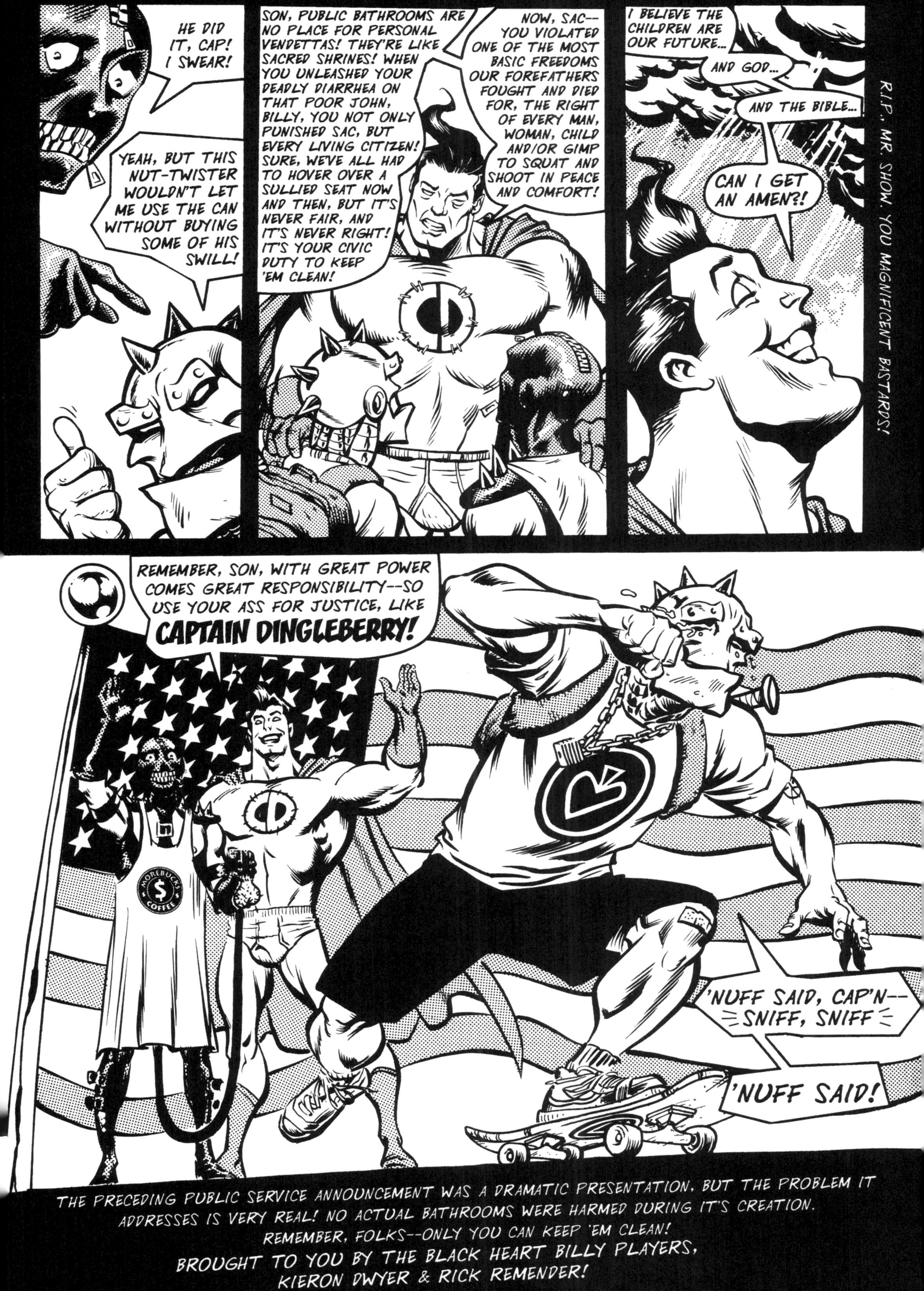
HE DID IT, CAP! I SWEAR!
YEAH, BUT THIS NUT-TWISTER WOULDN'T LET ME USE THE CAN WITHOUT BUYING SOME OF HIS SWILL!
SON, PUBLIC BATHROOMS ARE NO PLACE FOR PERSONAL VENDETTAS! THEY'RE LIKE SACRED SHRINES! WHEN YOU UNLEASHED YOUR DEADLY DIARRHEA ON THAT POOR JOHN, BILLY, YOU NOT ONLY PUNISHED SAC, BUT EVERY LIVING CITIZEN! SURE, WE'VE ALL HAD TO HOVER OVER A SULLIED SEAT NOW AND THEN, BUT IT'S NEVER FAIR, AND IT'S NEVER RIGHT! IT'S YOUR CIVIC DUTY TO KEEP 'EM CLEAN!
NOW, SAC-- YOU VIOLATED ONE OF THE MOST BASIC FREEDOMS OUR FOREFATHERS FOUGHT AND DIED FOR, THE RIGHT OF EVERY MAN, WOMAN, CHILD AND/OR GIMP TO SQUAT AND SHOOT IN PEACE AND COMFORT!
I BELIEVE THE CHILDREN ARE OUR FUTURE...
AND GOD...
AND THE BIBLE...
CAN I GET AN AMEN?!
R.I.P. MR. SHOW. YOU MAGNIFICENT BASTARDS!
REMEMBER, SON, WITH GREAT POWER COMES GREAT RESPONSIBILITY--SO USE YOUR ASS FOR JUSTICE, LIKE CAPTAIN DINGLEBERRY!
MOREBUCKS $ COFFEE
'NUFF SAID, CAP'N-- SNIFF, SNIFF
'NUFF SAID!
THE PRECEDING PUBLIC SERVICE ANNOUNCEMENT WAS A DRAMATIC PRESENTATION, BUT THE PROBLEM IT ADDRESSES IS VERY REAL! NO ACTUAL BATHROOMS WERE HARMED DURING IT'S CREATION.
REMEMBER, FOLKS--ONLY YOU CAN KEEP 'EM CLEAN!
BROUGHT TO YOU BY THE BLACK HEART BILLY PLAYERS, KIERON DWYER & RICK REMENDER!

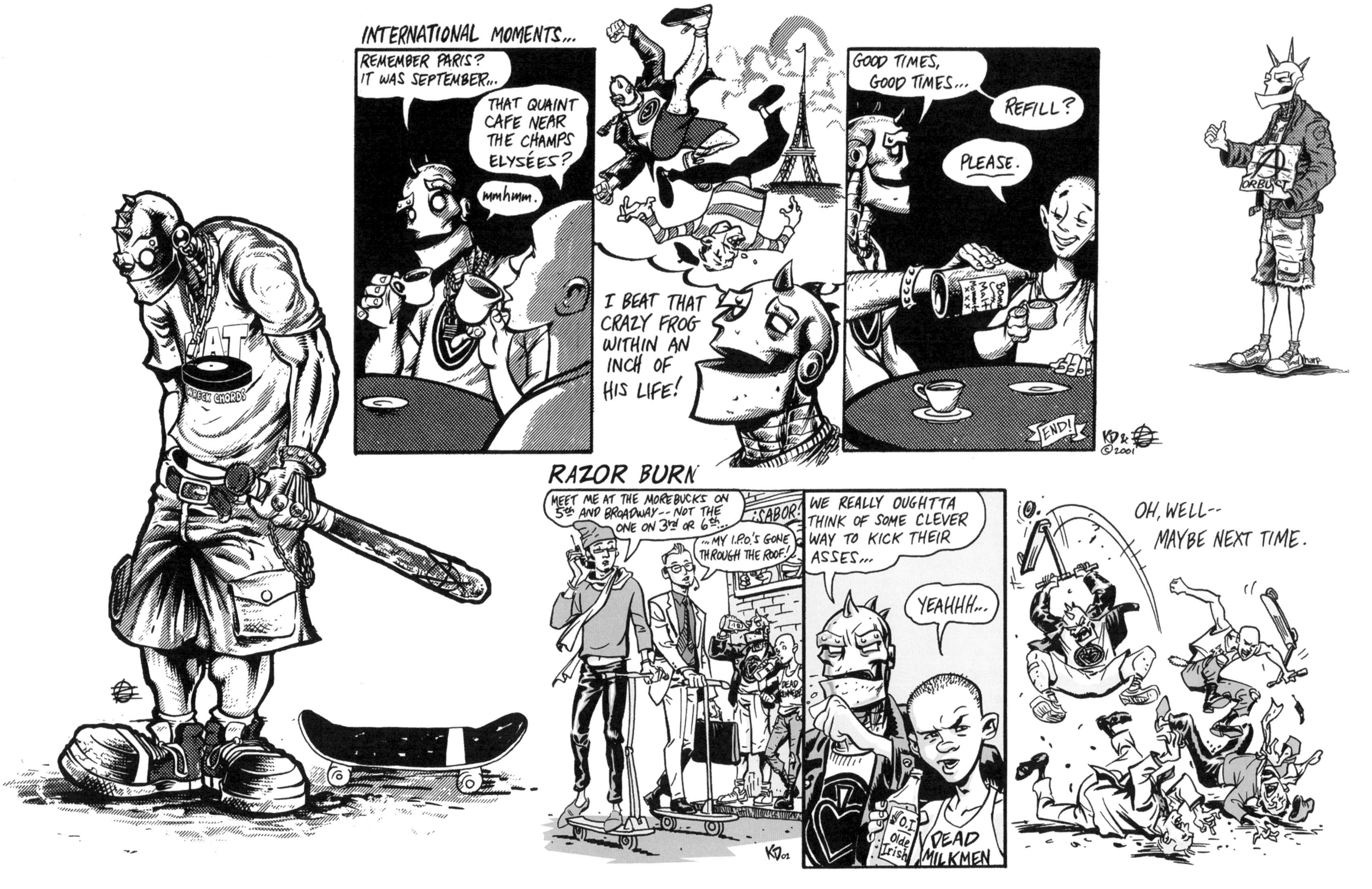
INTERNATIONAL MOMENTS...
REMEMBER PARIS? IT WAS SEPTEMBER...
THAT QUAINT CAFE NEAR THE CHAMPS ELYSÉES?
mmhmm.
I BEAT THAT CRAZY FROG WITHIN AN INCH OF HIS LIFE!
GOOD TIMES, GOOD TIMES...
REFILL?
PLEASE.
END!
KD & © 2001
WRECK CHORDS
ORBUST
RAZOR BURN
MEET ME AT THE MOREBUCKS ON 5th AND BROADWAY-- NOT THE ONE ON 3rd OR 6th...
...MY I.P.O.'S GONE THROUGH THE ROOF!
¡SABOR!
KD 02
WE REALLY OUGHTTA THINK OF SOME CLEVER WAY TO KICK THEIR ASSES...
YEAHHH...
O.I. Olde Irish
DEAD MILKMEN
OH, WELL--
MAYBE NEXT TIME.

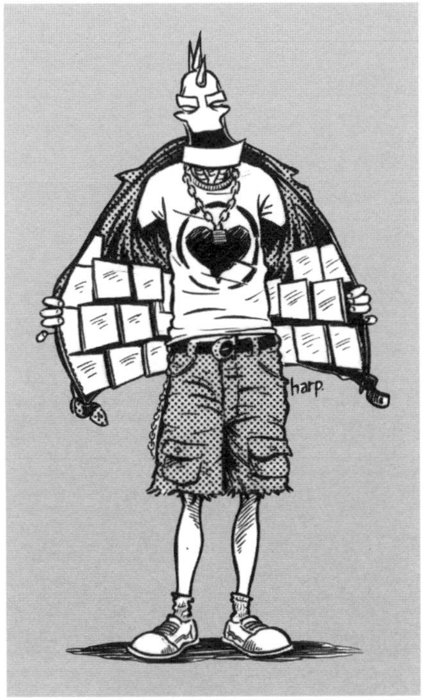

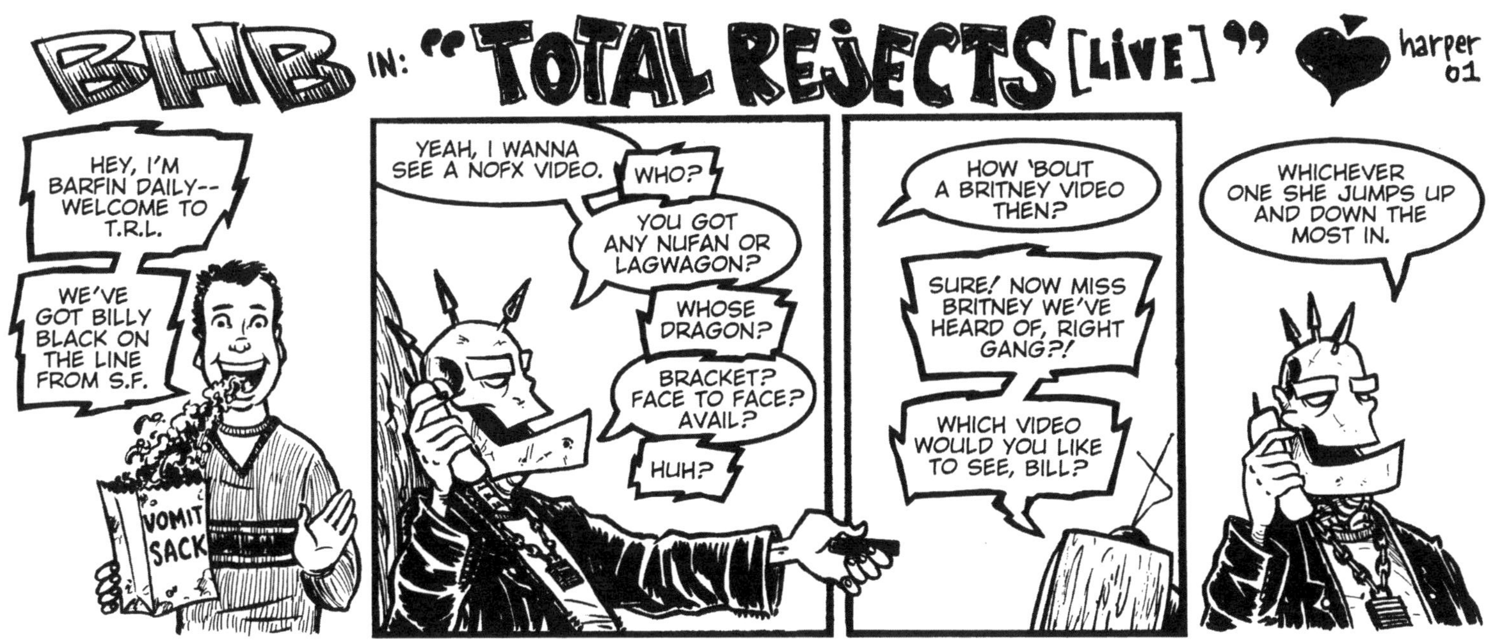
BHB IN: "TOTAL REJECTS [LIVE]"
harper 01
HEY, I'M BARFIN DAILY-- WELCOME TO T.R.L.
WE'VE GOT BILLY BLACK ON THE LINE FROM S.F.
VOMIT SACK
YEAH, I WANNA SEE A NOFX VIDEO.
WHO?
YOU GOT ANY NUFAN OR LAGWAGON?
WHOSE DRAGON?
BRACKET? FACE TO FACE? AVAIL?
HUH?
HOW 'BOUT A BRITNEY VIDEO THEN?
SURE! NOW MISS BRITNEY WE'VE HEARD OF, RIGHT GANG?!
WHICH VIDEO WOULD YOU LIKE TO SEE, BILL?
WHICHEVER ONE SHE JUMPS UP AND DOWN THE MOST IN.

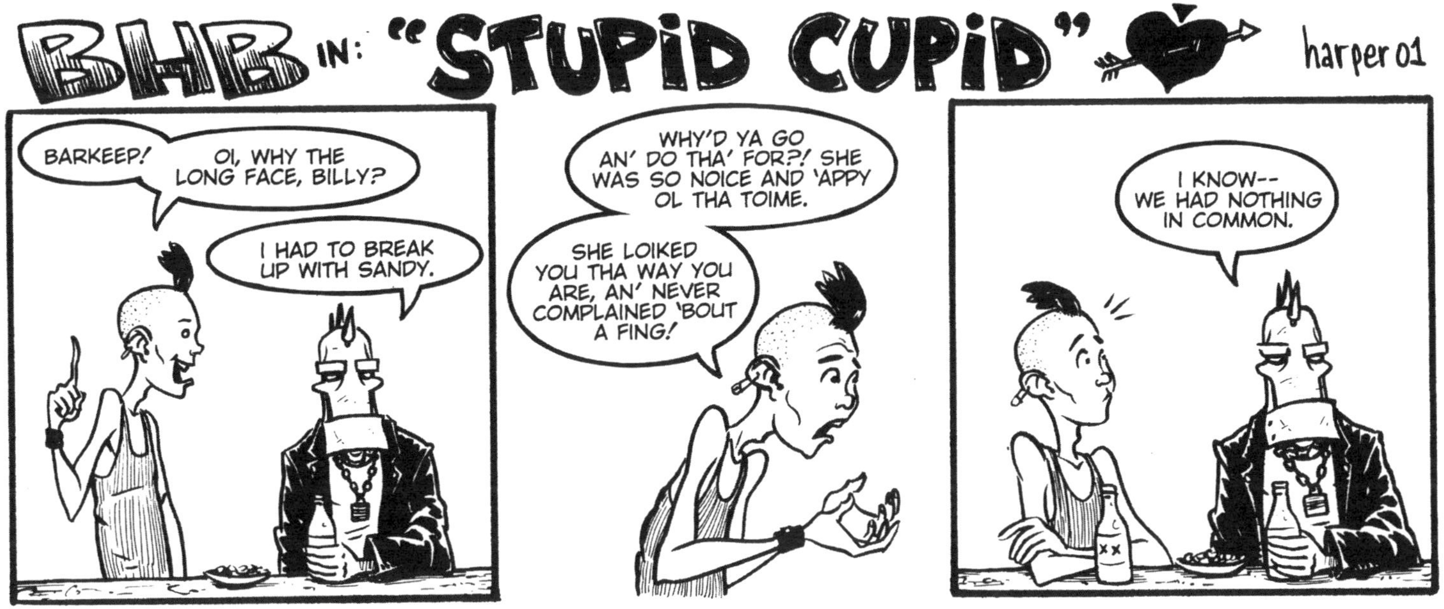
BHB IN: "STUPID CUPID"
harper 01
BARKEEP!
OI, WHY THE LONG FACE, BILLY?
I HAD TO BREAK UP WITH SANDY.
WHY'D YA GO AN' DO THA' FOR?! SHE WAS SO NOICE AND 'APPY OL THA TOIME.
SHE LOIKED YOU THA WAY YOU ARE, AN' NEVER COMPLAINED 'BOUT A FING!
I KNOW-- WE HAD NOTHING IN COMMON.

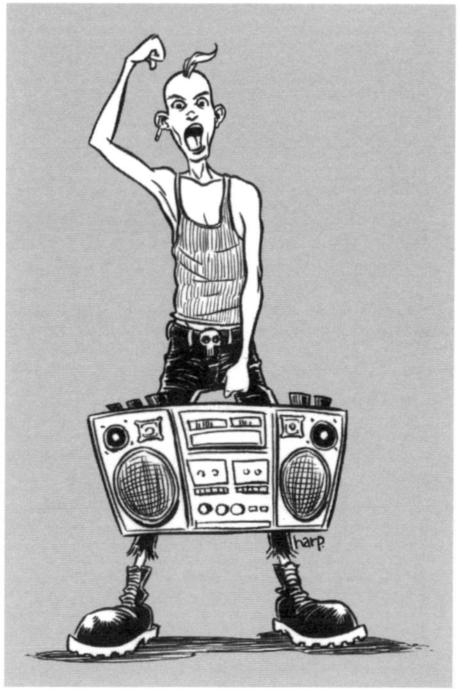

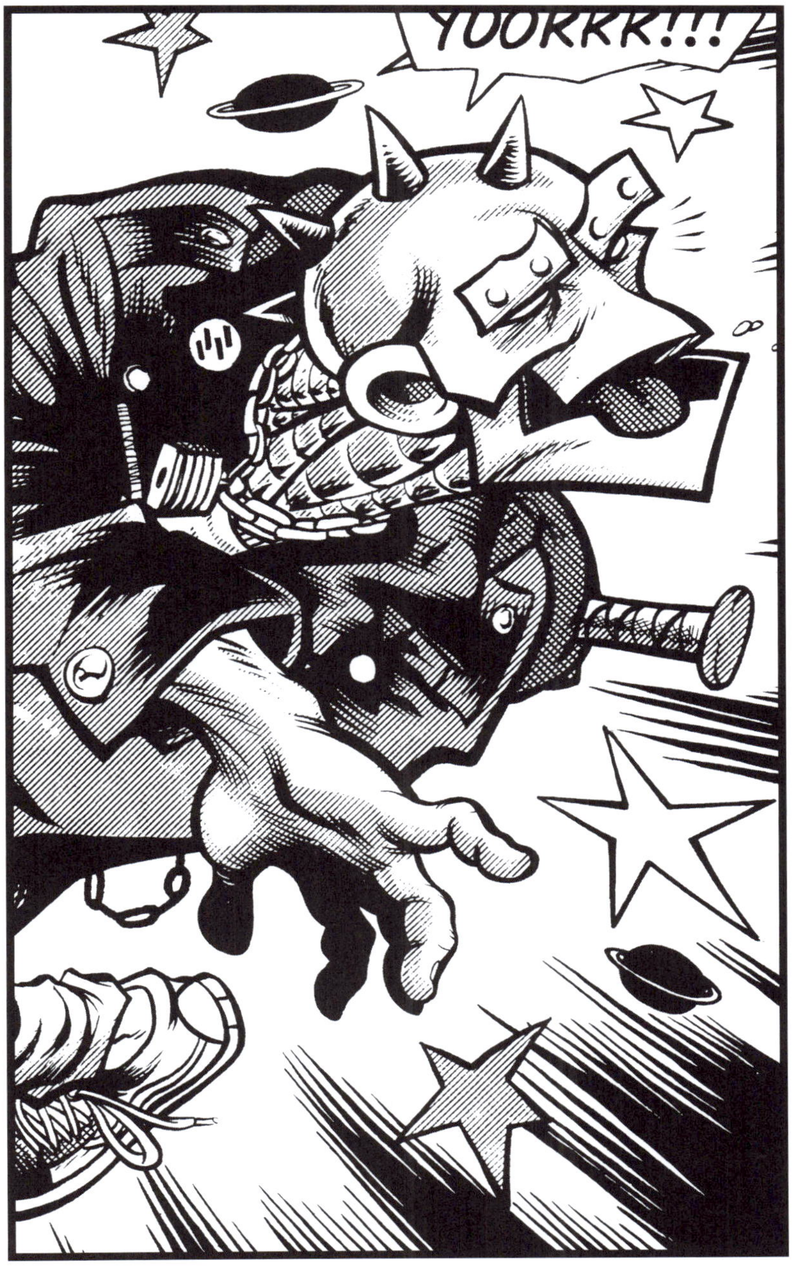
YUORRK!!!

FOUR

MY HEART BILL GO ON

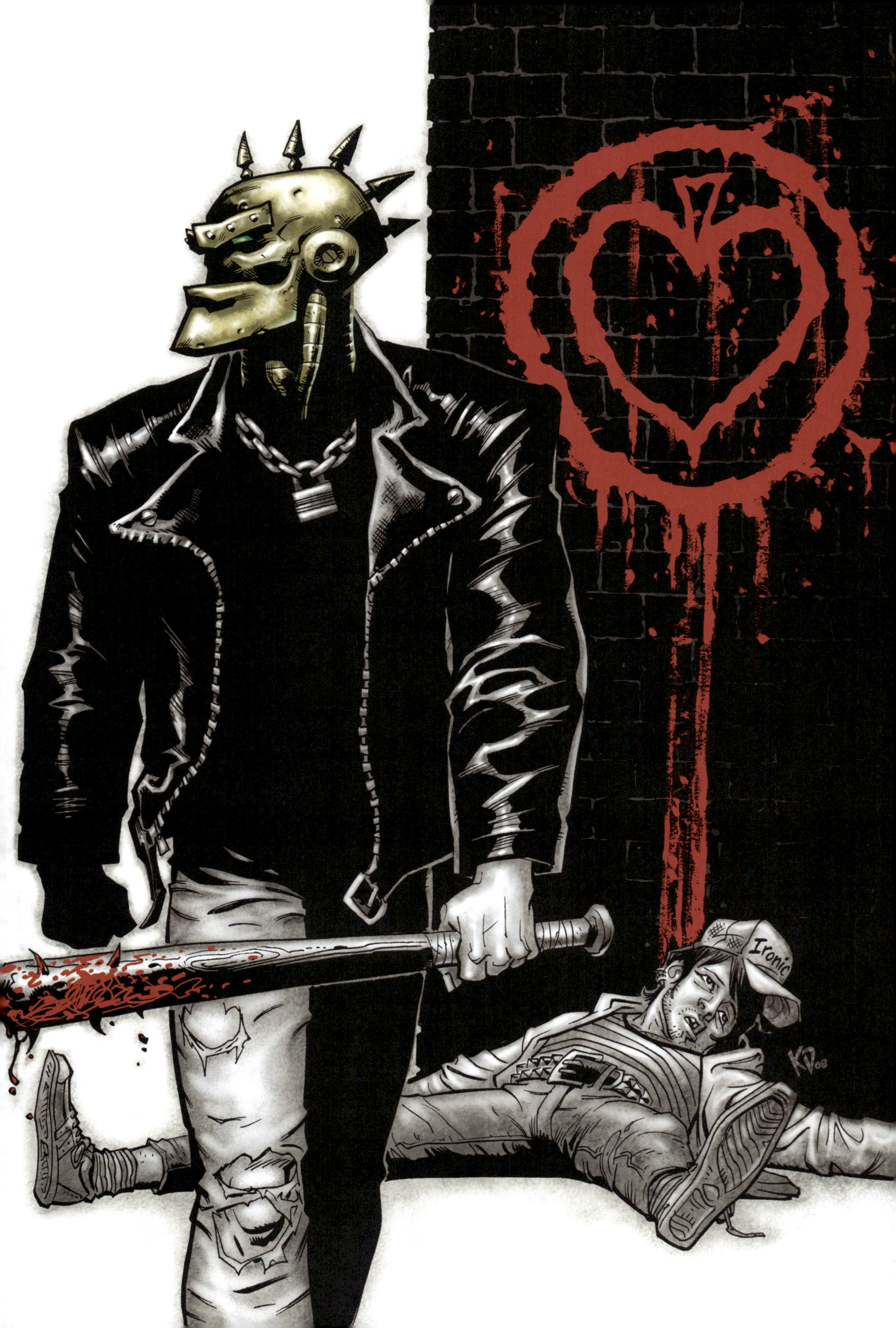
Ironic

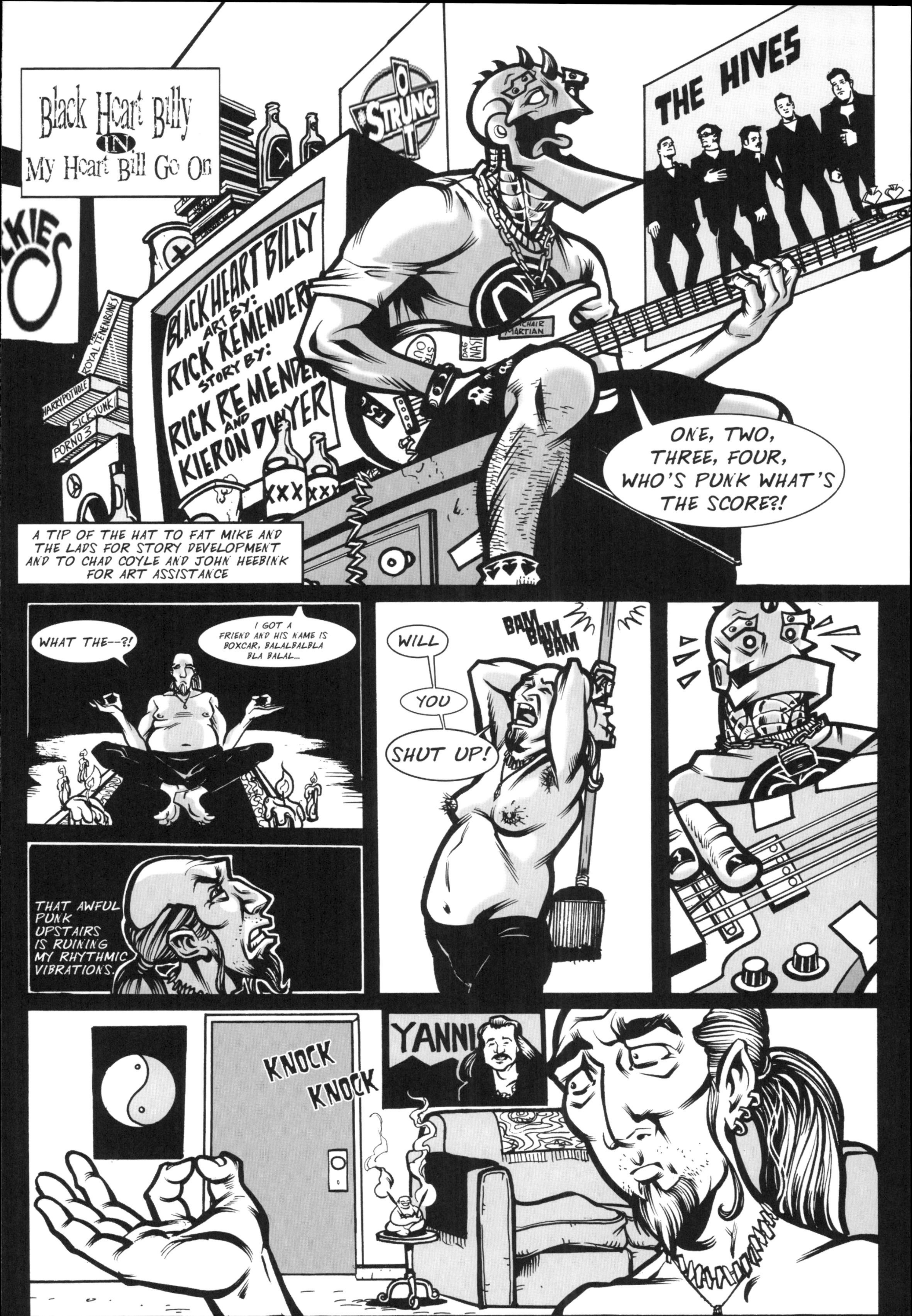

Black Heart Billy
IN
My Heart Bill Go On
BLACK HEART BILLY
ART BY: RICK REMENDER
STORY BY: RICK REMENDER AND KIERON DWYER
A TIP OF THE HAT TO FAT MIKE AND THE LADS FOR STORY DEVELOPMENT AND TO CHAD COYLE AND JOHN HEEBINK FOR ART ASSISTANCE
THE HIVES
STRUNG OUT
ONE, TWO, THREE, FOUR, WHO'S PUNK WHAT'S THE SCORE?!
WHAT THE--?!
I GOT A FRIEND AND HIS NAME IS BOXCAR, BALALBALBLA BLA BALAL...
THAT AWFUL PUNK UPSTAIRS IS RUINING MY RHYTHMIC VIBRATIONS.
BAM BAM BAM
WILL
YOU
SHUT UP!
YANNI
KNOCK
KNOCK

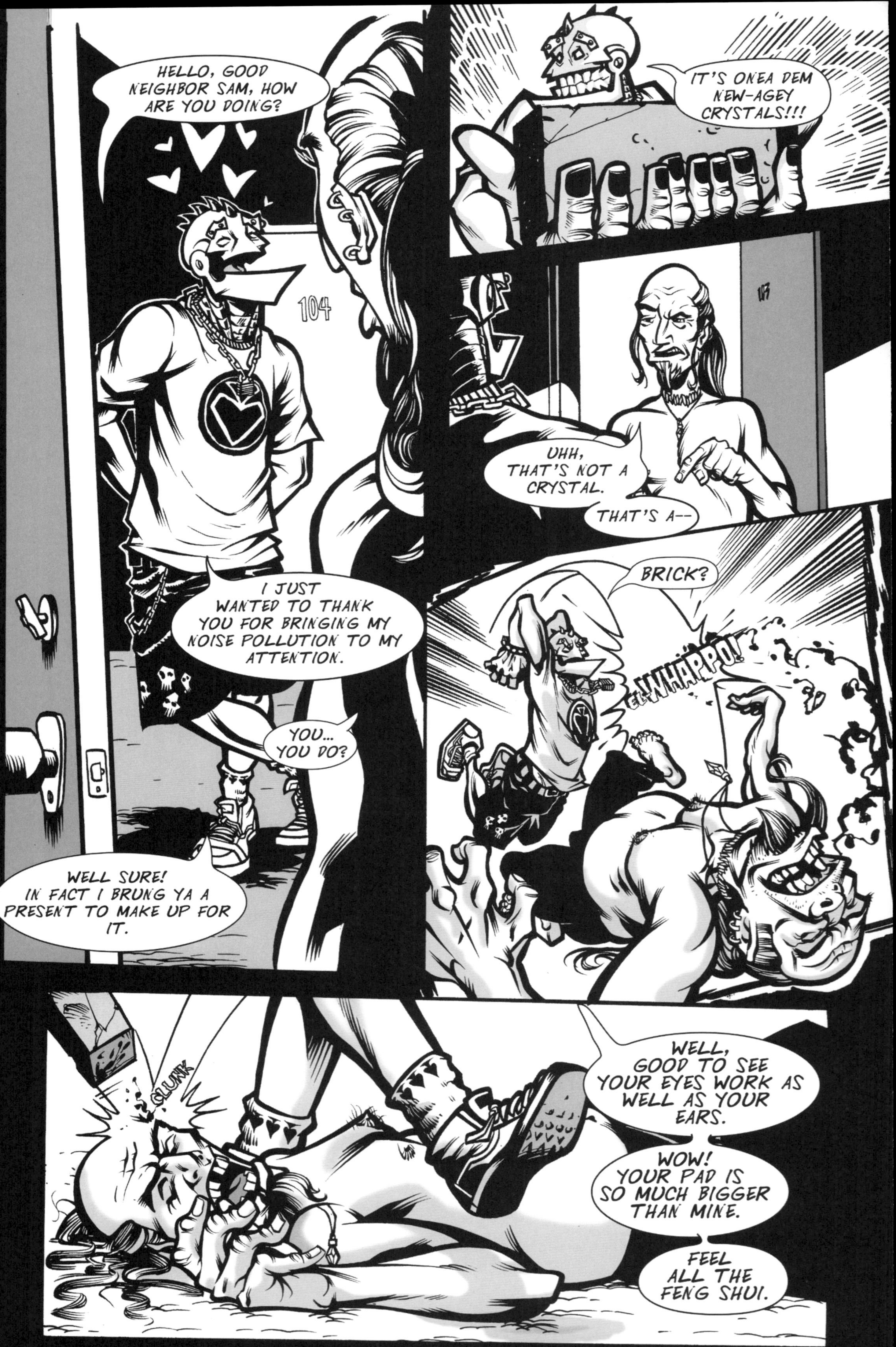
HELLO, GOOD NEIGHBOR SAM, HOW ARE YOU DOING?
104
I JUST WANTED TO THANK YOU FOR BRINGING MY NOISE POLLUTION TO MY ATTENTION.
YOU... YOU DO?
WELL SURE! IN FACT I BRUNG YA A PRESENT TO MAKE UP FOR IT.
IT'S ONEA DEM NEW-AGEY CRYSTALS!!!
103
UHH, THAT'S NOT A CRYSTAL.
THAT'S A--
BRICK?
WHAPPO!
CLUNK
WELL, GOOD TO SEE YOUR EYES WORK AS WELL AS YOUR EARS.
WOW! YOUR PAD IS SO MUCH BIGGER THAN MINE.
FEEL ALL THE FENG SHUI.

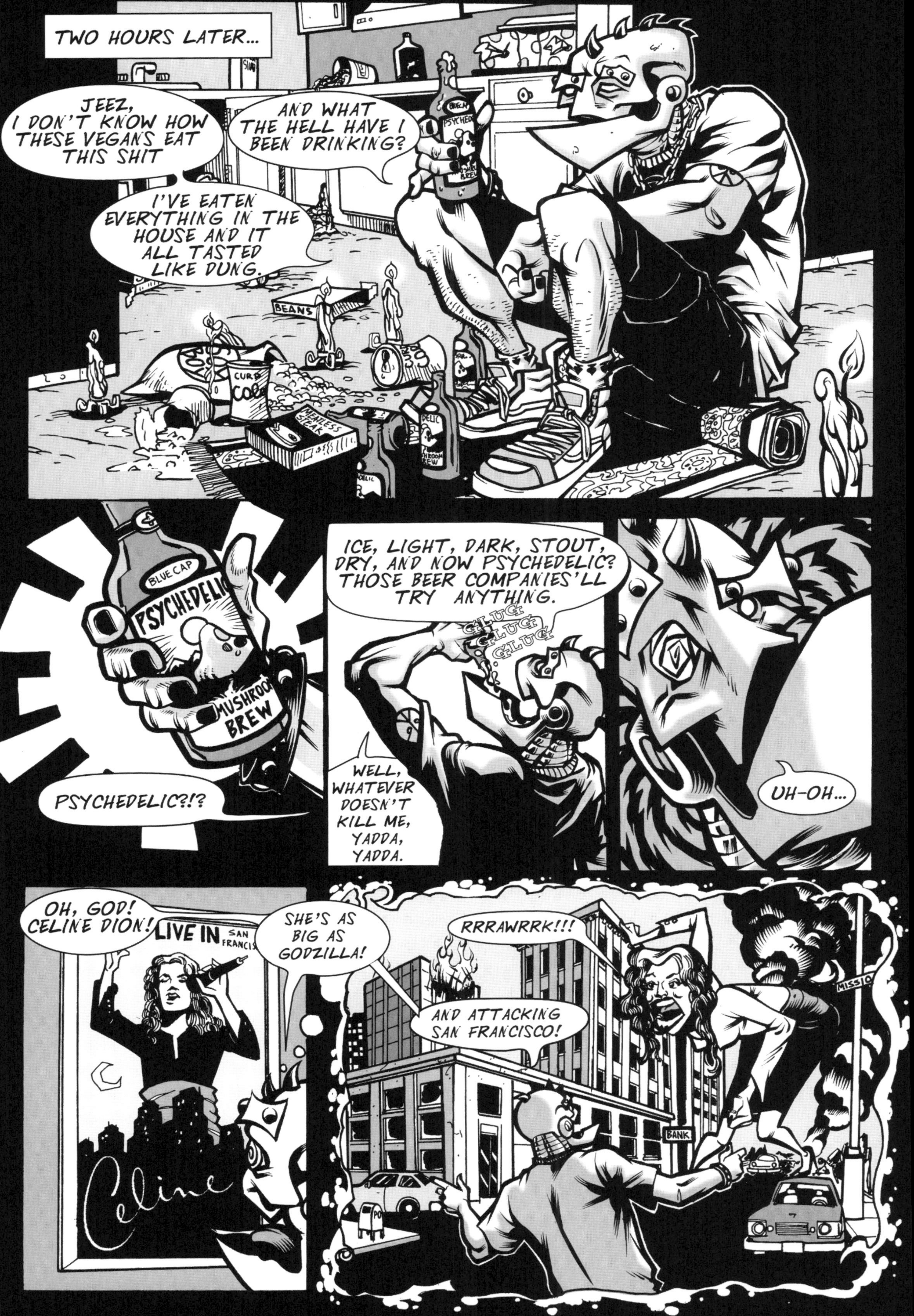
TWO HOURS LATER...
JEEZ, I DON'T KNOW HOW THESE VEGANS EAT THIS SHIT
AND WHAT THE HELL HAVE I BEEN DRINKING?
I'VE EATEN EVERYTHING IN THE HOUSE AND IT ALL TASTED LIKE DUNG.
BEANS
MEATLESS STEAK
BLUE CAP
PSYCHEDELIC
MUSHROOM BREW
PSYCHEDELIC?!?
ICE, LIGHT, DARK, STOUT, DRY, AND NOW PSYCHEDELIC? THOSE BEER COMPANIES'LL TRY ANYTHING.
GLUG GLUG GLUG
WELL, WHATEVER DOESN'T KILL ME, YADDA, YADDA.
UH-OH...
OH, GOD! CELINE DION!
LIVE IN SAN FRANCIS
Celine
SHE'S AS BIG AS GODZILLA!
RRRAWRRK!!!
AND ATTACKING SAN FRANCISCO!
BANK

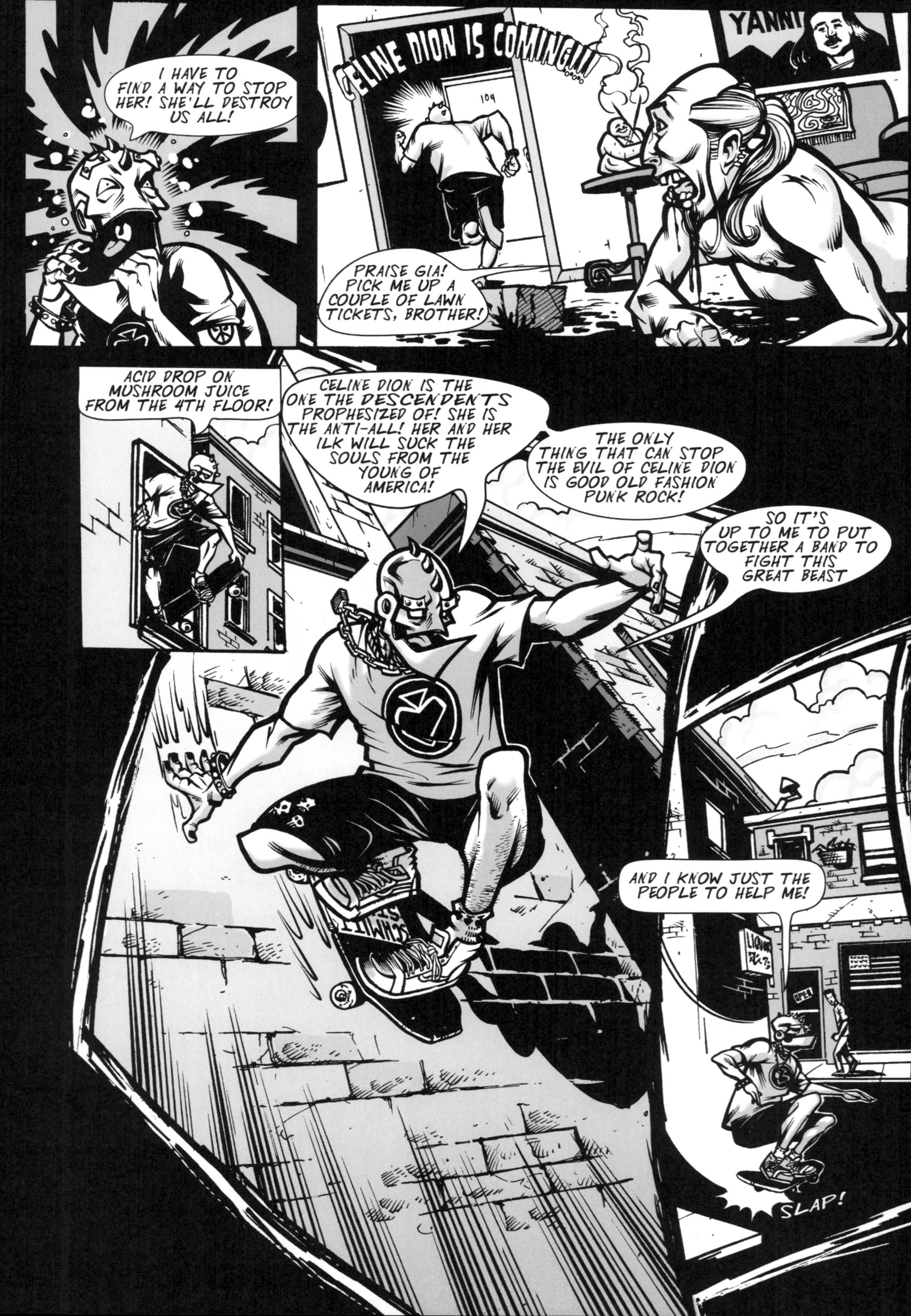
I HAVE TO FIND A WAY TO STOP HER! SHE'LL DESTROY US ALL!
YANNI
CELINE DION IS COMING!!!
PRAISE GIA! PICK ME UP A COUPLE OF LAWN TICKETS, BROTHER!
ACID DROP ON MUSHROOM JUICE FROM THE 4TH FLOOR!
CELINE DION IS THE ONE THE DESCENDENTS PROPHESIZED OF! SHE IS THE ANTI-ALL! HER AND HER ILK WILL SUCK THE SOULS FROM THE YOUNG OF AMERICA!
THE ONLY THING THAT CAN STOP THE EVIL OF CELINE DION IS GOOD OLD FASHION PUNK ROCK!
SO IT'S UP TO ME TO PUT TOGETHER A BAND TO FIGHT THIS GREAT BEAST
AND I KNOW JUST THE PEOPLE TO HELP ME!
SLAP!

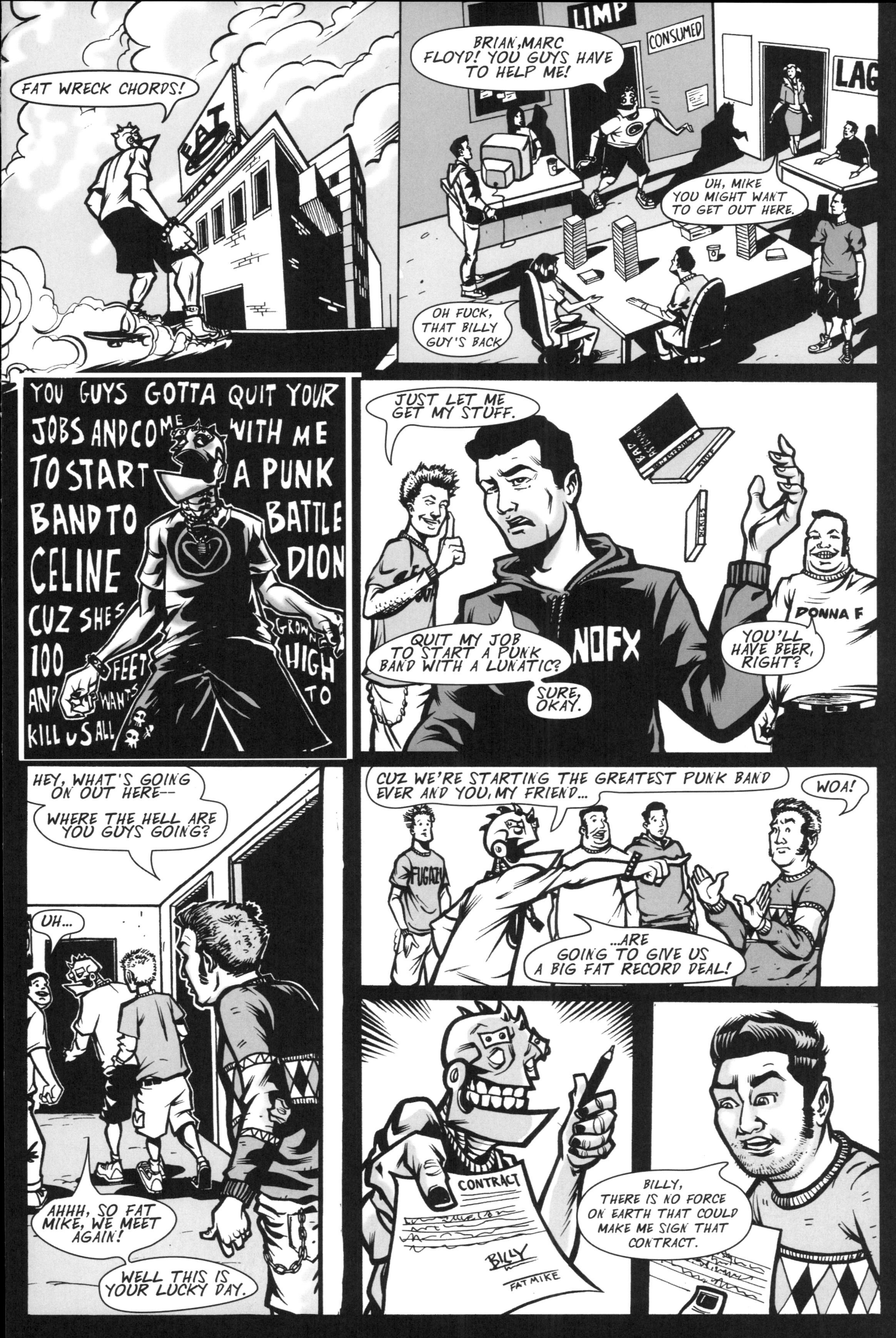
FAT WRECK CHORDS!
FAT
LIMP
CONSUMED
LAG
BRIAN, MARC FLOYD! YOU GUYS HAVE TO HELP ME!
UH, MIKE YOU MIGHT WANT TO GET OUT HERE.
OH FUCK, THAT BILLY GUY'S BACK
YOU GUYS GOTTA QUIT YOUR JOBS AND COME WITH ME TO START A PUNK BAND TO BATTLE CELINE DION CUZ SHE'S GROWN 100 FEET HIGH AND WANTS TO KILL US ALL
JUST LET ME GET MY STUFF.
QUIT MY JOB TO START A PUNK BAND WITH A LUNATIC?
SURE, OKAY.
YOU'LL HAVE BEER, RIGHT?
NOFX
DONNA F
DICKIES
HEY, WHAT'S GOING ON OUT HERE--
WHERE THE HELL ARE YOU GUYS GOING?
UH...
AHHH, SO FAT MIKE, WE MEET AGAIN!
WELL THIS IS YOUR LUCKY DAY.
CUZ WE'RE STARTING THE GREATEST PUNK BAND EVER AND YOU, MY FRIEND...
WOA!
FUGAZI
...ARE GOING TO GIVE US A BIG FAT RECORD DEAL!
CONTRACT
BILLY
FAT MIKE
BILLY, THERE IS NO FORCE ON EARTH THAT COULD MAKE ME SIGN THAT CONTRACT.

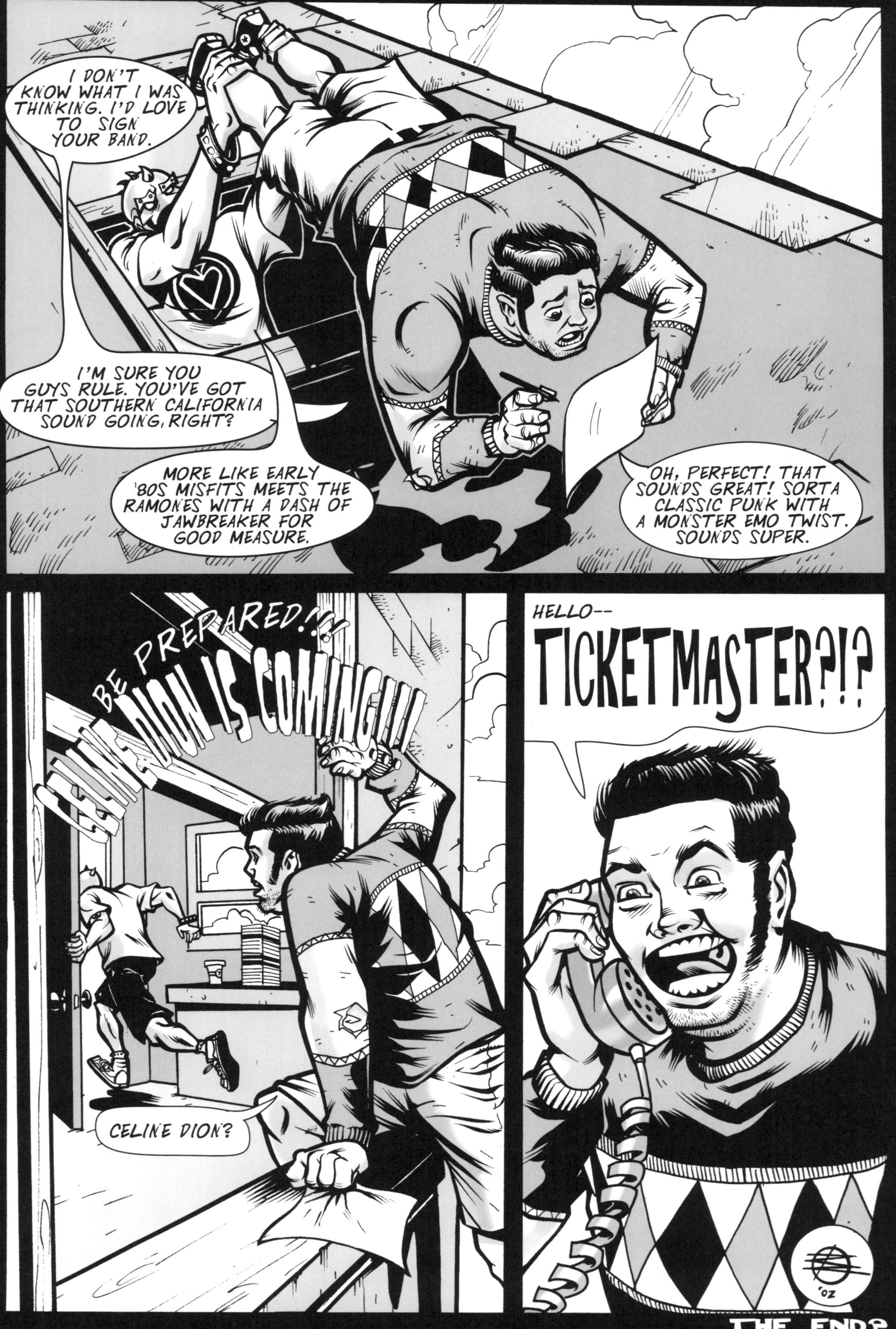
I DON'T KNOW WHAT I WAS THINKING. I'D LOVE TO SIGN YOUR BAND.
I'M SURE YOU GUYS RULE. YOU'VE GOT THAT SOUTHERN CALIFORNIA SOUND GOING, RIGHT?
MORE LIKE EARLY '80S MISFITS MEETS THE RAMONES WITH A DASH OF JAWBREAKER FOR GOOD MEASURE.
OH, PERFECT! THAT SOUNDS GREAT! SORTA CLASSIC PUNK WITH A MONSTER EMO TWIST. SOUNDS SUPER.
BE PREPARED!!!
CELINE DION IS COMING!!!
CELINE DION?
HELLO--
TICKETMASTER?!?
'02

THE END?

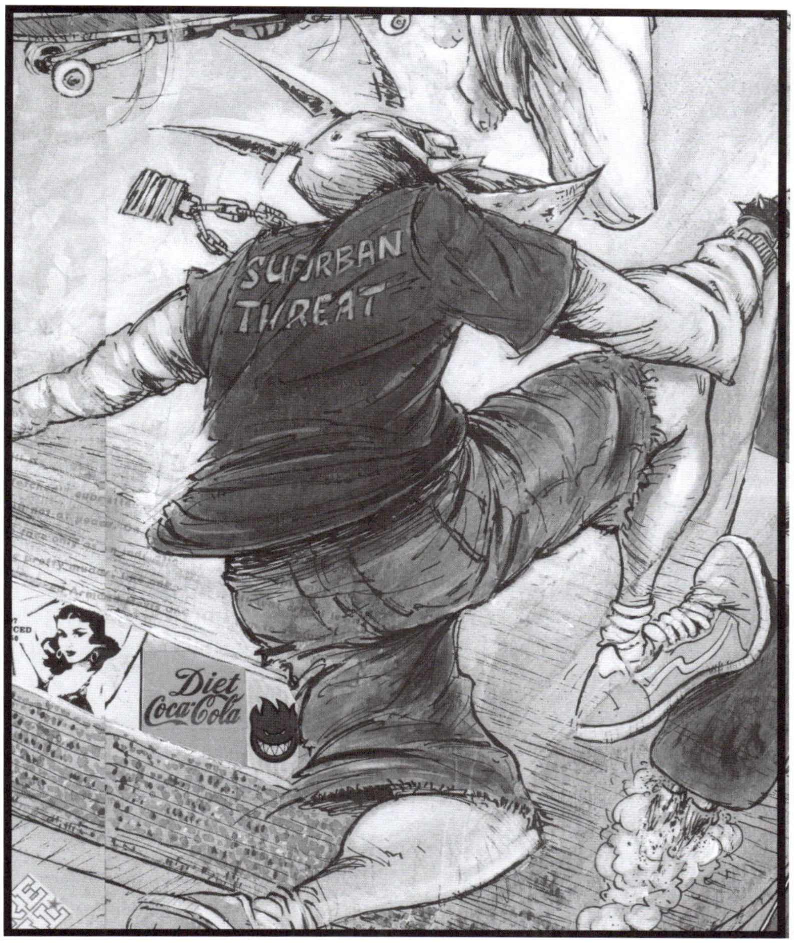
SUBURBAN
THREAT
Diet
Coca-Cola

FIVE

BLACK HEART BILLY 2099

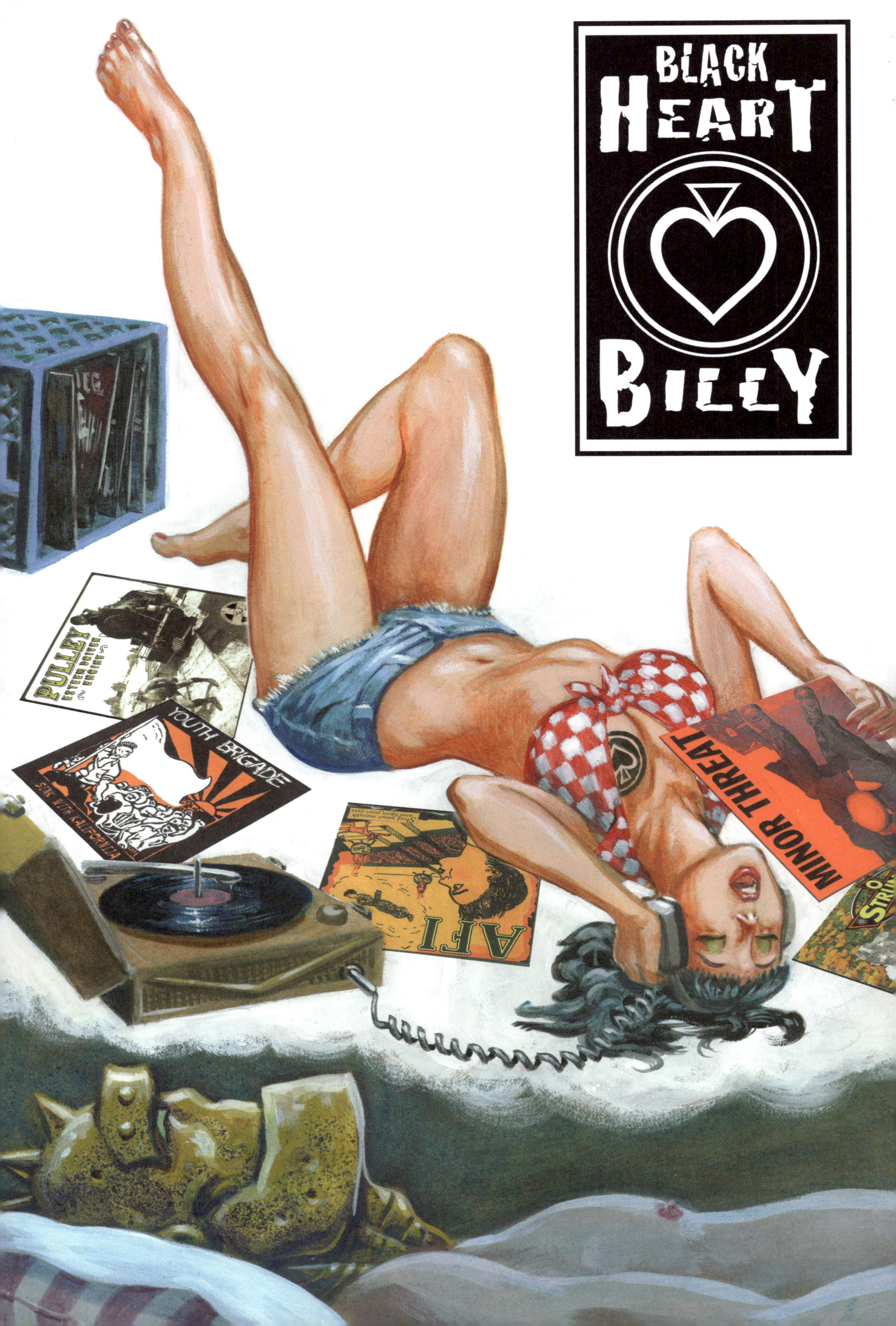
BLACK HEART BILLY
PULLEY
ESTEEM DRIVEN ENGINE
YOUTH BRIGADE
MINOR THREAT
AFI
Shut your mouth and open your eyes

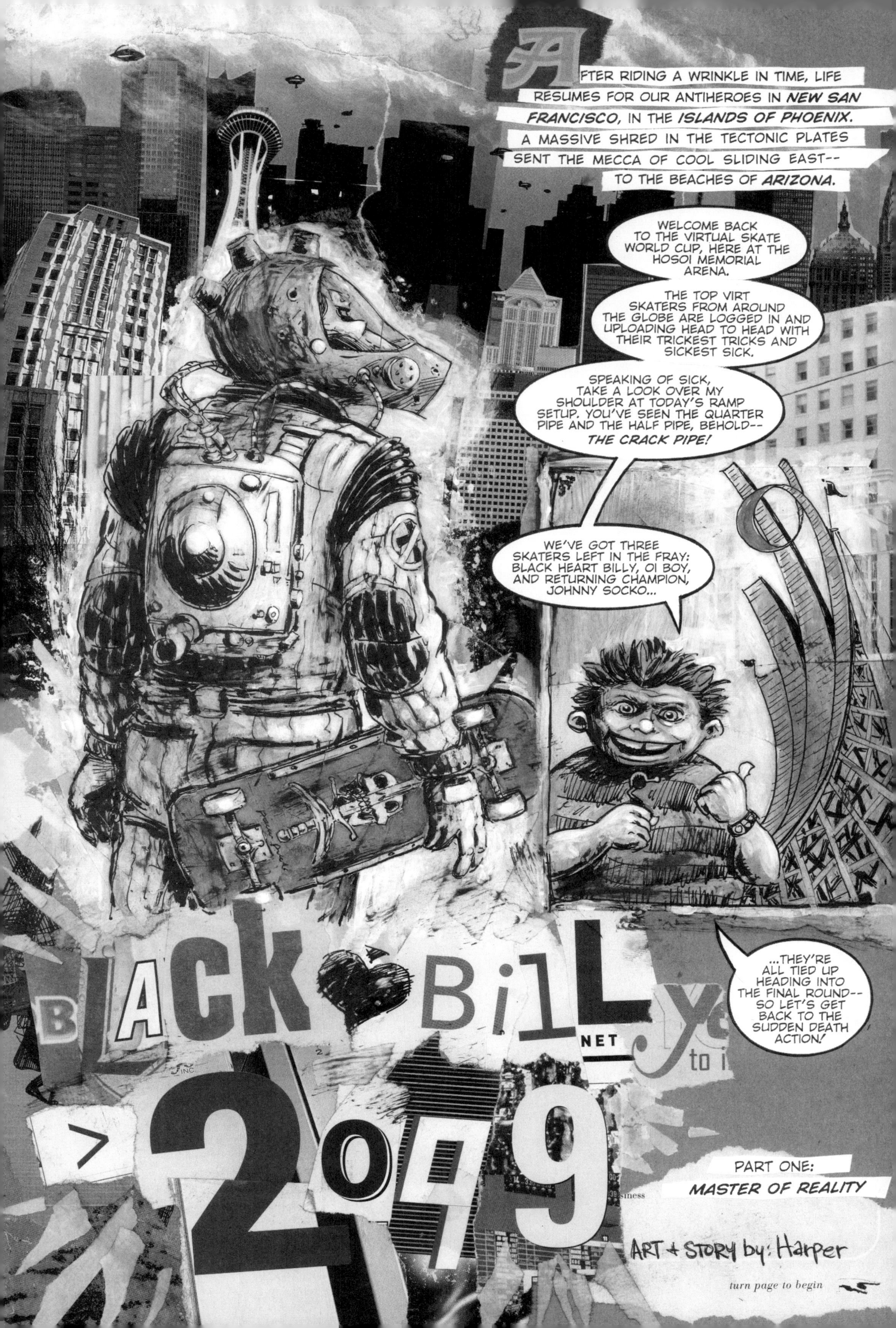
AFTER RIDING A WRINKLE IN TIME, LIFE RESUMES FOR OUR ANTIHEROES IN NEW SAN FRANCISCO, IN THE ISLANDS OF PHOENIX. A MASSIVE SHRED IN THE TECTONIC PLATES SENT THE MECCA OF COOL SLIDING EAST-- TO THE BEACHES OF ARIZONA.
WELCOME BACK TO THE VIRTUAL SKATE WORLD CUP, HERE AT THE HOSOI MEMORIAL ARENA.
THE TOP VIRT SKATERS FROM AROUND THE GLOBE ARE LOGGED IN AND UPLOADING HEAD TO HEAD WITH THEIR TRICKEST TRICKS AND SICKEST SICK.
SPEAKING OF SICK, TAKE A LOOK OVER MY SHOULDER AT TODAY'S RAMP SETUP. YOU'VE SEEN THE QUARTER PIPE AND THE HALF PIPE, BEHOLD-- THE CRACK PIPE!
WE'VE GOT THREE SKATERS LEFT IN THE FRAY: BLACK HEART BILLY, OI BOY, AND RETURNING CHAMPION, JOHNNY SOCKO...
...THEY'RE ALL TIED UP HEADING INTO THE FINAL ROUND-- SO LET'S GET BACK TO THE SUDDEN DEATH ACTION!
BLACK BILLY
NET
>2 OF 9
PART ONE:
MASTER OF REALITY
ART + STORY by: Harper
turn page to begin

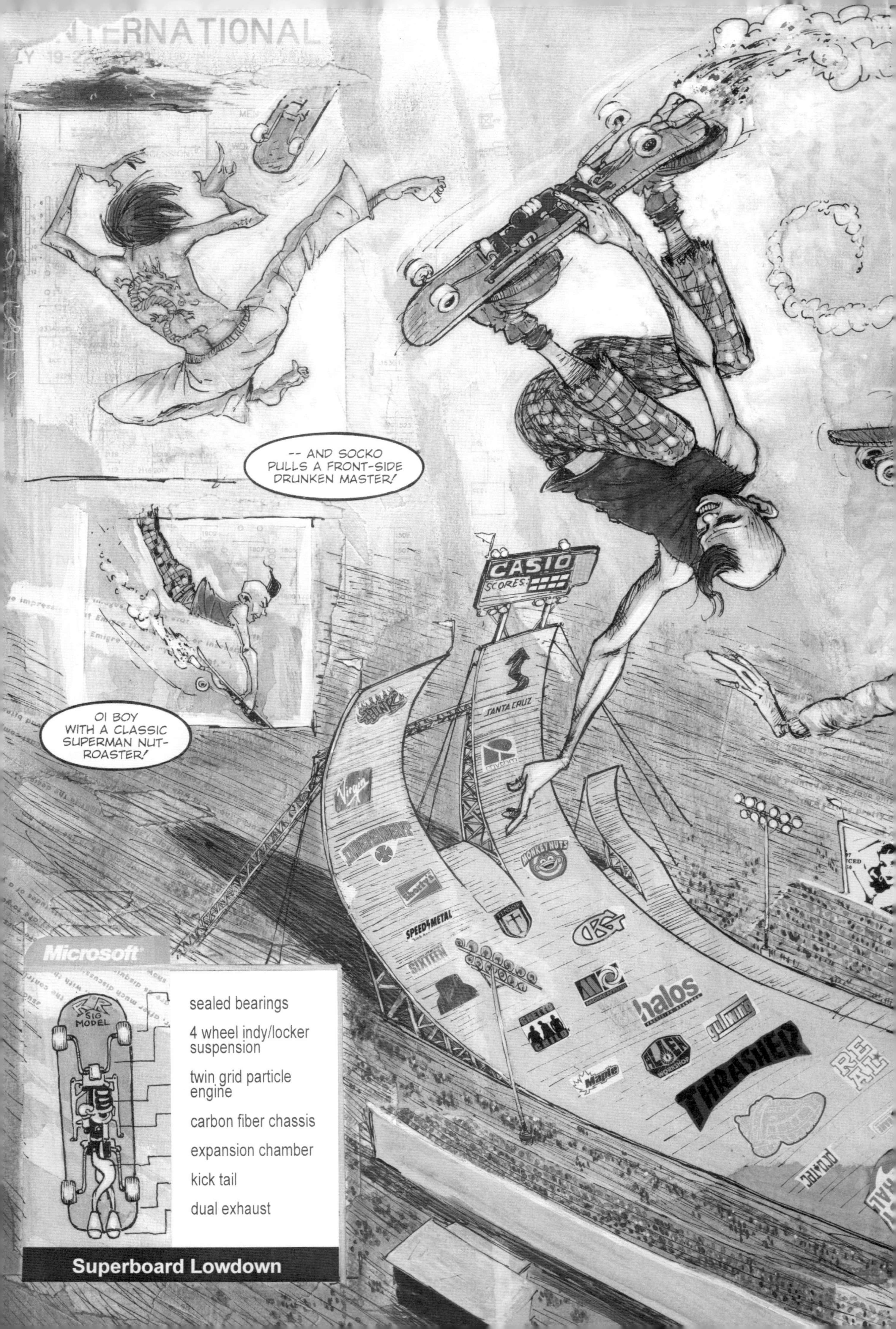
-- AND SOCKO PULLS A FRONT-SIDE DRUNKEN MASTER!
OI BOY WITH A CLASSIC SUPERMAN NUT-ROASTER!
CASIO
SCORES
SANTA CRUZ
Virgin
MONKEYNUTS
SPEED METAL
SIXTEEN
halos
THRASHER
Microsoft
SIG MODEL
sealed bearings
4 wheel indy/locker suspension
twin grid particle engine
carbon fiber chassis
expansion chamber
kick tail
dual exhaust
Superboard Lowdown

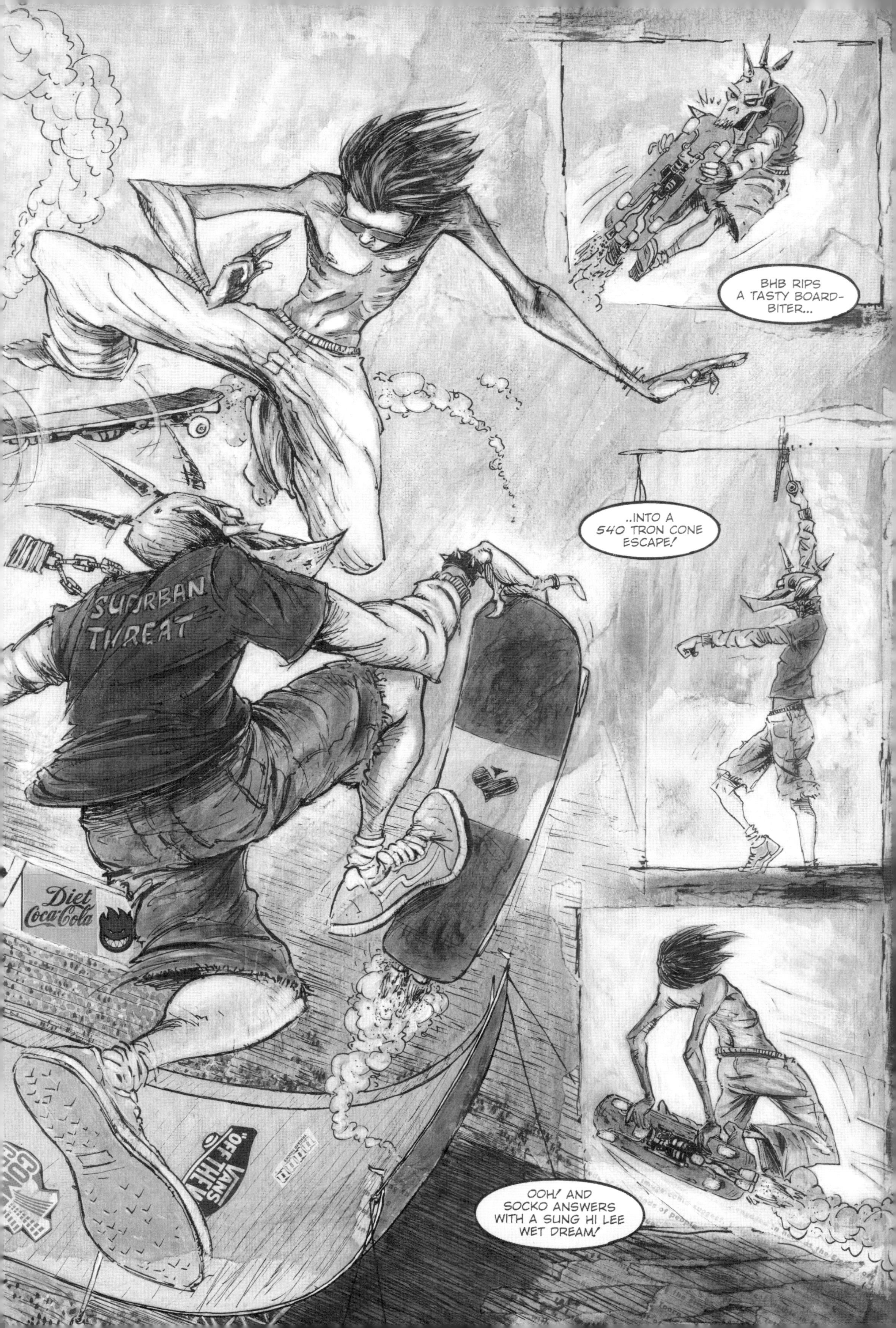

BHB RIPS A TASTY BOARD-BITER...
..INTO A 540 TRON CONE ESCAPE!
OOH! AND SOCKO ANSWERS WITH A SUNG HI LEE WET DREAM!
SUBURBAN THREAT
Diet Coca-Cola
VANS "OFF THE W

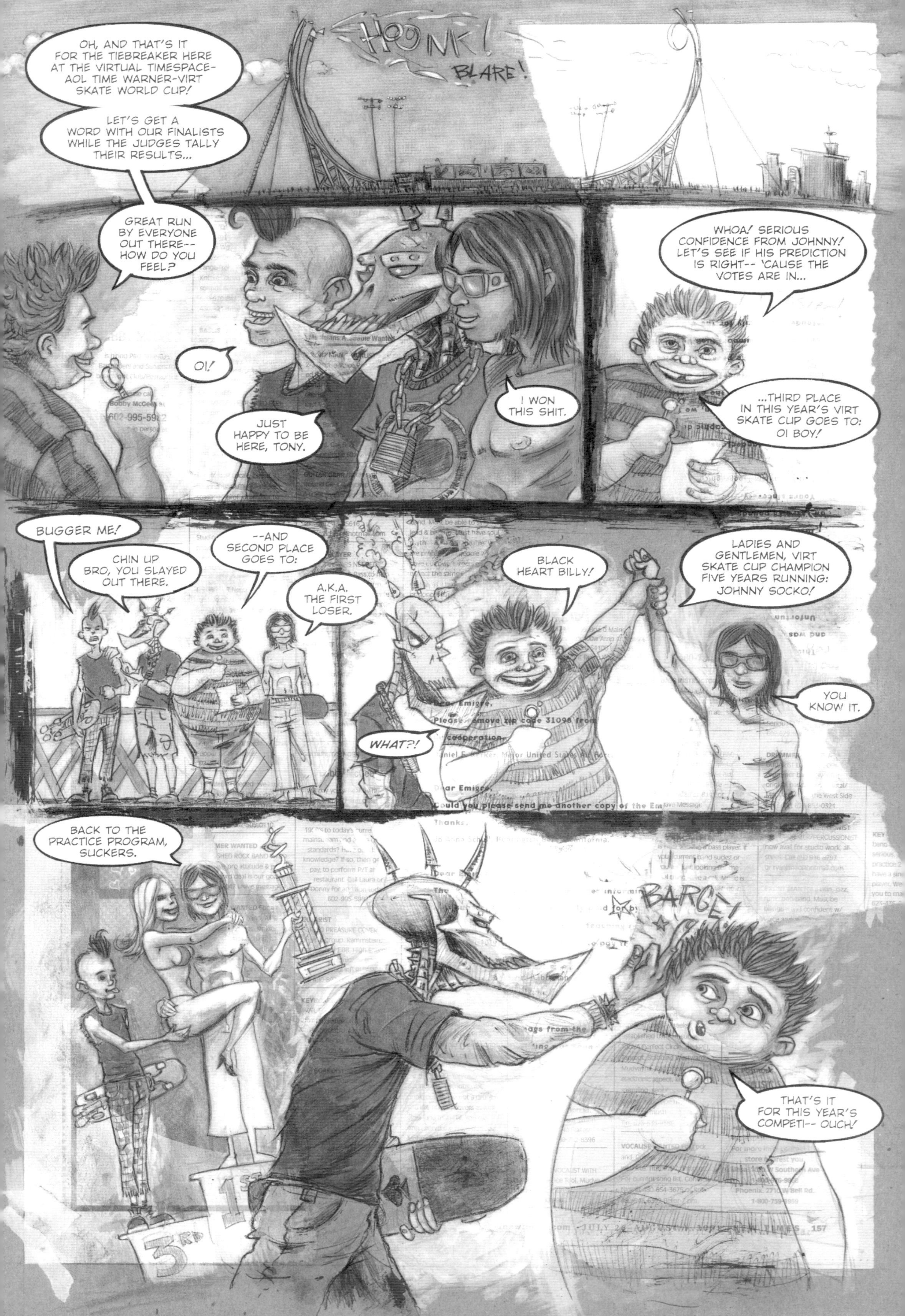
HOONK!
BLARE!
OH, AND THAT'S IT FOR THE TIEBREAKER HERE AT THE VIRTUAL TIMESPACE-AOL TIME WARNER-VIRT SKATE WORLD CUP!
LET'S GET A WORD WITH OUR FINALISTS WHILE THE JUDGES TALLY THEIR RESULTS...
GREAT RUN BY EVERYONE OUT THERE-- HOW DO YOU FEEL?
OI!
JUST HAPPY TO BE HERE, TONY.
I WON THIS SHIT.
WHOA! SERIOUS CONFIDENCE FROM JOHNNY! LET'S SEE IF HIS PREDICTION IS RIGHT-- 'CAUSE THE VOTES ARE IN...
...THIRD PLACE IN THIS YEAR'S VIRT SKATE CUP GOES TO: OI BOY!
BUGGER ME!
CHIN UP BRO, YOU SLAYED OUT THERE.
--AND SECOND PLACE GOES TO:
A.K.A. THE FIRST LOSER.
BLACK HEART BILLY!
WHAT?!
LADIES AND GENTLEMEN, VIRT SKATE CUP CHAMPION FIVE YEARS RUNNING: JOHNNY SOCKO!
YOU KNOW IT.
BACK TO THE PRACTICE PROGRAM, SUCKERS.
BARGE!
THAT'S IT FOR THIS YEAR'S COMPETI-- OUCH!
1ST
3RD

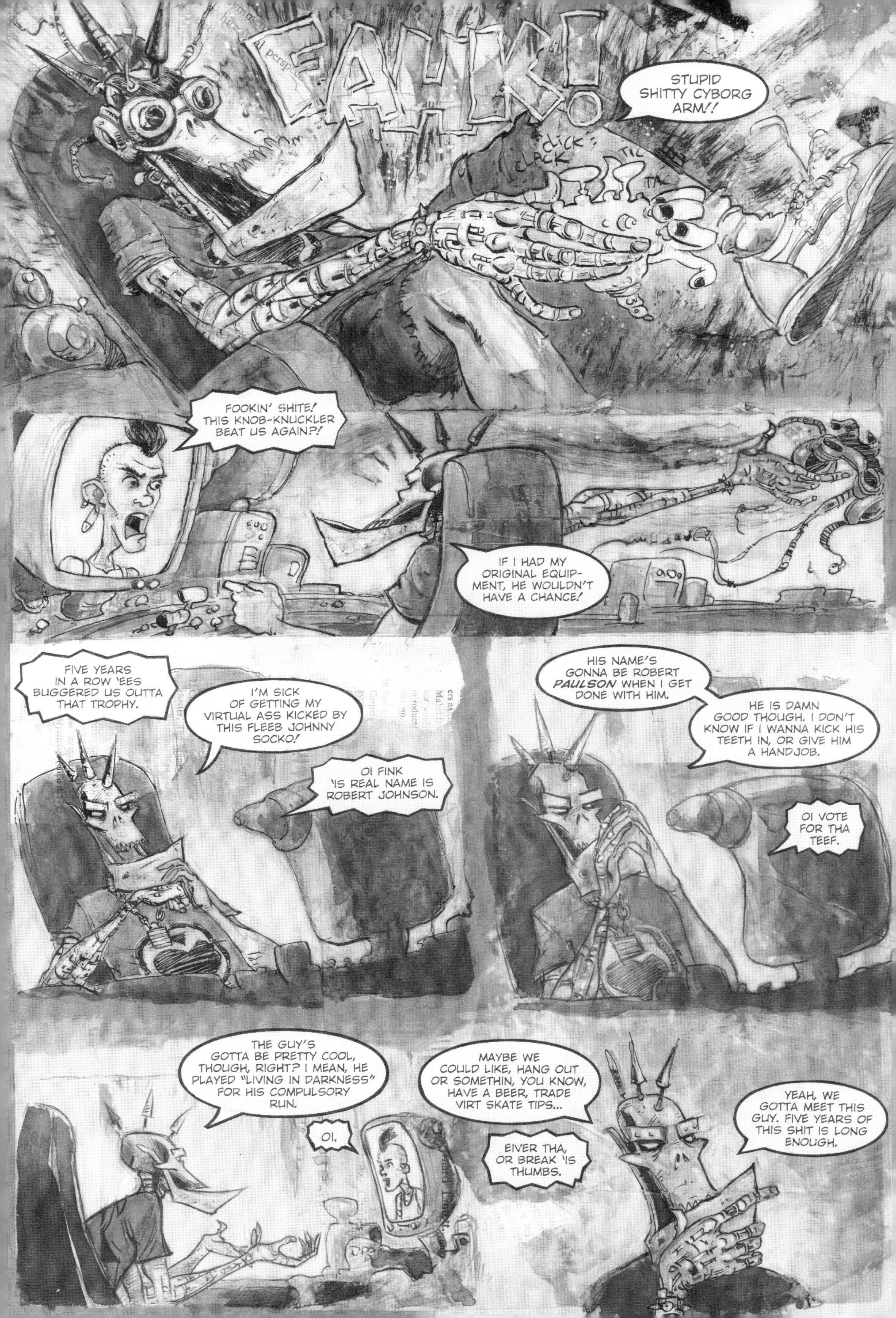
STUPID SHITTY CYBORG ARM!!
CLICK CLACK
TIC TAC
FOOKIN' SHITE! THIS KNOB-KNUCKLER BEAT US AGAIN?!
IF I HAD MY ORIGINAL EQUIP-MENT, HE WOULDN'T HAVE A CHANCE!
FIVE YEARS IN A ROW 'EES BUGGERED US OUTTA THAT TROPHY.
I'M SICK OF GETTING MY VIRTUAL ASS KICKED BY THIS FLEEB JOHNNY SOCKO!
OI FINK 'IS REAL NAME IS ROBERT JOHNSON.
HIS NAME'S GONNA BE ROBERT ***PAULSON*** WHEN I GET DONE WITH HIM.
HE IS DAMN GOOD THOUGH. I DON'T KNOW IF I WANNA KICK HIS TEETH IN, OR GIVE HIM A HANDJOB.
OI VOTE FOR THA TEEF.
THE GUY'S GOTTA BE PRETTY COOL, THOUGH, RIGHT? I MEAN, HE PLAYED "LIVING IN DARKNESS" FOR HIS COMPULSORY RUN.
MAYBE WE COULD LIKE, HANG OUT OR SOMETHIN, YOU KNOW, HAVE A BEER, TRADE VIRT SKATE TIPS...
OI.
EIVER THA, OR BREAK 'IS THUMBS.
YEAH, WE GOTTA MEET THIS GUY. FIVE YEARS OF THIS SHIT IS LONG ENOUGH.

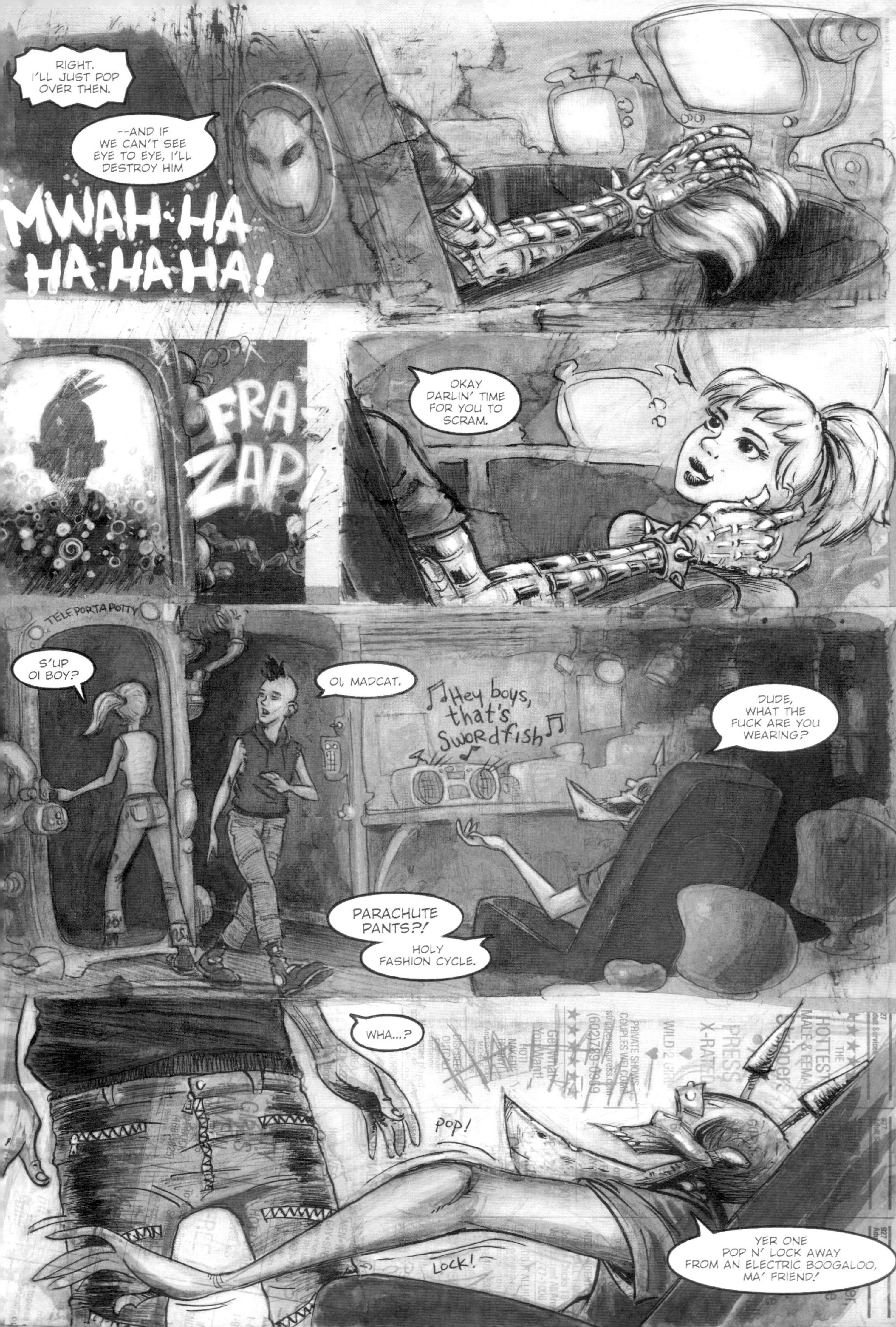
RIGHT. I'LL JUST POP OVER THEN.
--AND IF WE CAN'T SEE EYE TO EYE, I'LL DESTROY HIM
MWAH-HA HA-HA-HA!
FRA-ZAP!
OKAY DARLIN' TIME FOR YOU TO SCRAM.
TELEPORTA POTTY
S'UP OI BOY?
OI, MADCAT.
Hey boys, that's Swordfish
DUDE, WHAT THE FUCK ARE YOU WEARING?
PARACHUTE PANTS?!
HOLY FASHION CYCLE.
WHA...?
POP!
LOCK!
YER ONE POP N' LOCK AWAY FROM AN ELECTRIC BOOGALOO, MA' FRIEND!

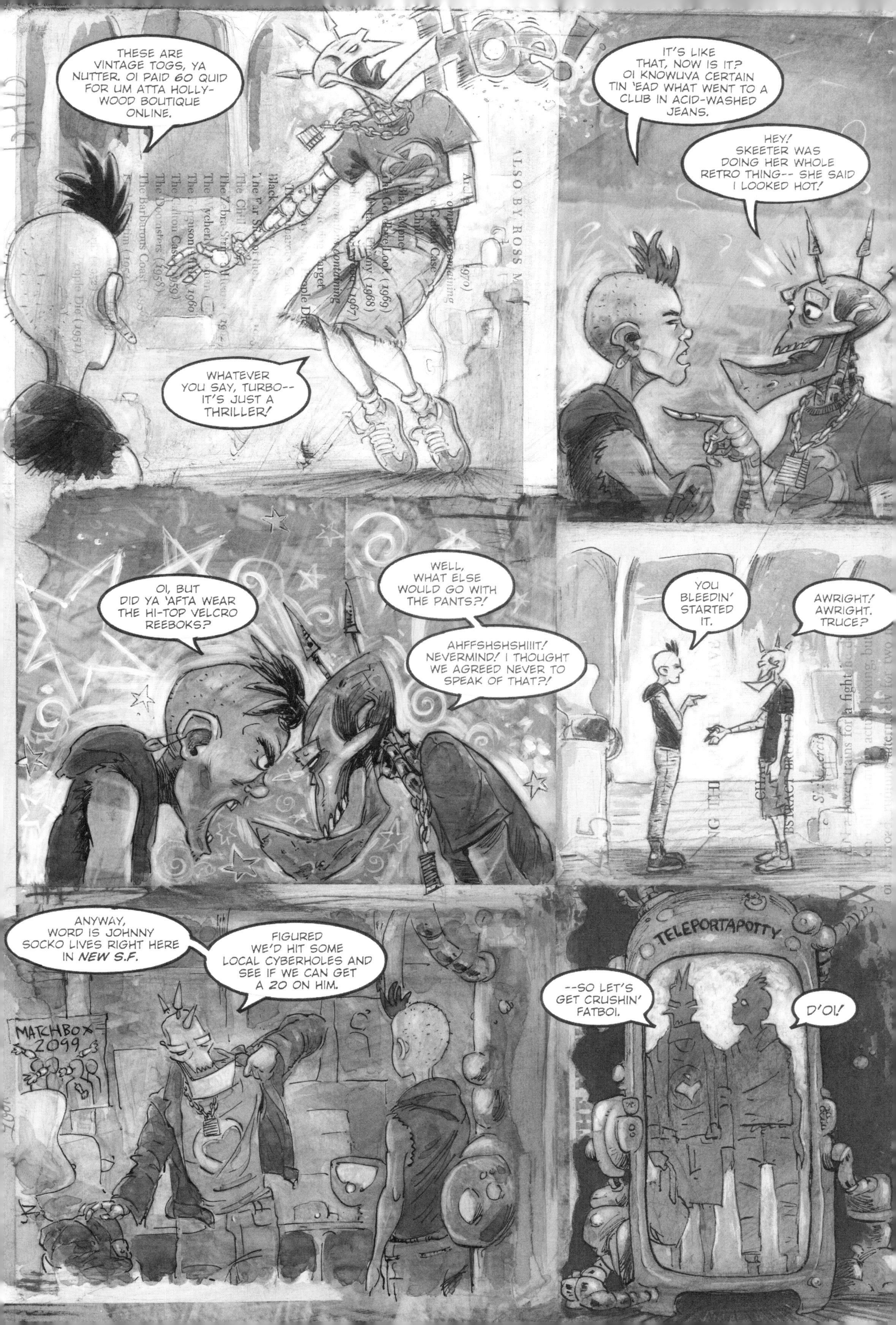
THESE ARE VINTAGE TOGS, YA NUTTER. OI PAID 60 QUID FOR UM ATTA HOLLY-WOOD BOUTIQUE ONLINE.
WHATEVER YOU SAY, TURBO-- IT'S JUST A THRILLER!
IT'S LIKE THAT, NOW IS IT? OI KNOWUVA CERTAIN TIN 'EAD WHAT WENT TO A CLUB IN ACID-WASHED JEANS.
HEY! SKEETER WAS DOING HER WHOLE RETRO THING-- SHE SAID I LOOKED HOT!
OI, BUT DID YA 'AFTA WEAR THE HI-TOP VELCRO REEBOKS?
WELL, WHAT ELSE WOULD GO WITH THE PANTS?!
AHFFSHSHSHIIIT! NEVERMIND! I THOUGHT WE AGREED NEVER TO SPEAK OF THAT?!
YOU BLEEDIN' STARTED IT.
AWRIGHT! AWRIGHT. TRUCE?
ANYWAY, WORD IS JOHNNY SOCKO LIVES RIGHT HERE IN NEW S.F.
FIGURED WE'D HIT SOME LOCAL CYBERHOLES AND SEE IF WE CAN GET A 20 ON HIM.
MATCHBOX 2099
TELEPORTAPOTTY
--SO LET'S GET CRUSHIN' FATBOI.
D'OI!

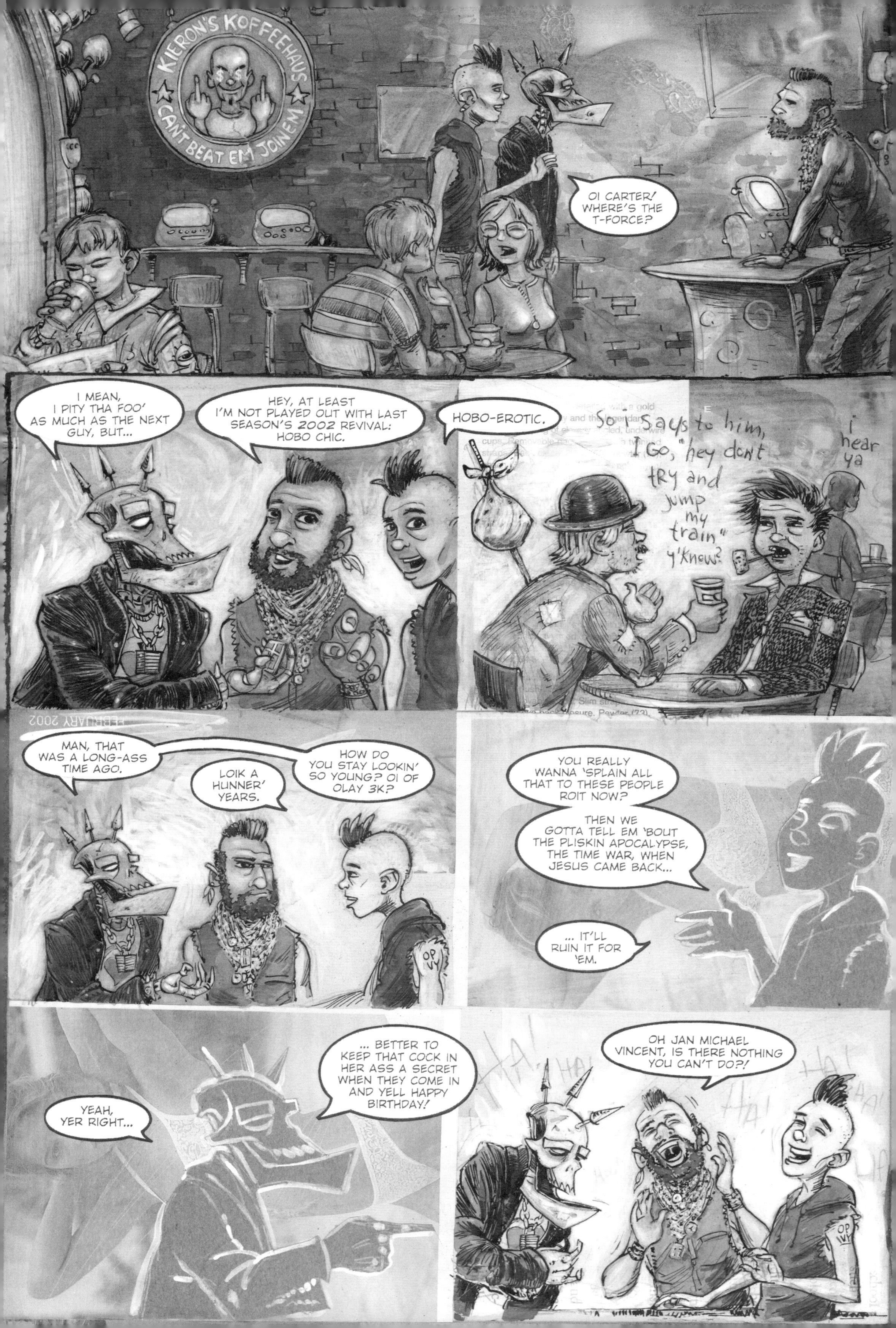
KIERON'S KOFFEEHAUS
CAN'T BEAT EM JOIN EM
OI CARTER! WHERE'S THE T-FORCE?
I MEAN, I PITY THA FOO' AS MUCH AS THE NEXT GUY, BUT...
HEY, AT LEAST I'M NOT PLAYED OUT WITH LAST SEASON'S 2002 REVIVAL: HOBO CHIC.
HOBO-EROTIC.
So i Says to him, I Go, "hey don't TRY and jump my train" y'know?
i hear ya
MAN, THAT WAS A LONG-ASS TIME AGO.
LOIK A HUNNER' YEARS.
HOW DO YOU STAY LOOKIN' SO YOUNG? OI OF OLAY 3K?
YOU REALLY WANNA 'SPLAIN ALL THAT TO THESE PEOPLE ROIT NOW?
THEN WE GOTTA TELL EM 'BOUT THE PLISKIN APOCALYPSE, THE TIME WAR, WHEN JESUS CAME BACK...
... IT'LL RUIN IT FOR 'EM.
YEAH, YER RIGHT...
... BETTER TO KEEP THAT COCK IN HER ASS A SECRET WHEN THEY COME IN AND YELL HAPPY BIRTHDAY!
OH JAN MICHAEL VINCENT, IS THERE NOTHING YOU CAN'T DO?!

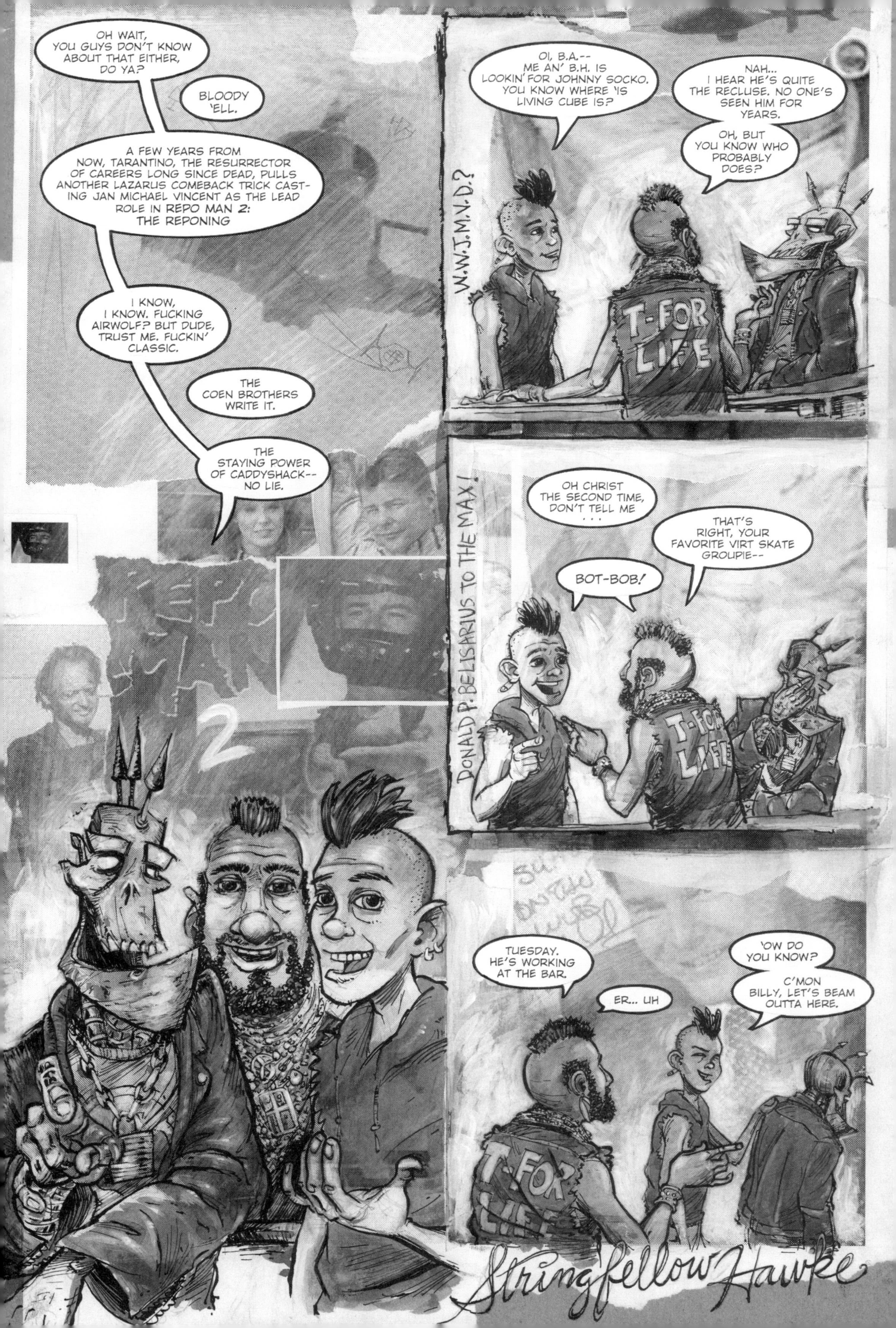
OH WAIT, YOU GUYS DON'T KNOW ABOUT THAT EITHER, DO YA?
BLOODY 'ELL.
A FEW YEARS FROM NOW, TARANTINO, THE RESURRECTOR OF CAREERS LONG SINCE DEAD, PULLS ANOTHER LAZARUS COMEBACK TRICK CASTING JAN MICHAEL VINCENT AS THE LEAD ROLE IN REPO MAN 2: THE REPONING
I KNOW, I KNOW. FUCKING AIRWOLF? BUT DUDE, TRUST ME. FUCKIN' CLASSIC.
THE COEN BROTHERS WRITE IT.
THE STAYING POWER OF CADDYSHACK-- NO LIE.
OI, B.A.-- ME AN' B.H. IS LOOKIN' FOR JOHNNY SOCKO. YOU KNOW WHERE 'IS LIVING CUBE IS?
NAH... I HEAR HE'S QUITE THE RECLUSE. NO ONE'S SEEN HIM FOR YEARS.
OH, BUT YOU KNOW WHO PROBABLY DOES?
W.W.J.M.V.D.?
T-FOR LIFE
OH CHRIST THE SECOND TIME, DON'T TELL ME . . .
THAT'S RIGHT, YOUR FAVORITE VIRT SKATE GROUPIE--
BOT-BOB!
DONALD P. BELISARIUS TO THE MAX!
TUESDAY. HE'S WORKING AT THE BAR.
'OW DO YOU KNOW?
C'MON BILLY, LET'S BEAM OUTTA HERE.
ER... UH
Stringfellow Hawke

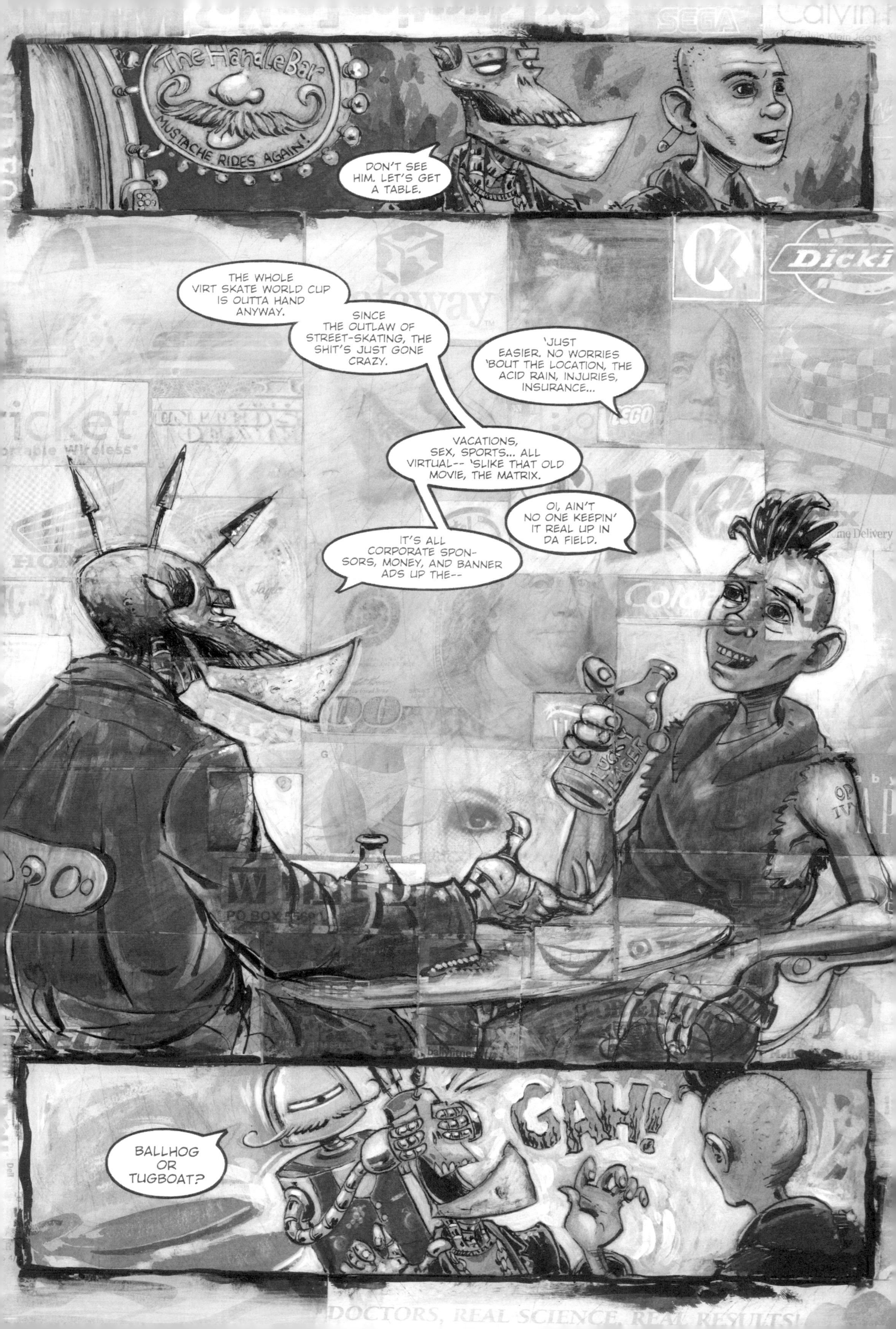

The HandleBar
MUSTACHE RIDES AGAIN!
DON'T SEE HIM. LET'S GET A TABLE.
THE WHOLE VIRT SKATE WORLD CUP IS OUTTA HAND ANYWAY.
SINCE THE OUTLAW OF STREET-SKATING, THE SHIT'S JUST GONE CRAZY.
'JUST EASIER. NO WORRIES 'BOUT THE LOCATION, THE ACID RAIN, INJURIES, INSURANCE...
VACATIONS, SEX, SPORTS... ALL VIRTUAL-- 'SLIKE THAT OLD MOVIE, THE MATRIX.
OI, AIN'T NO ONE KEEPIN' IT REAL UP IN DA FIELD.
IT'S ALL CORPORATE SPON-SORS, MONEY, AND BANNER ADS UP THE--
LUCKY LAGER
BALLHOG OR TUGBOAT?
GAH!
DOCTORS, REAL SCIENCE, REAL RESULTS!

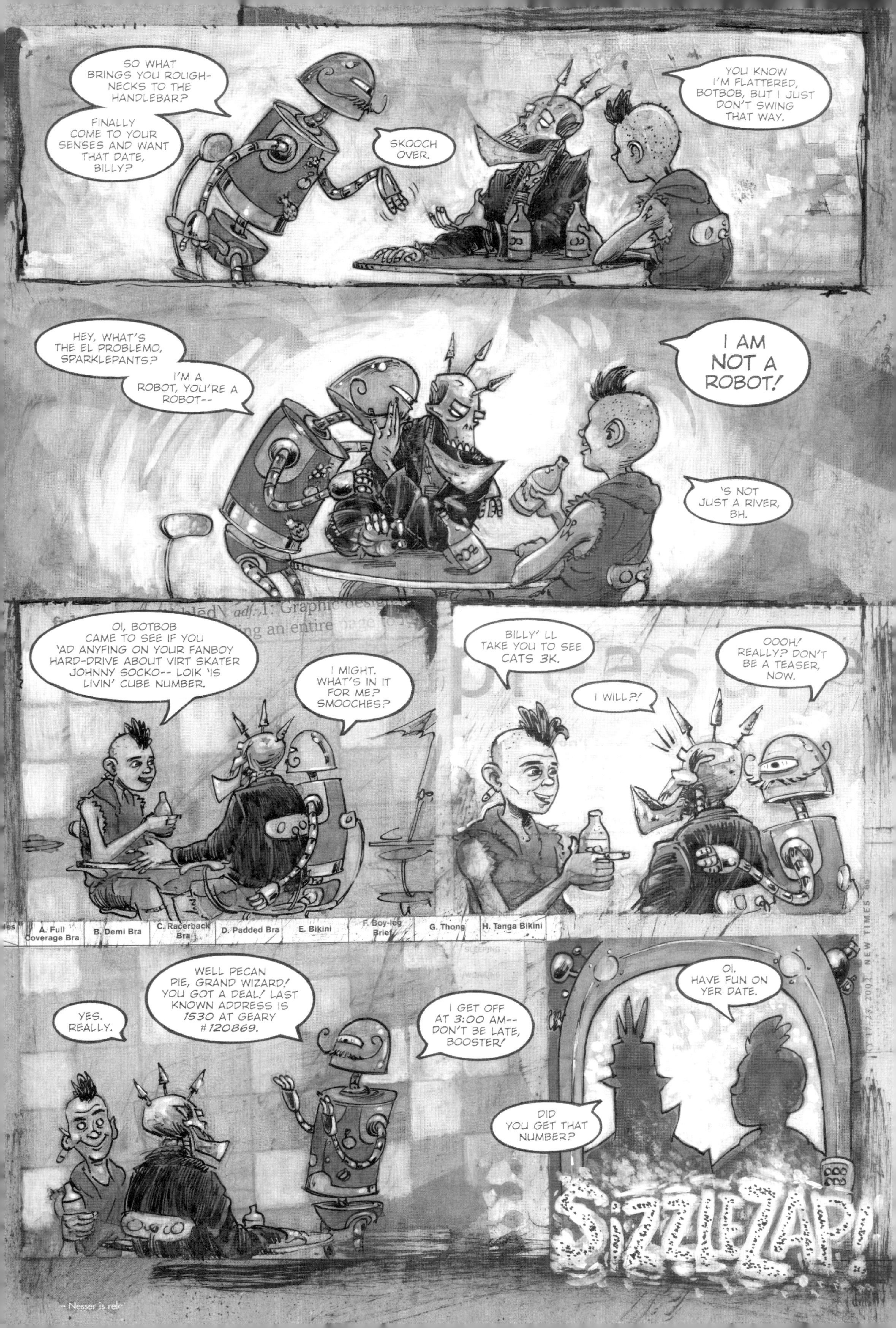
SO WHAT BRINGS YOU ROUGH-NECKS TO THE HANDLEBAR?
FINALLY COME TO YOUR SENSES AND WANT THAT DATE, BILLY?
SKOOCH OVER.
YOU KNOW I'M FLATTERED, BOTBOB, BUT I JUST DON'T SWING THAT WAY.
HEY, WHAT'S THE EL PROBLEMO, SPARKLEPANTS?
I'M A ROBOT, YOU'RE A ROBOT--
I AM NOT A ROBOT!
'S NOT JUST A RIVER, BH.
OI, BOTBOB CAME TO SEE IF YOU 'AD ANYFING ON YOUR FANBOY HARD-DRIVE ABOUT VIRT SKATER JOHNNY SOCKO-- LOIK 'IS LIVIN' CUBE NUMBER.
I MIGHT. WHAT'S IN IT FOR ME? SMOOCHES?
BILLY' LL TAKE YOU TO SEE CATS 3K.
I WILL?!
OOOH! REALLY? DON'T BE A TEASER, NOW.
A. Full Coverage Bra
B. Demi Bra
C. Racerback Bra
D. Padded Bra
E. Bikini
F. Boy-leg Brief
G. Thong
H. Tanga Bikini
YES. REALLY.
WELL PECAN PIE, GRAND WIZARD! YOU GOT A DEAL! LAST KNOWN ADDRESS IS 1530 AT GEARY #120869.
I GET OFF AT 3:00 AM-- DON'T BE LATE, BOOSTER!
OI. HAVE FUN ON YER DATE.
DID YOU GET THAT NUMBER?
SIZZLEZAP!
NEW TIMES 65

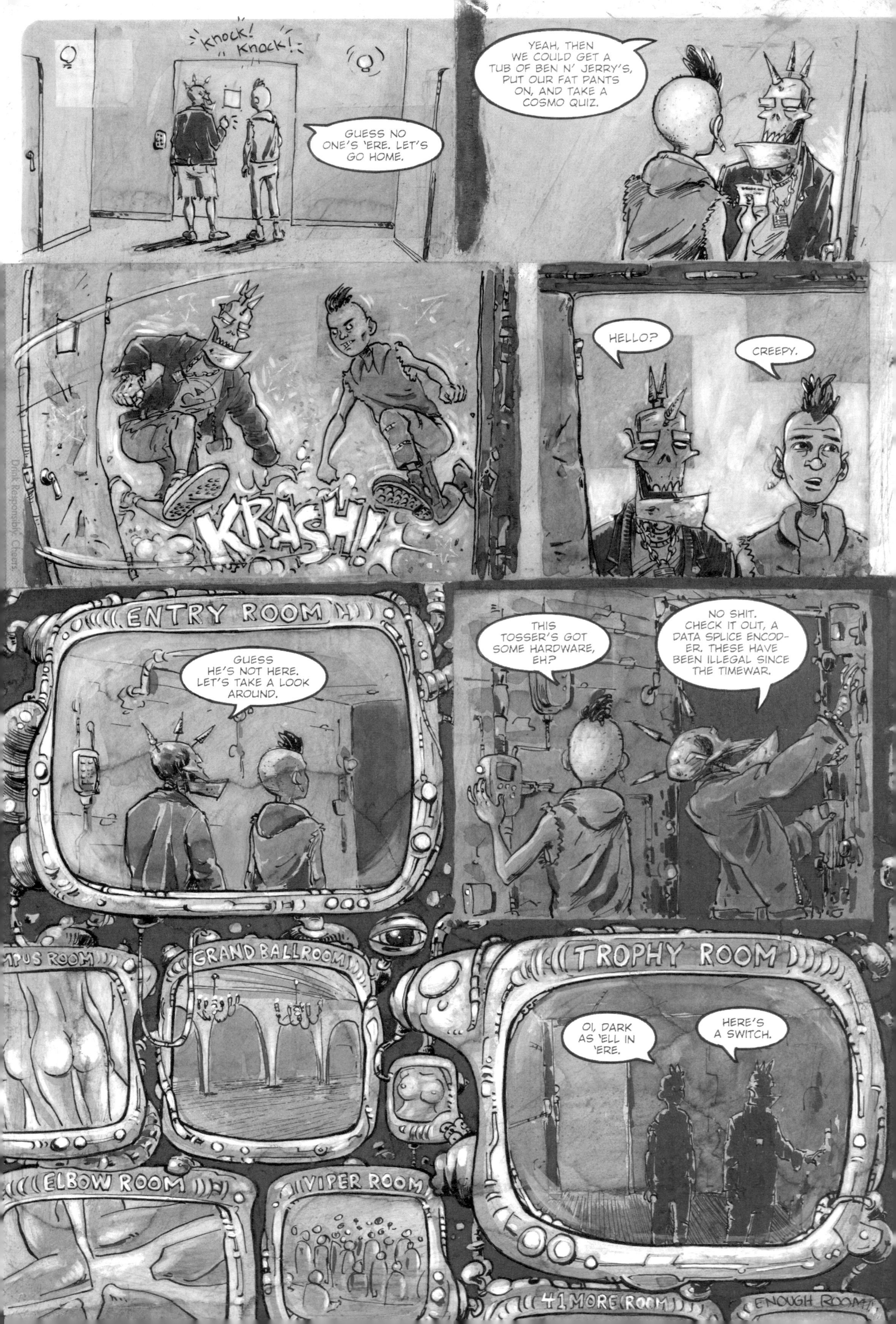
Knock! Knock!
GUESS NO ONE'S 'ERE. LET'S GO HOME.
YEAH, THEN WE COULD GET A TUB OF BEN N' JERRY'S, PUT OUR FAT PANTS ON, AND TAKE A COSMO QUIZ.
KRASH!
HELLO?
CREEPY.
ENTRY ROOM
GUESS HE'S NOT HERE. LET'S TAKE A LOOK AROUND.
THIS TOSSER'S GOT SOME HARDWARE, EH?
NO SHIT. CHECK IT OUT, A DATA SPLICE ENCODER. THESE HAVE BEEN ILLEGAL SINCE THE TIMEWAR.
GRAND BALLROOM
TROPHY ROOM
OI, DARK AS 'ELL IN 'ERE.
HERE'S A SWITCH.
ELBOW ROOM
VIPER ROOM
41 MORE ROOM
ENOUGH ROOM!
Drink Responsibly. Cheers.

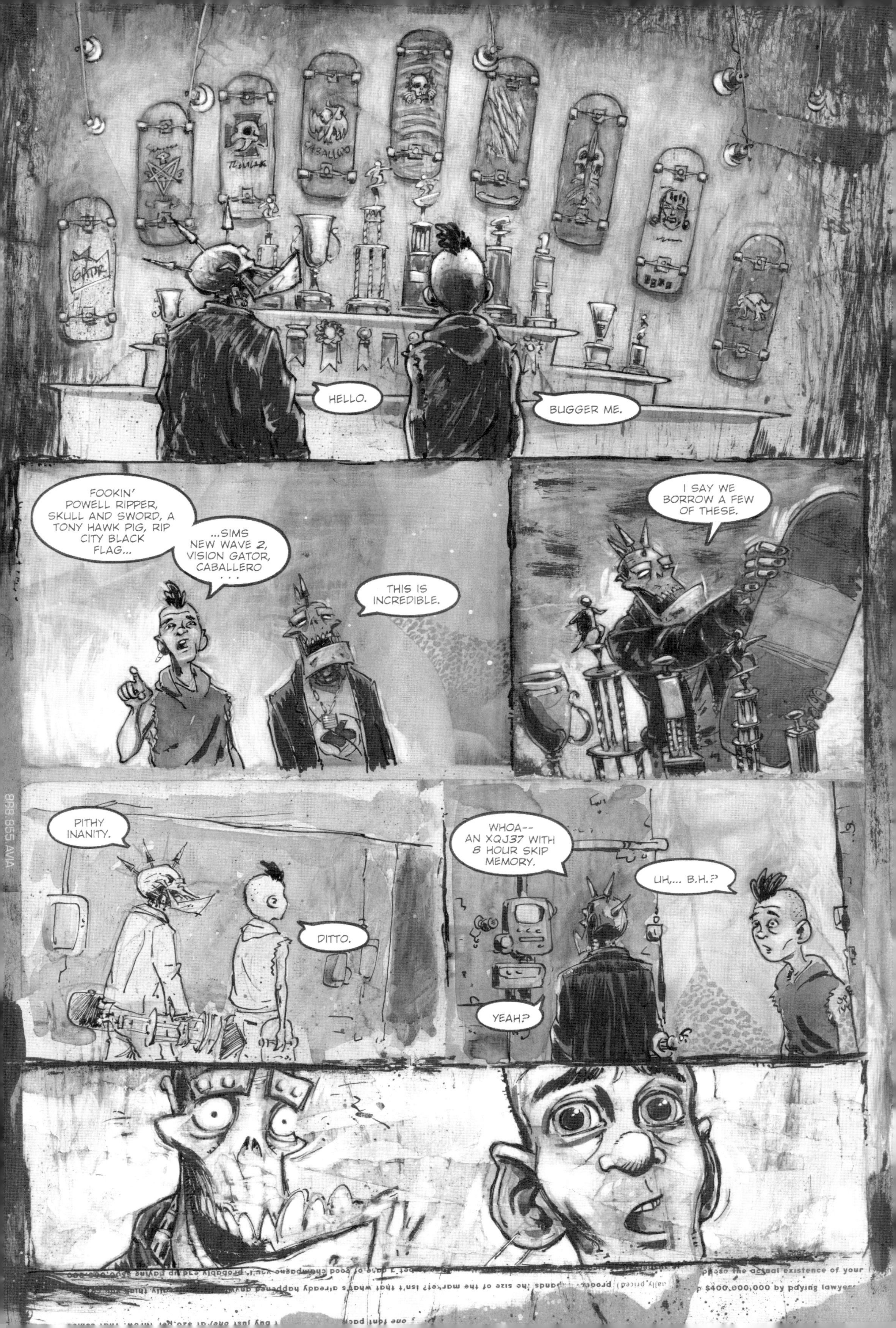
HELLO.
BUGGER ME.
FOOKIN' POWELL RIPPER, SKULL AND SWORD, A TONY HAWK PIG, RIP CITY BLACK FLAG...
...SIMS NEW WAVE 2, VISION GATOR, CABALLERO . . .
THIS IS INCREDIBLE.
I SAY WE BORROW A FEW OF THESE.
PITHY INANITY.
DITTO.
WHOA-- AN XQJ37 WITH 8 HOUR SKIP MEMORY.
UH,... B.H.?
YEAH?

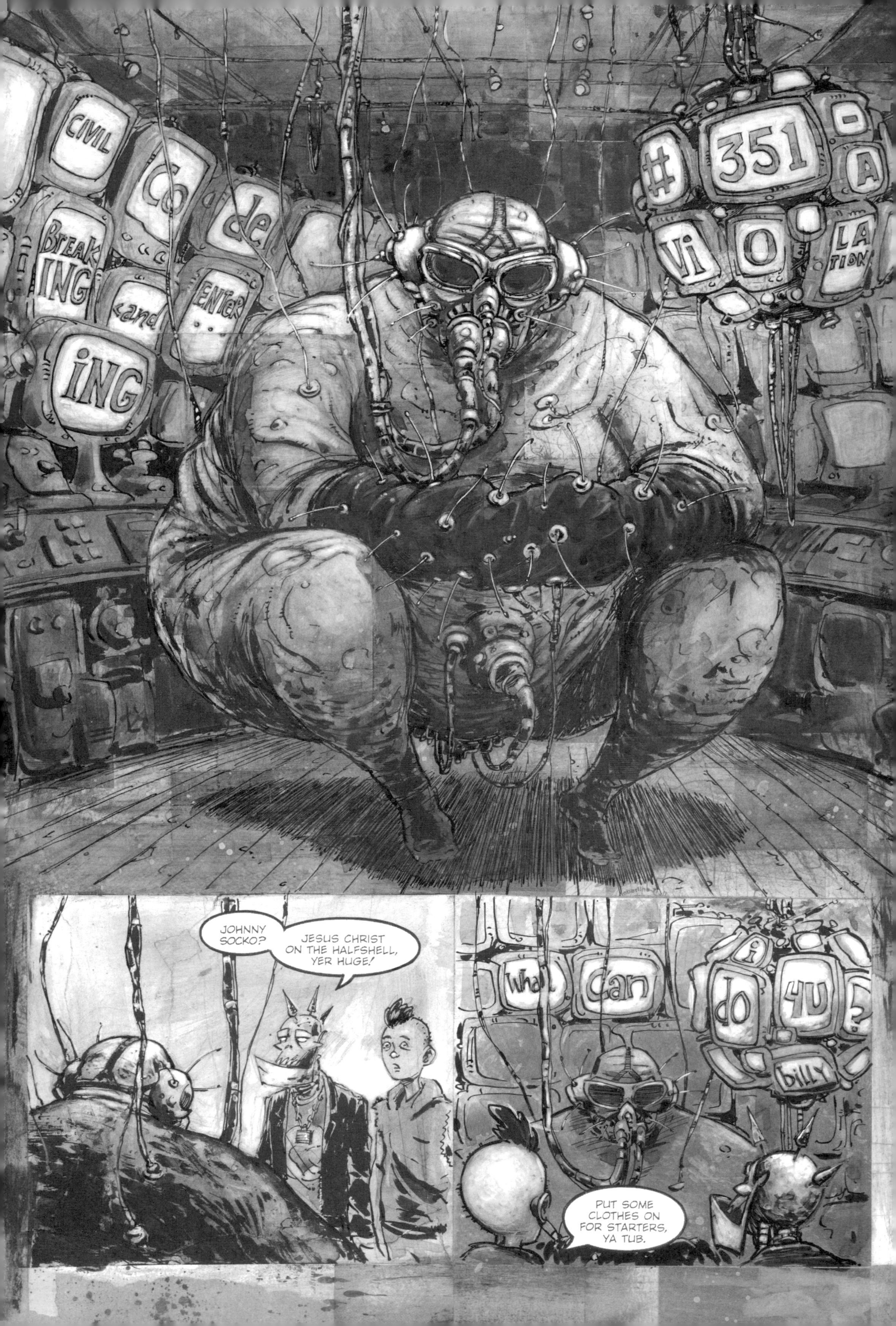
CIVIL Co de BREAKING and ENTERing
#351-A ViOLATION
JOHNNY SOCKO?
JESUS CHRIST ON THE HALFSHELL, YER HUGE!
what can i do 4U ?
billy
PUT SOME CLOTHES ON FOR STARTERS, YA TUB.

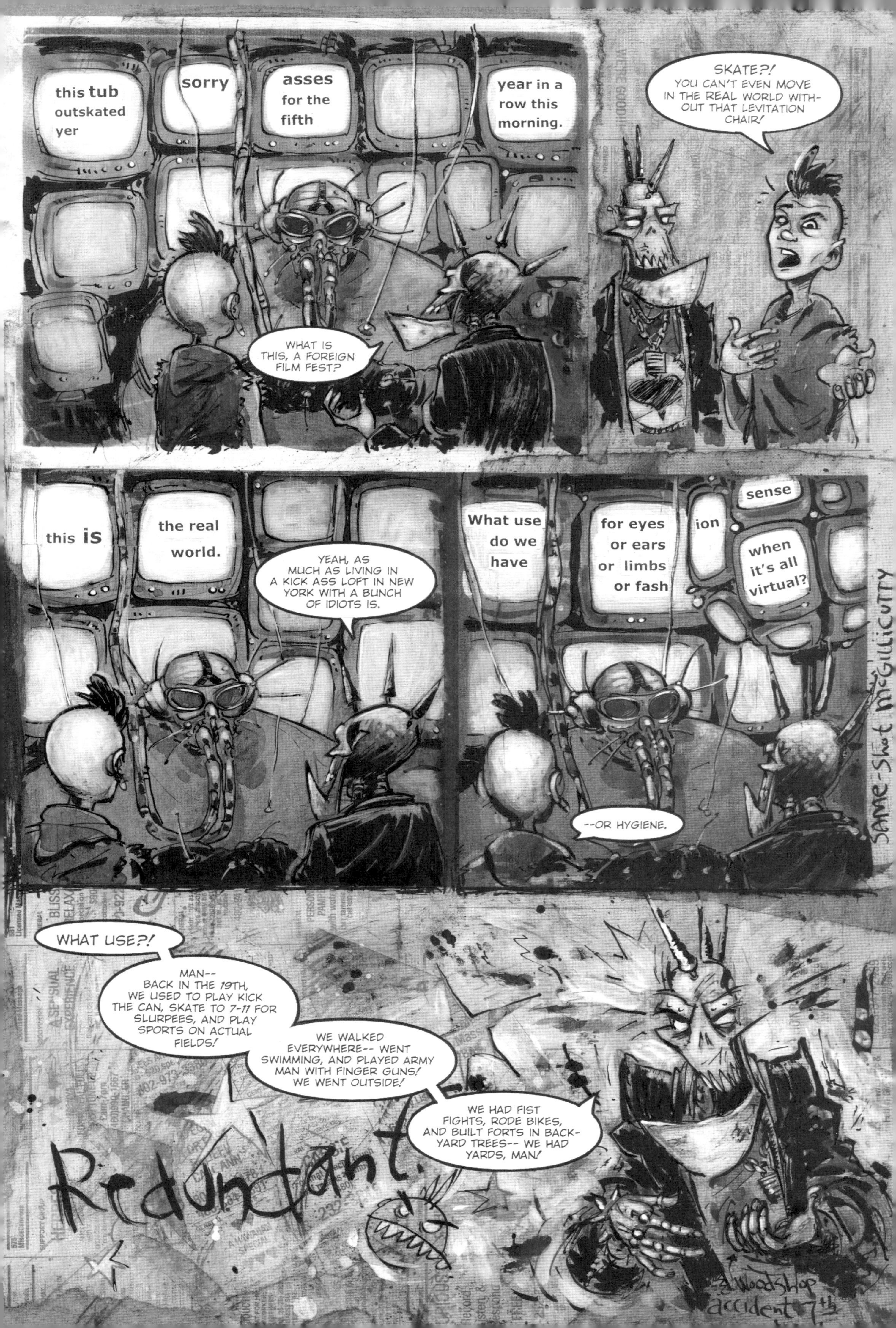
this tub outskated yer
sorry
asses for the fifth
year in a row this morning.
WHAT IS THIS, A FOREIGN FILM FEST?
SKATE?! YOU CAN'T EVEN MOVE IN THE REAL WORLD WITH-OUT THAT LEVITATION CHAIR!
this is
the real world.
YEAH, AS MUCH AS LIVING IN A KICK ASS LOFT IN NEW YORK WITH A BUNCH OF IDIOTS IS.
What use do we have
for eyes or ears or limbs or fash
ion
sense
when it's all virtual?
--OR HYGIENE.
SAME-SHOT McGILLICUTTY
WHAT USE?!
MAN-- BACK IN THE 19TH, WE USED TO PLAY KICK THE CAN, SKATE TO 7-11 FOR SLURPEES, AND PLAY SPORTS ON ACTUAL FIELDS!
WE WALKED EVERYWHERE-- WENT SWIMMING, AND PLAYED ARMY MAN WITH FINGER GUNS! WE WENT OUTSIDE!
WE HAD FIST FIGHTS, RODE BIKES, AND BUILT FORTS IN BACK-YARD TREES-- WE HAD YARDS, MAN!
Redundant.
Woodshop accident 7th

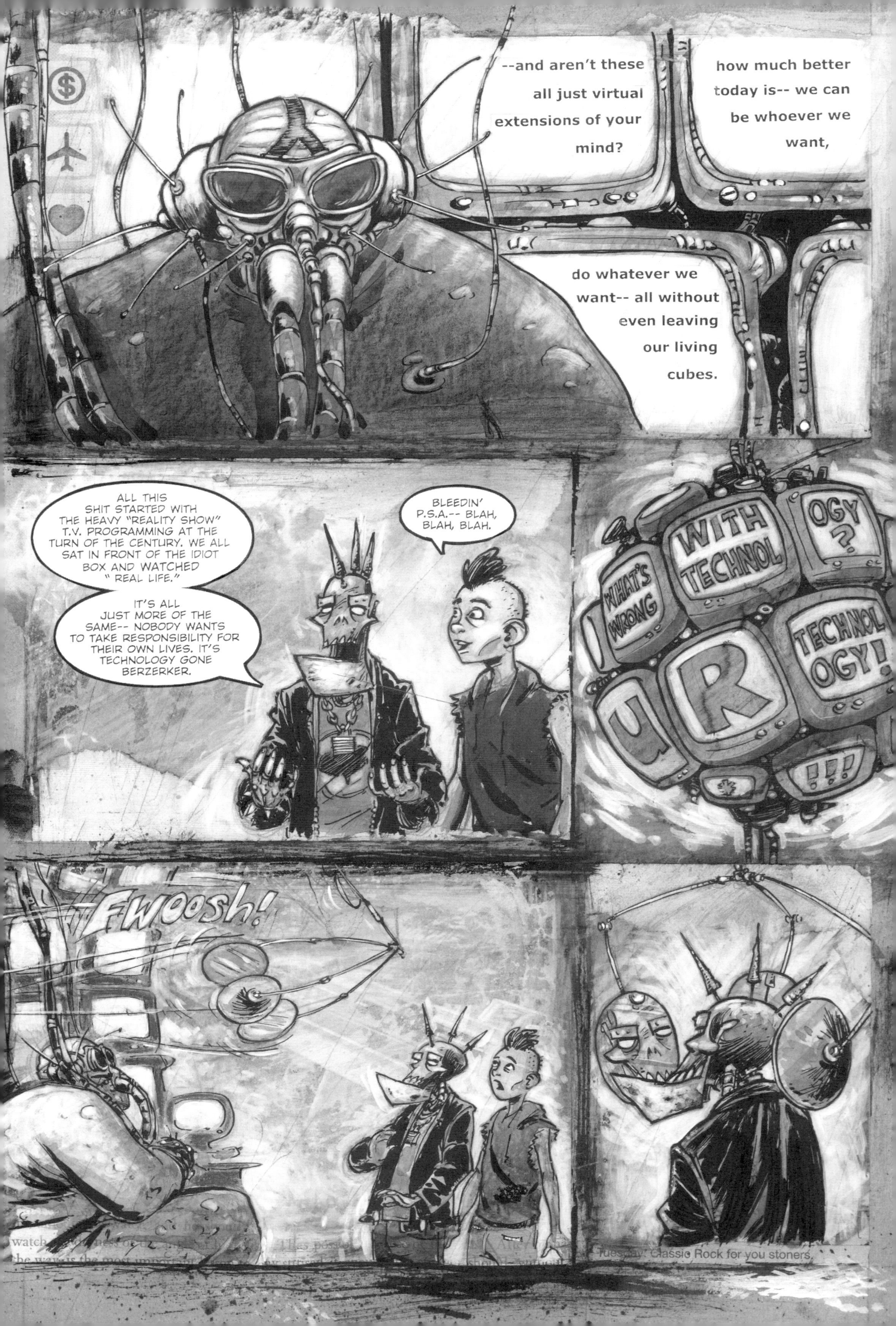
--and aren't these all just virtual extensions of your mind?
how much better today is-- we can be whoever we want,
do whatever we want-- all without even leaving our living cubes.
ALL THIS SHIT STARTED WITH THE HEAVY "REALITY SHOW" T.V. PROGRAMMING AT THE TURN OF THE CENTURY. WE ALL SAT IN FRONT OF THE IDIOT BOX AND WATCHED " REAL LIFE."
BLEEDIN' P.S.A.-- BLAH, BLAH, BLAH.
IT'S ALL JUST MORE OF THE SAME-- NOBODY WANTS TO TAKE RESPONSIBILITY FOR THEIR OWN LIVES. IT'S TECHNOLOGY GONE BERZERKER.
WHAT'S WRONG
WITH TECHNOL
OGY ?
U
R
TECHNOL OGY!
!!!
FWOOSH!
Tuesday: Classic Rock for you stoners.

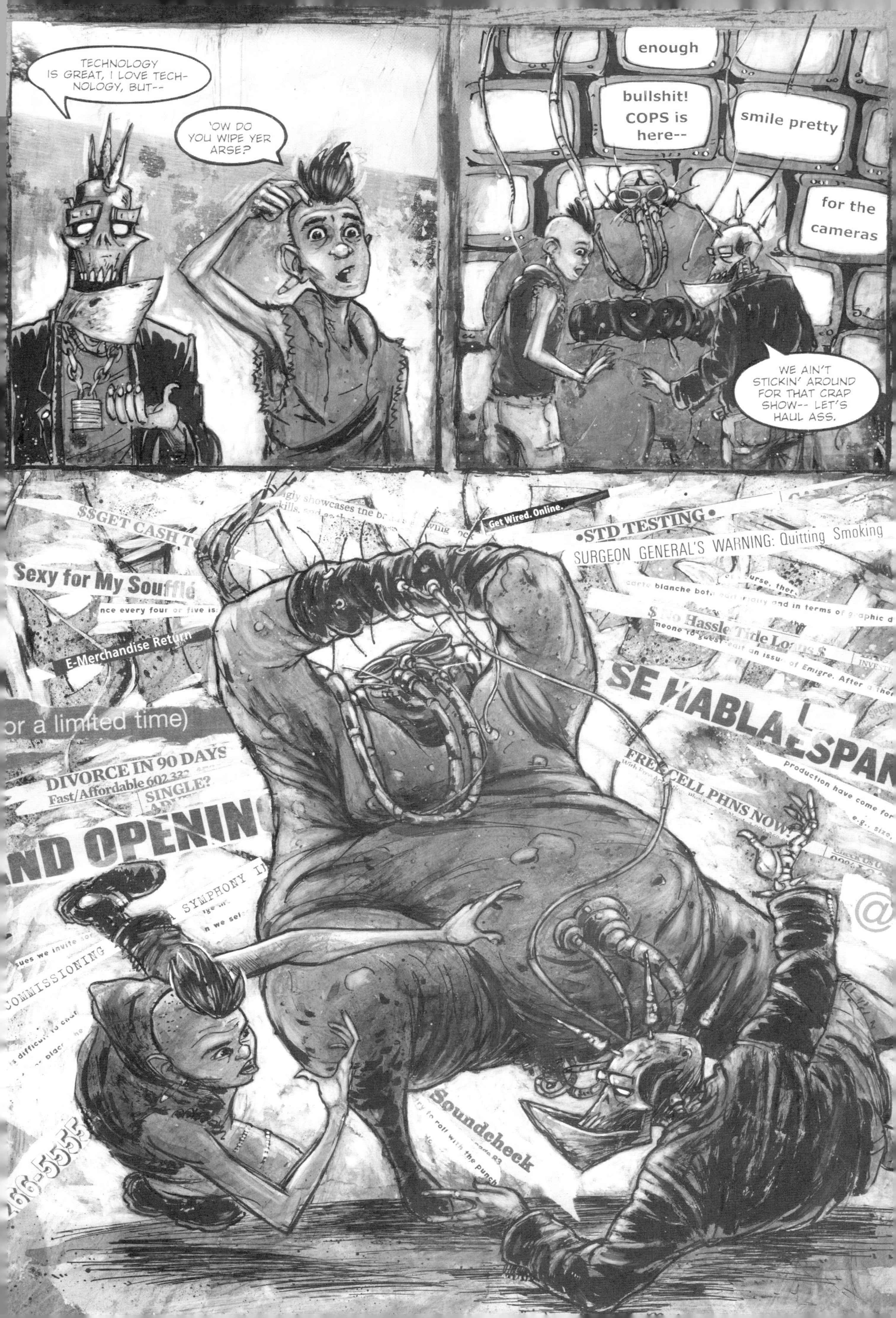
TECHNOLOGY IS GREAT, I LOVE TECHNOLOGY, BUT--
'OW DO YOU WIPE YER ARSE?
enough
bullshit! COPS is here--
smile pretty
for the cameras
WE AIN'T STICKIN' AROUND FOR THAT CRAP SHOW-- LET'S HAUL ASS.
$$GET CASH TO
Get Wired. Online.
•STD TESTING•
SURGEON GENERAL'S WARNING: Quitting Smoking
Sexy for My Soufflé
E-Merchandise Return
$ No Hassle Title Loans $
SE HABLA ESPAN
or a limited time)
DIVORCE IN 90 DAYS
Fast/Affordable 602
SINGLE?
FREE CELL PHNS NOW
ND OPENIN
A SYMPHONY
COMMISSIONING
@
Soundcheck
roll with the punch
66-555

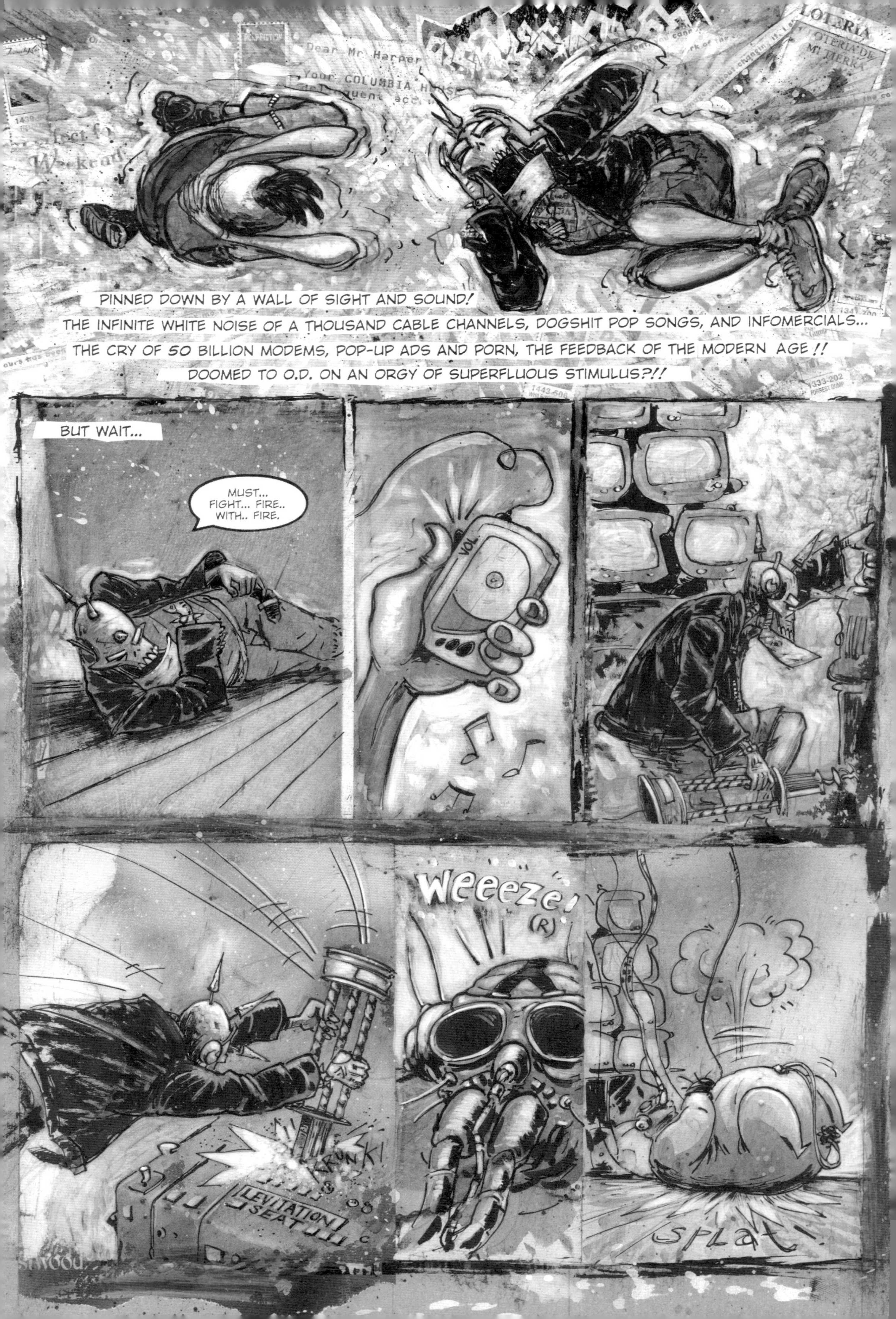
PINNED DOWN BY A WALL OF SIGHT AND SOUND!
THE INFINITE WHITE NOISE OF A THOUSAND CABLE CHANNELS, DOGSHIT POP SONGS, AND INFOMERCIALS...
THE CRY OF 50 BILLION MODEMS, POP-UP ADS AND PORN, THE FEEDBACK OF THE MODERN AGE!!
DOOMED TO O.D. ON AN ORGY OF SUPERFLUOUS STIMULUS?!!
BUT WAIT...
MUST... FIGHT... FIRE.. WITH.. FIRE.
VOL.
KRUNK!
LEVITATION SEAT
Weeeze!
(R)
SPLAT

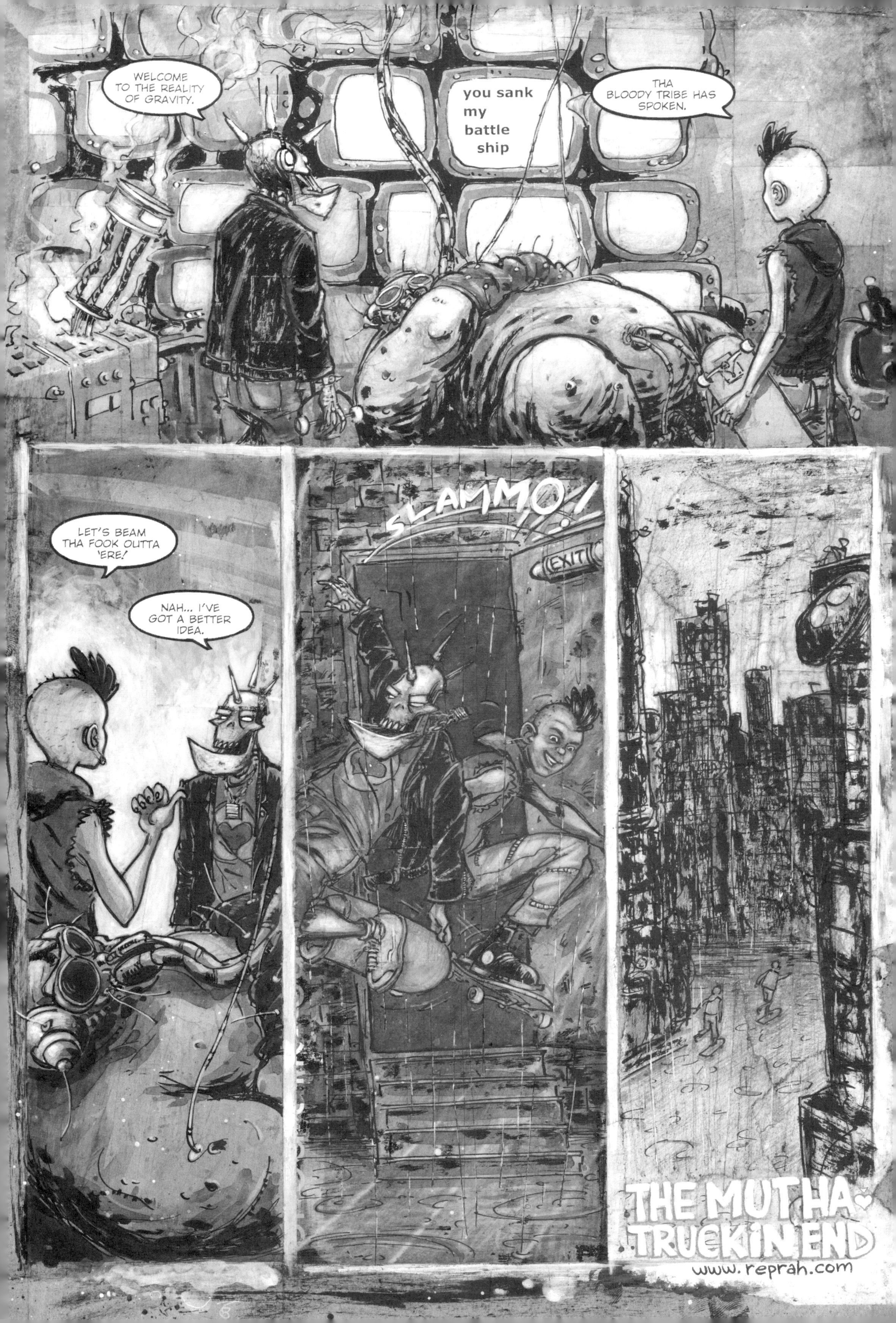
WELCOME TO THE REALITY OF GRAVITY.
you sank my battle ship
THA BLOODY TRIBE HAS SPOKEN.
LET'S BEAM THA FOOK OUTTA 'ERE!
NAH... I'VE GOT A BETTER IDEA.
SLAMMO!
EXIT
THE MUTHA TRUCKIN END
www.reprah.com

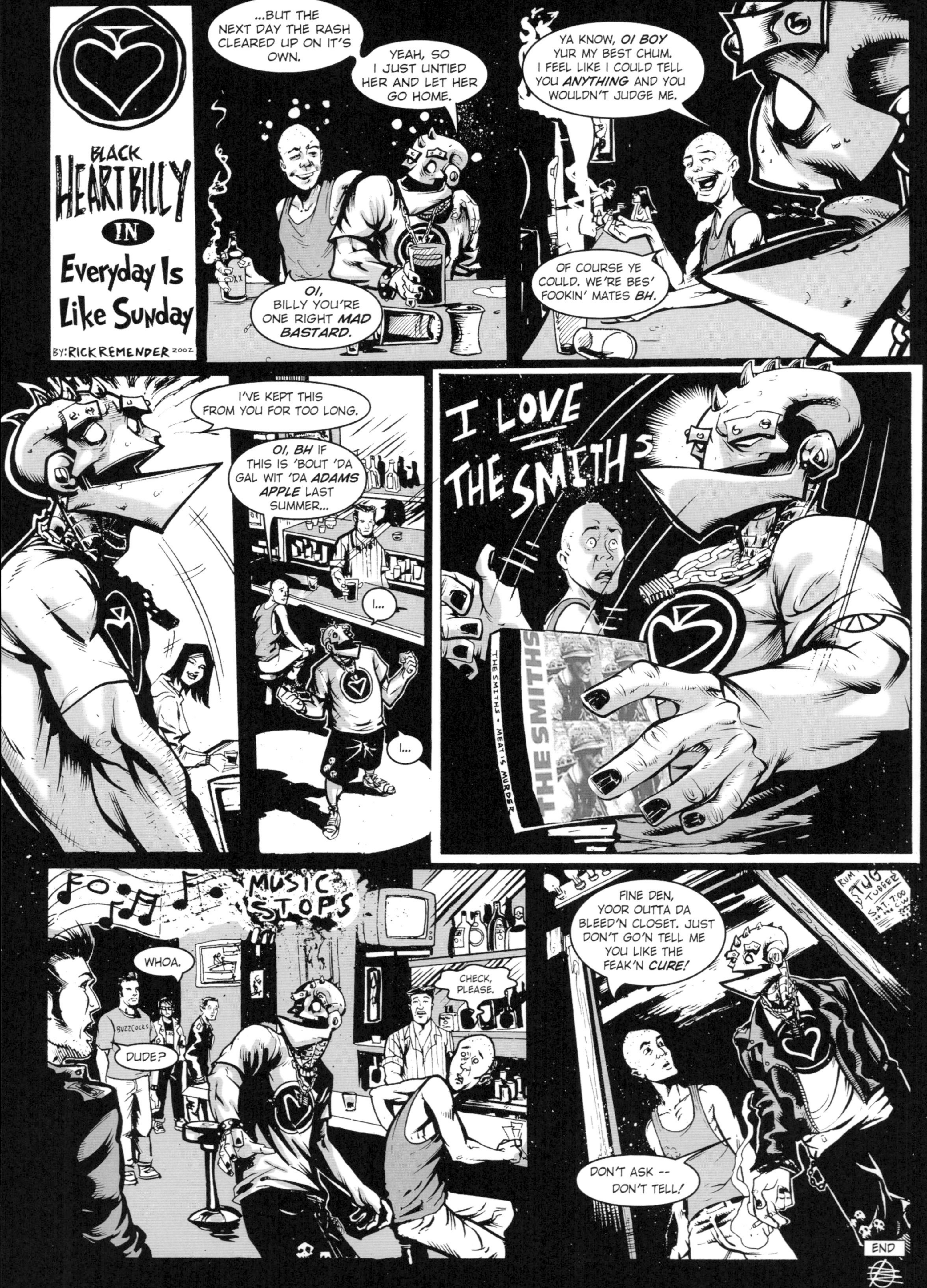

BLACK HEARTBILLY IN
Everyday Is Like Sunday
BY: RICK REMENDER 2002
...BUT THE NEXT DAY THE RASH CLEARED UP ON IT'S OWN.
YEAH, SO I JUST UNTIED HER AND LET HER GO HOME.
OI, BILLY YOU'RE ONE RIGHT MAD BASTARD.
YA KNOW, OI BOY YUR MY BEST CHUM. I FEEL LIKE I COULD TELL YOU ANYTHING AND YOU WOULDN'T JUDGE ME.
OF COURSE YE COULD. WE'RE BES' FOOKIN' MATES BH.
I'VE KEPT THIS FROM YOU FOR TOO LONG.
OI, BH IF THIS IS 'BOUT 'DA GAL WIT 'DA ADAMS APPLE LAST SUMMER...
I...
I...
I LOVE THE SMITHS
THE SMITHS • MEAT IS MURDER
THE SMITHS
MUSIC STOPS
WHOA.
DUDE?
BUZZCOCKS
CHECK, PLEASE.
FINE DEN, YOOR OUTTA DA BLEED'N CLOSET. JUST DON'T GO'N TELL ME YOU LIKE THE FEAK'N CURE!
DON'T ASK -- DON'T TELL!
END

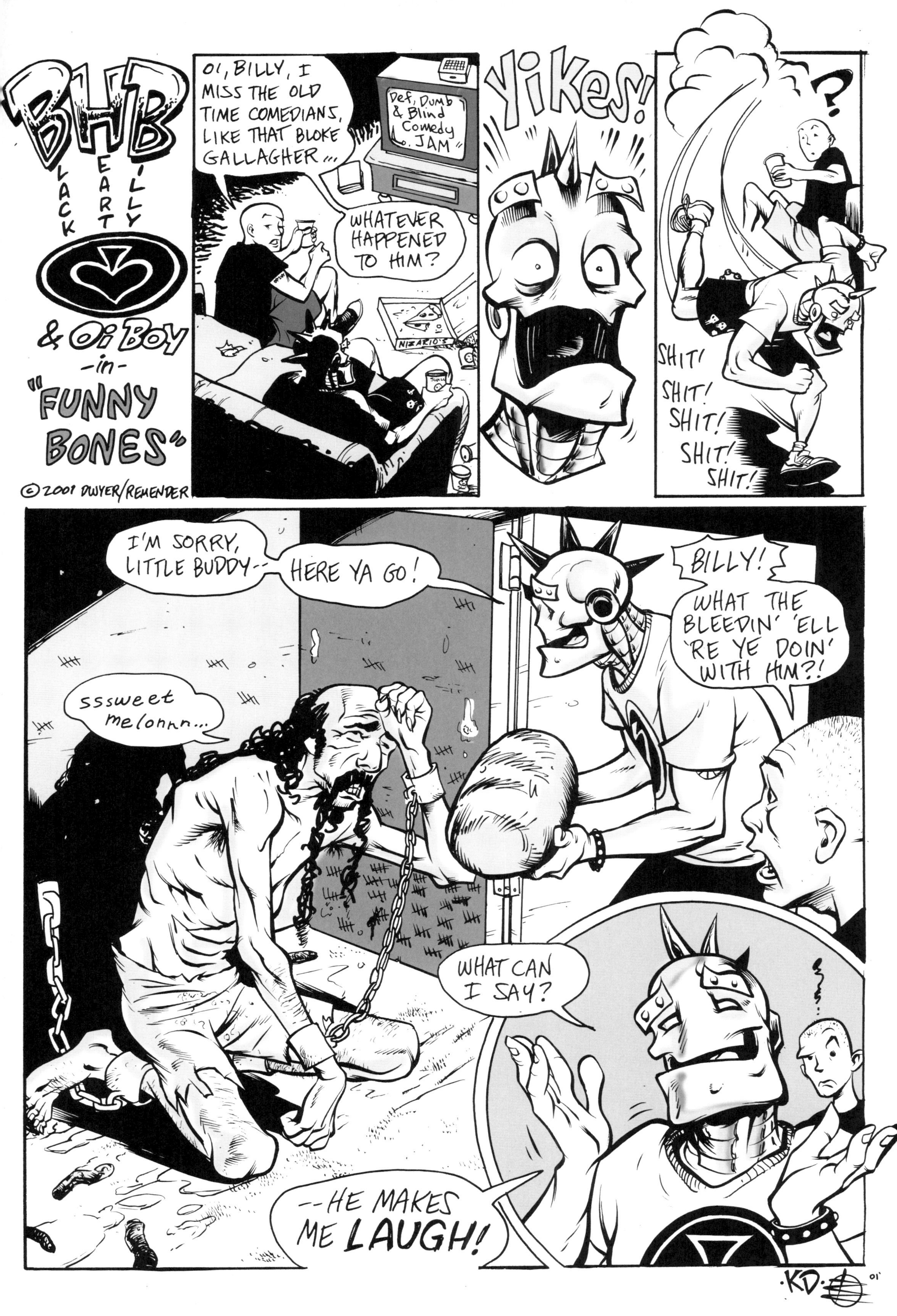
BHB
BLACK HEART BILLY
& Oi Boy
-in-
"FUNNY BONES"
© 2001 DWYER/REMENDER
OI, BILLY, I MISS THE OLD TIME COMEDIANS, LIKE THAT BLOKE GALLAGHER...
Def, Dumb & Blind Comedy JAM
WHATEVER HAPPENED TO HIM?
NIZARIO'S
YIKES!
?
SHIT! SHIT! SHIT! SHIT! SHIT!
I'M SORRY, LITTLE BUDDY--
HERE YA GO!
BILLY!
WHAT THE BLEEDIN' 'ELL 'RE YE DOIN' WITH HIM?!
sssweet melonnn...
WHAT CAN I SAY?
--HE MAKES ME LAUGH!
KD '01

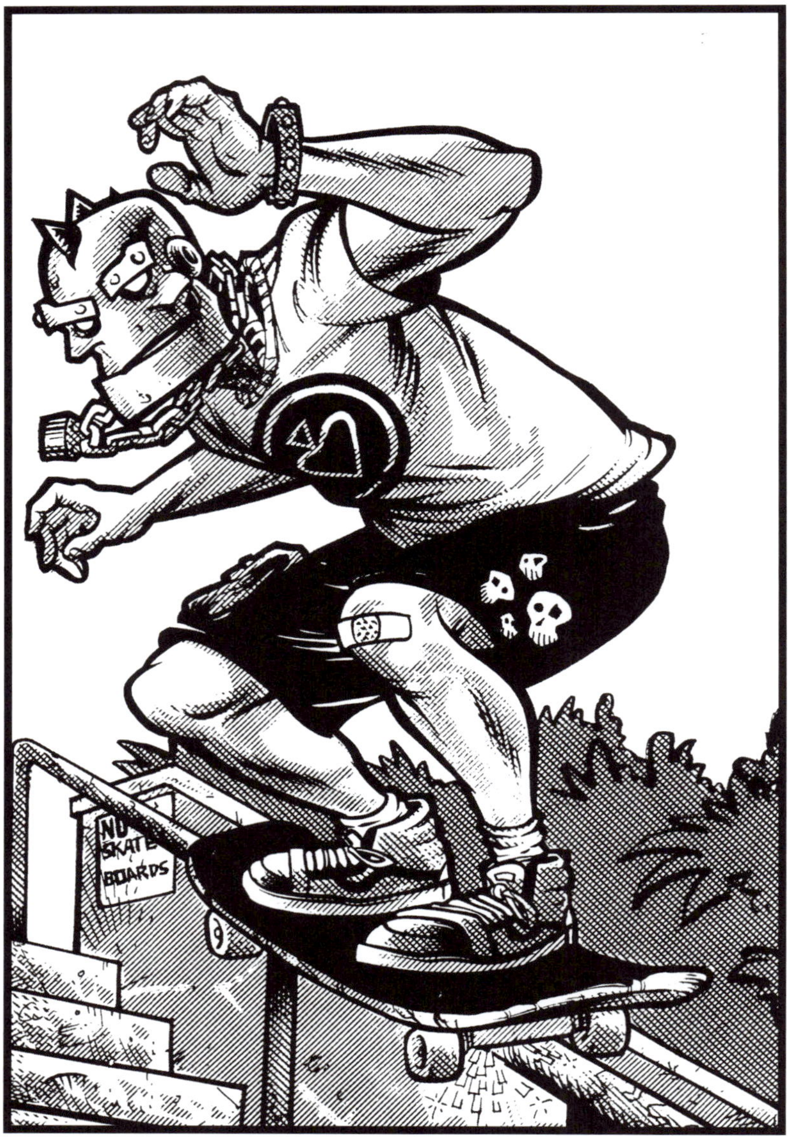
NO SKATE BOARDS

SIX
ANTI-FASHION

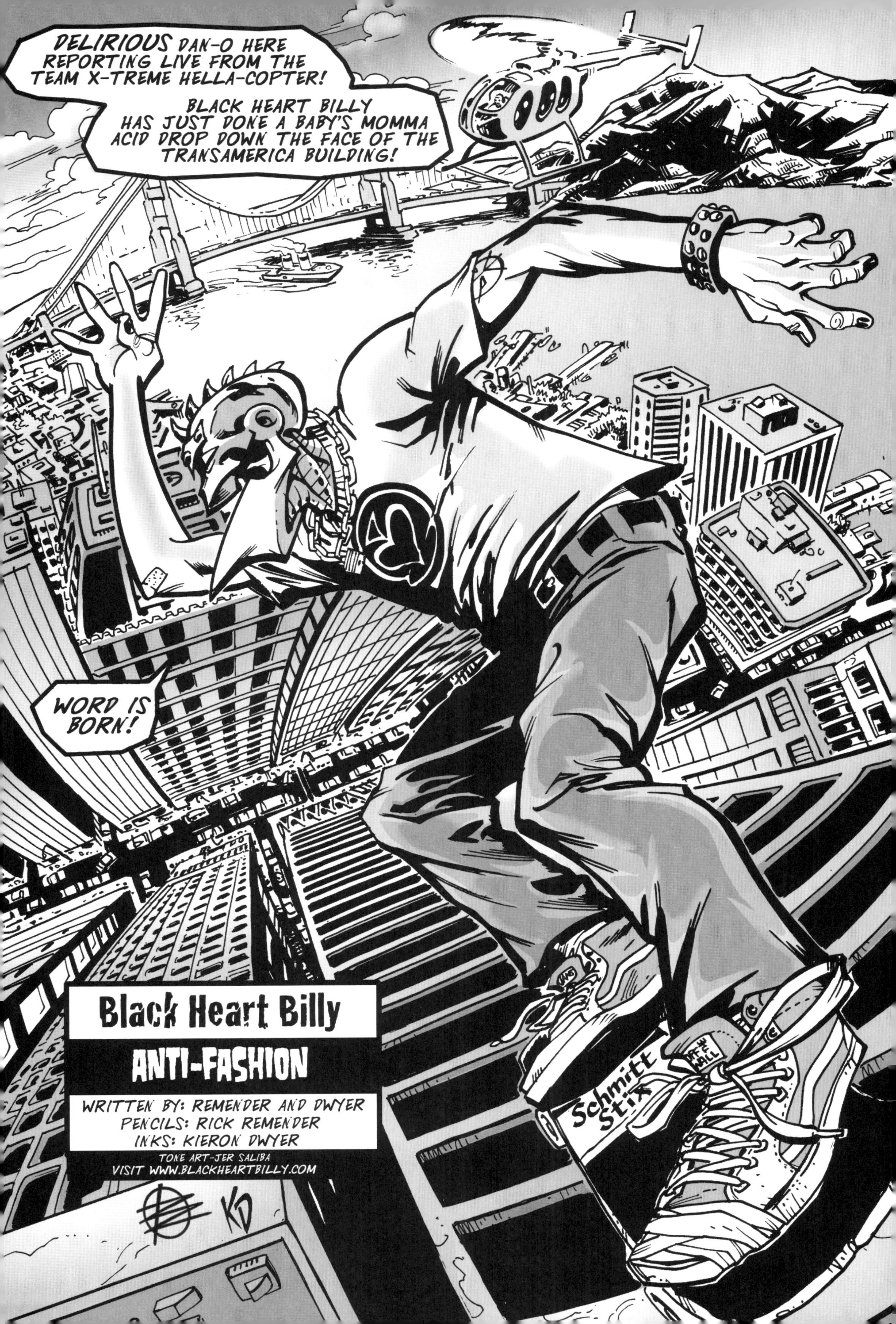
DELIRIOUS DAN-O HERE REPORTING LIVE FROM THE TEAM X-TREME HELLA-COPTER!
BLACK HEART BILLY HAS JUST DONE A BABY'S MOMMA ACID DROP DOWN THE FACE OF THE TRANSAMERICA BUILDING!
WORD IS BORN!
Black Heart Billy
ANTI-FASHION
WRITTEN BY: REMENDER AND DWYER
PENCILS: RICK REMENDER
INKS: KIERON DWYER
TONE ART-JER SALIBA
VISIT WWW.BLACKHEARTBILLY.COM
Schmitt Stix

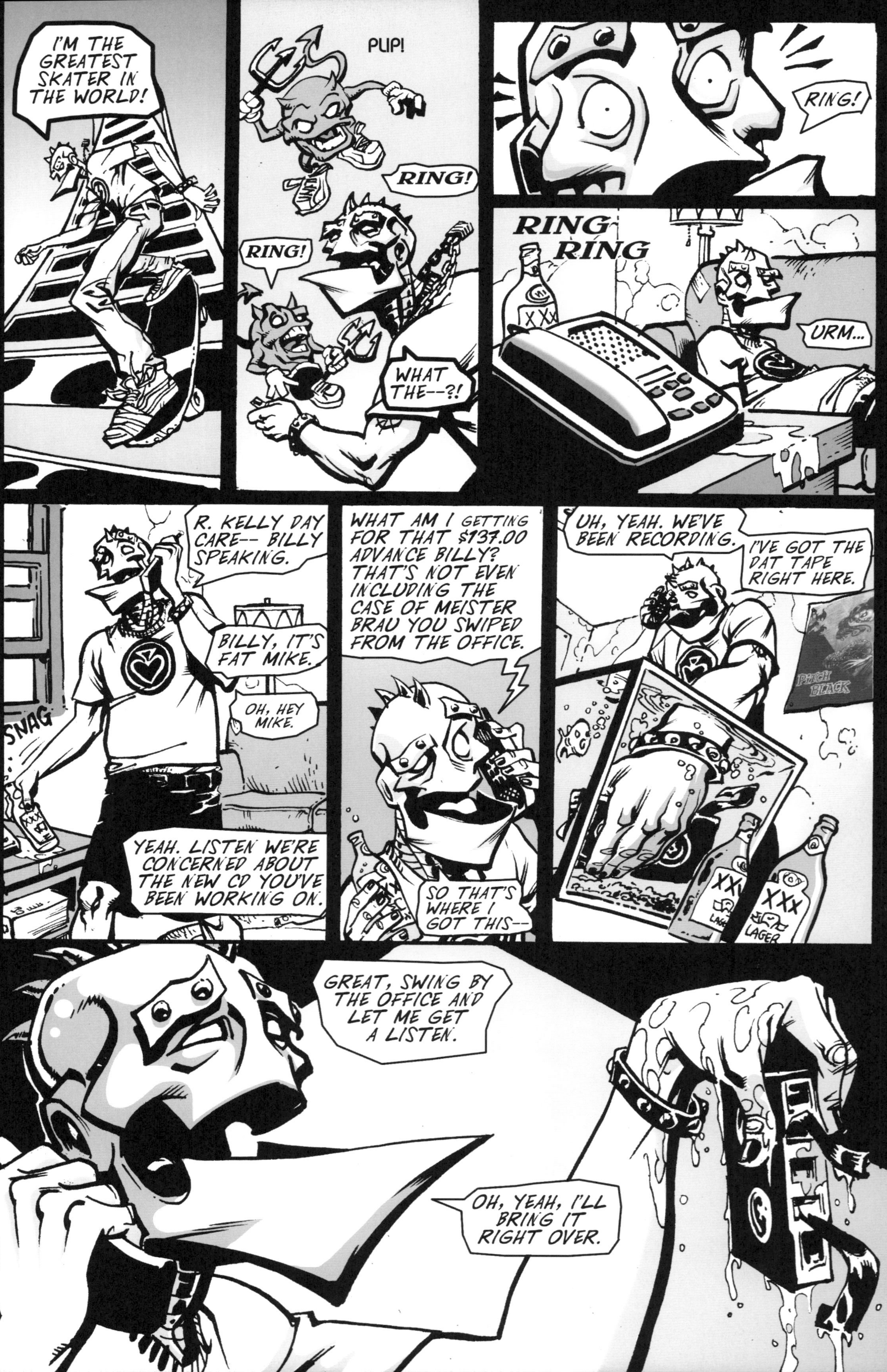
I'M THE GREATEST SKATER IN THE WORLD!
PLIP!
RING!
RING!
WHAT THE--?!
RING!
RING RING
URM...
R. KELLY DAY CARE-- BILLY SPEAKING.
BILLY, IT'S FAT MIKE.
OH, HEY MIKE.
SNAG
YEAH. LISTEN WE'RE CONCERNED ABOUT THE NEW CD YOU'VE BEEN WORKING ON.
WHAT AM I GETTING FOR THAT $137.00 ADVANCE BILLY? THAT'S NOT EVEN INCLUDING THE CASE OF MEISTER BRAU YOU SWIPED FROM THE OFFICE.
SO THAT'S WHERE I GOT THIS--
UH, YEAH. WE'VE BEEN RECORDING.
I'VE GOT THE DAT TAPE RIGHT HERE.
PITCH BLACK
XXX LAGER
GREAT, SWING BY THE OFFICE AND LET ME GET A LISTEN.
OH, YEAH, I'LL BRING IT RIGHT OVER.

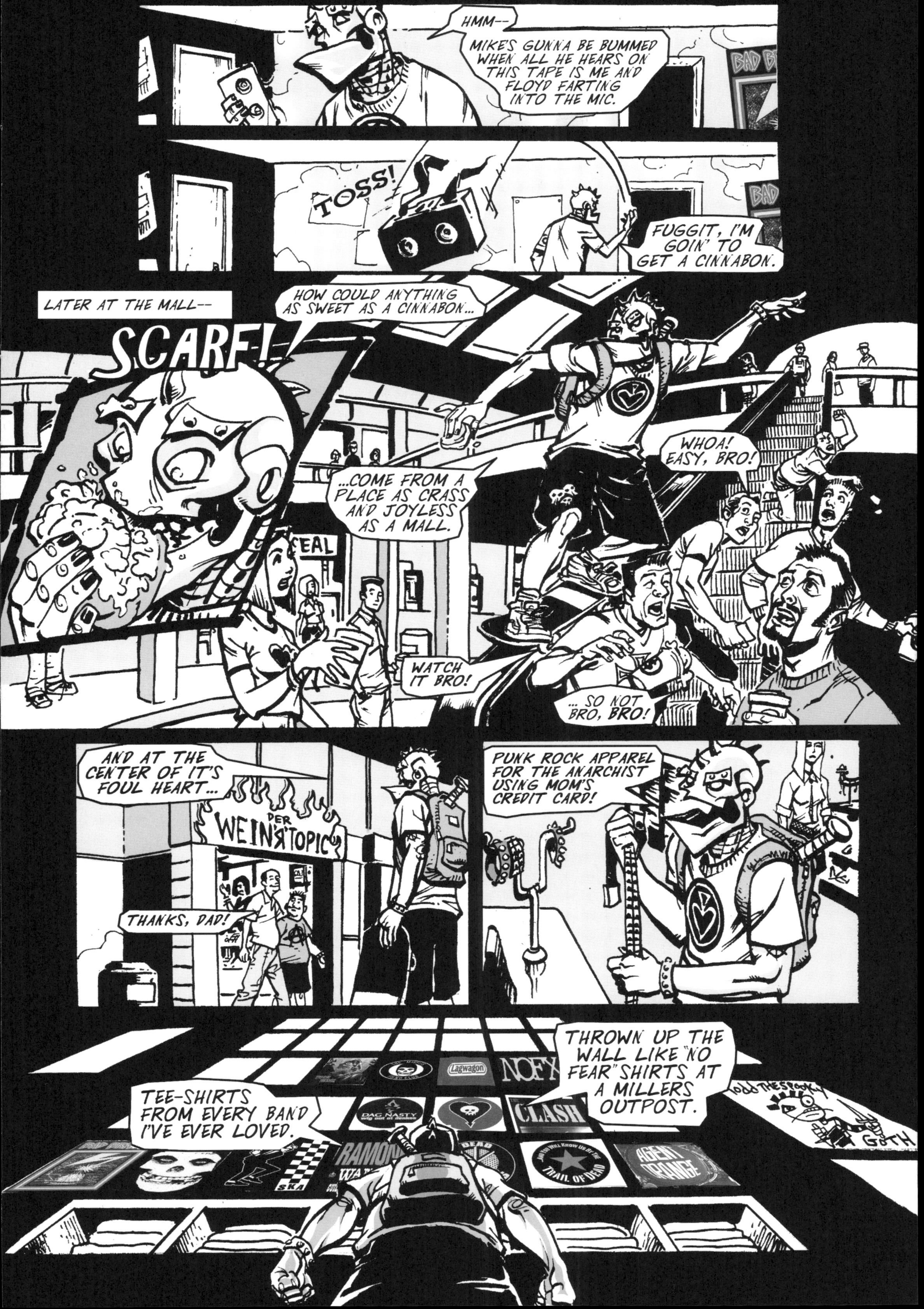
HMM--
MIKE'S GUNNA BE BUMMED WHEN ALL HE HEARS ON THIS TAPE IS ME AND FLOYD FARTING INTO THE MIC.
TOSS!
FUGGIT, I'M GOIN' TO GET A CINNABON.
LATER AT THE MALL--
HOW COULD ANYTHING AS SWEET AS A CINNABON...
SCARF!
...COME FROM A PLACE AS CRASS AND JOYLESS AS A MALL.
WHOA! EASY, BRO!
WATCH IT BRO!
...SO NOT BRO, BRO!
AND AT THE CENTER OF IT'S FOUL HEART...
WEIN DER 'R' TOPIC
THANKS, DAD!
PUNK ROCK APPAREL FOR THE ANARCHIST USING MOM'S CREDIT CARD!
TEE-SHIRTS FROM EVERY BAND I'VE EVER LOVED.
THROWN UP THE WALL LIKE "NO FEAR" SHIRTS AT A MILLERS OUTPOST.
Lagwagon
NOFX
DAG NASTY
CLASH
RAMONES
SKA
TRAIL OF DEAD
AGENT ORANGE

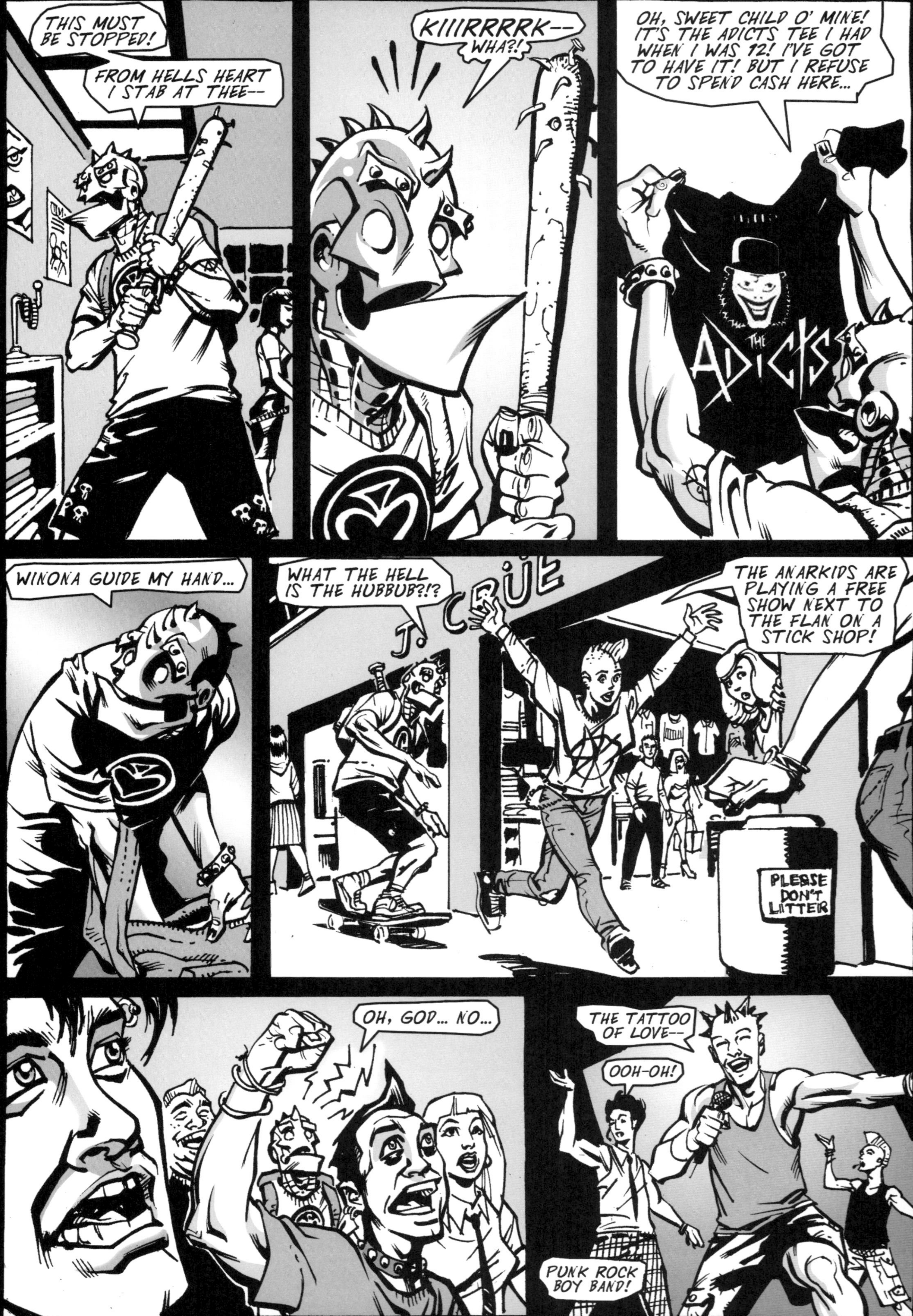

THIS MUST BE STOPPED!
FROM HELLS HEART I STAB AT THEE--
KIIIRRRRK--
WHA?!
OH, SWEET CHILD O' MINE! IT'S THE ADICTS TEE I HAD WHEN I WAS 12! I'VE GOT TO HAVE IT! BUT I REFUSE TO SPEND CASH HERE...
THE ADICTS
WINONA GUIDE MY HAND...
WHAT THE HELL IS THE HUBBUB?!?
J. CRÜE
THE ANARKIDS ARE PLAYING A FREE SHOW NEXT TO THE FLAN ON A STICK SHOP!
PLEASE DON'T LITTER
OH, GOD... NO...
THE TATTOO OF LOVE--
OOH-OH!
PUNK ROCK BOY BAND!

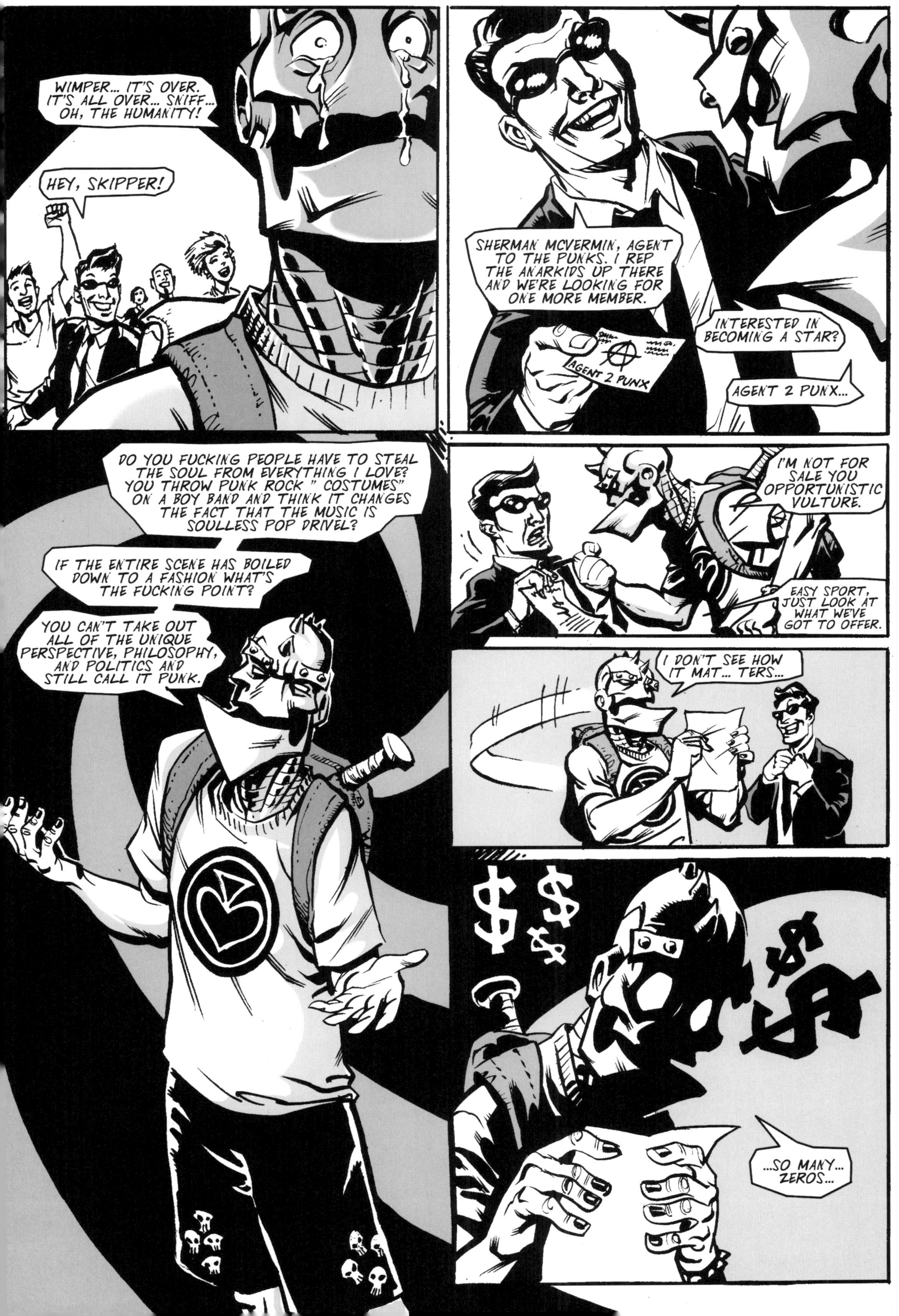
WIMPER... IT'S OVER. IT'S ALL OVER... SNIFF... OH, THE HUMANITY!
HEY, SKIPPER!
SHERMAN MCVERMIN, AGENT TO THE PUNKS. I REP THE ANARKIDS UP THERE AND WE'RE LOOKING FOR ONE MORE MEMBER.
INTERESTED IN BECOMING A STAR?
AGENT 2 PUNX
AGENT 2 PUNX...
DO YOU FUCKING PEOPLE HAVE TO STEAL THE SOUL FROM EVERYTHING I LOVE? YOU THROW PUNK ROCK "COSTUMES" ON A BOY BAND AND THINK IT CHANGES THE FACT THAT THE MUSIC IS SOULLESS POP DRIVEL?
IF THE ENTIRE SCENE HAS BOILED DOWN TO A FASHION WHAT'S THE FUCKING POINT?
YOU CAN'T TAKE OUT ALL OF THE UNIQUE PERSPECTIVE, PHILOSOPHY, AND POLITICS AND STILL CALL IT PUNK.
I'M NOT FOR SALE YOU OPPORTUNISTIC VULTURE.
EASY SPORT, JUST LOOK AT WHAT WE'VE GOT TO OFFER.
I DON'T SEE HOW IT MAT... TERS...
...SO MANY... ZEROS...

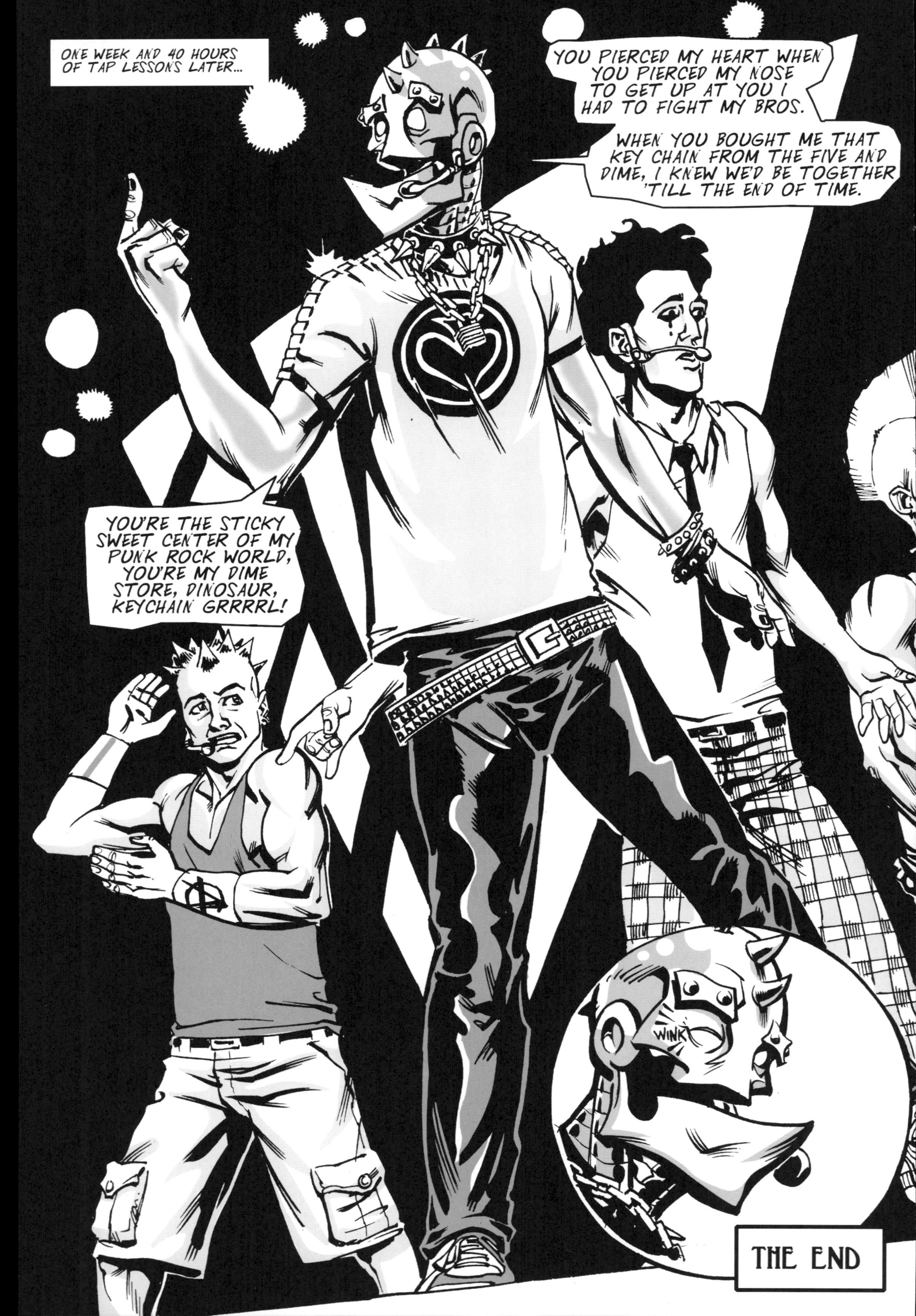

ONE WEEK AND 40 HOURS OF TAP LESSONS LATER...
YOU PIERCED MY HEART WHEN YOU PIERCED MY NOSE TO GET UP AT YOU I HAD TO FIGHT MY BROS.
WHEN YOU BOUGHT ME THAT KEY CHAIN FROM THE FIVE AND DIME, I KNEW WE'D BE TOGETHER 'TILL THE END OF TIME.
YOU'RE THE STICKY SWEET CENTER OF MY PUNK ROCK WORLD, YOU'RE MY DIME STORE, DINOSAUR, KEYCHAIN GRRRRL!
WINK
THE END

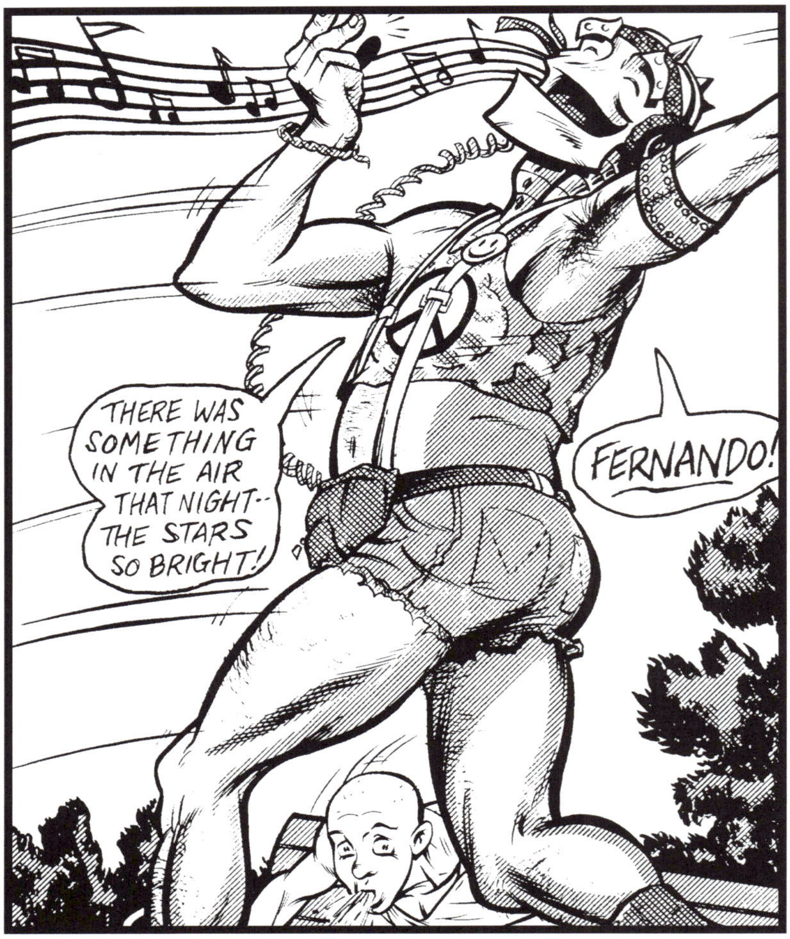
THERE WAS SOMETHING IN THE AIR THAT NIGHT-- THE STARS SO BRIGHT!
FERNANDO!

SEVEN
I LOVE LIVIN' IN THE CITY

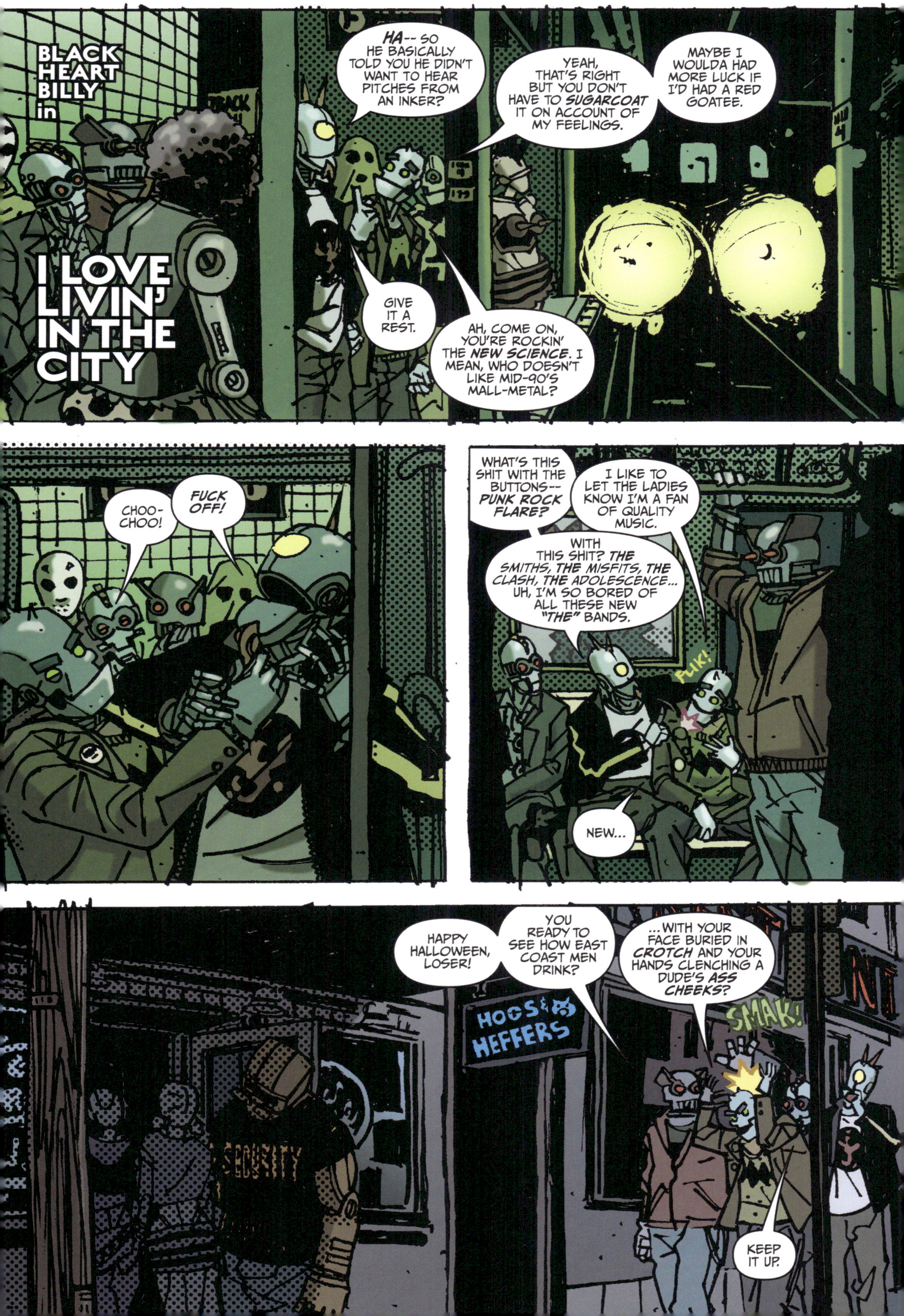

BLACK HEART BILLY in
I LOVE LIVIN' IN THE CITY
HA-- SO HE BASICALLY TOLD YOU HE DIDN'T WANT TO HEAR PITCHES FROM AN INKER?
YEAH, THAT'S RIGHT BUT YOU DON'T HAVE TO SUGARCOAT IT ON ACCOUNT OF MY FEELINGS.
MAYBE I WOULDA HAD MORE LUCK IF I'D HAD A RED GOATEE.
GIVE IT A REST.
AH, COME ON, YOU'RE ROCKIN' THE NEW SCIENCE. I MEAN, WHO DOESN'T LIKE MID-90'S MALL-METAL?
CHOO-CHOO!
FUCK OFF!
WHAT'S THIS SHIT WITH THE BUTTONS-- PUNK ROCK FLARE?
I LIKE TO LET THE LADIES KNOW I'M A FAN OF QUALITY MUSIC.
WITH THIS SHIT? THE SMITHS, THE MISFITS, THE CLASH, THE ADOLESCENCE... UH, I'M SO BORED OF ALL THESE NEW "THE" BANDS.
FLIK!
NEW...
HAPPY HALLOWEEN, LOSER!
YOU READY TO SEE HOW EAST COAST MEN DRINK?
...WITH YOUR FACE BURIED IN CROTCH AND YOUR HANDS CLENCHING A DUDE'S ASS CHEEKS?
HOGS & HEFFERS
SMAK!
SECURITY
KEEP IT UP.

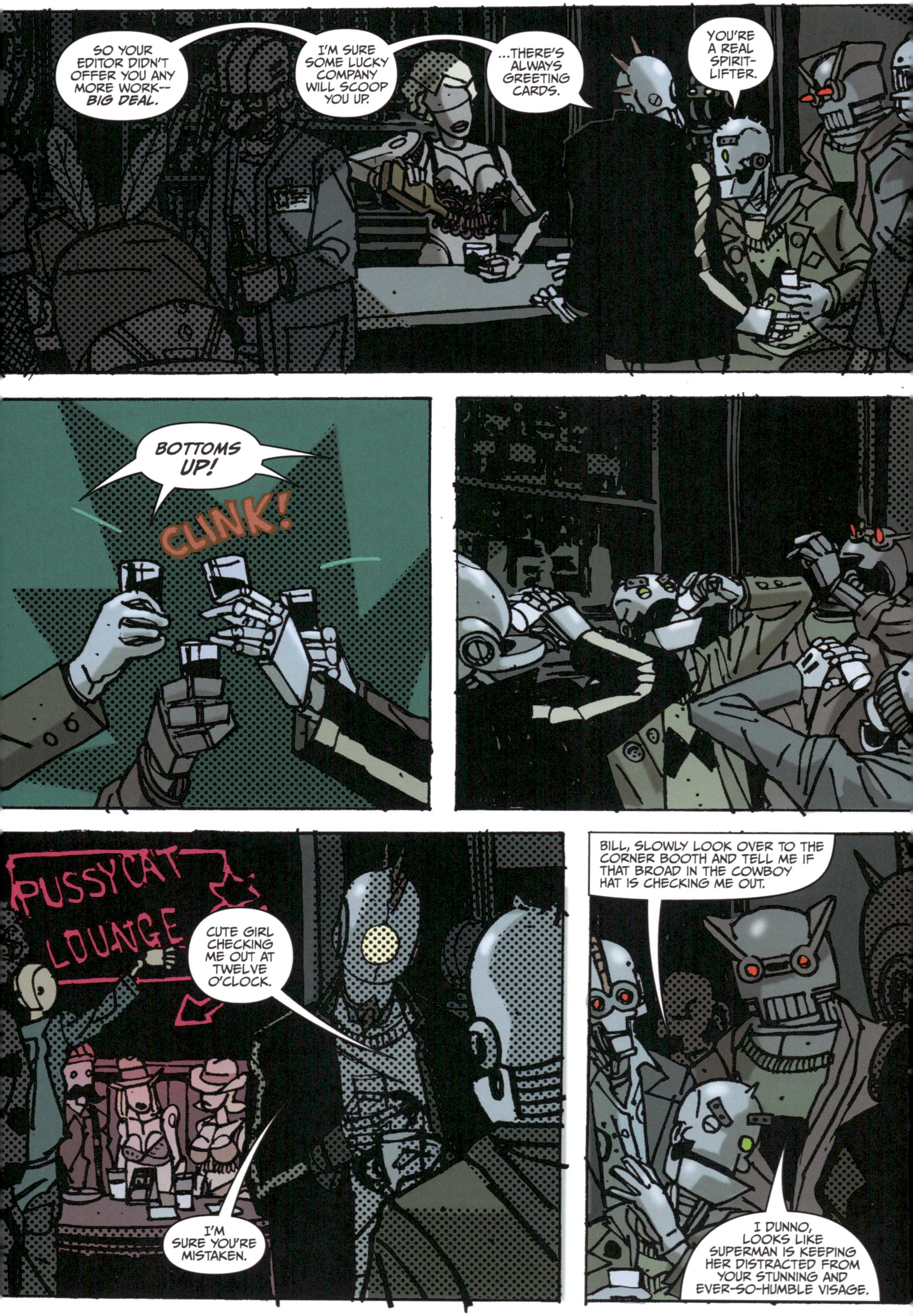
SO YOUR EDITOR DIDN'T OFFER YOU ANY MORE WORK-- BIG DEAL.
I'M SURE SOME LUCKY COMPANY WILL SCOOP YOU UP.
...THERE'S ALWAYS GREETING CARDS.
YOU'RE A REAL SPIRIT-LIFTER.
BOTTOMS UP!
CLINK!
PUSSYCAT LOUNGE
CUTE GIRL CHECKING ME OUT AT TWELVE O'CLOCK.
I'M SURE YOU'RE MISTAKEN.
BILL, SLOWLY LOOK OVER TO THE CORNER BOOTH AND TELL ME IF THAT BROAD IN THE COWBOY HAT IS CHECKING ME OUT.
I DUNNO, LOOKS LIKE SUPERMAN IS KEEPING HER DISTRACTED FROM YOUR STUNNING AND EVER-SO-HUMBLE VISAGE.

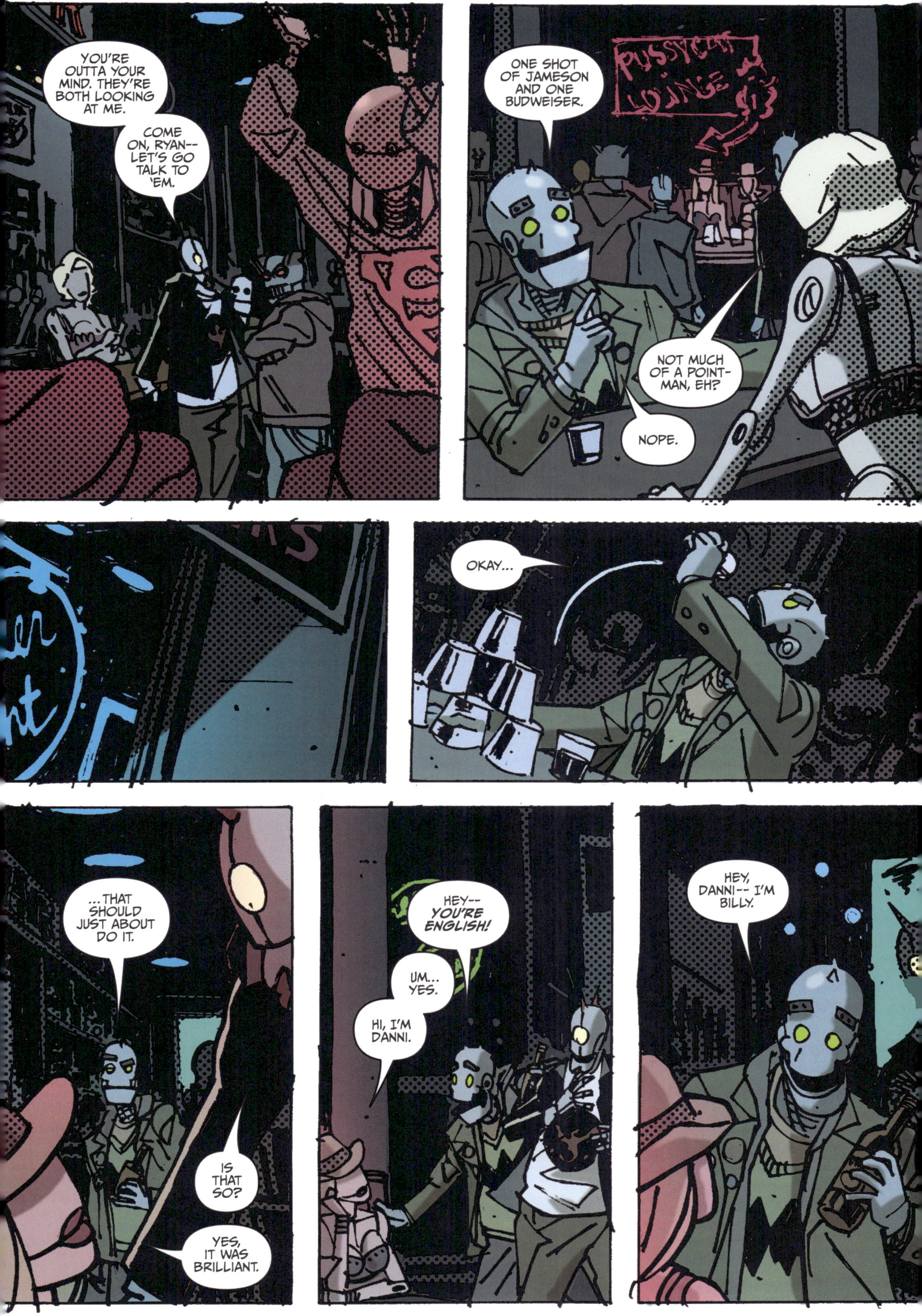

YOU'RE OUTTA YOUR MIND. THEY'RE BOTH LOOKING AT ME.
COME ON, RYAN-- LET'S GO TALK TO 'EM.
PUSSYCAT LOUNGE
ONE SHOT OF JAMESON AND ONE BUDWEISER.
NOT MUCH OF A POINT-MAN, EH?
NOPE.
OKAY...
...THAT SHOULD JUST ABOUT DO IT.
IS THAT SO?
YES, IT WAS BRILLIANT.
HEY-- YOU'RE ENGLISH!
UM... YES.
HI, I'M DANNI.
HEY, DANNI-- I'M BILLY.

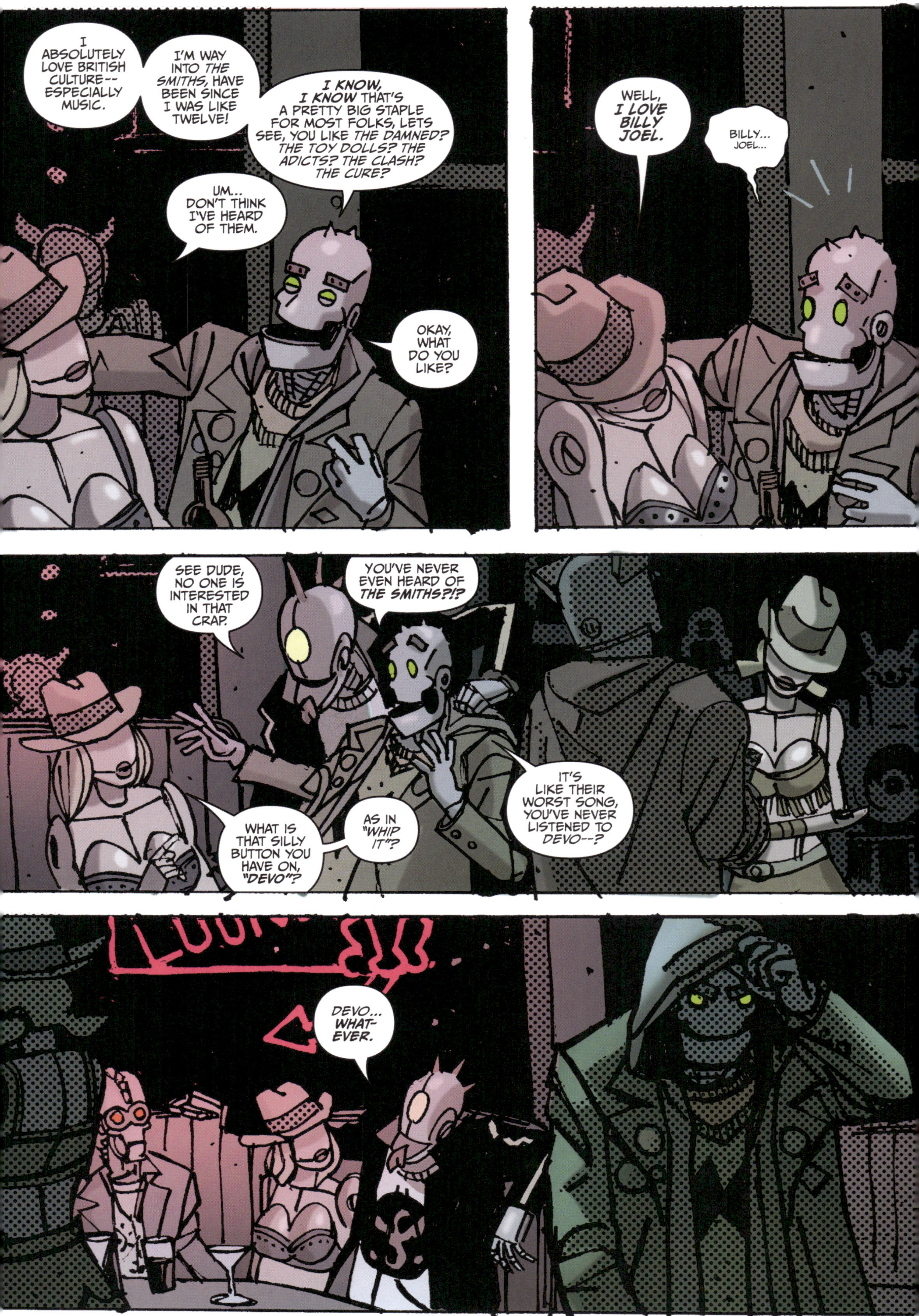
I ABSOLUTELY LOVE BRITISH CULTURE-- ESPECIALLY MUSIC.
I'M WAY INTO *THE SMITHS*, HAVE BEEN SINCE I WAS LIKE TWELVE!
UM... DON'T THINK I'VE HEARD OF THEM.
I KNOW, I KNOW THAT'S A PRETTY BIG STAPLE FOR MOST FOLKS, LETS SEE, YOU LIKE *THE DAMNED? THE TOY DOLLS? THE ADICTS? THE CLASH? THE CURE?*
OKAY, WHAT DO YOU LIKE?
WELL, ***I LOVE BILLY JOEL.***
BILLY... JOEL...
SEE DUDE, NO ONE IS INTERESTED IN THAT CRAP.
YOU'VE NEVER EVEN HEARD OF ***THE SMITHS?!?***
WHAT IS THAT SILLY BUTTON YOU HAVE ON, ***"DEVO"?***
AS IN *"WHIP IT"?*
IT'S LIKE THEIR WORST SONG, YOU'VE NEVER LISTENED TO *DEVO--?*
DEVO... ***WHAT-EVER.***

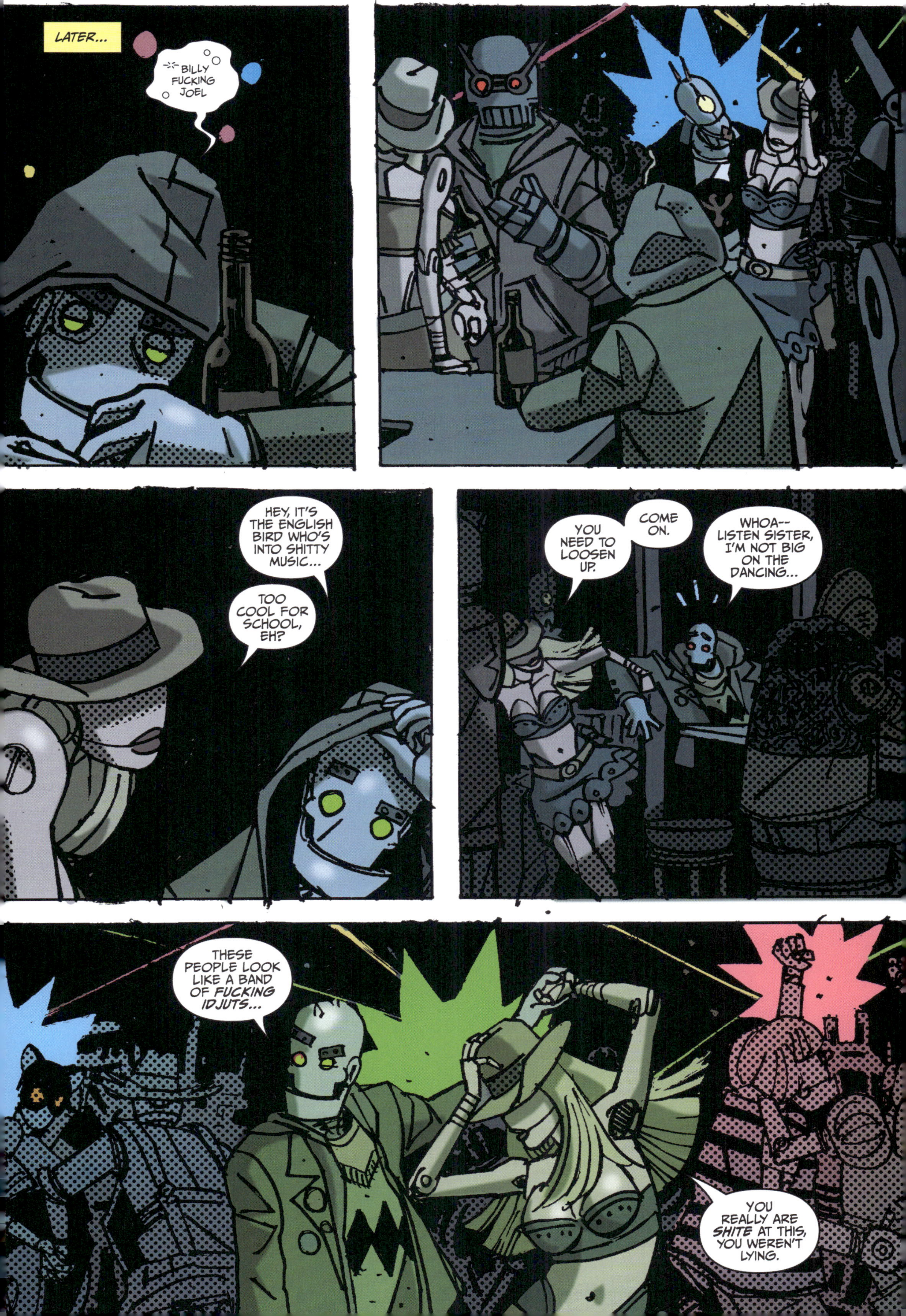
LATER...
BILLY FUCKING JOEL
HEY, IT'S THE ENGLISH BIRD WHO'S INTO SHITTY MUSIC...
TOO COOL FOR SCHOOL, EH?
YOU NEED TO LOOSEN UP.
COME ON.
WHOA-- LISTEN SISTER, I'M NOT BIG ON THE DANCING...
THESE PEOPLE LOOK LIKE A BAND OF *FUCKING IDJUTS*...
YOU REALLY ARE *SHITE* AT THIS, YOU WEREN'T LYING.

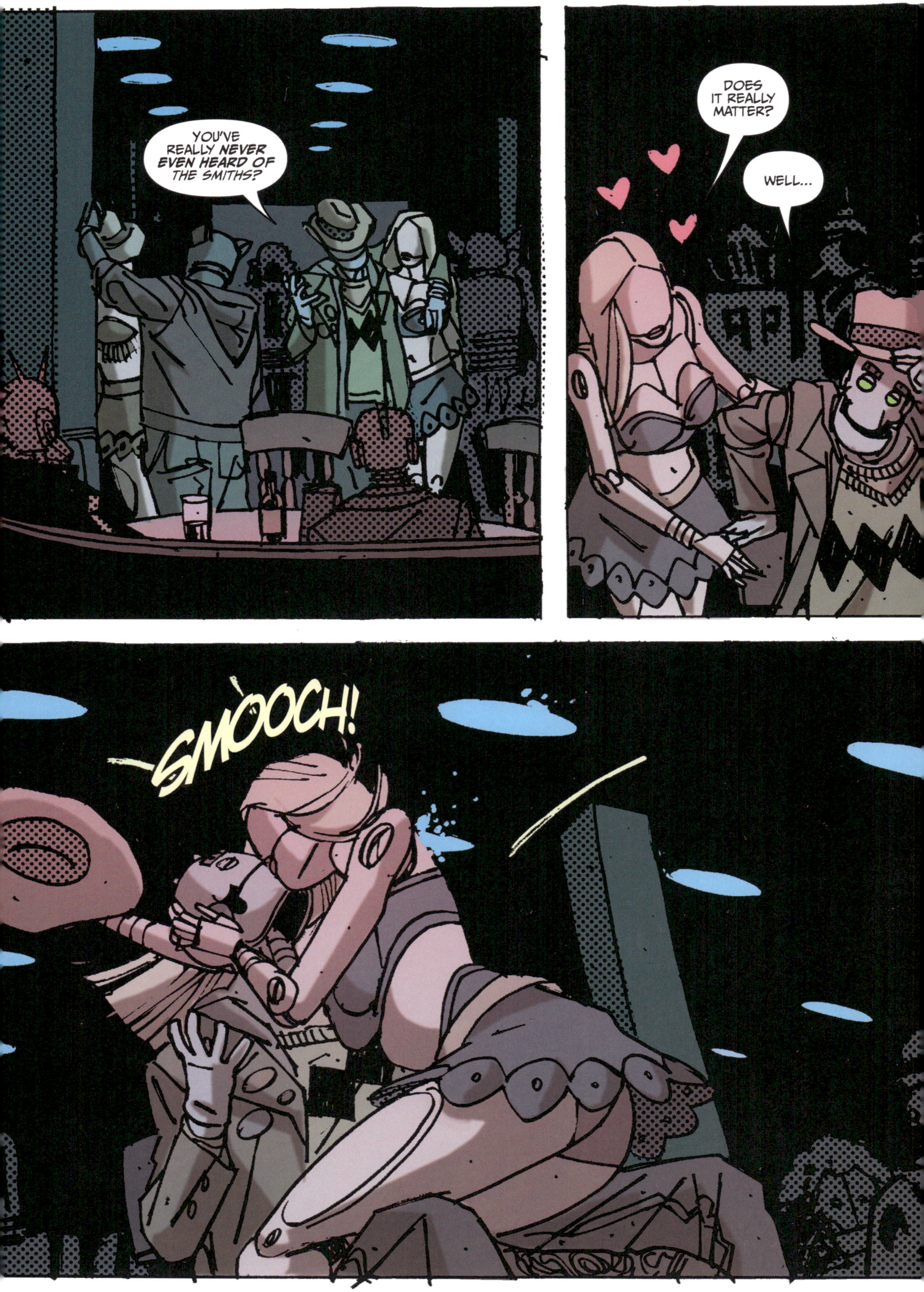
YOU'VE REALLY NEVER EVEN HEARD OF THE SMITHS?
DOES IT REALLY MATTER?
WELL...
SMOOCH!

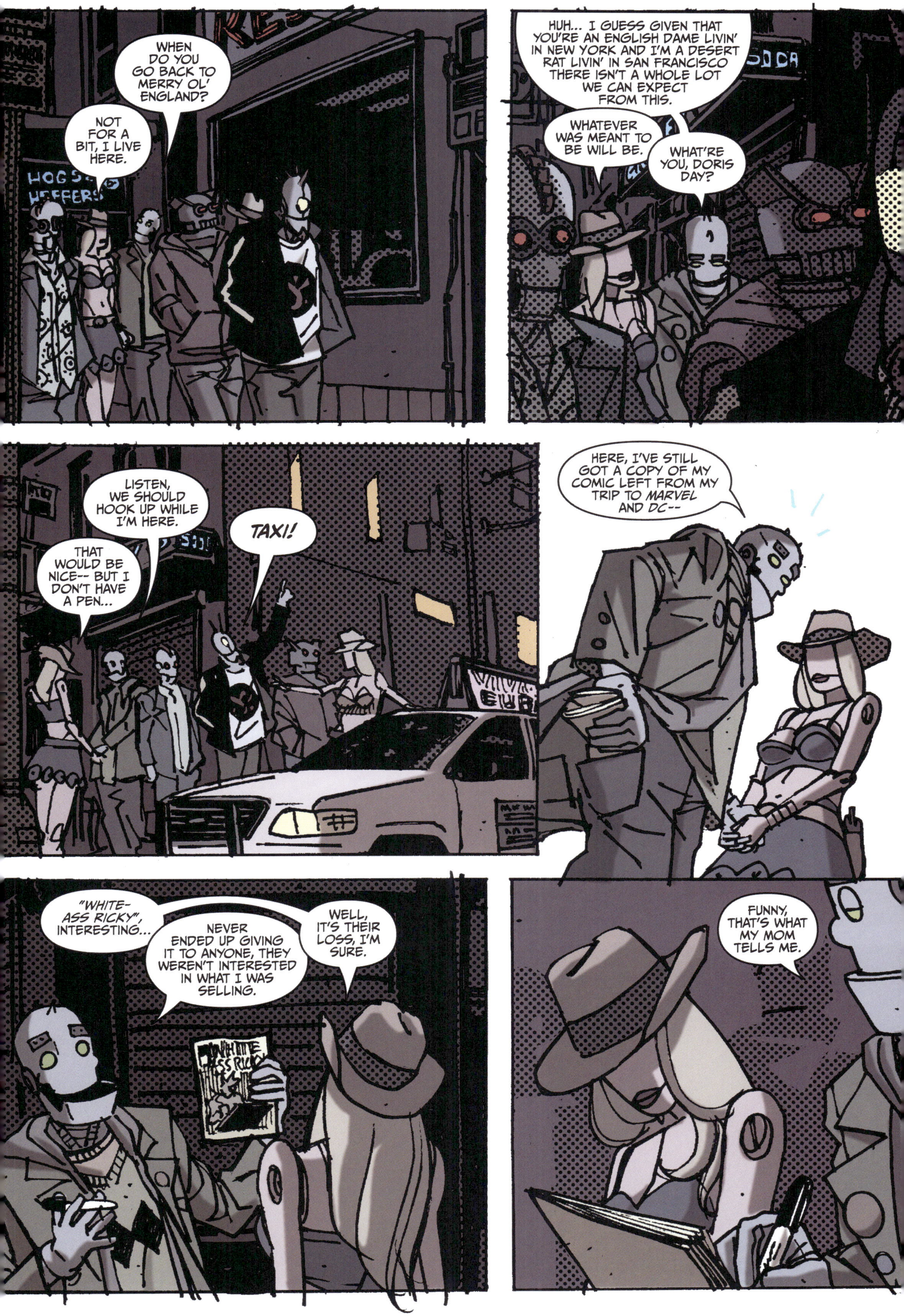
WHEN DO YOU GO BACK TO MERRY OL' ENGLAND?
NOT FOR A BIT, I LIVE HERE.
HUH... I GUESS GIVEN THAT YOU'RE AN ENGLISH DAME LIVIN' IN NEW YORK AND I'M A DESERT RAT LIVIN' IN SAN FRANCISCO THERE ISN'T A WHOLE LOT WE CAN EXPECT FROM THIS.
WHATEVER WAS MEANT TO BE WILL BE.
WHAT'RE YOU, DORIS DAY?
LISTEN, WE SHOULD HOOK UP WHILE I'M HERE.
THAT WOULD BE NICE-- BUT I DON'T HAVE A PEN...
TAXI!
HERE, I'VE STILL GOT A COPY OF MY COMIC LEFT FROM MY TRIP TO *MARVEL* AND *DC*--
"WHITE-ASS RICKY", INTERESTING...
NEVER ENDED UP GIVING IT TO ANYONE, THEY WEREN'T INTERESTED IN WHAT I WAS SELLING.
WELL, IT'S THEIR LOSS, I'M SURE.
FUNNY, THAT'S WHAT MY MOM TELLS ME.

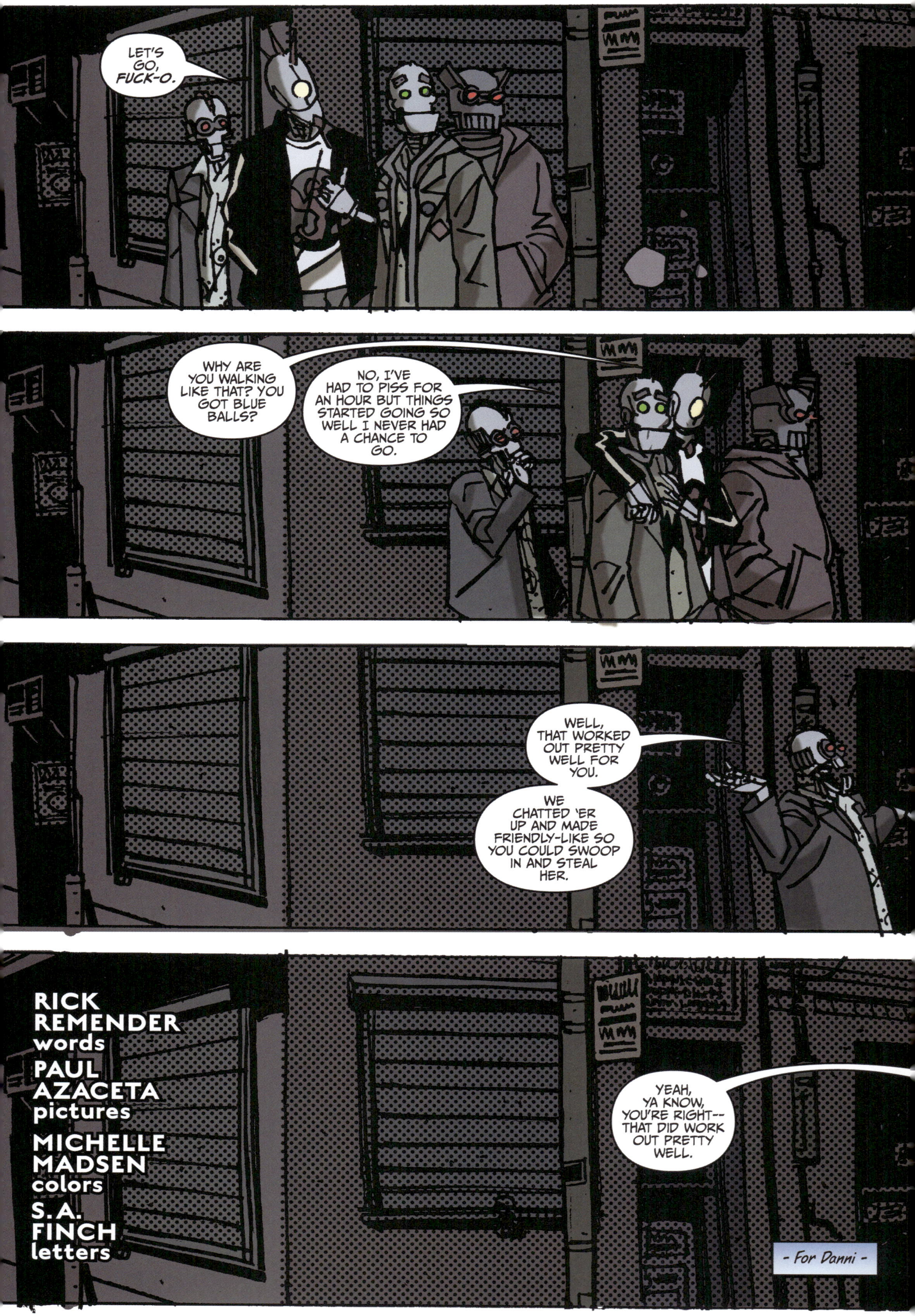
LET'S GO, FUCK-O.
WHY ARE YOU WALKING LIKE THAT? YOU GOT BLUE BALLS?
NO, I'VE HAD TO PISS FOR AN HOUR BUT THINGS STARTED GOING SO WELL I NEVER HAD A CHANCE TO GO.
WELL, THAT WORKED OUT PRETTY WELL FOR YOU.
WE CHATTED 'ER UP AND MADE FRIENDLY-LIKE SO YOU COULD SWOOP IN AND STEAL HER.
RICK REMENDER words
PAUL AZACETA pictures
MICHELLE MADSEN colors
S.A. FINCH letters
YEAH, YA KNOW, YOU'RE RIGHT-- THAT DID WORK OUT PRETTY WELL.
- For Danni -

EIGHT
HOW TO MISTAKE YOUR WAY INTO COMICS! (SKETCHES, ROUGHS & LEFTOVERS)

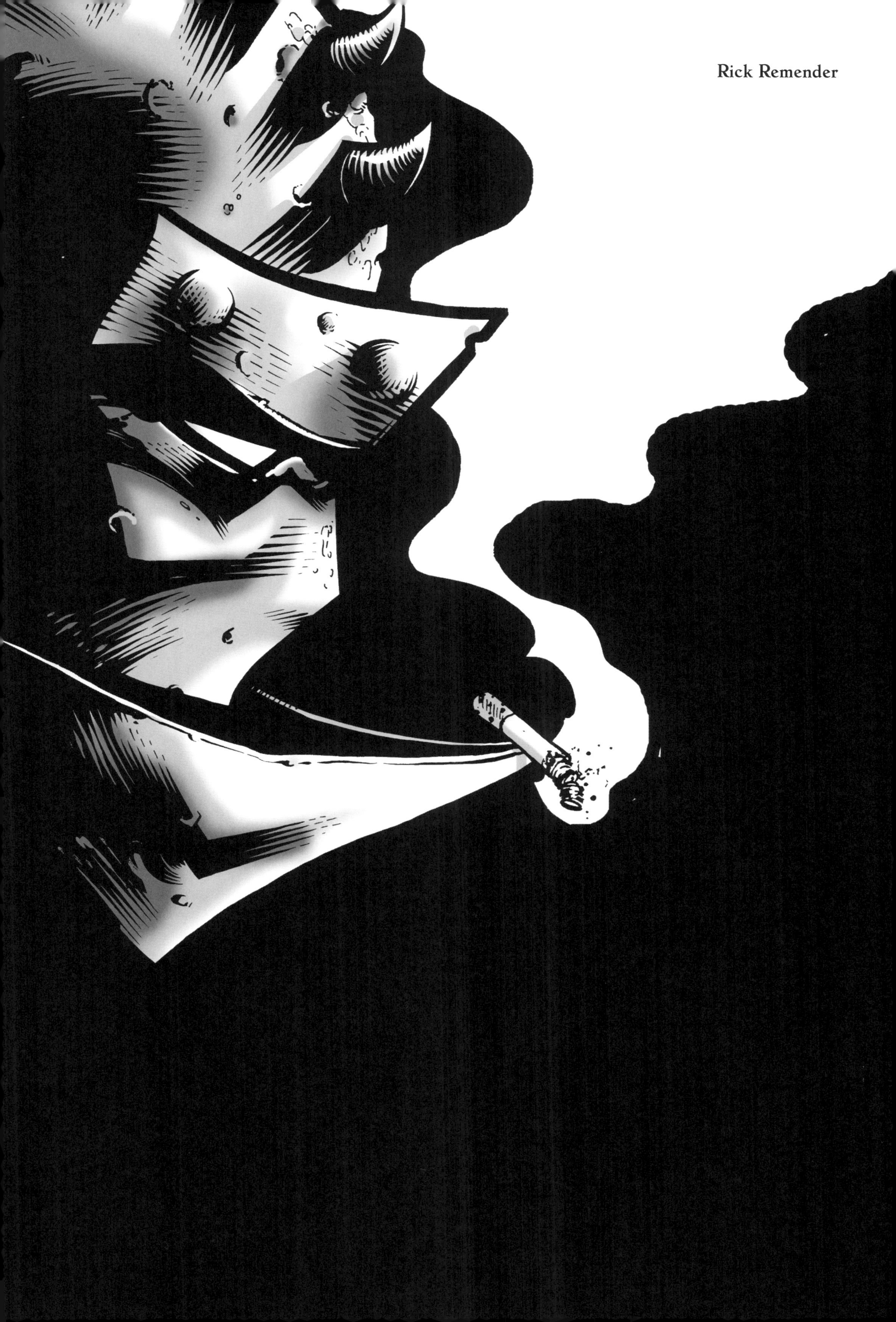

Rick Remender

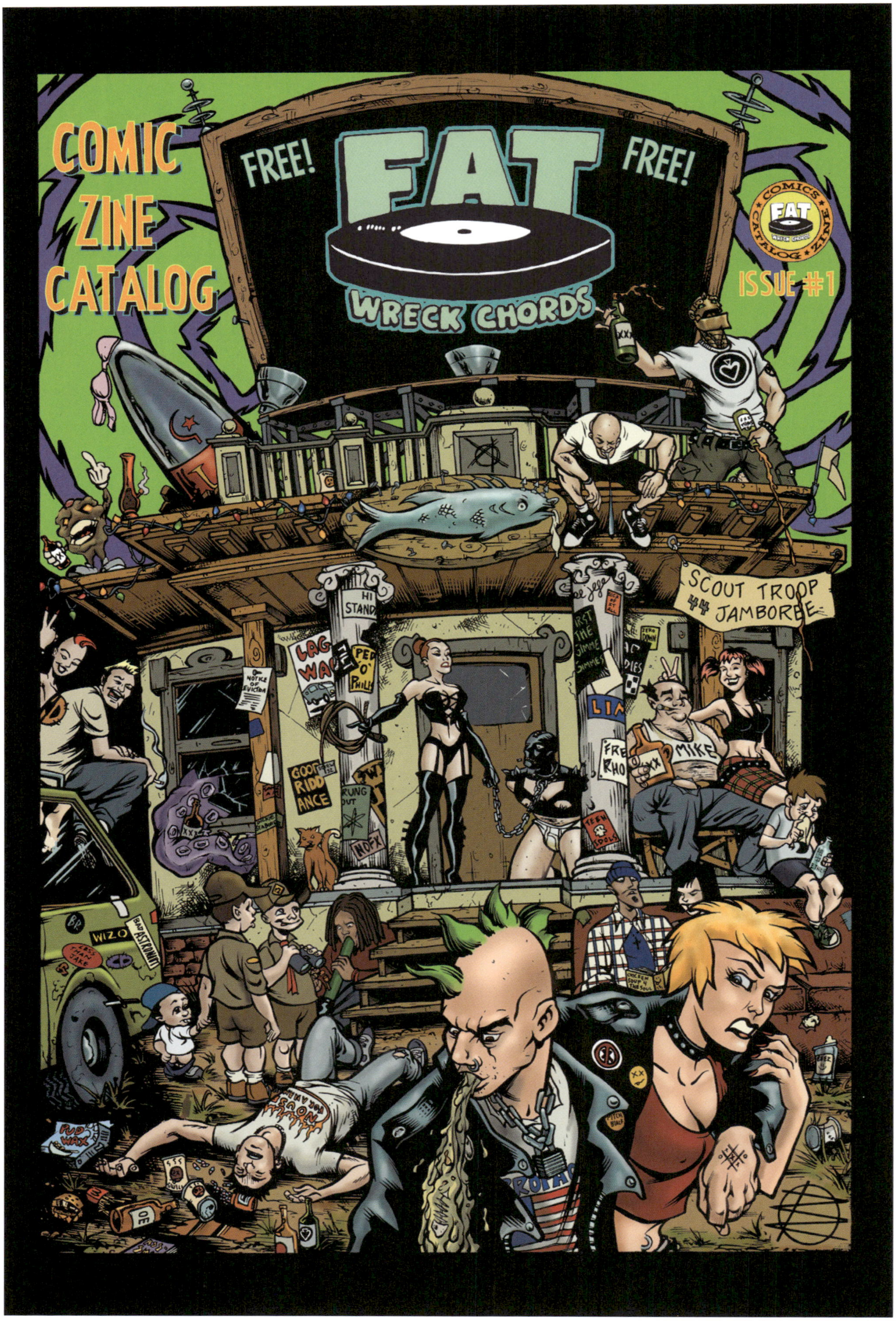
COMIC
ZINE
CATALOG
FREE!
FAT
WRECK CHORDS
FREE!
ISSUE #1
SCOUT TROOP
44 JAMBOREE
MIKE
WIZO
NOFX

Rick Remender

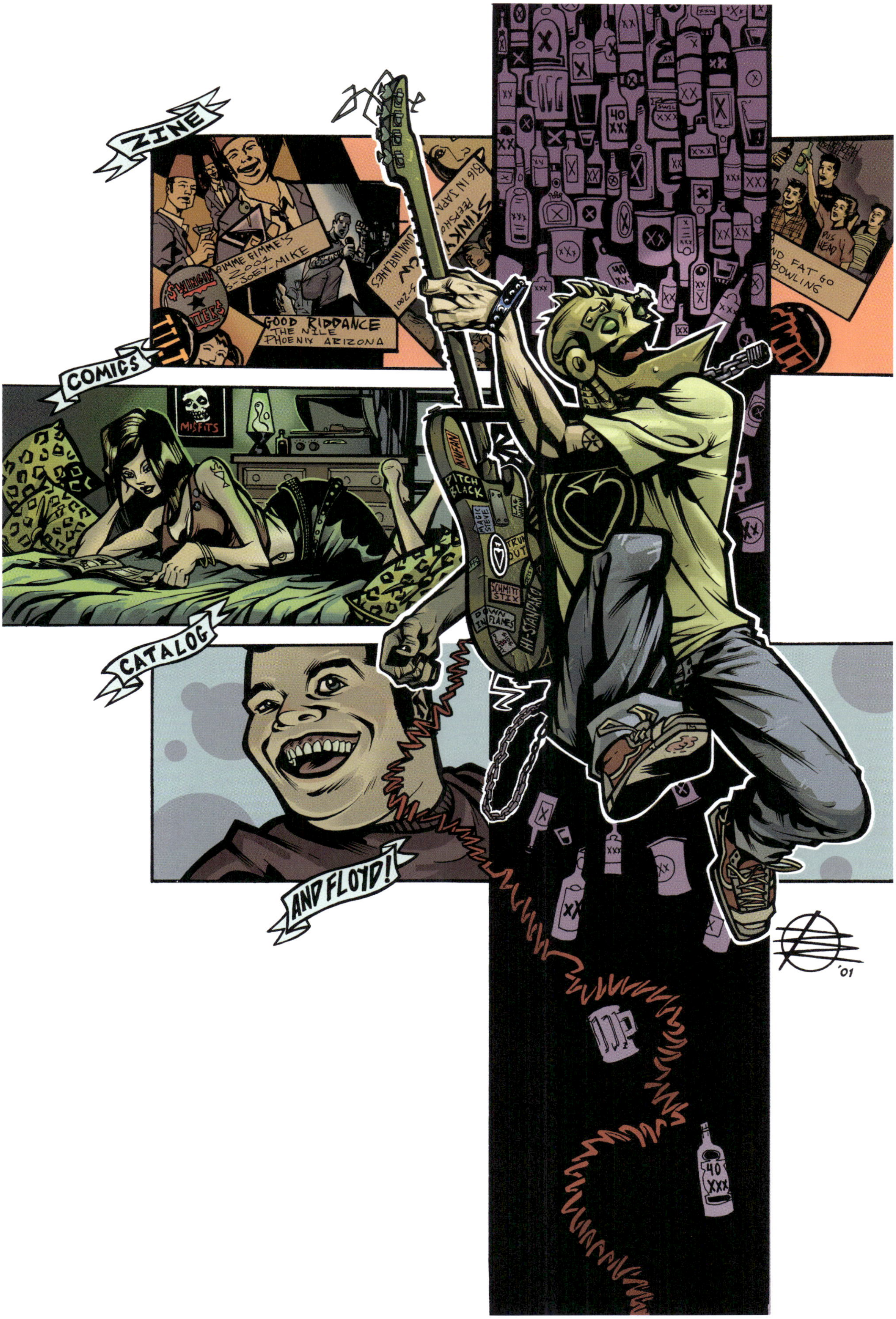
ZINE
GIMME GIMME'S
2001
S-JOEY-MIKE
GOOD RIDDANCE
THE NILE
PHOENIX ARIZONA
COMICS
MISFITS
PITCH BLACK
SCHMITT STIX
DOWN IN FLAMES
HI-STANDARD
CATALOG
AND FLOYD!
'01

Harper Jaten

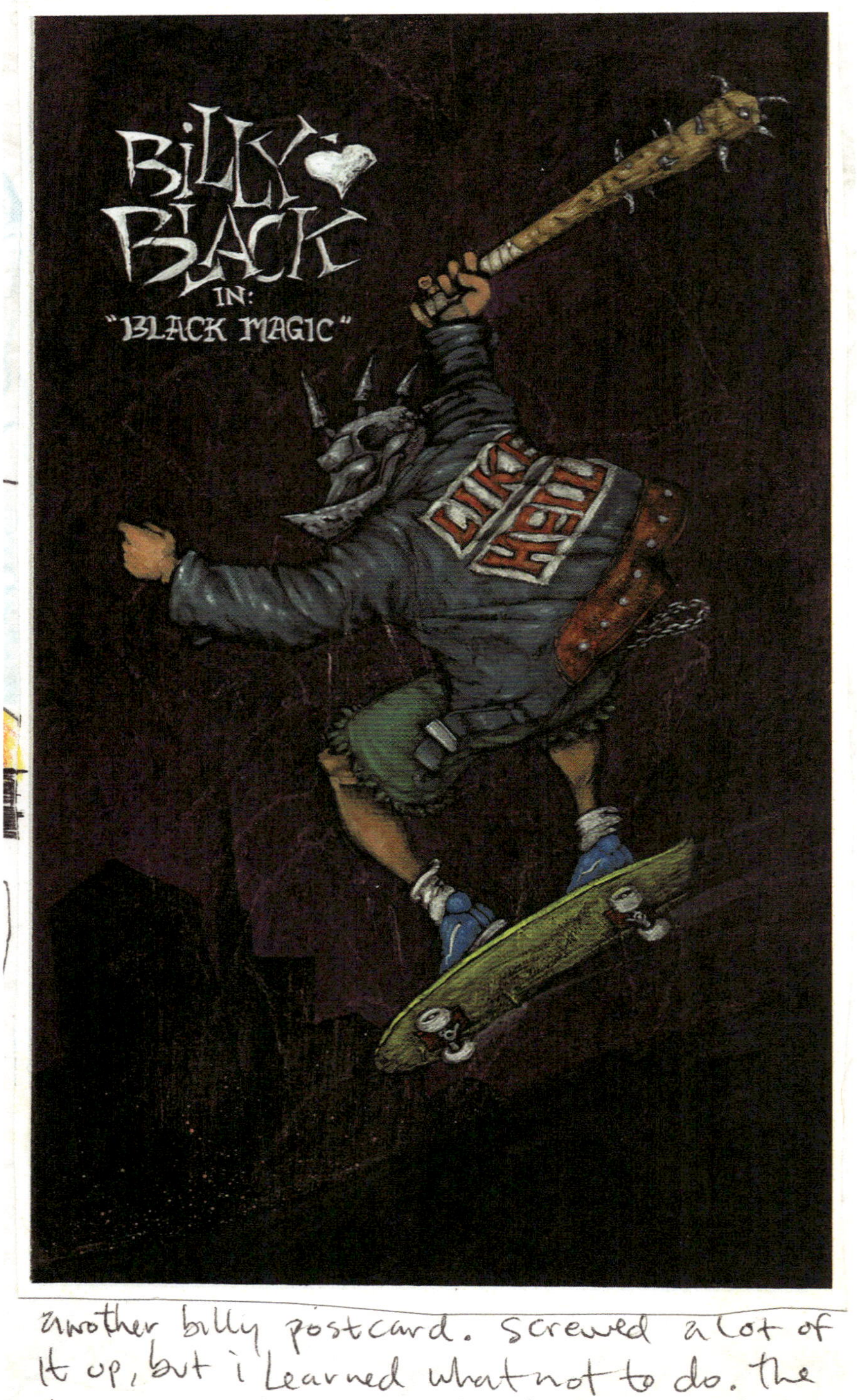
BILLY BLACK
IN:
"BLACK MAGIC"
LIKE HELL

another billy postcard. screwed a lot of
it up, but i learned what not to do. the

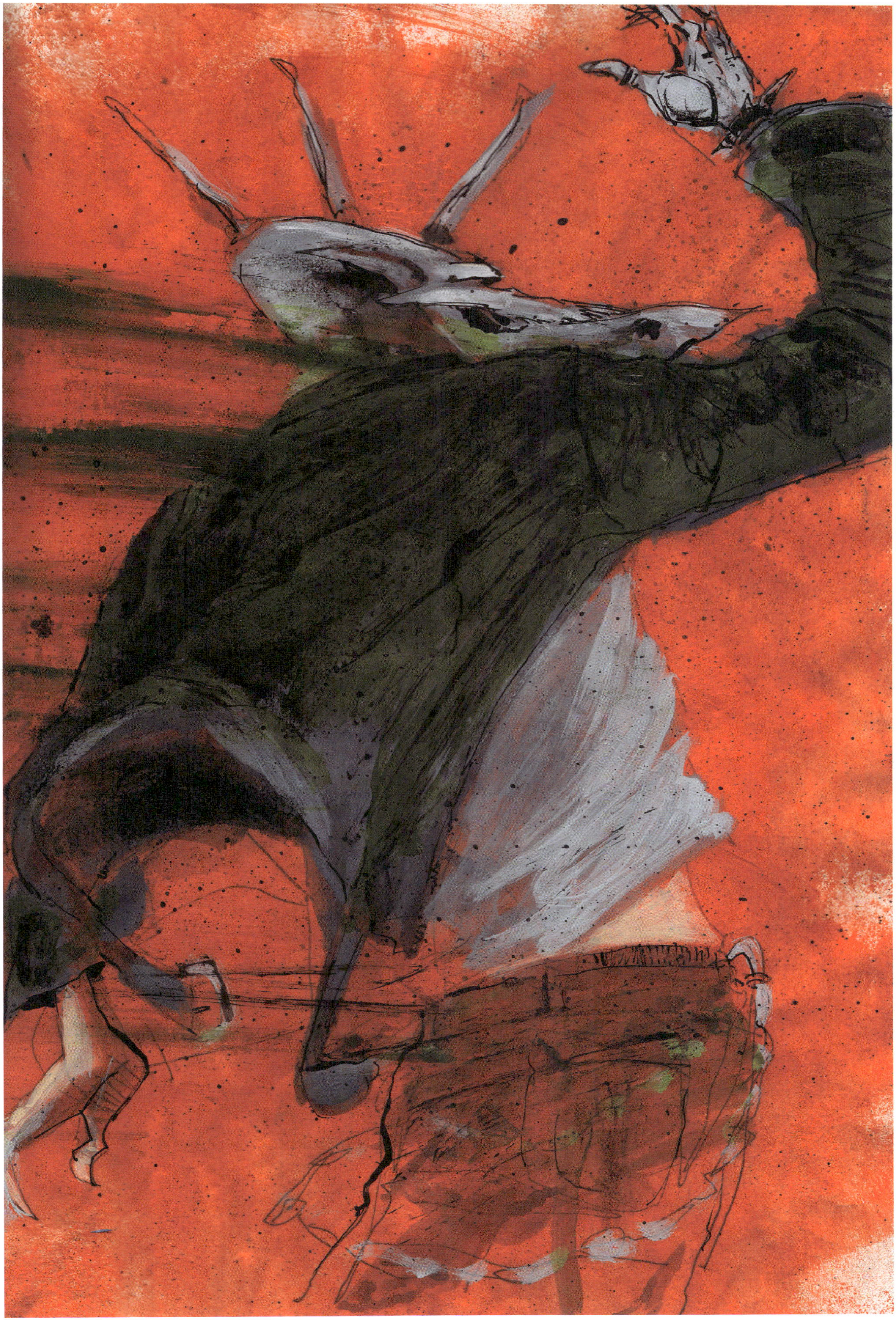

Rick Remender

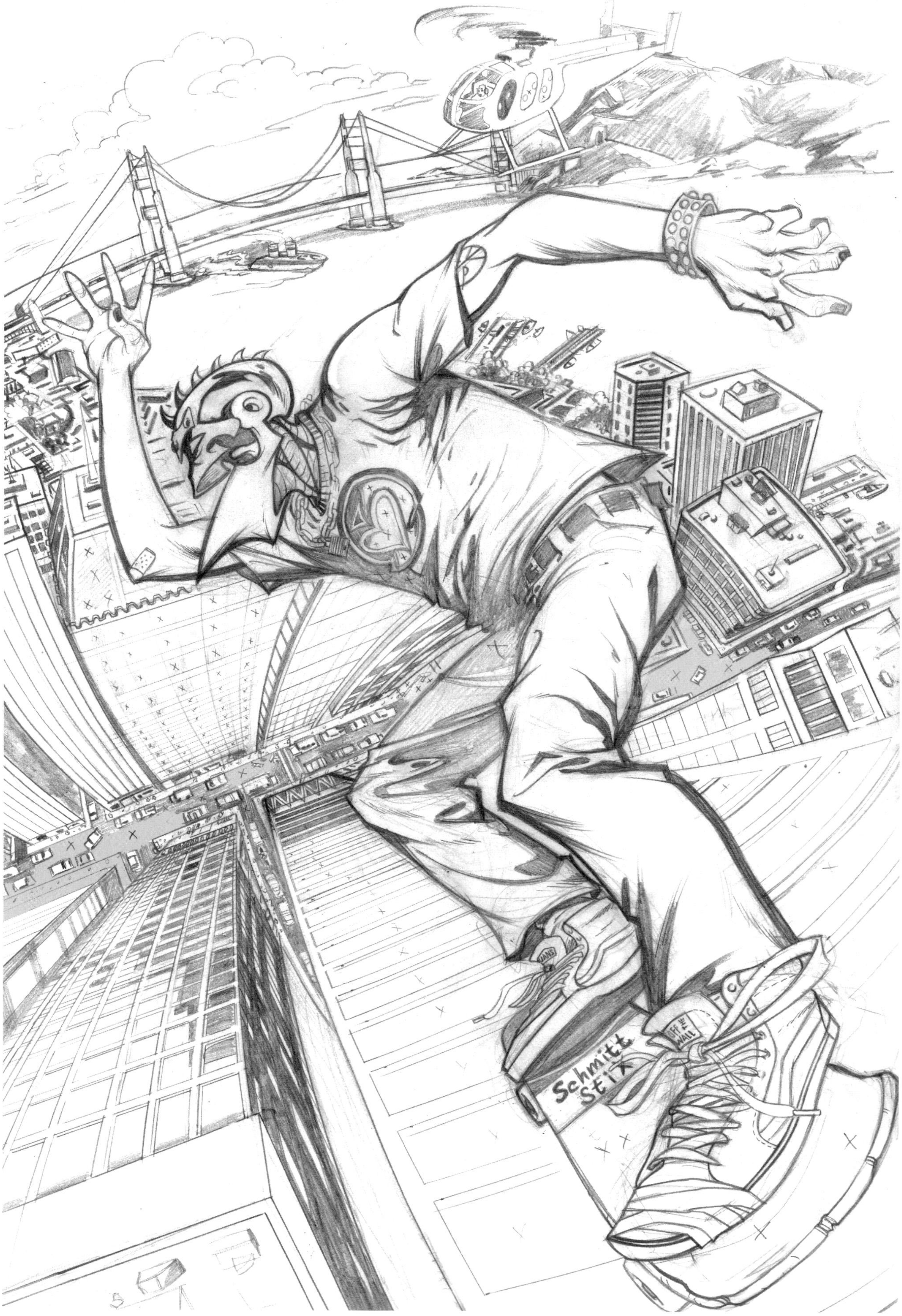
Schmitt Stix

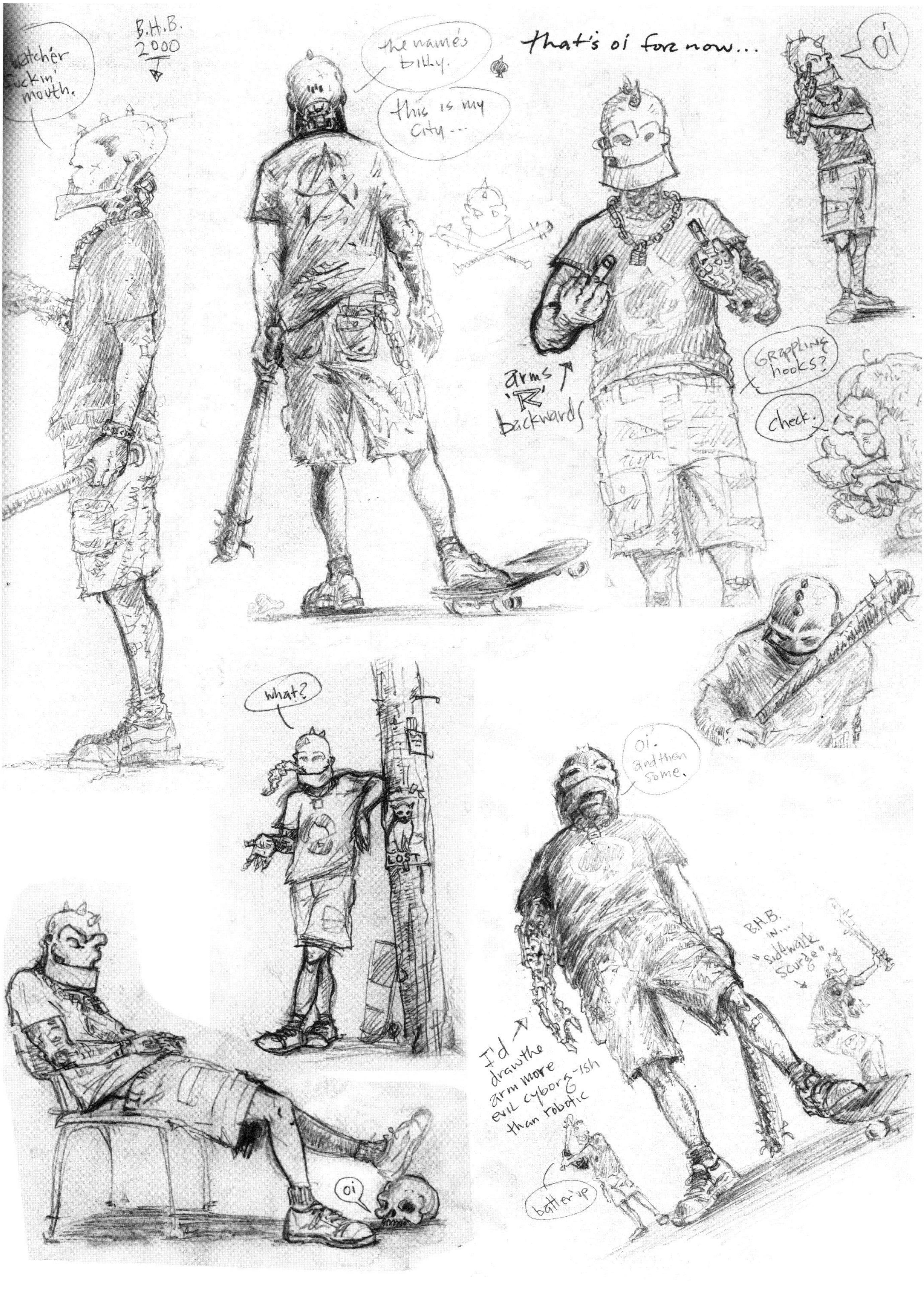
Watcher fuckin' mouth.
B.H.B. 2000
the name's billy.
this is my city...
that's oi for now...
oi
arms 'R' backwards
GRAPPLING hooks?
check.
what?
LOST
oi. and then some.
B.H.B. in... "sidewalk scurge"
I'd draw the arm more evil cyborg-ish than robotic
batter up
oi

Harper Jaten

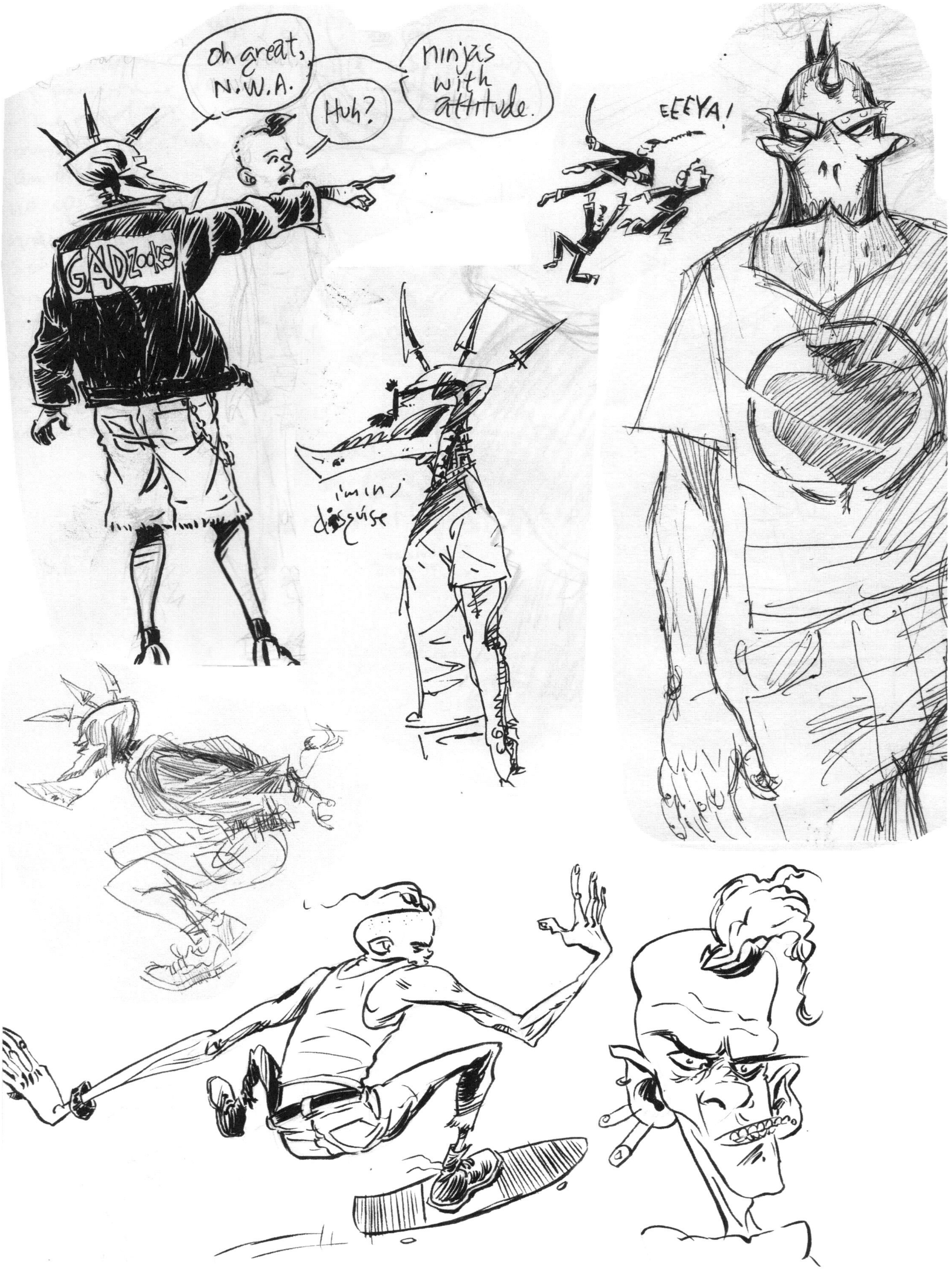
oh great, N.W.A.
Huh?
ninjas with attitude.
EEEYA!
GADZooks
i'm in disguise

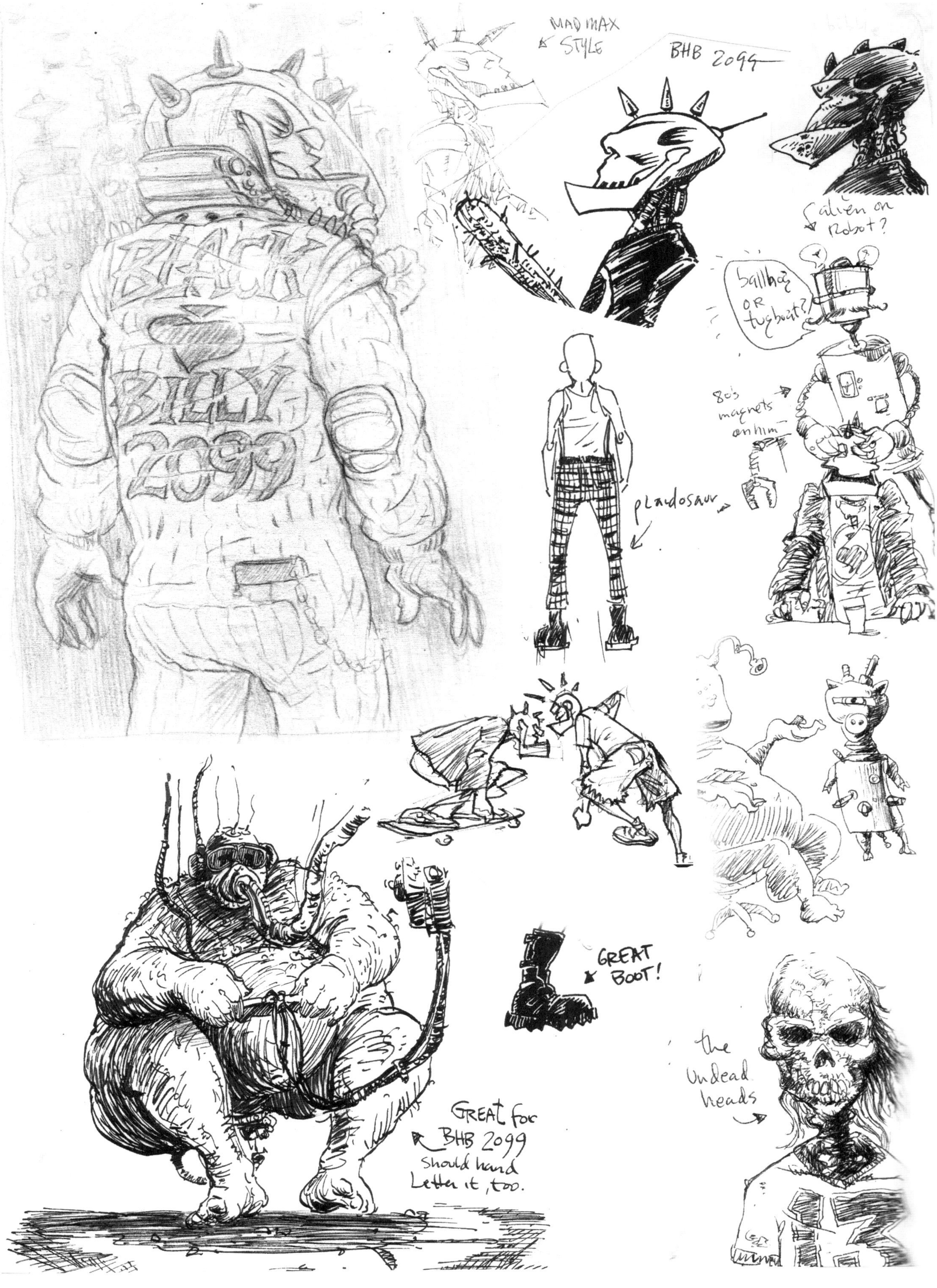
BLACK
BILLY
2099
MAD MAX STYLE
BHB 2099
alien on Robot?
ballhog or tugboat?
80's magnets on him
plaidosaur
GREAT BOOT!
the Undead heads
GREAT for BHB 2099 should hand Letter it, too.

long shot of sky high.

bh + oi: "Sky Highverson?"

Jc ½ shell when they see him

sky, projected: CIVIL code 32461 BREAKING and entering

bh: holy shit, yer a tub!

sky: this tub outskated your ass for the 3rd year in a row this morning...

bh: skate?! you can't even walk in the real world.

sky: this is the real world billy.

bh: huh?

sky: what use have we for limbs, or eyes ears or hygiene fashion sense when it's all virtual?

bh: back in the 19th, man we used to go outside. play kick the can, skate swimming to 7-11, ride bikes, play have fist fights in the front yard — we had yards, man.

sky: how much better today is – we never even have to leave our cubes. you can be anyone you want to be!

bh: how is that better? wouldn't want to be you

sky: and what is your problem w/technology, billy? you are technology. I looked in the mirror lately or machine head!

bh: tech is great. I love tech. but this is ridiculous but i'm not a couch rider watching someone else live. Reality TV? Shit ha!

So is this dialogue

bh: time for a reality check (smashes GRAVITATION chair)

sky falls to ground flopping beached whale

oi: (moves to teleporter) Let's beam tha fook outta 'ere...

bh: "nah, Let's go home old skool style"

cut to bust out the back door — steal skate boards + skate off in the acid rain.

Probably take more like 7 pgs to tell it right, but f. that S!!!

dear diary: i got some new fancy papermate med pt. pens at the store today and they suck asssss! No where near as black as that last magic one i had
Fok!
— oh i almost forgot, for some odd reason i'm wearing cowboy bootz! What. The?!!

LAST
SHOT

Berzerker
meow!
BAT OUTTA HELL!

2nd 2 Last

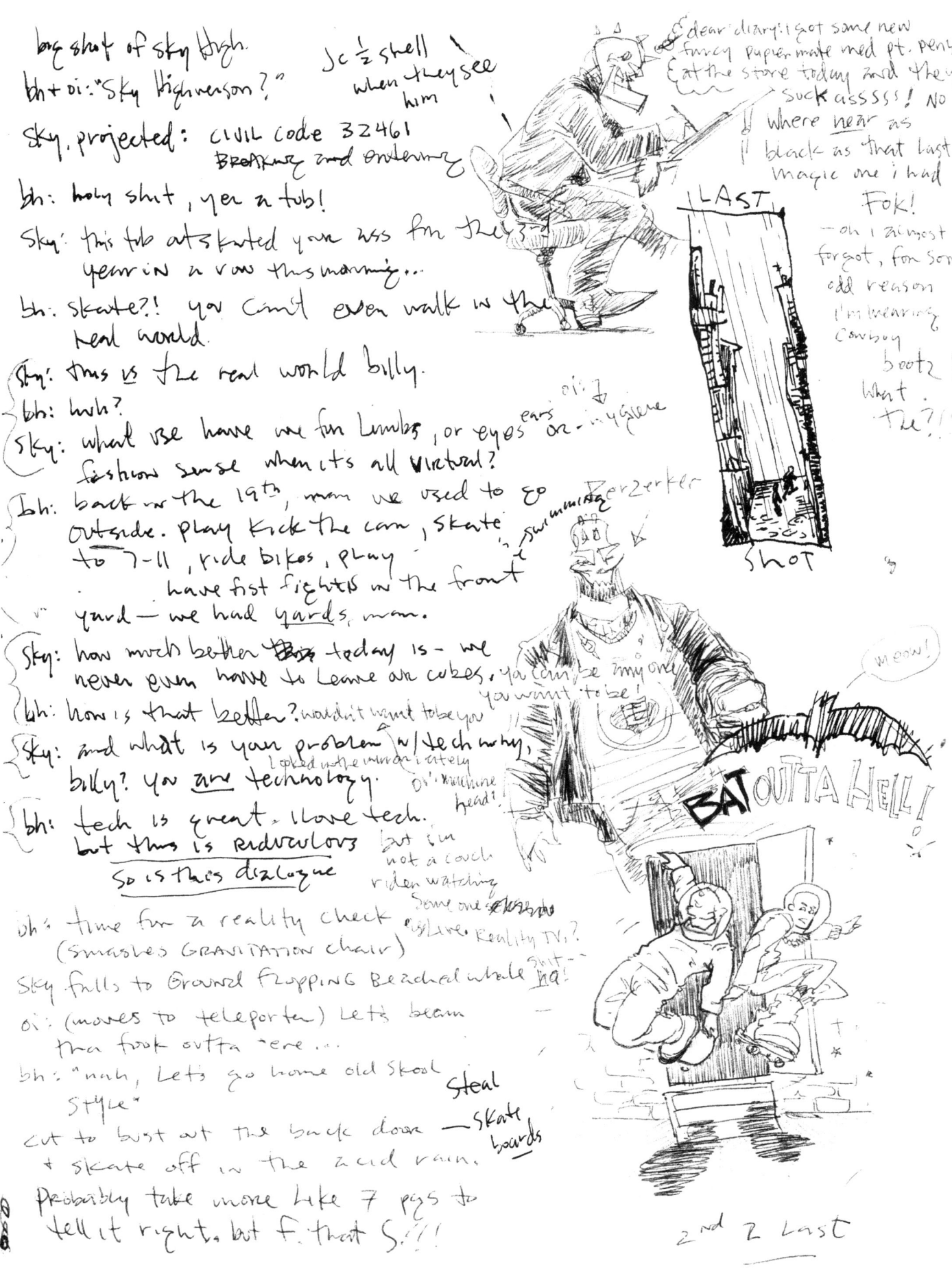

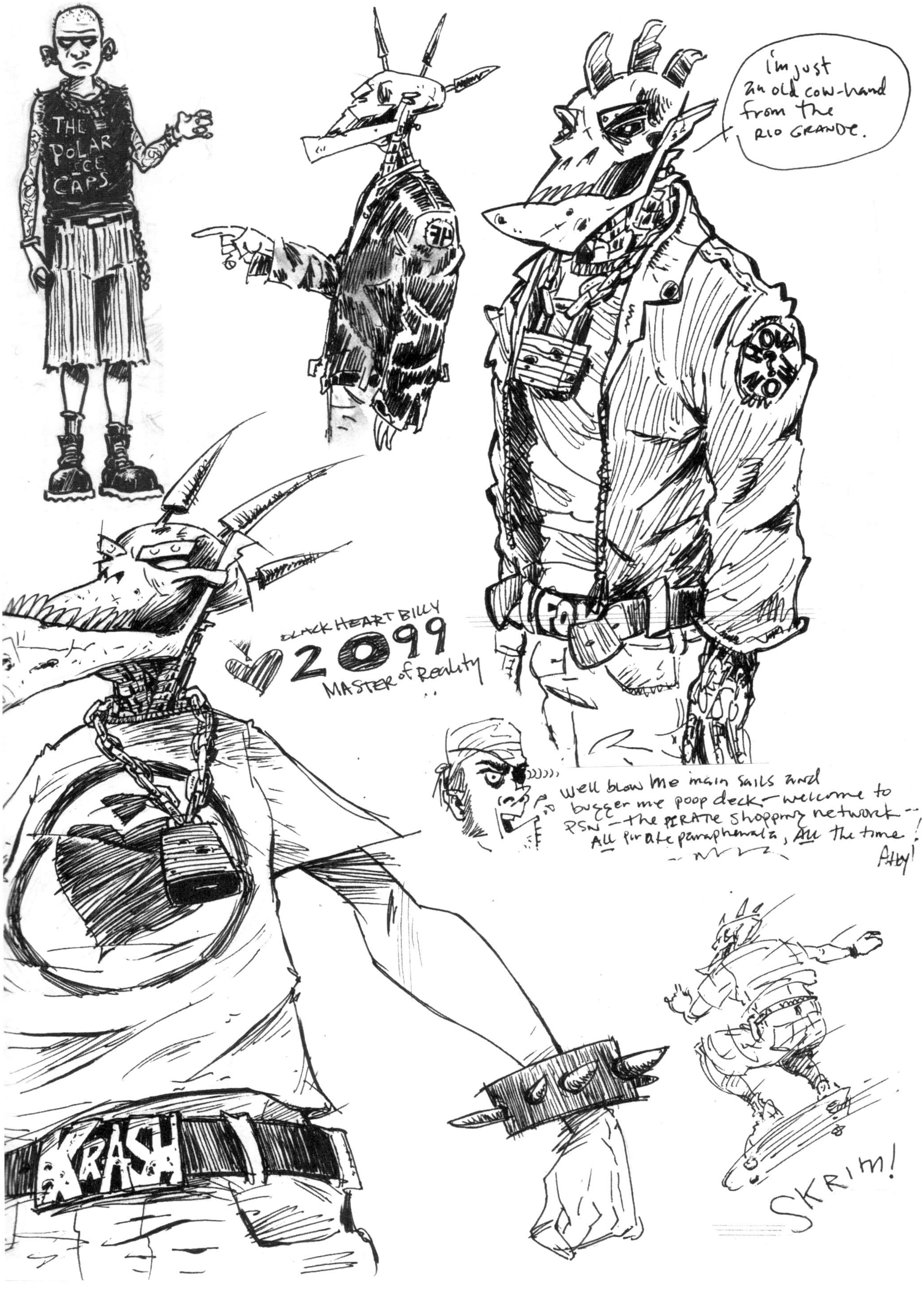
THE POLAR ICE CAPS
I'm just an old cow-hand from the RIO GRANDE.
HOW NOW
FOK
BLACK HEART BILLY
2099
MASTER of Reality
Well blow me main sails and bugger me poop deck — welcome to PSN — the PIRATE shopping network — All pirate paraphenalia, ALL the time!
Ahoy!
KRASH
SKRIM!

Harper Jaten

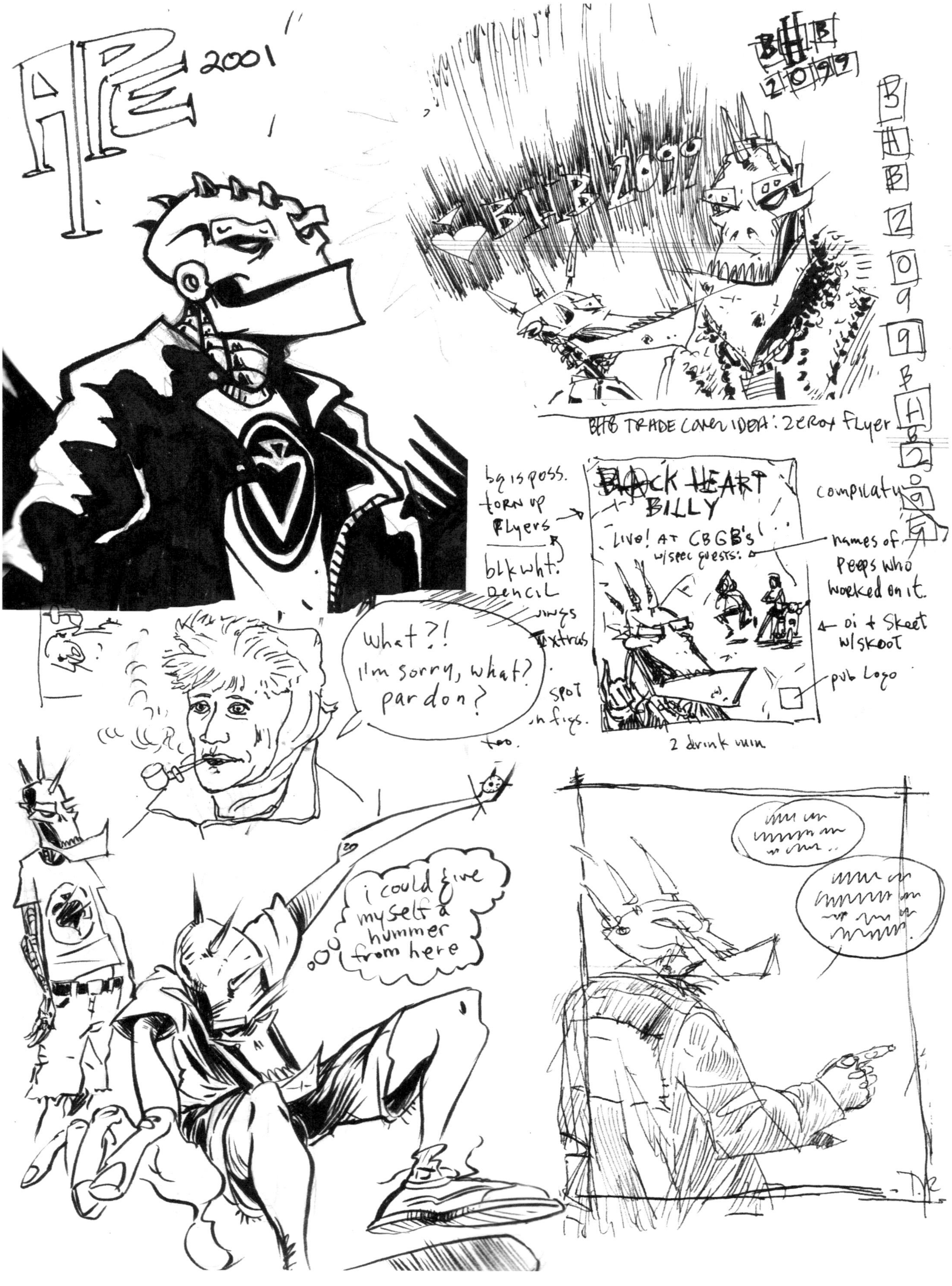

APE 2001
BHB 2099
BHB 2099
BHB TRADE COVER IDEA: ZEROX FLYER
bg is poss. torn up flyers
blk wht. pencil
BLACK HEART BILLY
LIVE! AT CBGB's
w/spec guests:
names of peeps who worked on it.
oi + Skeet w/skoot
pub logo
2 drink min
What?! I'm sorry, what? pardon?
i could give myself a hummer from here

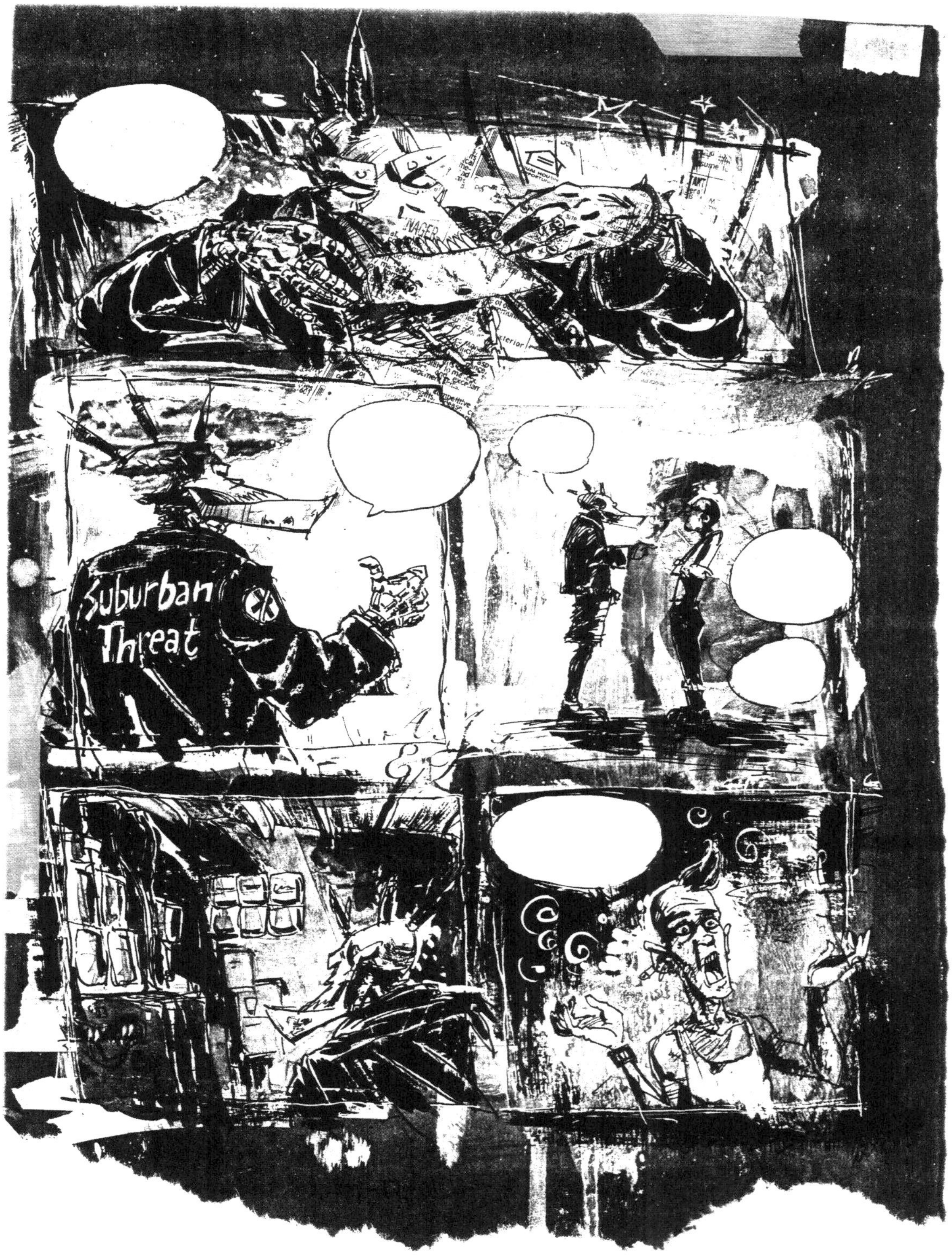
Suburban Threat

8-2-01 didn't do my hour in here yesterday or today. i was doing the page breakdown thumbnails for the billy 2099 story -- first 7 pages. this is a copy of a test page i did for this story. it's collage and pen/sumi brush ink on chipboard. i'm excited about it even though it'll probably print like shit. it's quite the departure -- and the whole thing only took 6 hours.

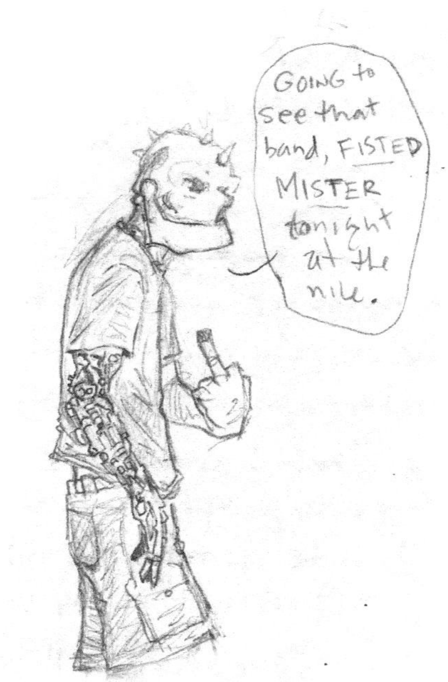
GOING to see that band, FISTED MISTER tonight at the nile.

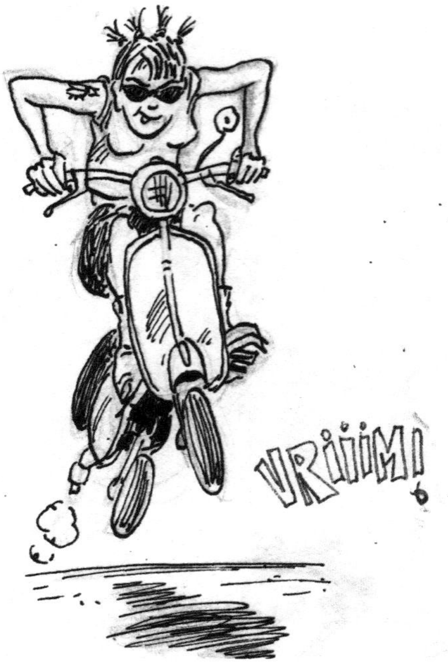
VRiiiM!

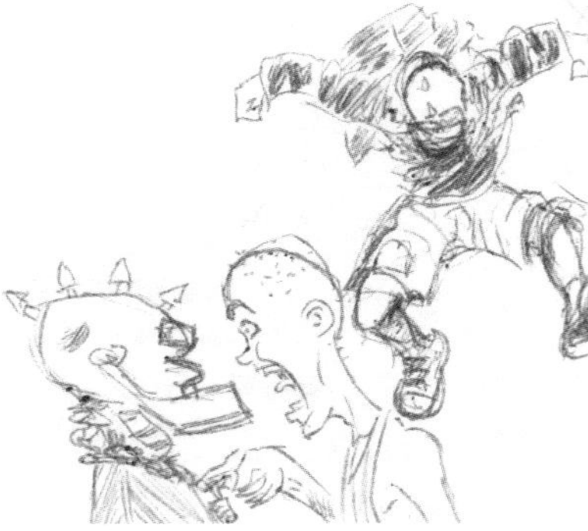

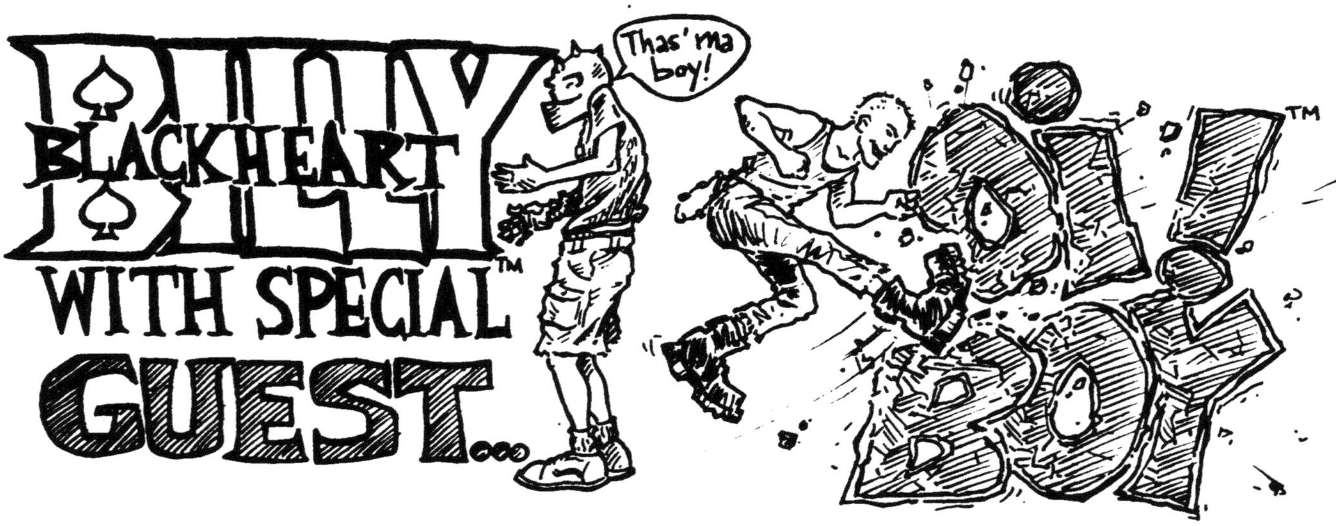
BILLY
BLACKHEART
WITH SPECIAL™
GUEST...
Thas' ma boy!
Oi! BOY!™

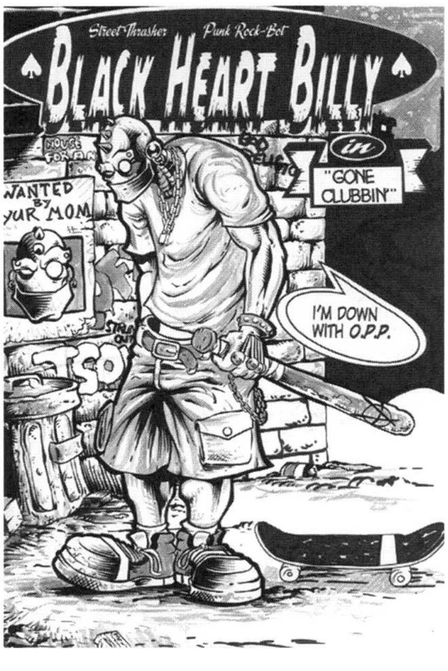
Street Thrasher
Punk Rock-Bot
BLACK HEART BILLY
in
"GONE CLUBBIN'"
WANTED BY YUR MOM
I'M DOWN WITH O.P.P.

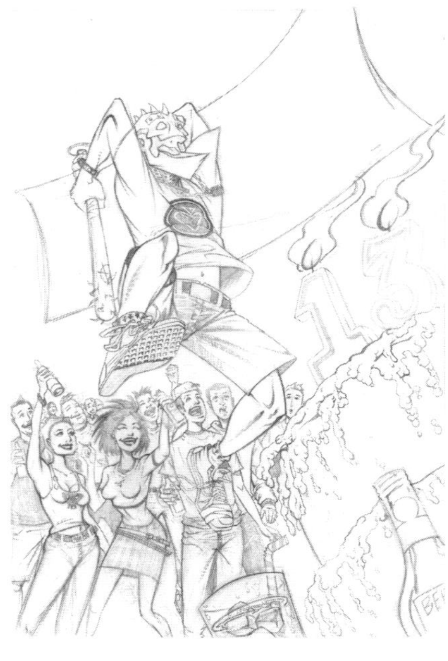

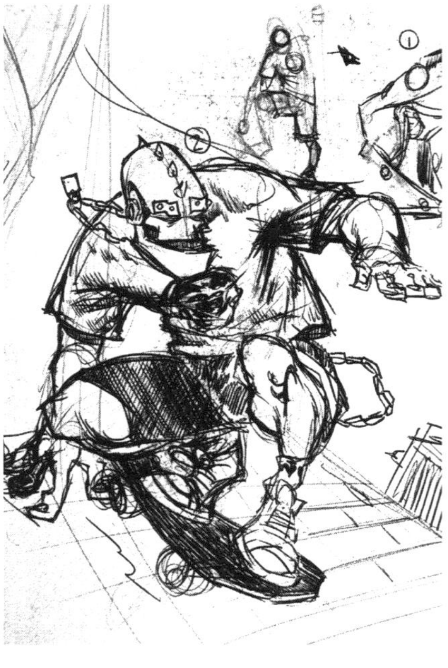

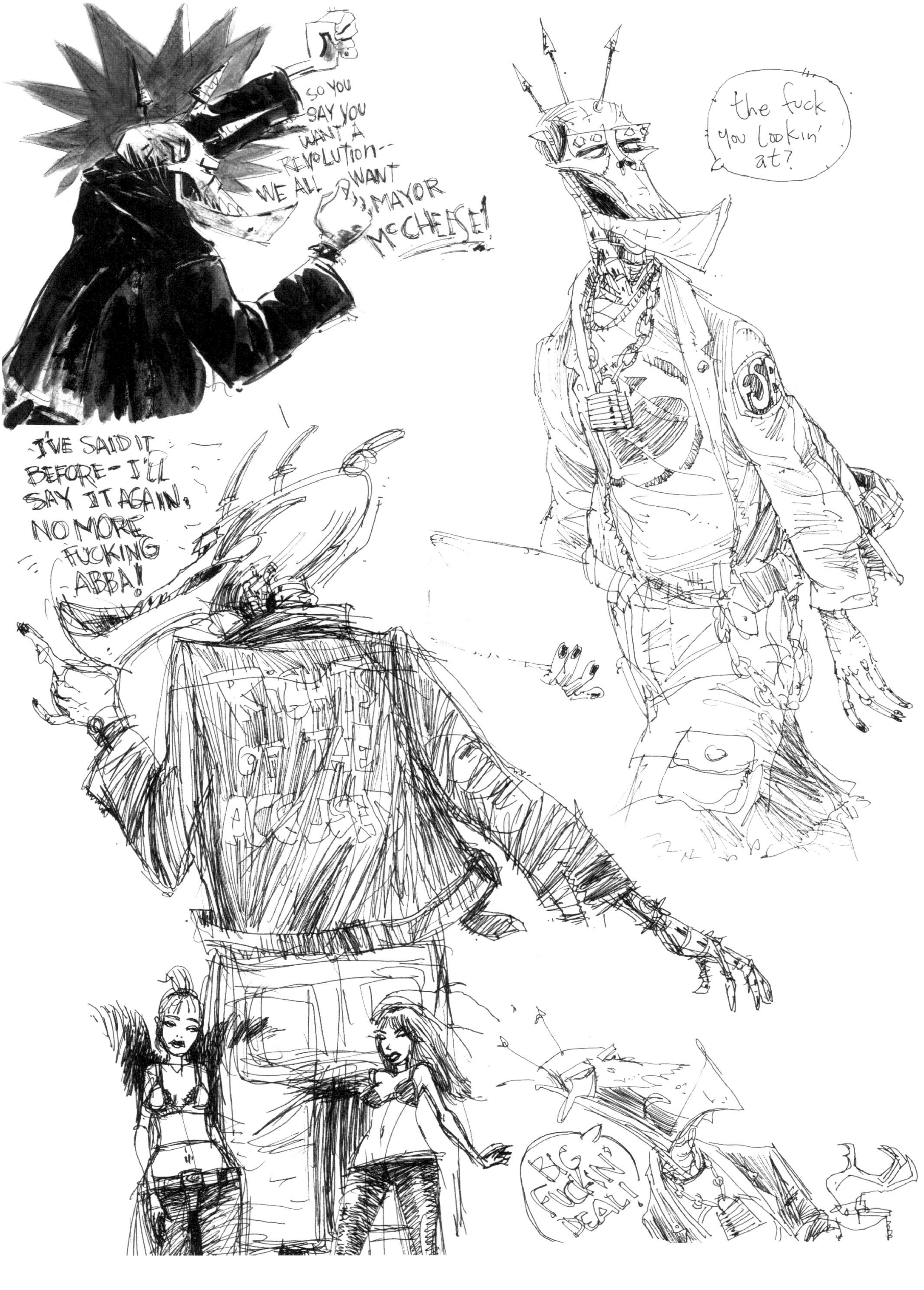
SO YOU SAY YOU WANT A REVOLUTION-- WE ALL WANT MAYOR McCHEESE!
the fuck you lookin' at?
I'VE SAID IT BEFORE- I'LL SAY IT AGAIN, NO MORE FUCKING ABBA!
BIG FUCKIN' DEAL!

Harper Jaten

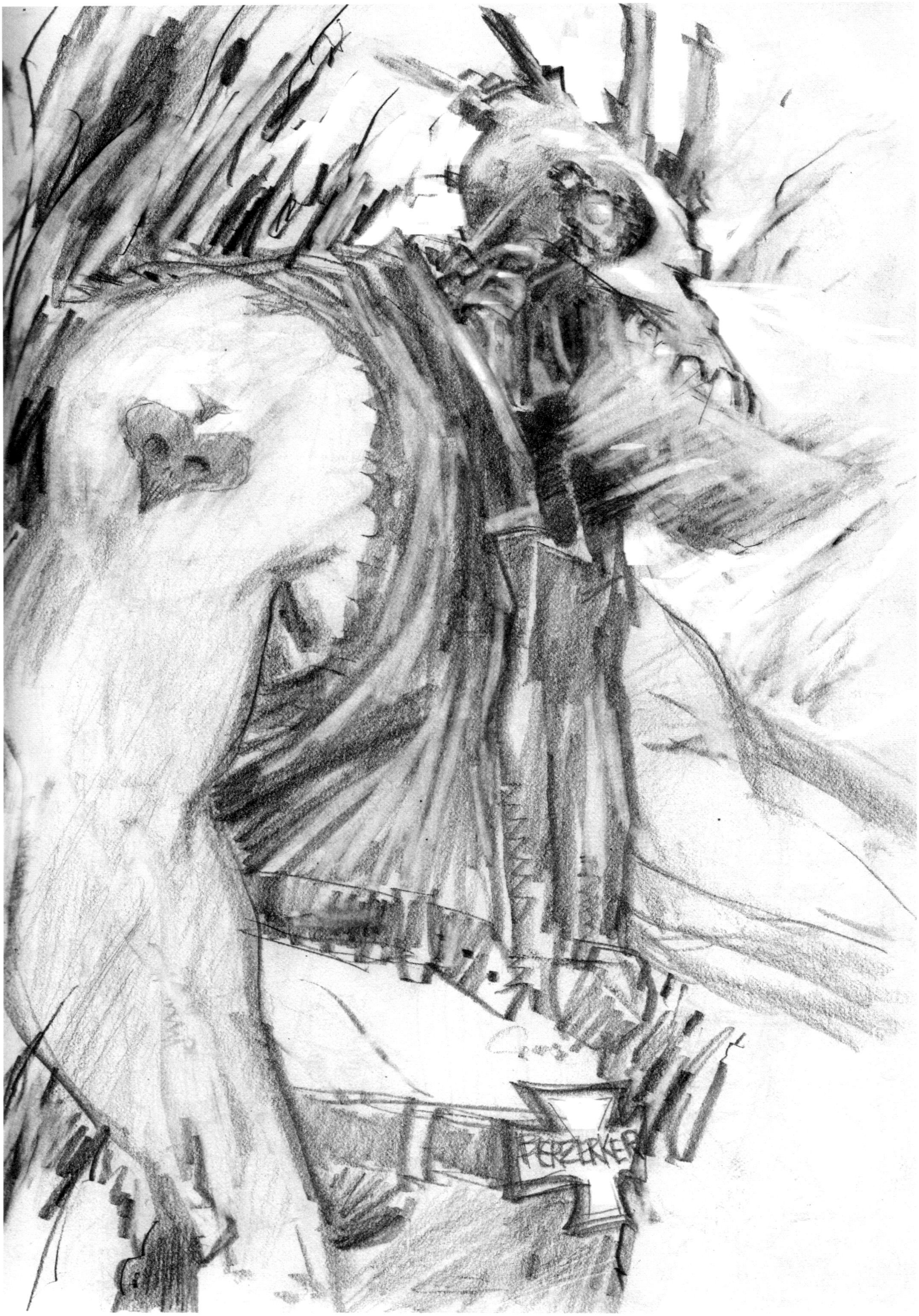
BERZERKER

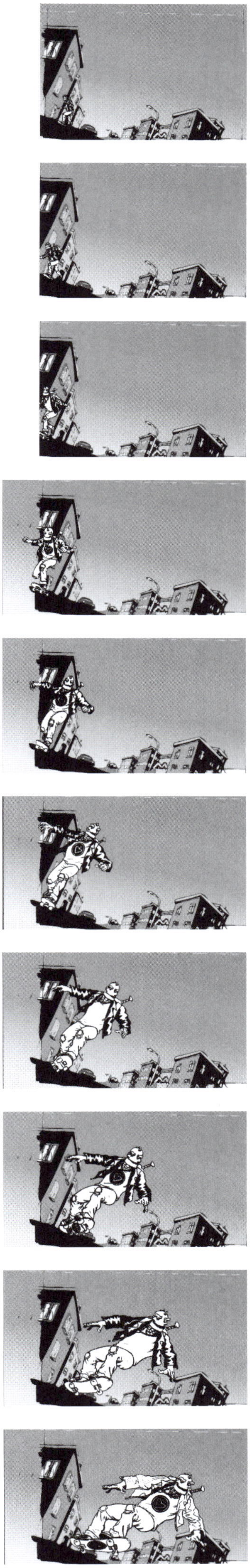

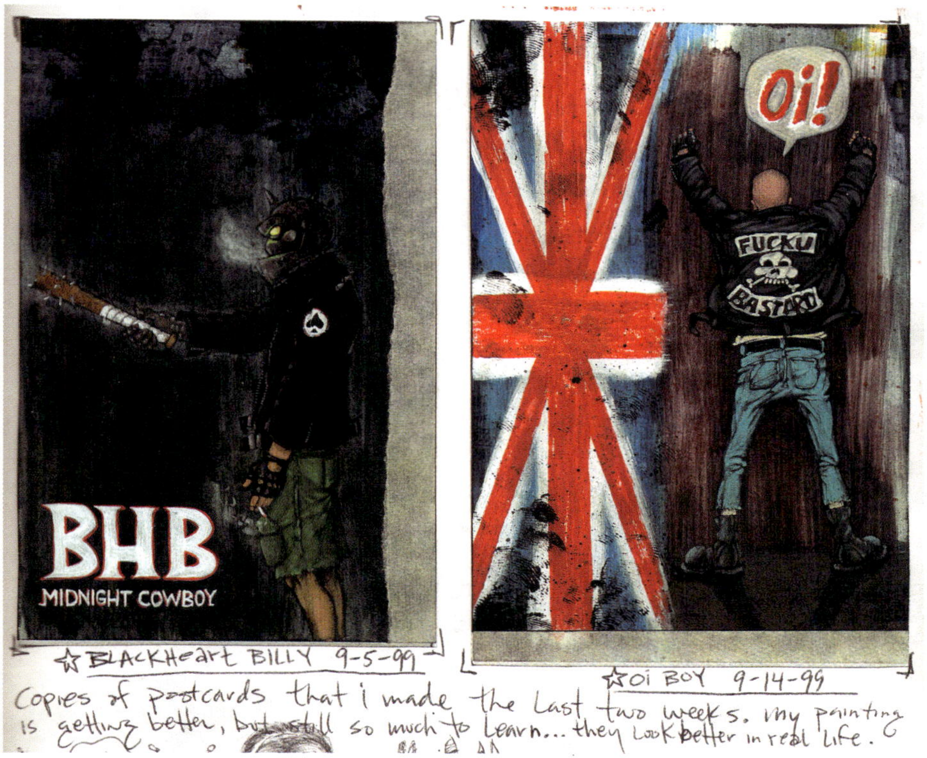

BHB
MIDNIGHT COWBOY
☆BLACKHEART BILLY 9-5-99
Oi!
FUCKU
BASTARD
☆OI BOY 9-14-99
Copies of postcards that i made the last two weeks. my painting is getting better, but still so much to learn... they look better in real life.

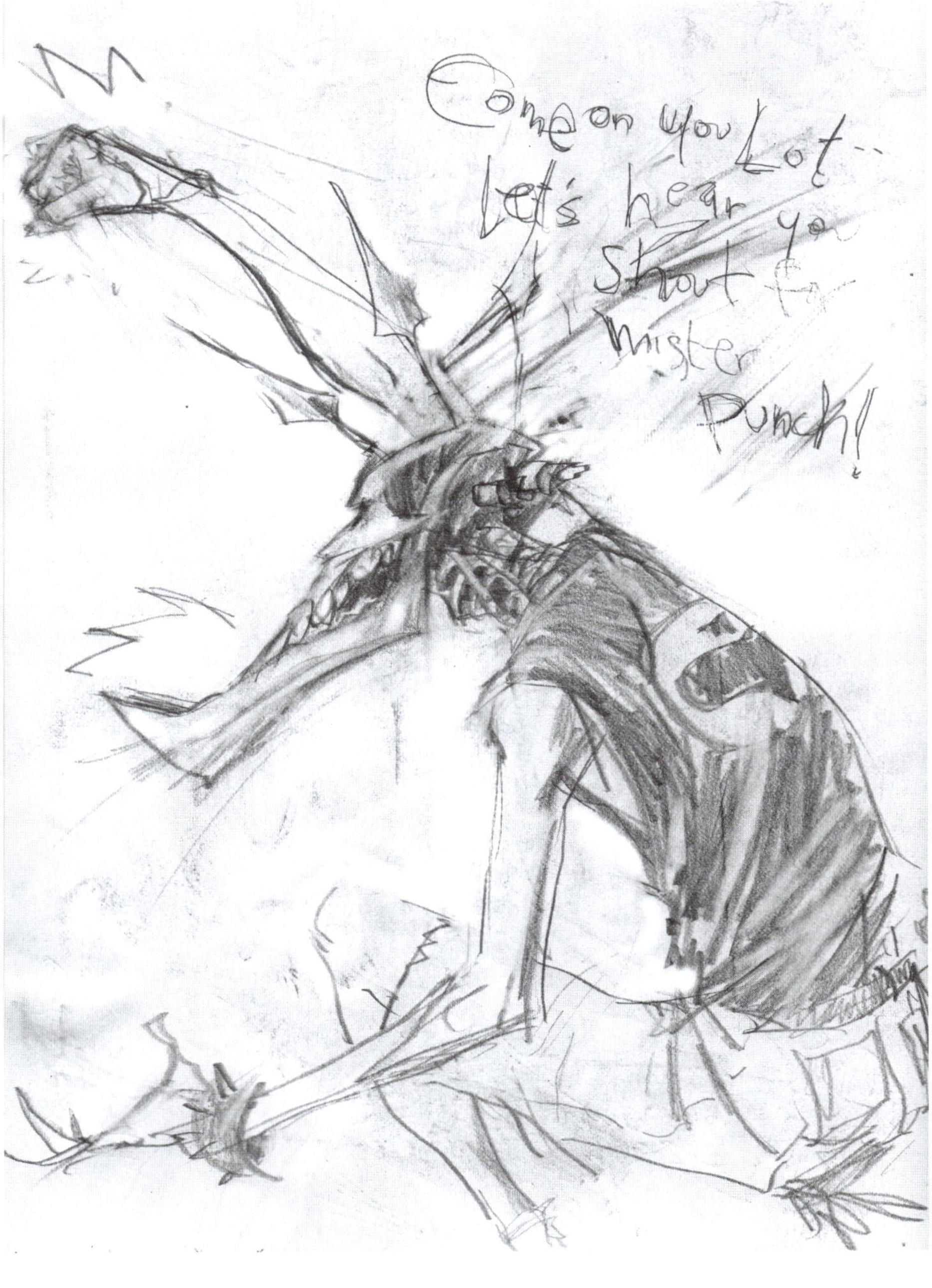

Come on you lot..
let's hear you
shout for
mister
Punch!

Rick Remender

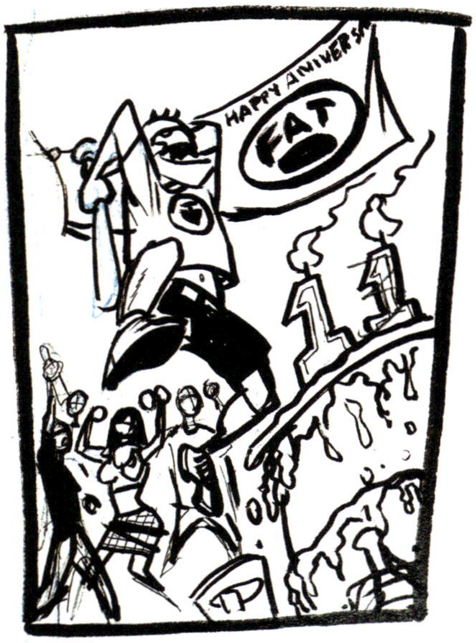
HAPPY ANIVERS
FAT

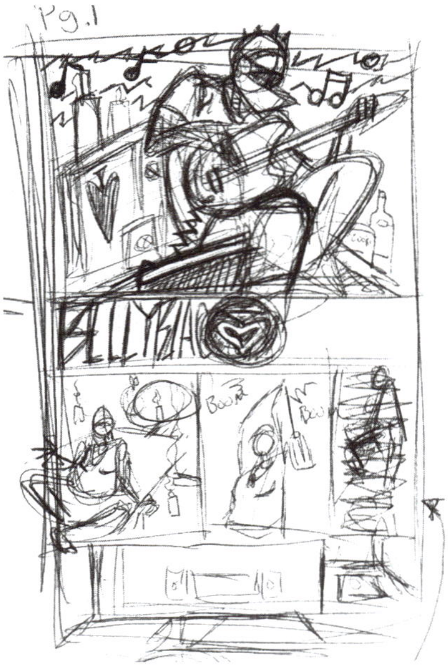

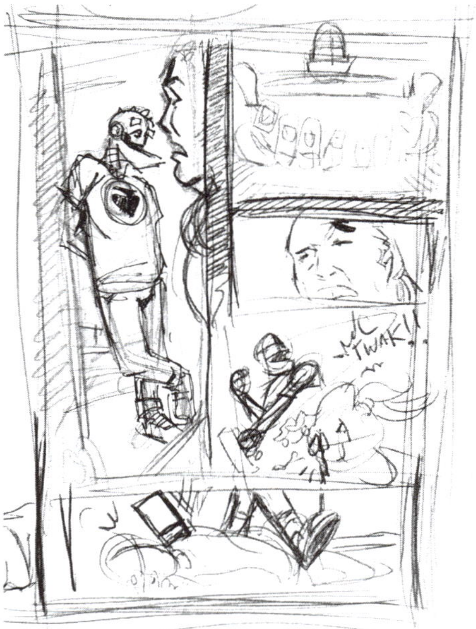

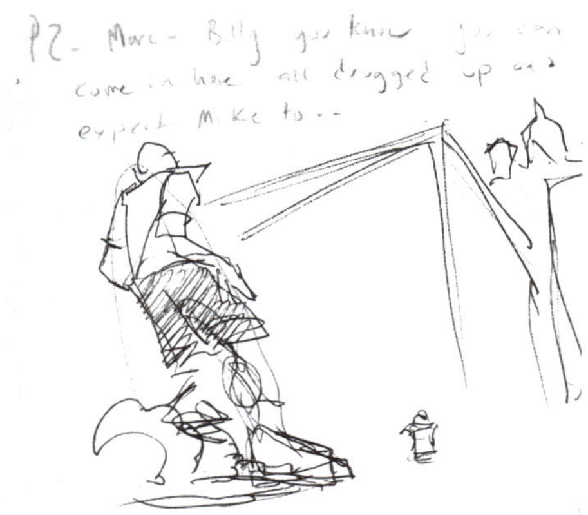

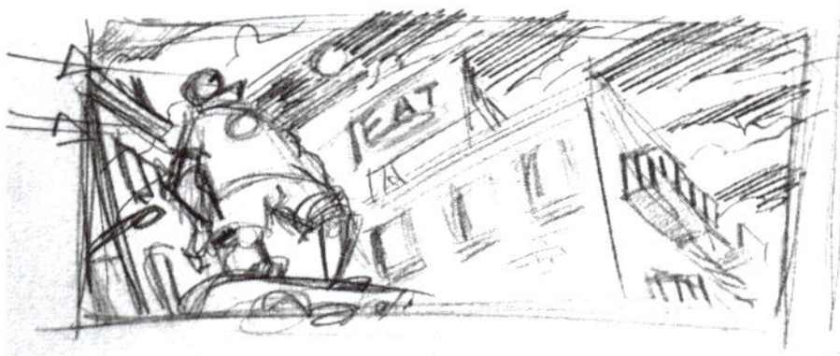

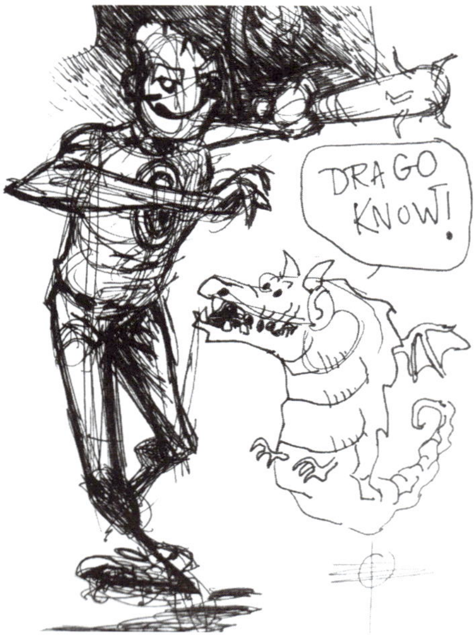
DRAGO KNOW!

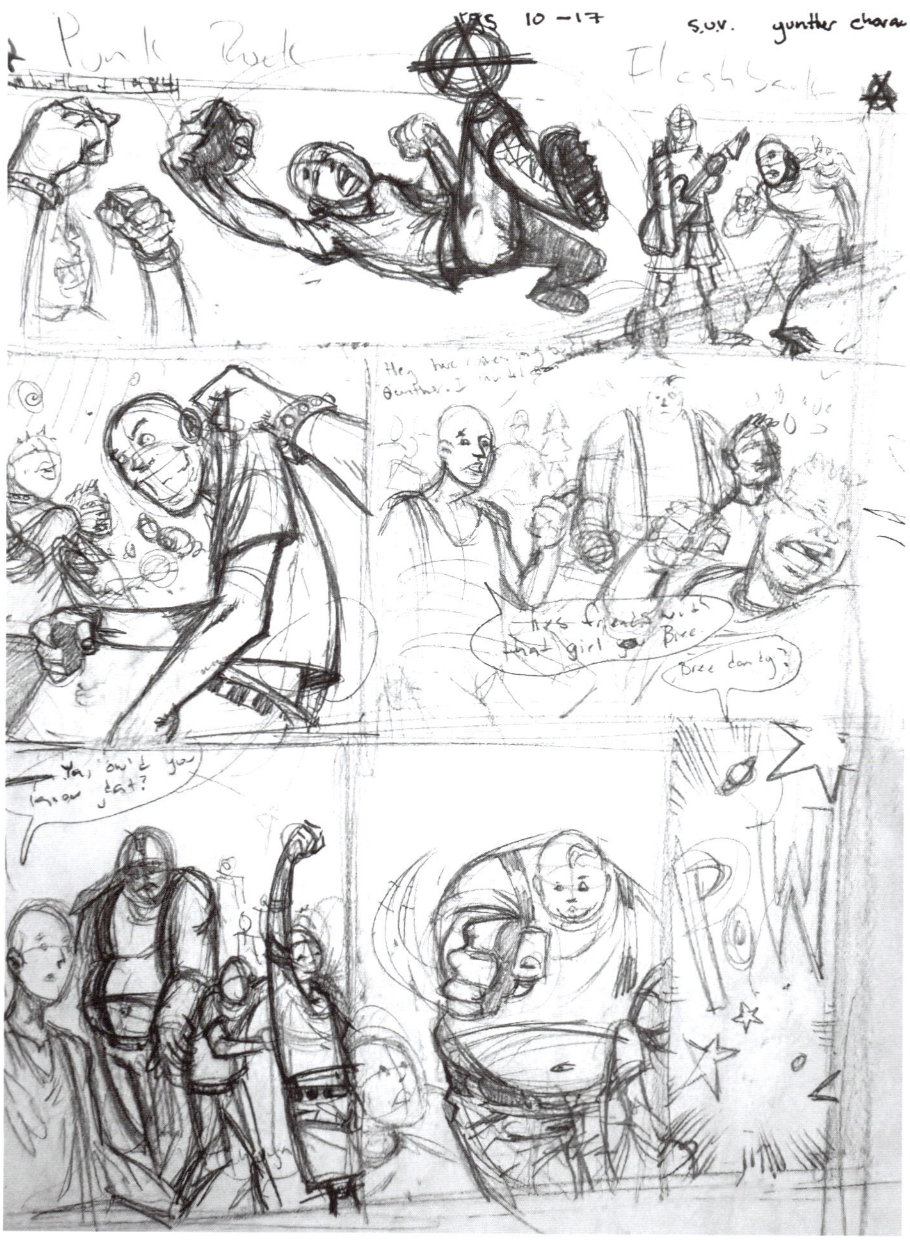
POW

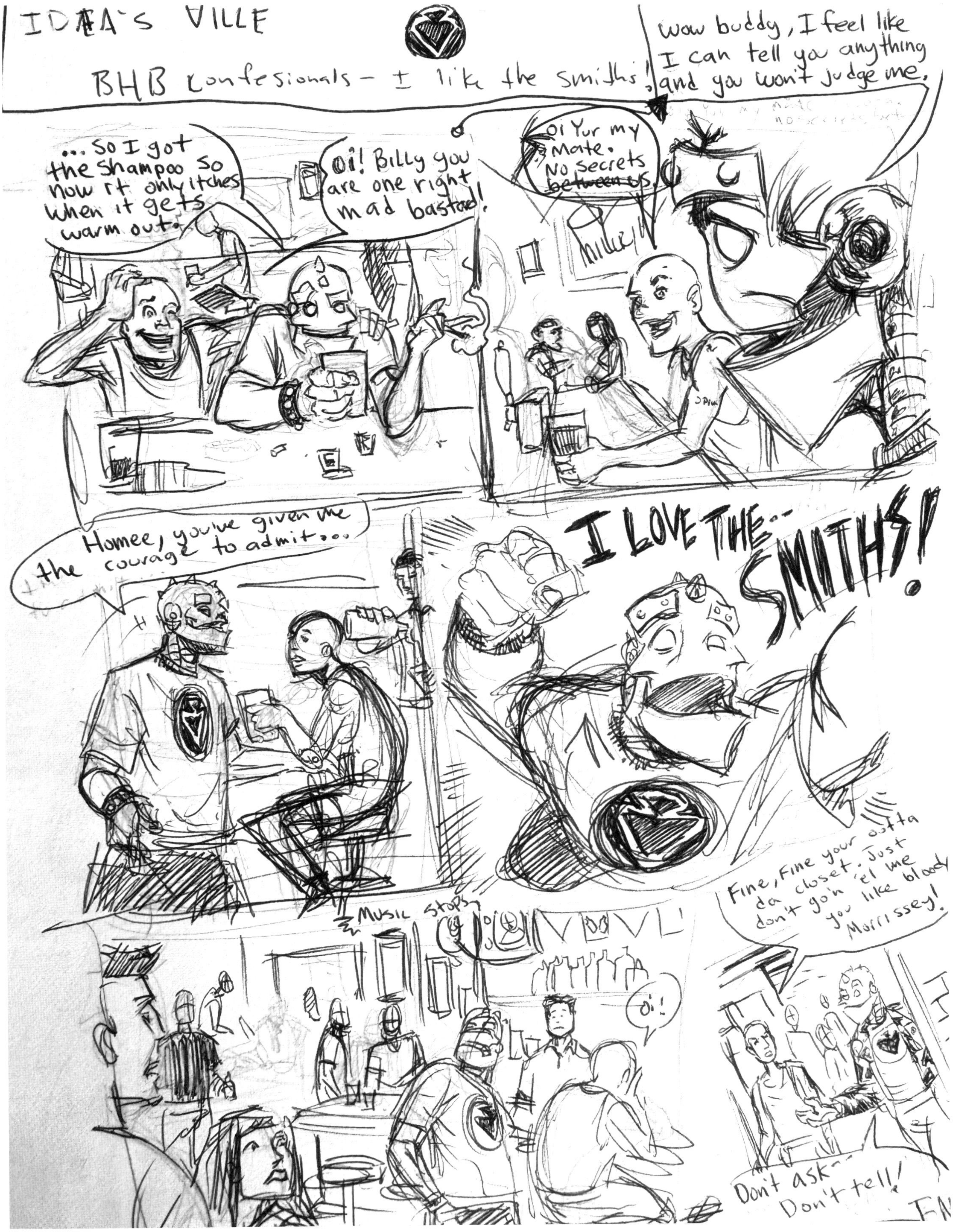
IDEA'S VILLE
BHB confesionals — I like the smiths!
Wow buddy, I feel like I can tell you anything and you won't judge me.
...So I got the shampoo so now it only itches when it gets warm out.
Oi! Billy you are one right mad bastard!
Oi Yur my Mate. No secrets between us.
Homee, you've given me the courage to admit...
I LOVE THE... SMITHS!
MUSIC STOPS
Oi!
Fine, Fine your outta da closet. Just don't go'n 'el me you like bloody Morrissey!
Don't ask— Don't tell!
FIN

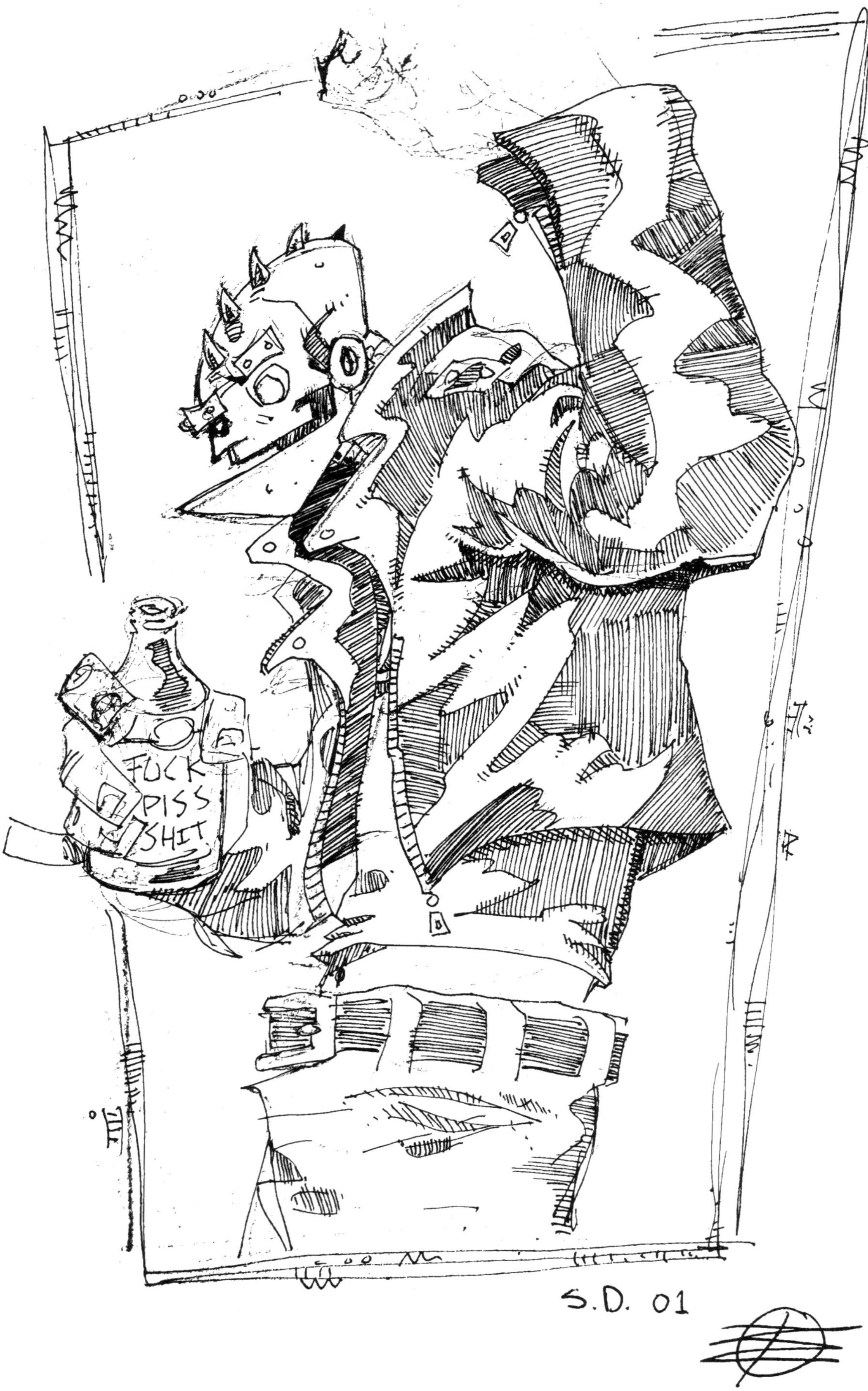
FUCK
PISS
SHIT
S.D. 01

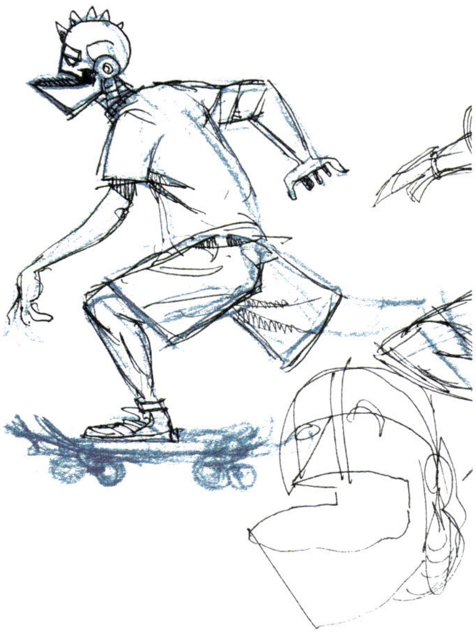

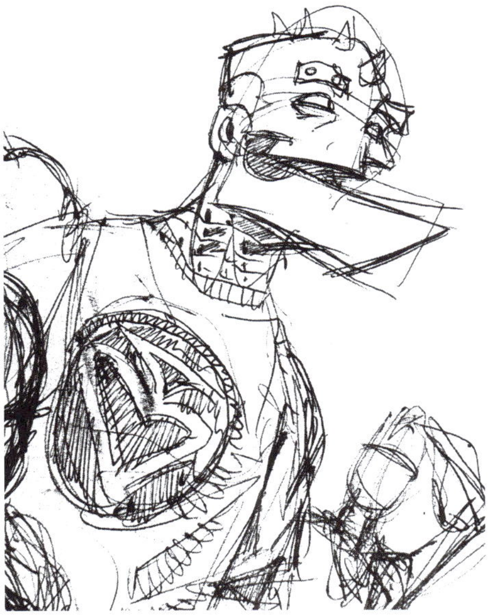

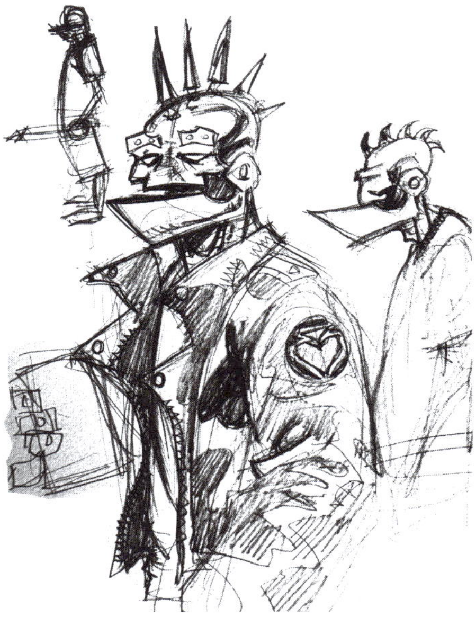

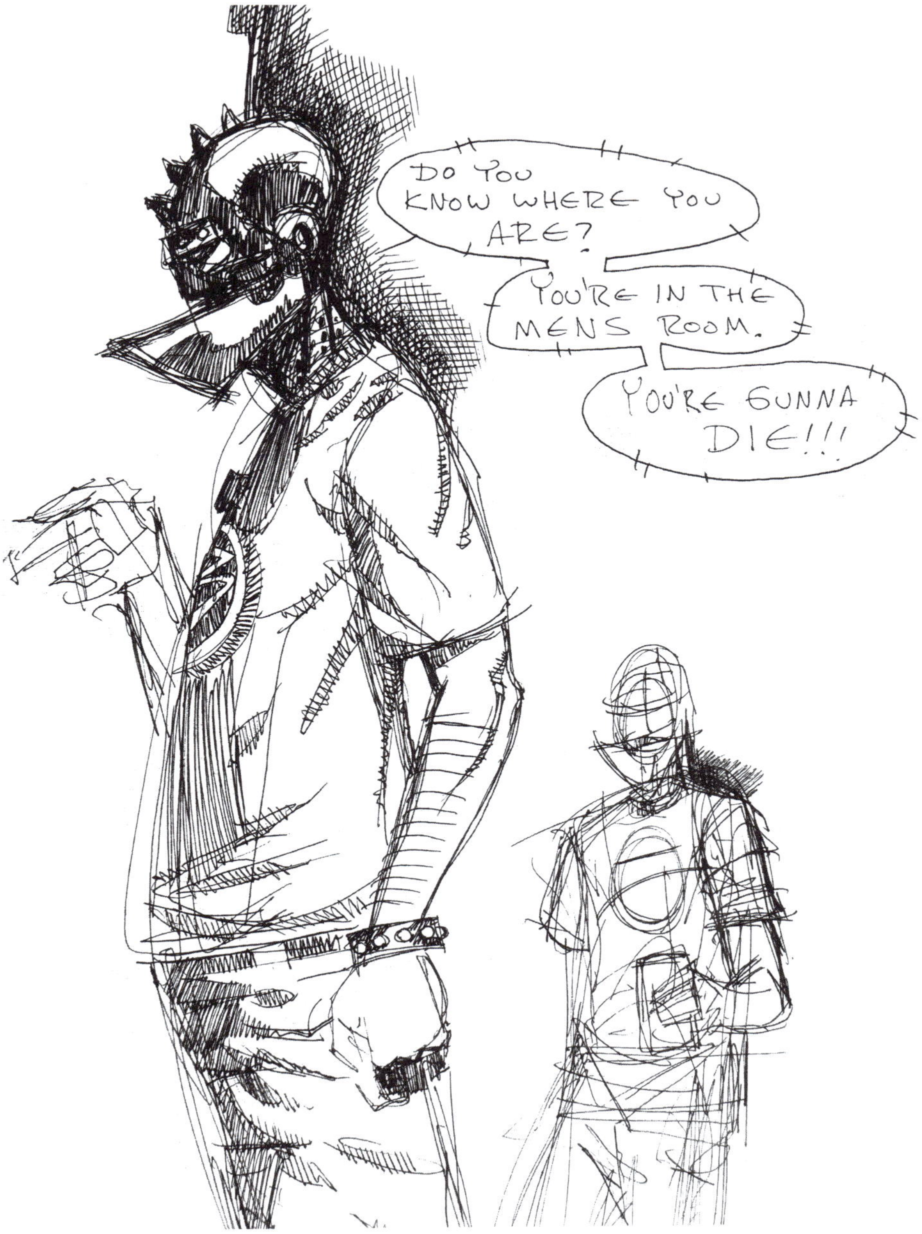
DO YOU KNOW WHERE YOU ARE?
YOU'RE IN THE MENS ROOM.
YOU'RE GUNNA DIE!!!

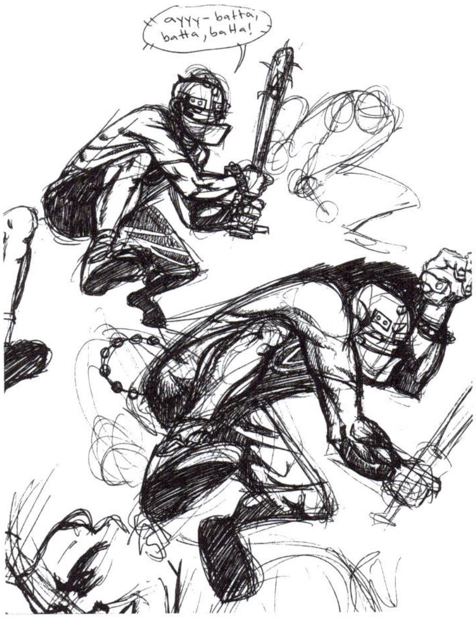
ayyy-batta, batta, batta!

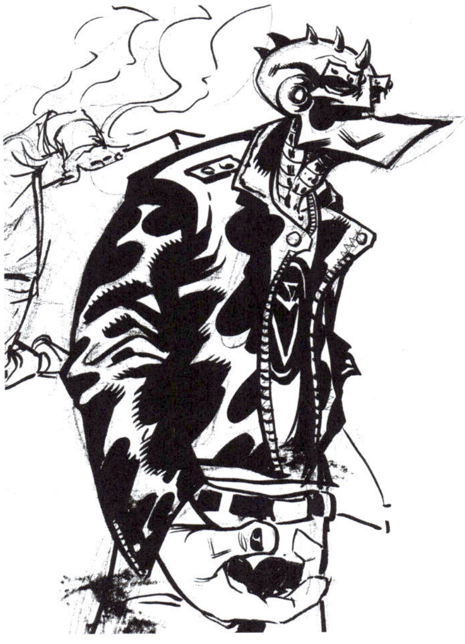

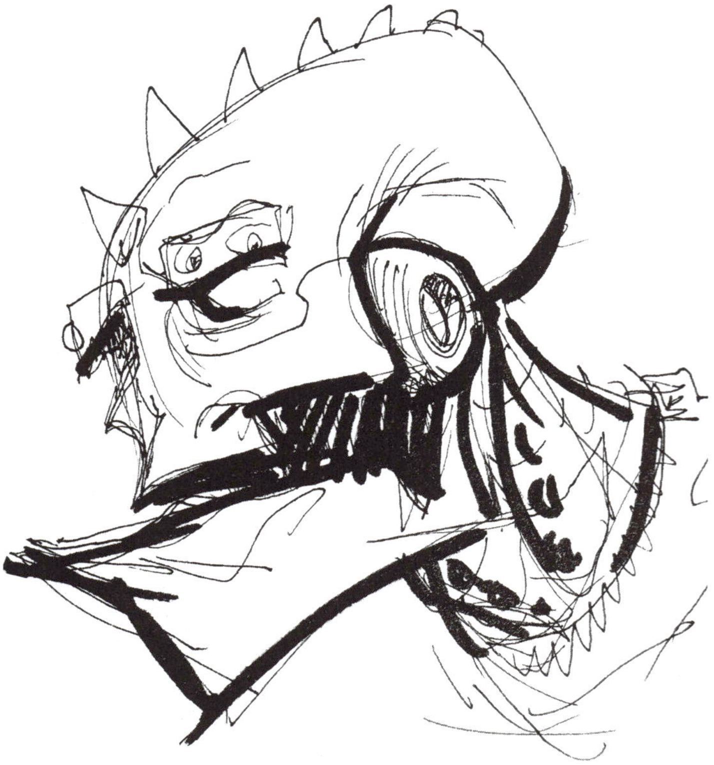

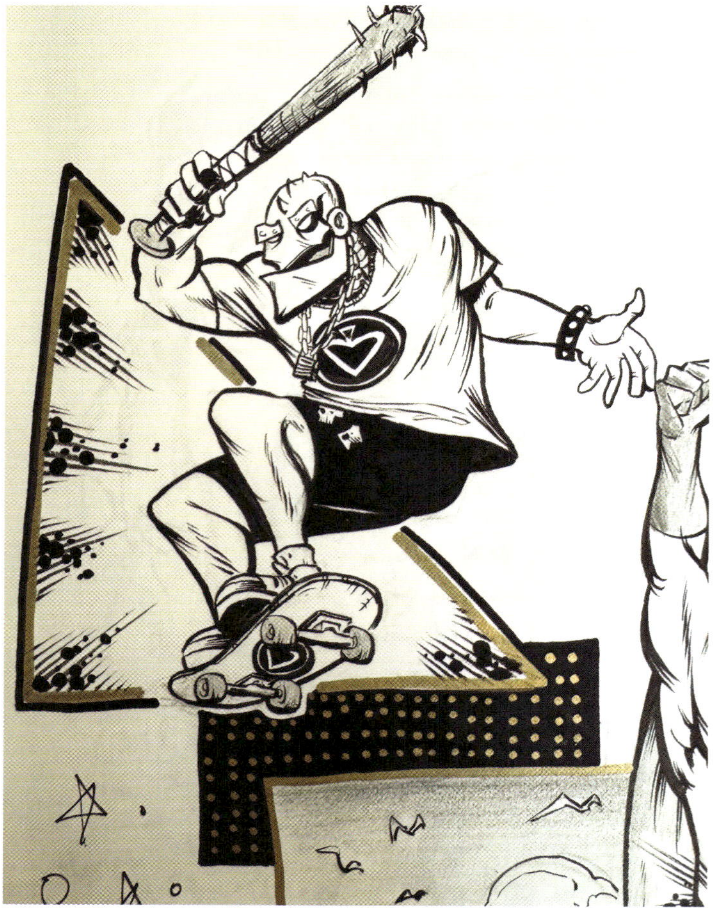

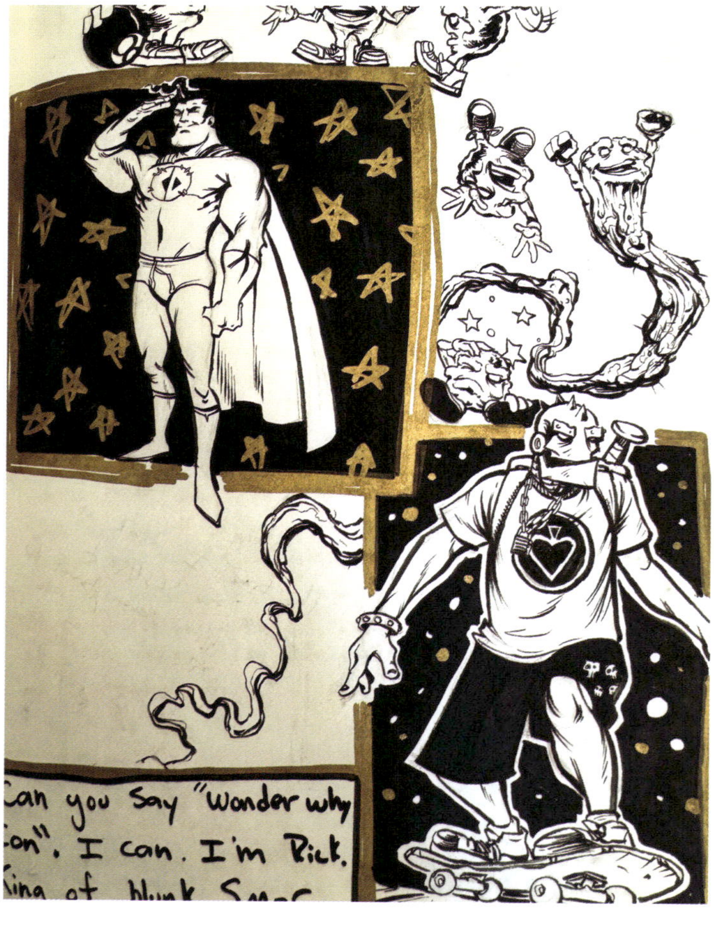
an you Say "Wonder why
on". I can. I'm Rick.

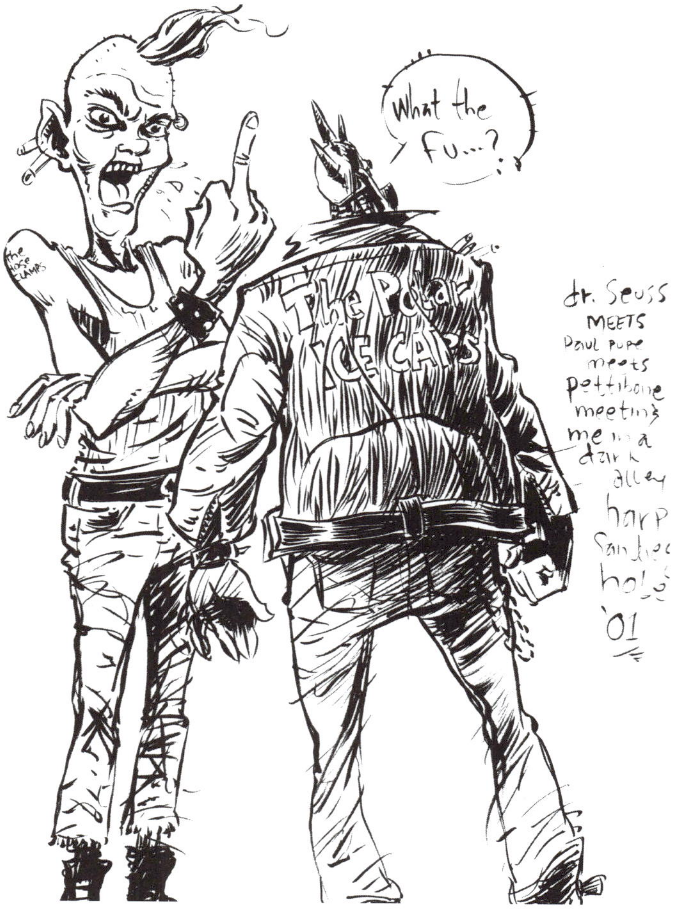
What the Fu...?
The Polar ICE CAPS
dr. Seuss MEETS Paul Pope meets pettibone meeting me a dark alley
'01

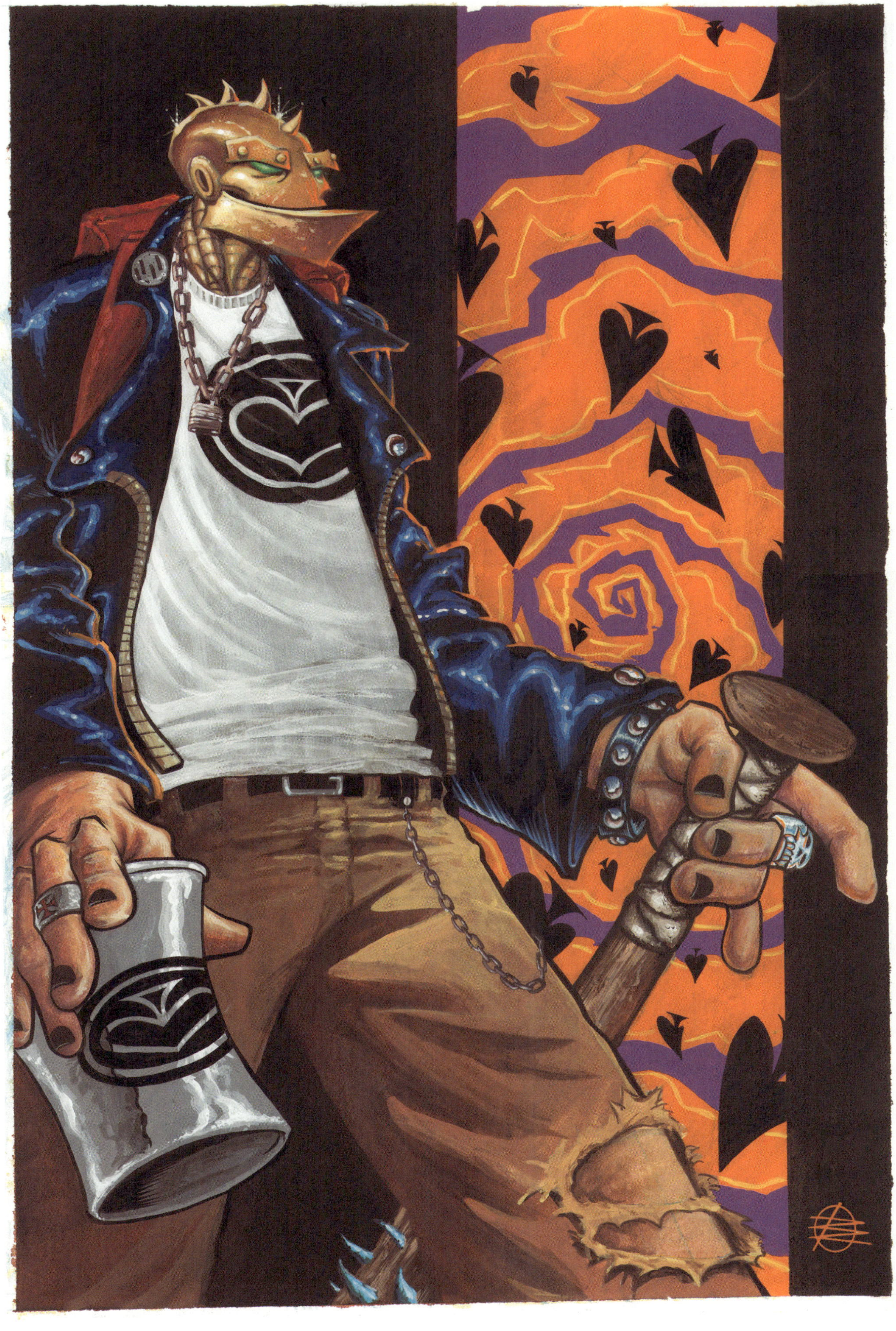

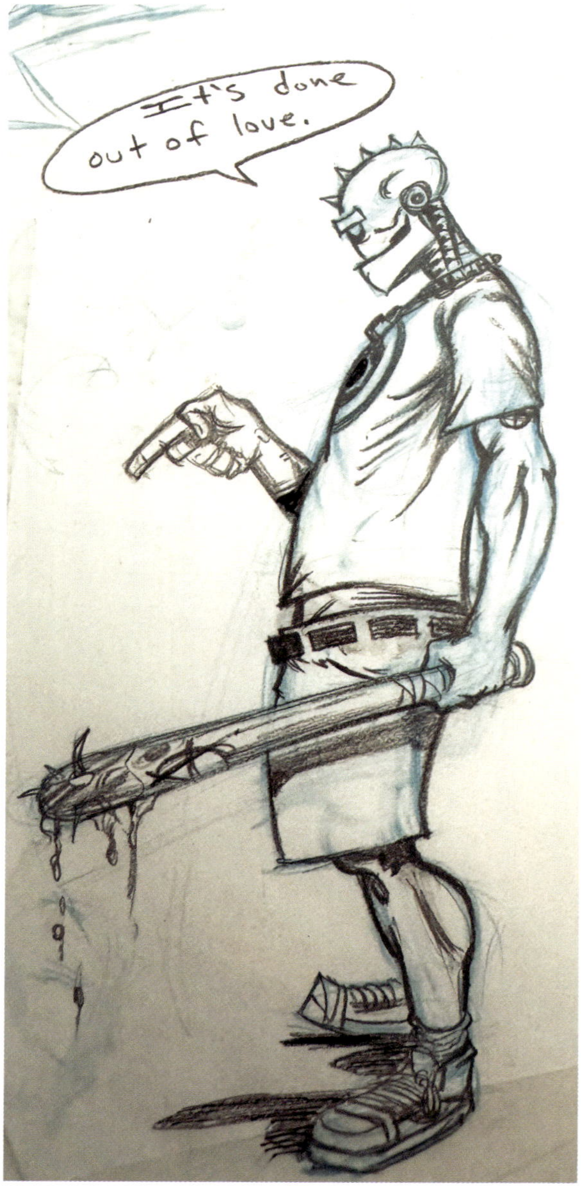
It's done out of love.

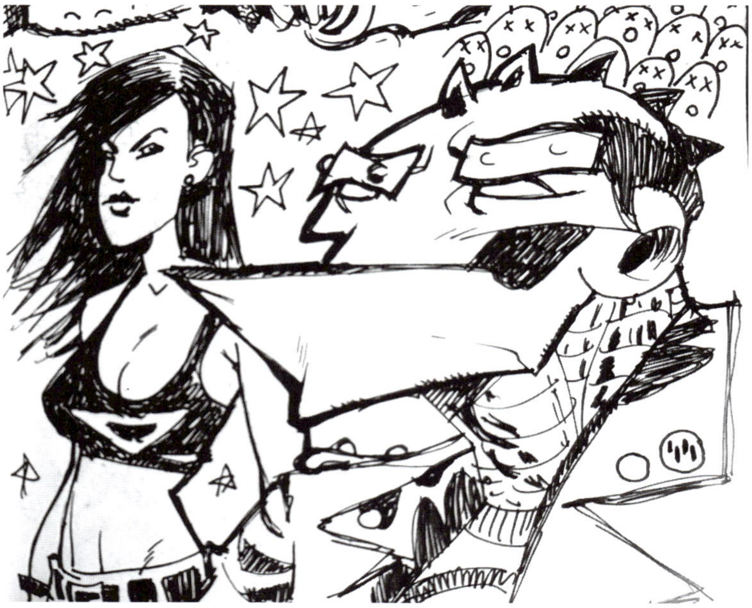

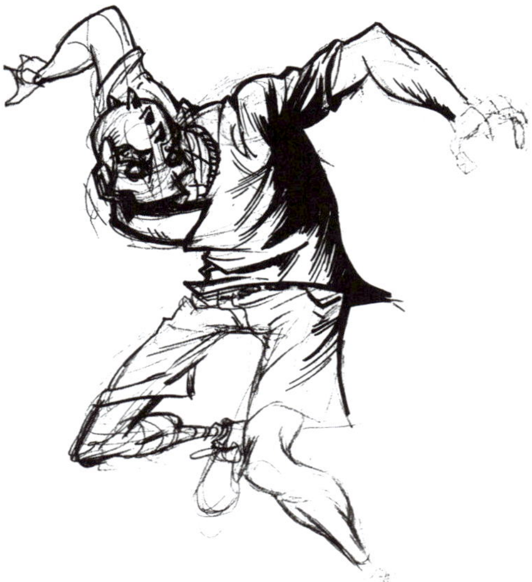

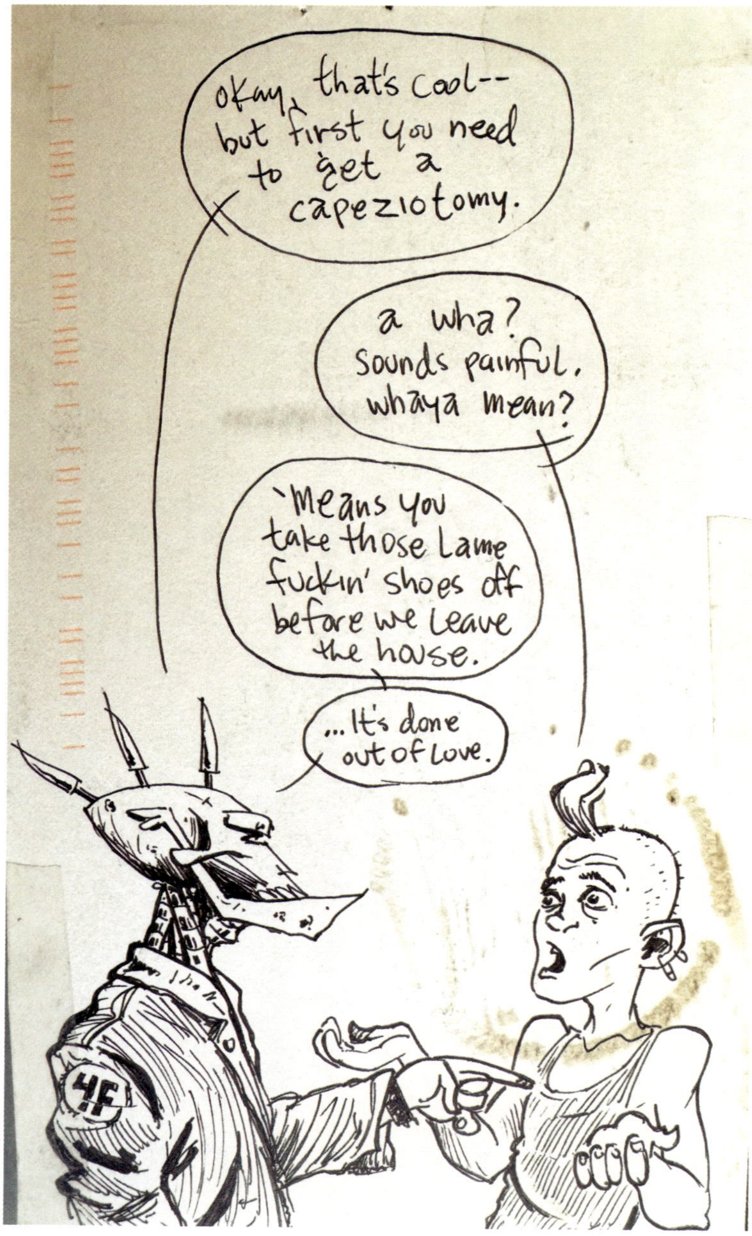
okay, that's cool-- but first you need to get a capeziotomy.
a wha? sounds painful. whaya mean?
'Means you take those Lame fuckin' shoes off before we leave the house.
...It's done out of Love.

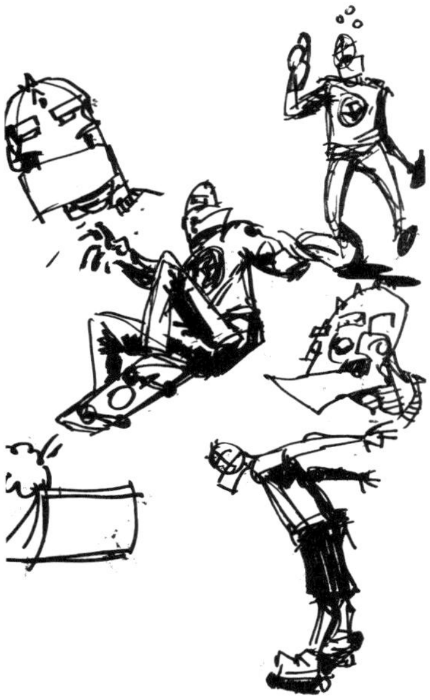

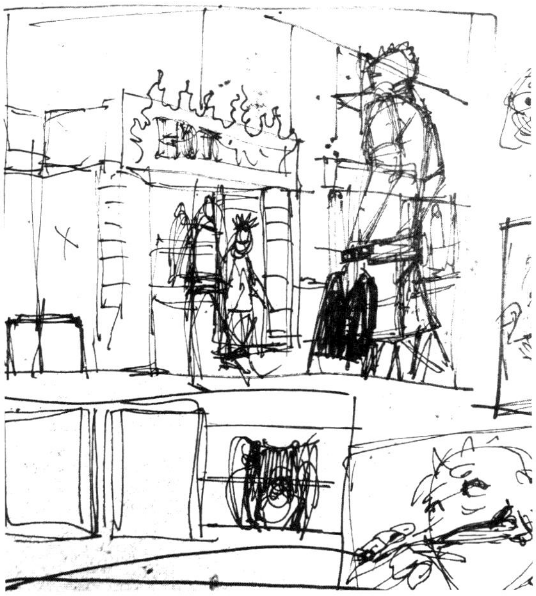

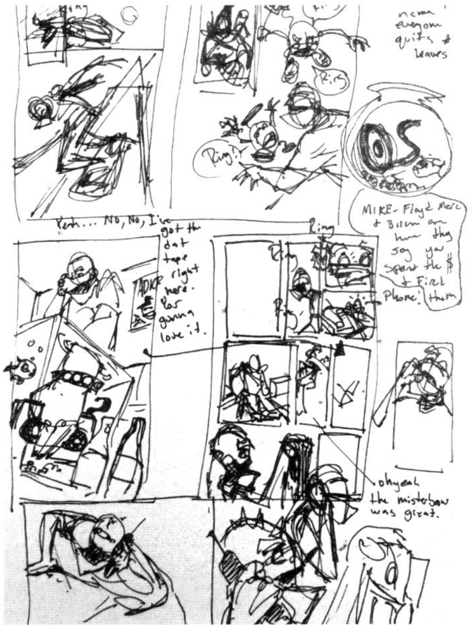
Ring
oh yeah the mistletoe was great.

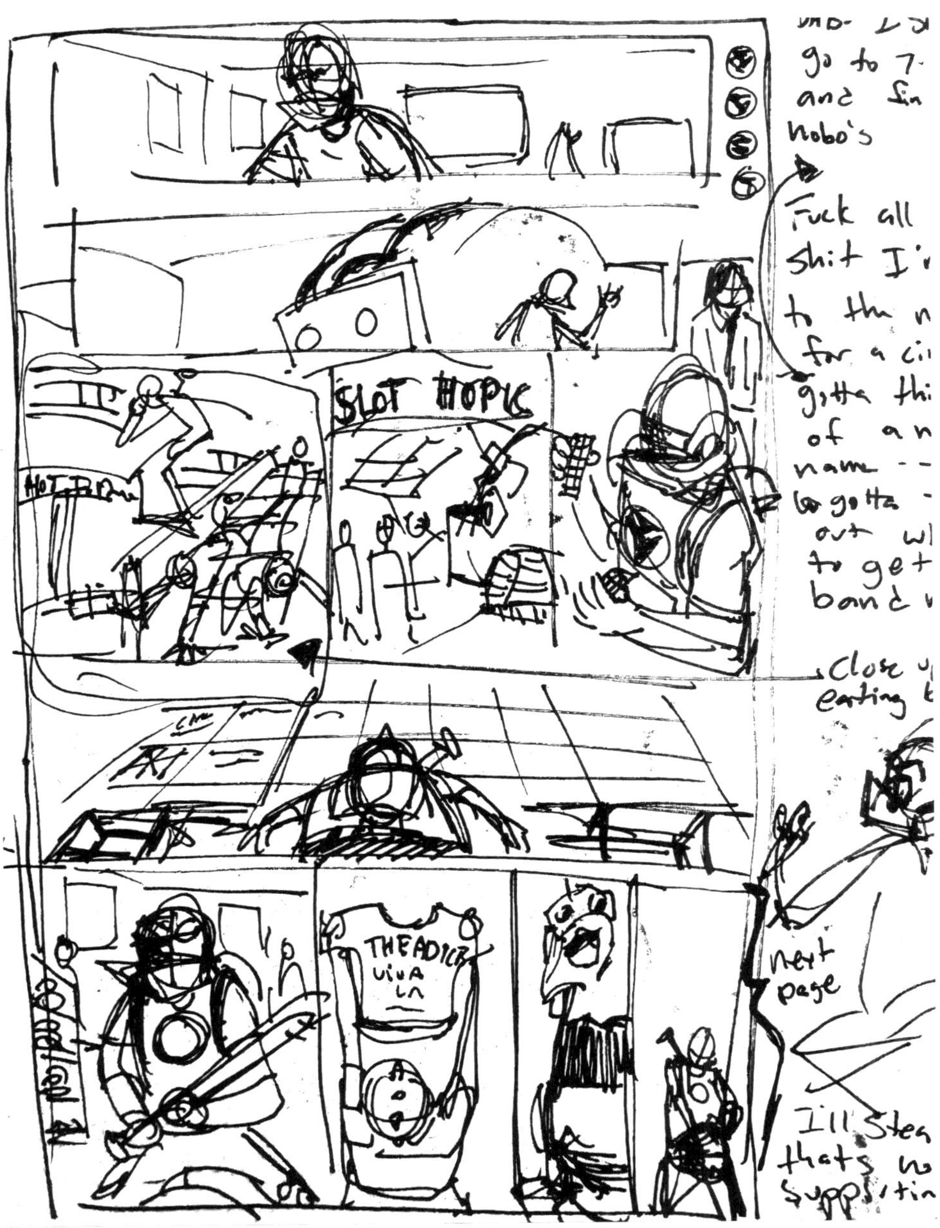
go to 7-
and fin
hobo's
Fuck all
shit I'
to the
for a ci
gotta thi
of a n
name --
gotta
out wh
to get
band
SLOT HOPIC
Close up
eating
THE ADICTS
VIVA LA
next page
I'll Stea
thats no

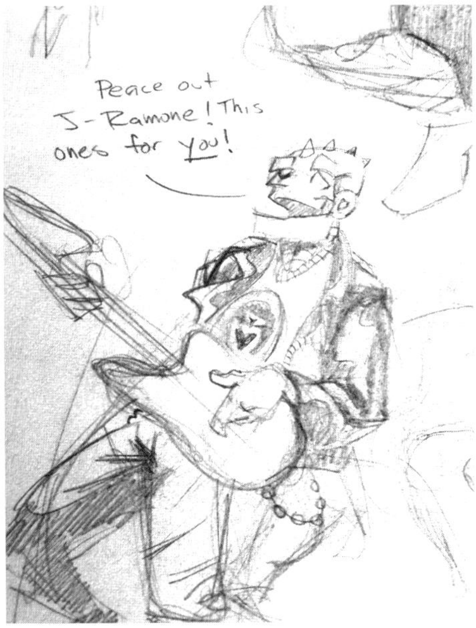
Peace out J-Ramone! This ones for you!

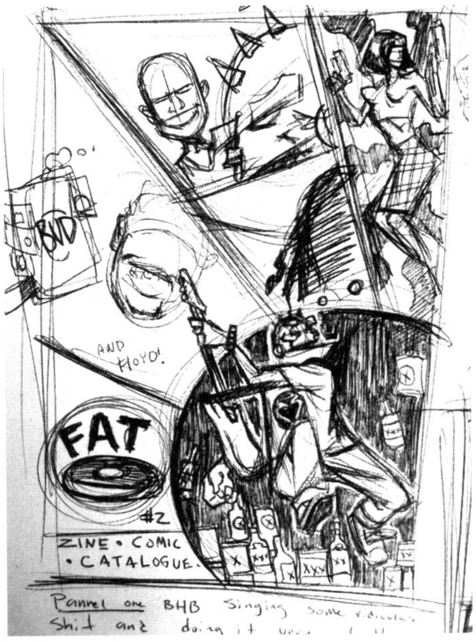
AND FLOYD!
FAT
#2
ZINE • COMIC • CATALOGUE

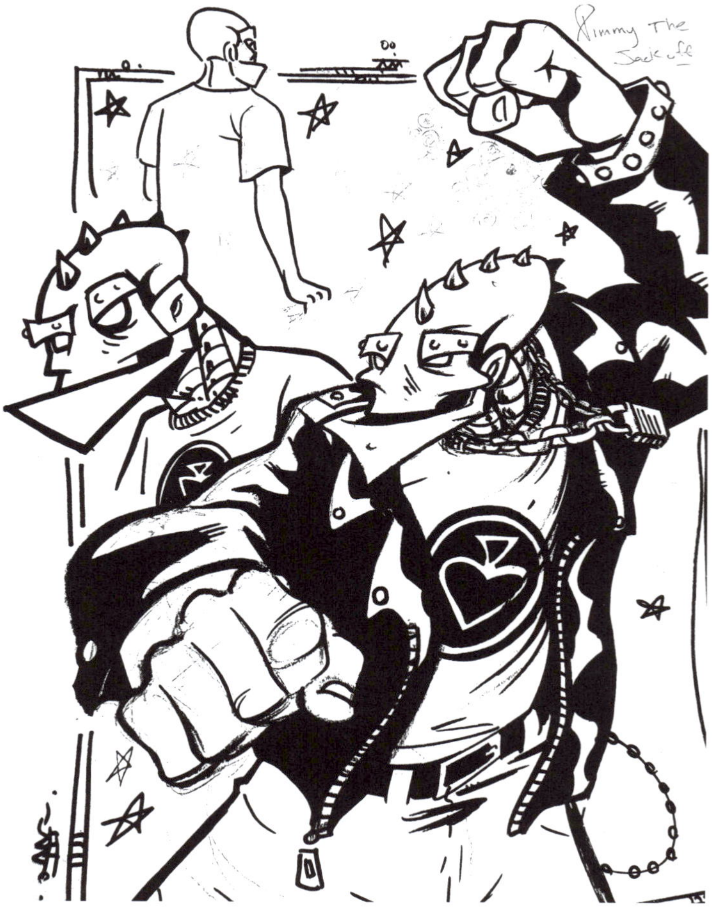

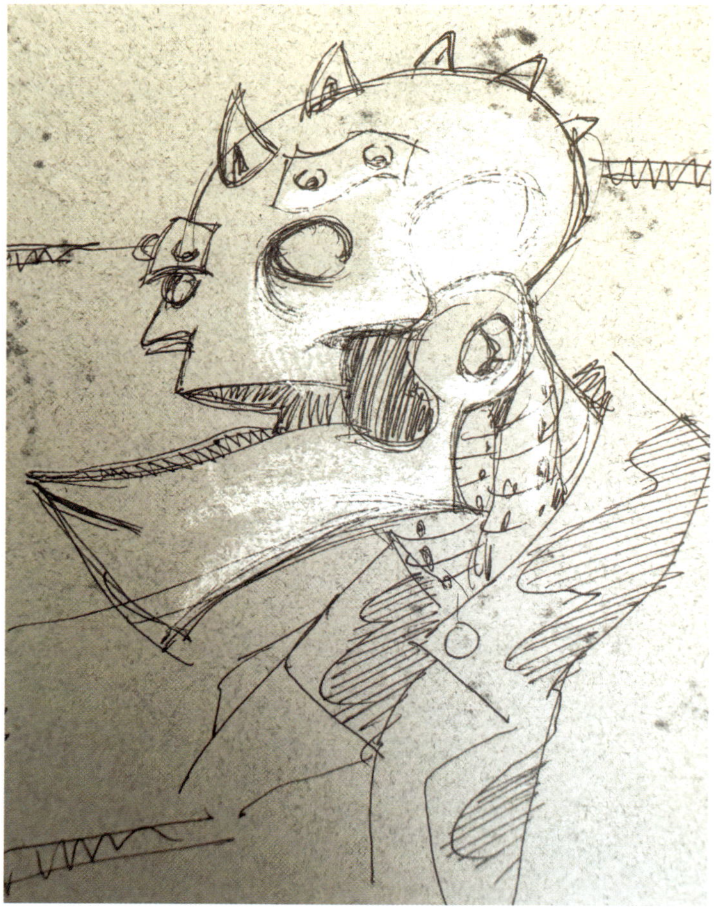

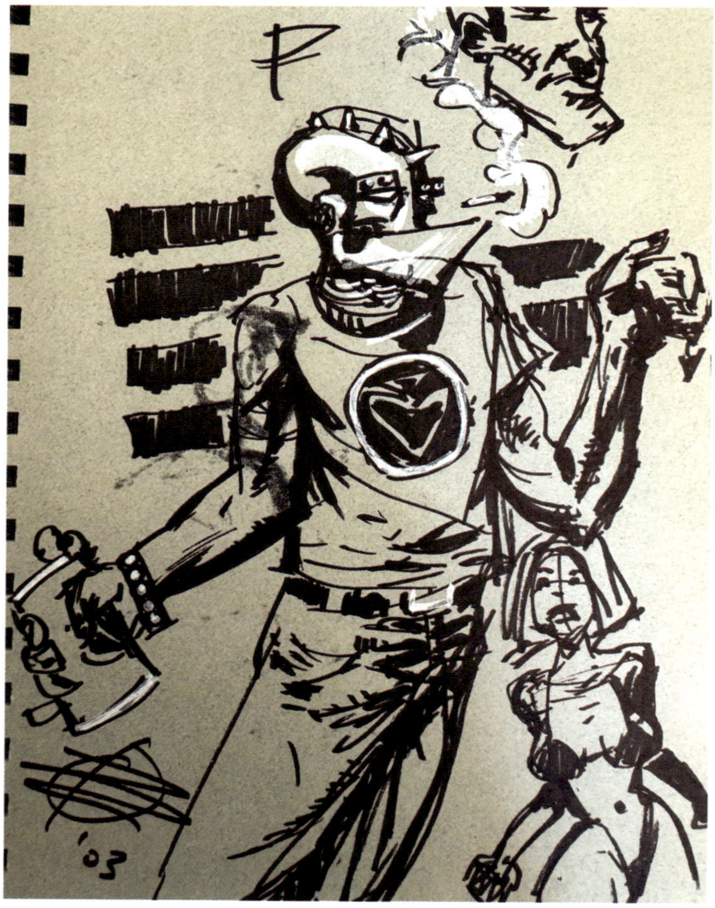
'03

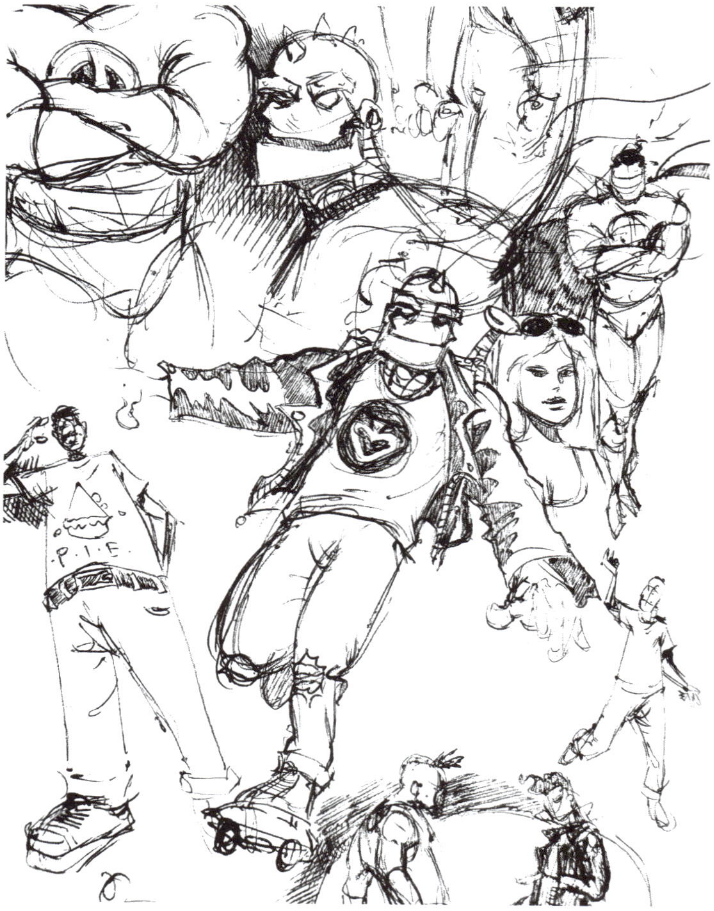
P.I.F.

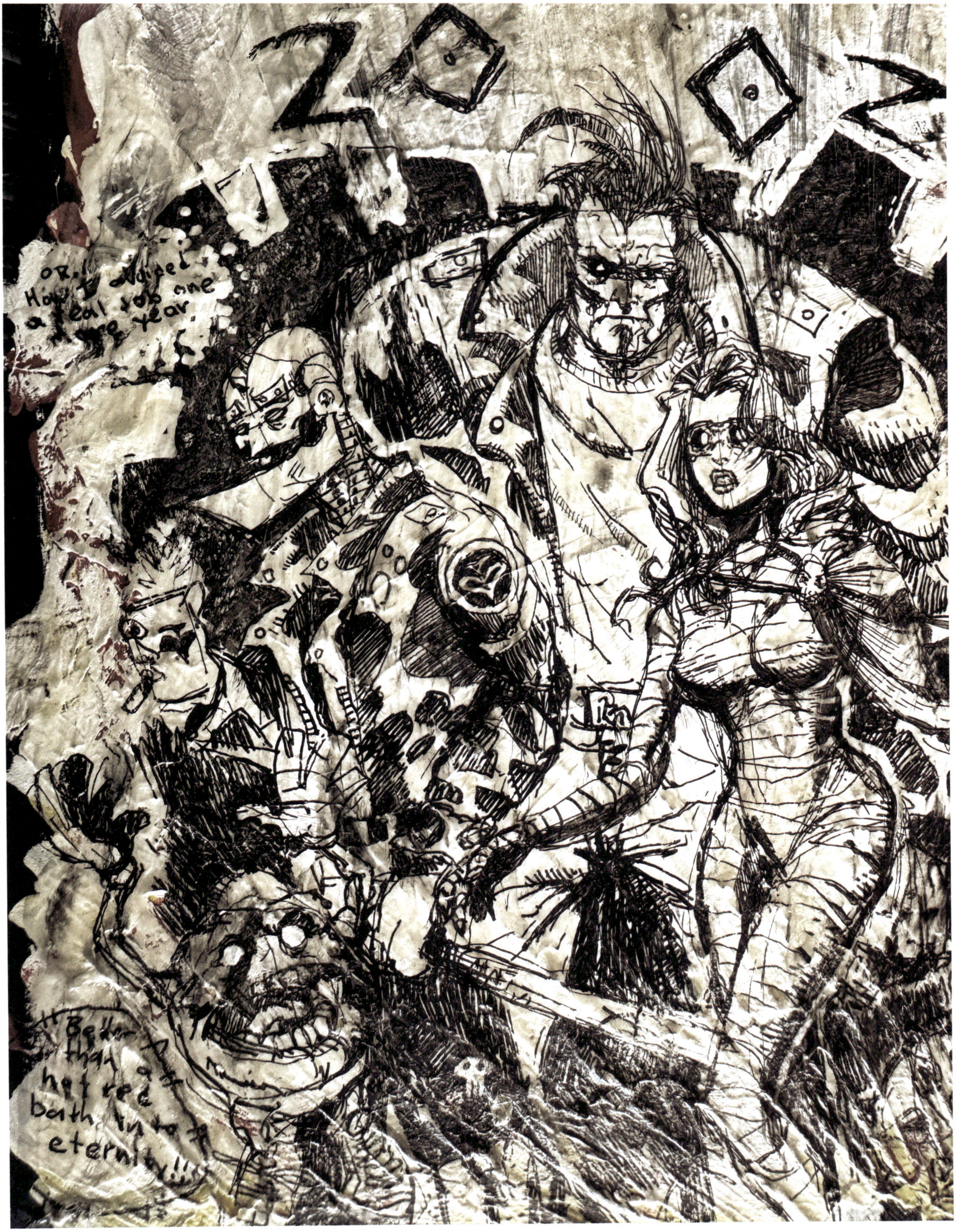
2002
OR..
a real job one
year
Better
than a
hot red
bath into
eternity!!

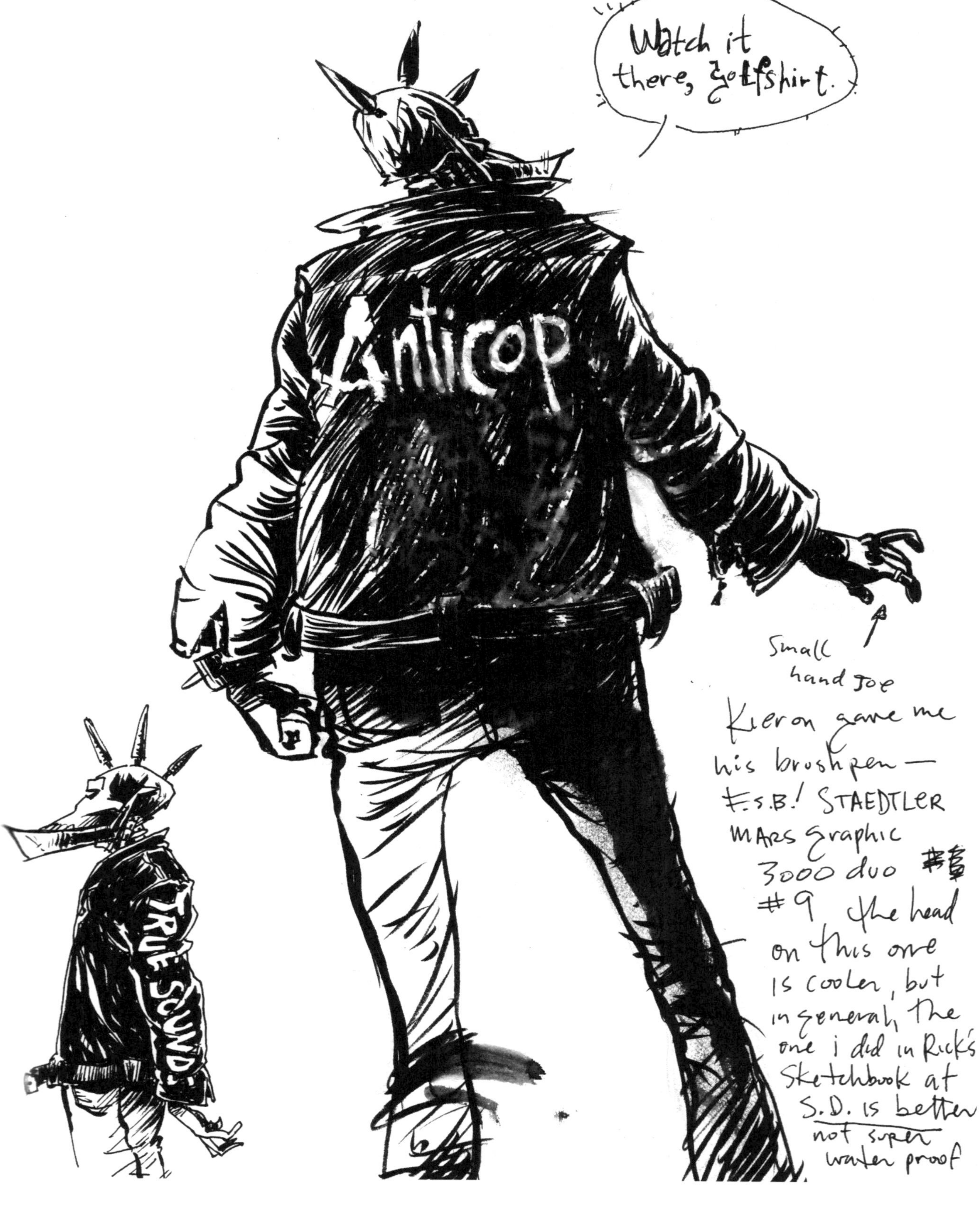
Watch it there, golfshirt.
Anticop
TRUE SOUNDS
Small hand Joe
Kieron gave me his brushpen — E.S.B! STAEDTLER MARS graphic 3000 duo #9 the head on this one is cooler, but in general, the one i did in Rick's Sketchbook at S.D. is better
not super water proof

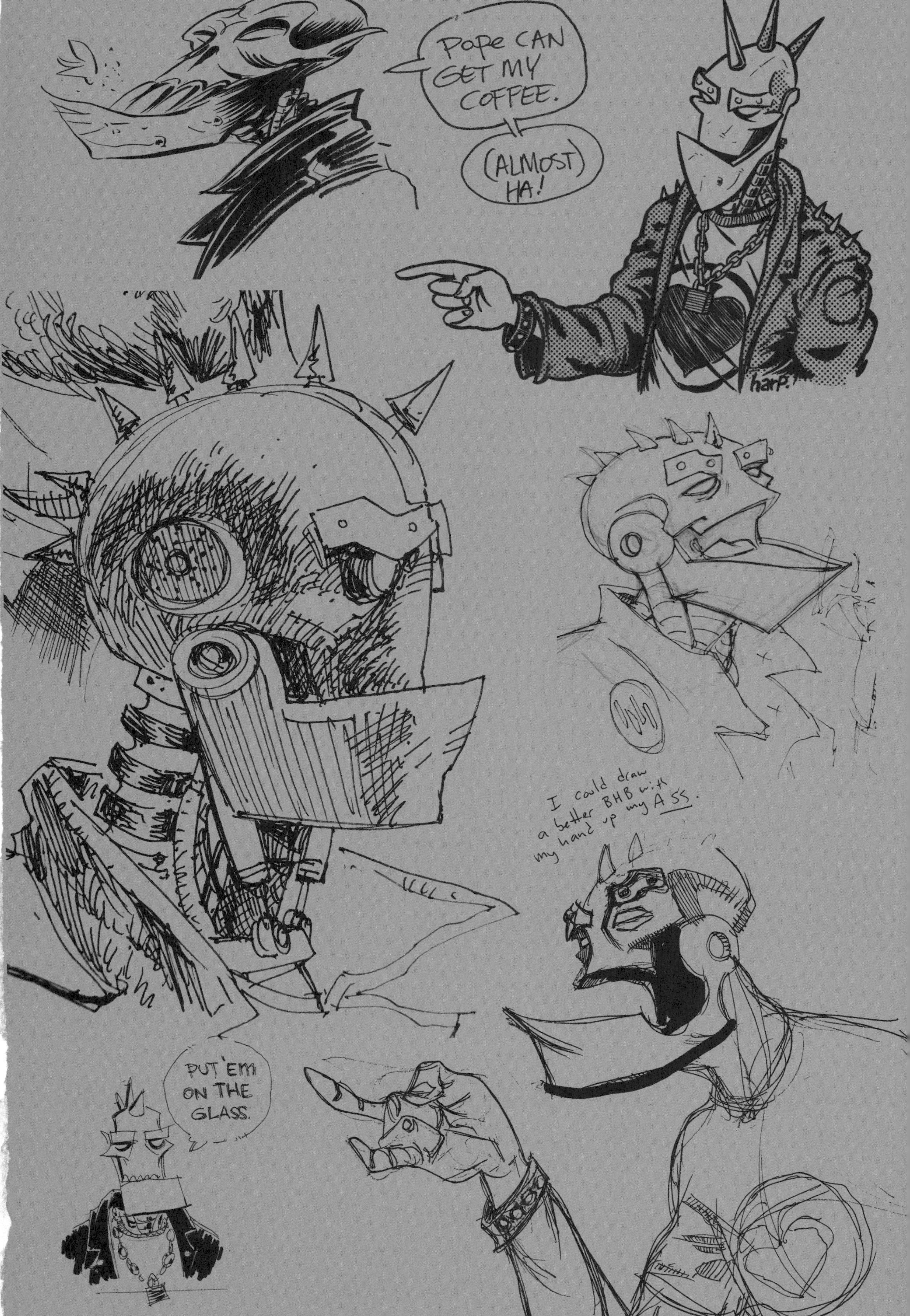

Pope CAN GET MY COFFEE.
(ALMOST) HA!
harP.
I could draw a better BHB with my hand up my ASS.
PUT'EM ON THE GLASS.

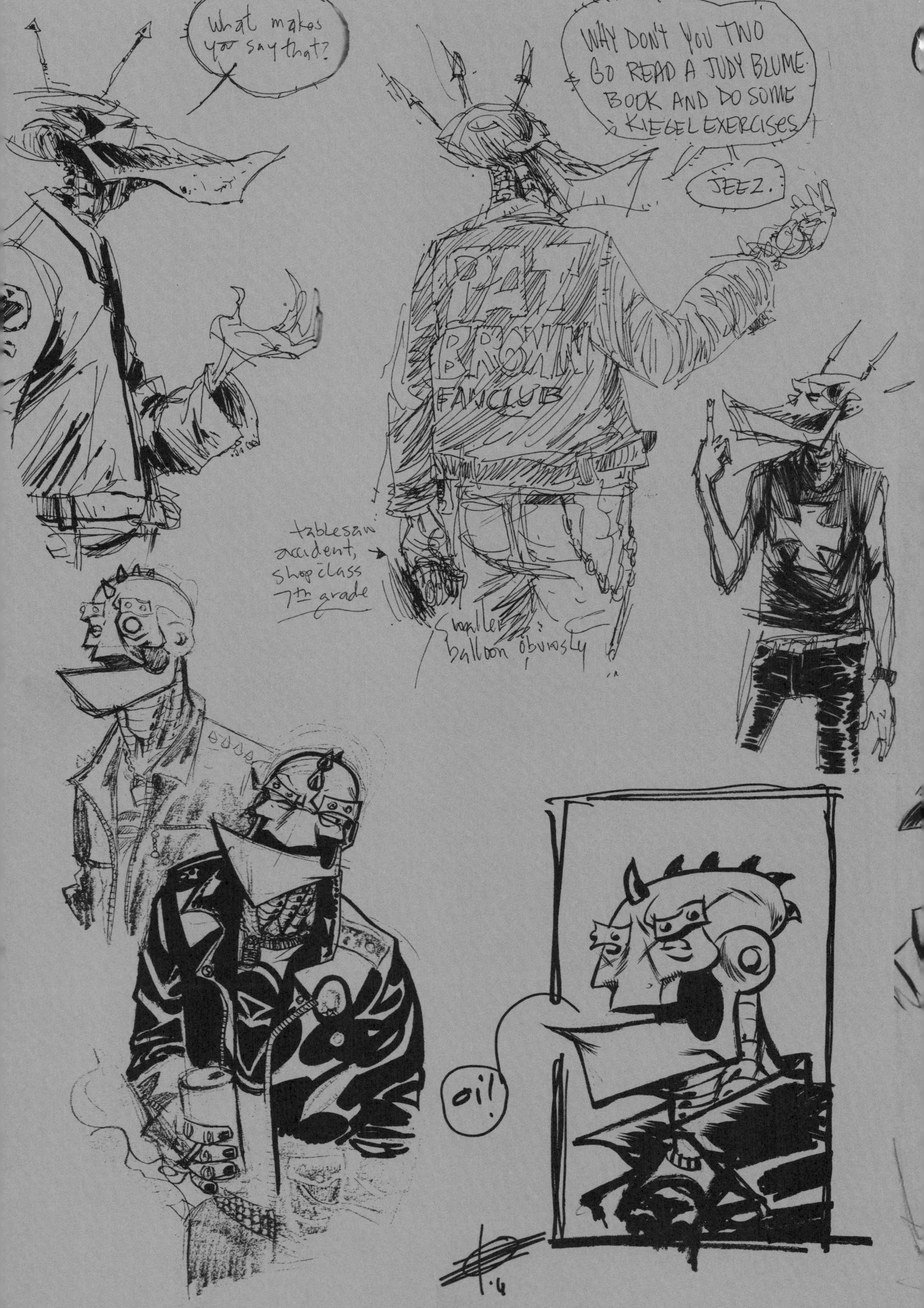
what makes you say that?
WHY DON'T YOU TWO GO READ A JUDY BLUME BOOK AND DO SOME KIEGEL EXERCISES
JEEZ.
FANCLUB
tablesaw accident, shop class 7th grade
smaller balloon obviously
oi!